Saving Diana

by

J. Lennington

Judy A. Lennington
Sept 2012

Marie and Jake –
Family is the most important
thing in life. I love you both.
Judy

DORRANCE PUBLISHING CO., INC.
PITTSBURGH, PENNSYLVANIA 15222

The contents of this work including, but not limited to, the accuracy of events, people, and places depicted; opinions expressed; permission to use previously published materials included; and any advice given or actions advocated are solely the responsibility of the author, who assumes all liability for said work and indemnifies the publisher against any claims stemming from publication of the work.

Dorrance Publishing Co., Inc.
701 Smithfield Street
Pittsburgh, PA 15222
Visit our website at www.dorrancebookstore.com

ISBN: 978-1-4349-1499-6
eISBN: 978-1-4349-1417-0

I would like to dedicate this book to my coworkers at USCan Ballonoff and Tecnocap LLC. It was a good thirty-eight years.

This novel is dedicated to all those hardworking men and women who I've had the pleasure of knowing and working alongside with. To all of my friends and co-workers of Ballonoff I remember.

Diana walked beside Gurdy, a milking cow. Wearing no shoes, the mud oozed between her toes. She looked to the sky, which was the brightest blue, with many white clouds.

To her right, she caught a glimpse of her older sister, Josephine, chasing a cow out of the underbrush to join the others. There were nine cows in all. It was time to milk them. Josie, Diana, and her younger sister, Regina, were assigned the duty of milking the cows, sometimes twice daily. Their father sold the milk to Sherman and Grace Hickman, who owned the general store in town.

Diana's father, William Lewis, had come to America from England. He settled here near the coast of Pennsylvania. He was a trapper by trade. Once, while selling his furs, he met a family who just arrived from England with their daughter, Agnus. One look at Agnus and he was in love. The courtship went quickly and he and his new bride moved deeper into the rich forest area of Pennsylvania, settling down amidst the mountains. There were Indians, but Will was a peaceable man and they managed to remain on friendly terms.

Will had always wanted a son. Agnus prayed that she might bless her husband with a son, to share in her husband's labors. However, for some unforeseen reason, the Lord blessed them with six daughters instead. The seventh child died at birth and Agnus nearly died, too. Since that time, Agnus was unable to have another child. It was hard raising six daughters. They took on the responsibility of the sons Will never had.

Josephine was the oldest. She was just thirteen now. Diana was twelve. Josephine and Diana were inseparable. They were more like twins joined at the hips than sisters, a year apart. Regina was ten. She was the spitting image of her mother, Agnus. Sofia was seven. She was the little lady of the house. Martha was four and Ruth Ann was three.

Will raised his cattle free range. This meant a constant struggle herding them in at milking time. Sometimes, the girls had to walk miles until they had all nine cows accounted for. Today was one of those days.

Diana looked around for a sign of her sister, Regina. She was nowhere in sight. She could hear cattle bawling off in a distance, but she could not see them. As they crested the hill, Diana could see the farm nestled in the valley below them. The house was an old log cabin that had two additional rooms added to it. The barn was a sod-covered fortress. It was small. When the girls milked the cows, it was very crowded, leaving them with bruised feet from being stepped on.

When the cows saw the barn, they quickened their pace. As they neared the fenced in area, which was just about as big as the barn itself, Diana saw Regina cresting the hill. She was ambling slowly toward them. Diana knew that Reggie was off in some daydream, no doubt wearing flowing skirts and fanning herself in the heat under a parasol. Diana pushed the cows faster. She wanted to get done early. There was much to do after the milking. She would scrub herself clean and load the milk onto a two-wheeled cart, to take to town.

Inside the barn, Will Lewis was shoving loose hay into a wooded area. The cows lined up to feed. Josie and Diana each grabbed a three-legged stool and began milking the cows. After Diana had started her second milking, Regina arrived with the rest of the cows. She too, began to milk. William also began to help. After each cow was milked, the bucket was emptied into a larger wooden barrel and a wooden lid was placed over it. Will measured the barrel's contents periodically. After a considerable amount of time, it was finished. He skimmed some of the cream off the top for dinner. He wheeled the barrel to the two-wheeled cart. Josephine and Diana both carried one side of the barrel, while their father carried the other. It took all three of them to hoist the barrel into the cart. The girls ran to the house to wash.

Josephine carried water from the stream in two buckets. They scrubbed themselves clean. They wore no shoes. They each had a pair of homemade shoes their father had made for them. They were to be worn on special occasions.

William had hitched their only horse, Buck, to the cart. Buck, being old, and sway backed. Josephine took the reins while Diana and Regina rode on each side of the barrel to steady it as they went. Their dog, Rudy, rode with them. They were off toward town on a dirt road that wound through the hills and across a wide but shallow stream.

Diana was grateful for the nice weather. Rain meant they would have to travel a considerable distance up stream to cross. Winter was even worse yet. She lifted her face toward the sky. The sun was warm. She felt the beads of sweat forming on her forehead.

There was always something new to see on the road to town. Sometimes it was a deer jumping across the road ahead of them. Once, they caught a glimpse of an Indian on horseback watching them. Diana looked from left to right as they went. The wooded area gave them shade. The coolness felt good. The girls talked as they went, and from time to time, they fell into silence. Josephine had a long barrel rifle tucked under the seat of the wagon. William had taught her how to shoot it, although she never had reason to. Diana was grateful for that, and hoped they would never have to use it. Rudy was also provided protection. No one would get close to the wagon as long as Rudy was there. However, they remained vigilant on their journey.

Soon, they made a sharp right turn into a clearing. Diana could see the small group of buildings ahead. It was Berlin. It consisted of a general store run by Sherman and Grace Hickman, a feed and grain store, which doubled as a livery stable and stagecoach stop. About five small sod-roofed houses scattered about.

Buck moved slowly; Diana watched the town grow larger as they approached it. Soon, they were on the main street. They stopped in front of the general store. Willy Hickman came out of the store. He was the eldest son of Sherman and Grace. He lifted the lid from the wooden barrel and called back into the store, "Hey there, Burt. Give me a hand, will ya?"

Burt Hickman came out of the store eating a piece of bread. By the aroma, Diana guessed it was fresh baked. He forced the entire piece into his mouth. Without saying a word, the two boys lifted the barrel onto the wooden porch of the store.

Soon, their younger sister, Concetta, came running to greet them. Concetta, or Connie as everyone called her, was the same age as Sofia. She looked around. She asked Josephine, who was tethering Buck to the hitching post. "Didn't Sofia come with you?"

Josie shook her head. Connie turned and went back into the store.

The girls followed the two older Hickman boys back into the store. Grace Hickman came through the curtained doorway wiping her hands on her apron. She went to the barrel and lifted the lid. She put her finger into the cream and tasted it. "How much we got here?" she asked her son.

Willy put a long stick they used to measure down into the barrel. "Almost four gallons," he said, looking at his mother.

Graced made a humming noise as she went to the counter. She pulled out a register book and wrote some figures in it. "I'm just going to take this amount off your father's bill. You tell him he owes me seventy-five cents now," she said, glaring at Josephine.

Diana looked at Josephine, who cleared her throat and said, "Pappa asked if we could have the money. He said he would settle up with you on the bill later next week." Diana looked back at Grace Hickman. She had folded her hands. She lowered her head but she kept her eyes on Josie.

"You tell your father the bill comes first. Anything leftover after the bill will be paid in cash," she said.

Josephine's face reddened. She smiled and said, "Yes, Ma'am, I will tell him. Thank you Ma'am."

Diana sighed in relief. Father said he knew they would not pay him the cash money, but there was no harm in asking. They all knew if it had been Sherman they were dealing with, they had a pretty good chance of getting the money. Grace, however, was another story. They waited until the barrel was emptied and loaded back into the cart. They began their journey home. It would be dark soon. They did not want to be late for dinner.

It seemed the sun was hotter during their trip home. They stopped at the stream and the girls waded in the water. They caught a few crayfishes, putting them in the cart. Agnus would boil them while Will ate their tails.

The girls began their journey back home. This trip was made every other day. Tomorrow, they would keep the milk for their own use. A household of eight used a lot of milk. Mother baked bread today so they would have bread pudding tomorrow. Soon, the homestead came into view. There was smoke coming from the chimney, which meant dinner was on. Josephine and Diana unhitched Buck and put him in the small wooden corral to graze. Most of the grass was tramped into mud, but Reggie had pulled some grass from the wooded area and threw it in to him. They washed their feet with water in a pan off the side of the porch and went inside.

The cabin had a dirt floor, which Agnus swept daily. It was packed down to a hard surface. There was a homemade table and eight three-legged stools for each of them to sit on. If company happened to come, they had a board used to secure the door at night that they placed over the stools to form a bench. The fireplace had a pot hanging over the coals. The house was hot from the warm weather and the daily baking. The stone fireplace had a hole in the side of it, which was the oven. There was a bucket of water sitting on a smaller homemade table. The dishes would be washed in that bucket.

All of their dishes were hand worked pieces of wood. Their only eating utensils were wooden spoons, made by their father. Their life was simple. There were no frills, for there was no money. Their clothes were all handmade, hand-me-downs, made from feed sacks and skins of animals. When they gathered around the table, a prayer was said, thanking the Lord for their many blessings. It was hard to imagine there were others who did not have a life as good as the Lewises.

After dinner, they all worked together to do the dishes. There were seldom any leftover. If there were, they were wrapped in cloths and skins and placed in a barrel buried in the floor under the table. The girls all had reading and writing lessons after dinner, all except for Martha and Ruth Ann who were too small. They all gathered around while Agnus read from the Bible and William smoked his pipe.

When the sun went down, they went to bed. There were two rooms off from the main portion of the house. One room had a loft. Josie, Diana, and Regina slept in the loft. Below them was a grass mattress where Sofia and Martha slept. Ruth Ann slept with William and Agnus.

In the loft, there were gaps between the logs where the dried mud had fallen out. At night, Diana liked to peek through those gaps. She could see the barn and the wooded glen to the left just near the hillside. The sky was full of stars this night. Her father had taught her where the Big Dipper was. She tried to locate it from peering through the gaps. This night she could not find it. She sighed and went to her grass mattress. She knelt and said a prayer before lying down. She pushed the cover back. It was too hot. She fell asleep listening to the steady breathing of her sisters as they slept.

Diana woke as Josephine was crawling over her. She sat up and watched Josie disappeared down the ladder. Regina was just waking. Diana rubbed her eyes and crawled toward the ladder. She heard the moans of Regina as she made her way to the bottom.

Martha and Ruth Ann were playing outside on the porch with Rudy and a couple of chicks. William sat on the porch steps smoking his homemade pipe. Inside, Agnus was boiling wheat in the pot over the fireplace. Josephine was crawling out from under the table where she had been getting a skin with some leftovers wrapped in it. Diana went to the barn. She began milking Gurdy. After Gurdy, she went to Jingles and Lulu. She turned each cow loose after it was milked. Regina had come out to help. They milked just enough for breakfast. The rest would be milked after the morning meal.

After breakfast, William went into the bedroom and came back with his long rifle. He took a second long rifle from above the fireplace and called Josephine. They were going hunting for dinner. Diana, Regina, and Sofia would have to finish the milking and barn work. When they were finished, Diana went to the creek that ran behind the house and collected two buckets of water. She set them on the porch. Sofia was helping her mother clean up after breakfast. Regina and Diana gathered up the laundry and carried them to the creek. They proceeded to wash the clothes in the stream. They carried the wet clothes back to the house and hung them to dry on a small line their father had stretched from the house to a tree.

After the laundry was finished and the breakfast dishes were washed, it was time for their sewing lesson. Diana, Regina, and Sofia were each working on a new dress. They had saved sacks from the feed mill and with the help of their mother, they were making their own dresses. Diana and Regina had each made their own dresses before. This was the first time for Sofia. They sat scattered about the porch, talking and sewing for a couple of hours.

Agnus said, "Diana, you go down stream to where the cattails are growing and gather some roots. You Paw will be home with some meat for dinner and the roots will help make a nice stew."

Diana smiled and took her sewing inside. She tucked it into a wooden box behind the door and retrieved a wooden bowl from the table. She went outside toward the back of the house. She sang to herself as she went.

She came upon a wide area where the stream spread out. Her father had dammed the stream with rocks here and the water was deeper. Cattails grew along the banks on both sides. Diana waded knee deep into the water. She reached down deep near the bottom, pulling the cattails up by their roots. She was ever vigilant for snakes. Luckily, she saw none this day. She crawled back up on the bank and gathered her cattails. She headed back toward the house. She laid the cattails down on a large limestone rock and wondered off into the wooded area. Here, she gathered some wild onions. She returned to collect her cattails and walked toward the house. Her mother was in the kitchen. She was making the bread pudding. Diana could smell it as she approached the house.

Diana spread the cattails on the stone step that went up onto the porch. She went inside and got a knife. She cut the tops off and spread them in the yard to dry. Nothing was wasted. The cattail would be dried and used to weave baskets. The roots were shaped like large bulbs. The roots themselves were cut off and the bulbs were scrubbed and cut up to be put into the pots. These would be used instead of potatoes, until the potatoes were ready for picking in the garden to the right of the house.

Diana helped her mother prepare the stew. It was soon all ready. All they needed was the meat. They went back outside. Regina and Sofia were weeding the garden. Diana went for the woods. "I am going to pick mushrooms, Momma," she said. She took her wooden bowl and disappeared into the thicket.

As she wandered about in the forest, she could hear the bell of one of the cows. She followed the noise just to make sure the cow was not in peril. It was Nelly. She was eating grass off the hillside along the edge of the forest. Diana looked around. It seemed to be safe there, so she went about looking for mushrooms again. She soon had collected about half a bowl full. It was enough for dinner. Never take more than you can use. Mushrooms did not keep well, and Mother Nature was always kind to them. Diana said a small prayer thanking the Lord for his graciousness. She went back toward the house.

As she approached the clearing, she saw her father and Josephine nearing the house. She quickened her pace. They were carrying some kind of a kill. That meant there would be meat in their stew tonight. She reached the porch. Martha and Ruth Ann were swinging on a homemade swing William had put up in a large maple tree near the garden. Diana went inside.

Josephine was putting the long rifle above the fireplace. She turned when she heard Diana enter the house.

"Paw and I killed us two squirrels," Josephine said.

"They will taste good in our stew, won't they Momma?" Diana asked.

Agnus smiled and nodded her head as she answered, "They sure will. These mushrooms will be a nice addition, too." Then she turned to Sofia and said, "Sofia, you take these mushrooms outside and wash them off. We need to get these here squirrels skinned and cut up so we can eat before sundown."

Sofia took the mushrooms outside. She began to wash them with some of the water from the buckets that sat on the porch. Diana grabbed an empty bucket and went to the stream to fill it. She passed her father who was in the process of skinning the squirrels. Regina was helping him.

After filling the water bucket, Diana went to the fields. She wanted to get an early start on fetching the cows. She found Bosie and Pie right away. She worked them back toward the barn. Nelly ambled out from the hillside where she had been grazing, to join them. On the way back, they passed Hughie. He was the only bull they owned. They never brought Hughie in. He stayed out all year round. He never went far from the cows. He bred them periodically. This replenished the herd, though it also reduced the amount of milk they could sell. At the present, there were two cows that were with calves.

On the way to the barn, Diana passed Josephine coming out to help. Regina had already started milking the cows as they entered the barn. William had joined her. Diana went back to help bring in the rest of the cows. This should be the last trip. The cows had a sense when it was time to come in. They usually started in the general direction on their own. They were not hard to find.

The milking was done and the cows were all out in the corral. The girls decided to go to the stream and wash off. They pulled their dresses off and waded into the shallow water. They splashed one another and made it a fun time. However, it was necessary to wash their feet one more time after they returned to the house.

They all enjoyed the stew they ate for dinner. They had bread pudding for desert. The clean up was a joint effort. Afterwards, they worked on their reading and writing. William had gone to the front porch to smoke his pipe. When Agnus began their nightly Bible reading, he re-entered the house. William liked the Bible stories. Then it was time for bed once again. Tomorrow was another trip to town.

The summer was long and hot. Soon, the leaves were beginning to change. William had collected enough pelts to cut each of the girls' two new pair of fur-lined shoes for winter. They had all finished their new dresses, which would be passed down from girl to girl until Ruth Ann had grown out of them. They would be patched and sewed over and over again. The creek water would yellow them until the patterns were no longer visible, but they did not mind. They were no worse off than any other of the homesteaders there abouts. If fact, there weren't many others their age for miles. The two Hickman boys were a little older than Josephine. Connie was the same age as Sophia. Diana could not remember ever seeing another child her age. There was no schoolhouse. There was no teacher. They were all taught at home reading and writing, and maybe a little arithmetic, but very little, for only those in town ever used arithmetic. However, her mother tried to teach them what little she knew on the subject.

Zachariah Dillon ran the feed store in town. His wife had died in childbirth. Edwin Morgan, who was better known as Stumpy, had a daughter, but she took the stage East to live with her aunt and uncle. She left when Diana was just a baby. Edwin helped Zachariah out when the stage came through. So did Marcus O'Hara. He was a bit dim witted, but he was an honest man.

The fall went by quickly. The girls continued their daily chores and their daily lessons. One day, they were on the road to town to make their milk delivery. As they approached the wide spot in the stream, they heard pounding. They crossed the stream and brought Buck to a halt. There in a clearing to the right were two men chopping down a tree. They watched for a while. The men noticed them and began to approach them. Rudy began to growl. Diana held her arms about his neck. The men did not come close. The largest and oldest of the two called out, "Where you girls going?"

Josephine called back. "We are fixin to deliver our milk here to the general store in Berlin,"

The older gentleman asked again, "Where you from?"

Again, Josephine called out. "Back yonder. We have a farm yonder. You fellows building a house?"

The older man answered. "Yes. My name is Porter Martin. I'm homesteading on this piece of land. You girls have a Father?"

Josephine called back, "Yes! His name is William Lewis. Our farm is back yonder as I said. Our mother's name is Agnus. You care if we cross the stream here?"

Mr. Martin nodded as he responded. "You can cross. It looks like we are going to be neighbors. This is my nephew, James. James Harris. You girls be careful now. Tell your daddy I will make a call on him when I have the time," he said.

Josephine clicked her tongue and Buck responded by crossing the stream slowly. They waved at the strangers as they crossed the stream and followed the dirt road on the other side. Soon, they wound through the trees and the homesteaders disappeared. The girls began chattering again as they approached Berlin.

Josephine pulled Buck to a halt at the hitching post in front of the general store. The girls jumped down from the cart. Regina tied Rudy inside the cart. Sofia had joined them this day, and she was anxious to see Connie.

They entered the store. Mrs. Hickman was talking to Marcus O'Hara. He had made a few purchases. He turned to greet the girls as they entered the store.

"Good day, girls. How's your ma and pa?" Marcus asked.

"They are fine," Josie replied.

"You tell them Marcus said hey," Marcus said. He then turned back to Mrs. Hickman once again. He pulled some change from his pocket. Grace Hickman counted the change, then counted it again. She nodded at Marcus and he took his purchases in his arms and, nodding to the girls as he passed, went through the front door.

Grace Hickman went to the curtained doorway and called out.

"Willy! Burt! Get out here!"

She came back to the counter. Taking a deep breath, she stared at the girls. Connie and Sofia had disappeared through the curtain. It was obvious that this displeased Mrs. Hickman. Soon, the boys came through the curtain. They nodded and went outside to lift the barrel down off the cart. Rudy barked at them as they approached. Diana went to the doorway and watched them lift the barrel onto the porch. Mrs. Hickman brushed past her and lifted the lid. Once again, she put her finger in the cream and tasted it. She nodded her approval to the boys. They carried the barrel inside and dumped its contents into the corner barrel inside the store.

Burt lowered the measuring stick into the milk. "Just under four gallons, Ma," he said.

Grace Hickman wrote it down in a ledger. She lowered her head and looked in Josephine's direction, as she said. "I can't give you credit for the forth gallon. Three gallons it is."

Josephine flushed. "Can't you give us credit for half a gallon, even though it is nearly a whole gallon?" she asked.

Mrs. Hickman shook her head. "You know better than that. How long have you girls been bringing milk to us? You know how it works by now. Three gallons it is." Grace Hickman nodded her head and went back to writing in her ledger. "That brings your father's bill down to thirty-five cents."

Josephine shuffled her feet. She swallowed hard. "Yes, Ma'am," she said. "Could we be getting some supplies?" she asked.

Mrs. Hickman put her pencil down. She looked directly at Josephine. "Not until the tab is paid in full. You know better than to ask me for more credit. If your father has a problem with that, you tell him to come talk to me himself," she said.

"Yes, Ma'am," Josephine said.

Burt had sat the barrel back in the cart. The girls crawled up into the cart. Josephine took the reins. Diana unhitched Buck and backed him up. She jumped into the back of the cart and Josephine clicked her tongue, spurring Buck into motion.

They began their trip home. They were quiet until they were out of hearing distance from the general store.

"Someday, that Mrs. Hickman is going to be on the other side of hard times. She will know what it is like to go home empty handed," Josephine said.

Diana looked over at Sofia. She knew Sofia was embarrassed because Concetta was her friend. Diana remained quiet. They rode in silence for a time. Then Regina asked, "What do you make of our new neighbors?"

"I can't wait to tell Pappa. He doesn't go to town often, and having another man nearby to visit would be good for him," Josephine said.

"What do you think about his nephew? He is a handsome young man, don't you think?" Regina asked.

Diana looked up at the back of Josie's head. She did not respond. Diana smiled and looked back at Regina and Sofia. "I thought he was a handsome young man," she said. She winked at her sisters. They smiled. Soon, Sofia began to sing a song. They all joined in. They sang until they approached the clearing where the stream widened. The two men were working on cutting the limbs off the tree they were cutting down when the girls first met them. The two men waved as the cart crossed the stream. The girls waved back.

The water was too cold to catch crayfish this time of year. Soon, there would be ice over the stream. They followed the dirt road toward home. Soon, they crested the hill and wound around the tree line until the farm came into view. Buck picked up his pace. Rudy jumped from the cart and ran to the house, barking. The girls saw their two youngest sisters come out onto the porch and waved to them as they approached.

Josephine stopped the cart in front of the house. Diana and Regina lifted the barrel down. Josephine clicked her tongue and Buck proceeded toward the barn. Josephine unhitched Buck and began to brush him down. Diana appeared with a bucket of water. Buck began to drink. Regina had pulled some of the grass from the wooded area and fed it to Buck. Then Josephine led him into the corral. The three girls went back to the house.

Agnus was stirring the remainder of the squirrel stew from the day before. William was working on a couple of coyote pelts on the table. The girls went into the kitchen all talking at once.

William slapped his hand on the table. Everyone became quiet. "What did the Hickmans say? Did they let you buy the items I told you to get?" he asked.

Josephine shook her head. "No, Pappa," she said. "Mrs. Hickman said you owe her thirty-five cents now. She wouldn't budge."

William shook his head. "That damn woman!" he said.

Agnus gasped. "Will! Watch your language in front of the girls!" she said.

Will swallowed hard and looked back at the pelts he had spread on the table. "Going to be sparse eatin for a couple of days," he commented.

"Pappa, we are getting new neighbors," Josie said.

Will looked up at her. "New neighbors? Where abouts is this happenin?" he asked.

The girls all began to answer at once. Will slammed his hand on the table once again. Again, it became quiet. He nodded at Josephine. She cleared her throat and answered. "Up yonder where the stream spreads out at the shallow part. There are two men clearing the trees and building a house. Porter Martin is his name. His nephew is working alongside of him. His nephew's name is James Harris. Mr. Martin said he would be calling on you when he has the time."

William frowned. "That could be bad. Ifin he decides to close that road off, we will have to cross somewheres else. Have to get the milk to Berlin before it sours," Will said.

"I asked him if it was all right to cross there. He said it would be fine. He seems like a real nice man, Pappa. I don't think he will be any trouble," Josephine said.

Will nodded and went back to his pelts. "Well, can't hardly do anything about it no how. Guess we will just have to wait until he comes a callin," he said as he worked.

Agnus spoke up, "You girls go wash up for dinner. Will, you get those dirty old furs off my table. It is time to eat."

The girls went through the open door. They jumped off the side of the porch and went toward the stream. The water was cold. Diana cringed as she slowly put each foot in the water. Reggie screamed and ran for the woods. "I have to pee!" she shouted as she went. Diana smiled. Sometimes, the water had that very affect on her, too. Soon, they would be breaking the ice to get to the water. They would do their washing inside then.

Diana walked toward the house slowly. She dreaded the winter. Times were so much more difficult then. The garden would be gone. There would be no mushrooms or wild onions from the forest. All they would have to eat would be what they managed to kill. Sometimes, that would be racoons or groundhogs that sometimes came out of hibernation. The winters were cold and long. She sighed heavily and went into the house. Dinner was almost ready. She heard Josie come in behind her.

"Where is Regina?" her mother asked.

Josie laughed and answered, "She went to the woods to pee." Diana smiled again as she began to set the table.

The days that followed were nothing out of the normal. Every day they chased down the cows and brought them in. They milked and fed them. Every other day, they made the trip into Berlin to sell the milk. Finally, the debt at the general store was paid off, and Josephine smiled as she handed Grace Sherman a list of supplies. Grace was huffy, but she gathered the items on the list and had Burt carry them to the cart. The girls sang all the way home. They would be eating good for a couple of weeks.

Every time they made the trip across the stream, they stretched their necks to see how far Mr. Porter Martin was coming with his house. Today, they noticed a strange looking contraption off to the right, near the woods that surrounded the clearing. The girls waved as they approached the stream. James waved back. Porter had his back to them and did not notice their presence. The machine had smoke coming from a stack and made a popping sound. It was loud enough that they could hear it from the stream.

James waved and started running in their direction. Josephine pulled Buck to a halt just before he stepped into the water. Diana noticed that Josie began adjusting her skirt and ran her fingers through her hair. James ran all the way to their cart.

"Miss Josephine. How nice it is to see you again. I mean it is nice to see all three of you again. How have you been?" James asked. He was panting as he spoke.

"We are all fine, Mr. Harris. How are you and Mr. Martin getting along these days?" Josephine asked.

"We are fine. The winter seems to be upon us soon. We were hoping to be a little further along on the house, but as you can see, we have a long way to go," he said. He was still smiling.

"What is the contraption?" Regina asked.

James Harris reached his hand out to pat Rudy. Diana held her breath. Rudy did not take to strangers. To her surprise, Rudy began licking James's hand. James said, "That is a sawmill. Uncle Porter had it brought in from Philadelphia. He had a sawmill there. He is using it to cut the lumber for his new house. When he is finished, he will set it up to cut lumber for the citizens of Berlin. That is how he made his money. Have you ladies not seen a sawmill before?"

All three girls shook their heads. James smiled. "Would you like to come watch it work?" he asked.

Josephine cleared her throat. "I think Pappa will be waiting for us. We better get home. We have chores to do. Thank you for the invitation though," she said.

"Sure. Anytime. You tell your pappa to allow you some extra time the next time you come this way. Uncle Porter would be glad to show you around," James said.

"Thank you," Josephine said. "We must be getting home now."

James stepped back and Josephine clicked her tongue. Buck raised his head and slowly started to pull the cart across the stream. Diana and Regina watched the sawmill puffing smoke until they had made the turn in the road and it was no longer visible.

"That James Harris is a nice young man," Diana called up to Josephine. There was no response, but Diana could see the back of her neck turning red. Diana smiled.

That evening, they tried to describe the machine to their father as they all sat around the dinner table. William frowned. "I have heard of those sawmills. I have never seen one, though." He ate his meal in silence. Diana got the impression that the news did not sit well with her father. If it bothered him, then there was a reason for it. William Lewis was an honest man. Something about this new neighbor seemed to have him unsettled.

That night, she lay in the bed staring at the ceiling. She could hear Regina's steady breathing. She whispered to Josephine. "Josie, are you awake?"

"I am now," Josephine whispered back.

"Do you like that Mr. Harris?" Diana asked.

Josephine raised herself up onto her elbow. "I think he is a nice enough fellow. Why do you ask?" she said.

"Well," Diana whispered, "Pappa seems unnerved by the news of his building a house there. Do you think there is going to be trouble?"

Josephine was quiet for a moment and then responded. "I think it will be all right. Sometimes, change is a good thing. Pappa has been here a long time. Every day is the same here. I think a change might be good. Who knows, maybe a sawmill is just what Berlin needs."

Diana rolled over on her side to face her sister. "I think James Harris is just what you need," she teased.

Josephine huffed. She rolled over with her back to Diana.

Diana whispered. "Don't get riled, Josie. I was just funnin' you." Josie did not respond. Soon, they were all asleep.

The days went by rather quickly as winter approached. It was a cold, windy day, with a few snow flurries blowing about. The girls had just finished their milking when they saw a black covered buggy with two men approaching the farm. Sofia ran into the house shouting, "Pappa! Pappa, someone's callin'!"

Will and Agnus both came out onto the porch. Agnus was holding a crying Ruth Ann in her arms. Martha was hanging onto Agnus's skirt, sucking her thumb, a habit they had all been trying to break her of. The buggy drew closer. It was Porter Martin. He had another man with him. It was a man Diana had never seen before. His skin was dark, almost black. His teeth gleamed the whitest white she had ever seen as he smiled at her and tipped his hat. The buggy stopped and the two men got down. Diana ran to the horse and tethered it to a hitching post. Porter approached the porch. The dark man stayed near the wagon.

Mr. Martin called out as he neared the porch. "Good afternoon. My name is Porter Martin. I have had the pleasure of meeting three of your daughters as they delivered your milk to Berlin. I have not made your acquaintance as of yet," he said. He stopped at the porch. He stood there looking up at Diana's parents.

Her father spoke as he looked down on the man. "My name is William Lewis. My friends call me Will. This here is my wife, Agnus. These are two of my youngest daughters, Martha and Ruth Ann. I have one more daughter, Sofia. She is somewhere abouts," Will replied.

Porter smiled and tipped his hat to Agnus and the smaller girls. "Ma'am. Glad to meet your acquaintance," he said smiling. Then he went on, "My nephew and myself are building a house up near the shallow crossing in the creek. I am sure your girls have mentioned as such."

"Yep. They mentioned it. What made you choose that particular spot to build your house?" Will asked.

"Available lumber, Mr. Lewis. Available lumber. You see, I am in the sawmill business. That is how I made my fortune in Philadelphia. I have a sawmill there, too. I was traveling through these parts on the stage once and thought it would be the perfect place for another mill. You ever seen a sawmill before, Mr. Lewis?" Porter asked.

William shook his head and replied. "Can't say I have. I heard of them, though."

"Well," Mr. Martin said, smiling, "you just come on over anytime you have the time and I will show you around. After all, we are going to be neighbors."

"Would you like to come in for a smoke?" Will asked.

Mr. Martin smiled and stepped up onto the porch. "Don't mind if I do," he said.

Will nodded back toward the buggy and asked, "That colored man there, is he your slave? I heard about slaves before."

Porter looked at the buggy and then back at William. He shook his head. "No. That is my associate, Thomas. I don't own no slaves, Mr. Lewis. Don't abide by it. Thomas is a free man. His daddy was a slave. Thomas worked for his freedom. Got papers to prove he is a free man. He has worked for me for some time now. Hell of a good worker. Works hard, that Thomas does," Porter Martin explained.

Agnus spoke up, "Then he might as well come up to the house and have a smoke with the two of you."

Porter turned toward the buggy and called out, "Thomas, come up here to the house and have a smoke with us." He waved his hand in the air.

Thomas tipped his hat to the girls who had gathered around to look at him. "Ladies," he said. He went to the porch and followed Porter into the house. Agnus and Will placed the plank they used to secure the door at night across two stools and formed a bench. The two strangers sat down. The girls gathered in the corner near the fireplace to listen. They all remained quiet. Even Ruth Ann had silenced her crying to stare at the colored man.

Will took out his tobacco pouch and handed it to the two men. They each pulled out a pipe and began stuffing the tobacco into it. When all three men had their pipes lit and had puffed a few times on it, Will spoke, "So you are fixin to start up one of them sawmills over yonder. You are building a house, too. What about the crossing? You gonna close it off?"

Porter shook his head. "Nah. I ain't aimin to make no changes like that. Your girls can cross there anytime. I don't have any reason to close off that crossing. I might use some of the water out of the stream for my steam machine. That is how I power up my sawmill. You really oughta come take a look at it for yourself. As soon as we finish the house, I will send for my wife, Margaret, who is an invalid. She was in a buggy crash in Philly and she has no use of her legs. She is staying with her sister right now. When I move her here, I may need some help looking after her. It would be a fine job for one or maybe even two of your girls. I will pay well. But that won't be for a while yet. I have a long way to go on the house," Porter said.

William cleared his throat. He did not respond right away. He just stared into the fireplace. Then, he said, "I am a cursed man, Mr. Martin. I have not been blessed with a son to help out here. Instead, I have six daughters. They are all good girls, and all hardworking girls, but still not the sons I would have liked to have had. Now, my Agnus is barren. Berlin doesn't offer much when it comes to available men. Not the marrying kind, if you get my drift. Feedin' eight mouths can be quite a hardship. A paying job for one or two of them would be very helpful." He nodded as he spoke, but never took his eyes off the fireplace.

"Well, Mr. Lewis. You can be sure I will be calling back on you as soon as I get that house finished and get my Margaret here. You can call on me anytime you have a notion to and take a look at my sawmill. This is pretty good tobacco you have here. What do you say, Thomas, pretty good tobacco, isn't it?" Porter said, turning to Thomas who had been sitting quietly as they talked.

"Yes, Mr. Martin. This is mighty fine tobacco, Mr. Lewis has here," Thomas said.

"I might be in the market for some mighty fine tobacco such as this. Do you have some to spare that you might consider selling, Mr. Lewis?" Porter asked.

William raised his eyebrows. For the first time, he took his eyes from the fireplace and looked at Porter Martin. He smiled while he clenched his teeth down on this pipe. "Yes, Sir, I believe I do have some to spare. I will send you off with some this very night ifin you be wantin' some," Will said.

"That would be mighty neighborly of you, Mr. Lewis." Porter said. He reached into his jacket pocket and pulled out a leather billfold. He withdrew a few paper bills and laid them on the table.

William turned to the girls. "Josephine, you fetch some tobacco leaves from the drying shed for Mr. Martin here," he said.

Josephine stood up. "Yes, Pappa," she said. She went outside. The girls shuffled closer together when she left, filling in the vacant spot. They remain silent and vigil as they crouched near the fireplace. Porter and Thomas both smiled at them.

Porter and Will talked about hunting and trapping in the area. Agnus busied herself near the fireplace preparing dinner. "Would you be staying for our evening meal, Mr. Martin?" she asked.

"Oh, no, Ma'am. Thank you for inviting us, but we have to be getting back. It will be getting dark soon, and we left my nephew, James, at the mill alone. Again, I thank you for the invite. Perhaps some other time," Porter Martin said, smiling.

Just then, Josephine came back into the house. She placed a few tobacco leaves on the table. Agnus wrapped them in an animal skin and placed them in front of Mr. Martin. Porter stood up. Thomas quickly followed.

"Well, Mr. Lewis, Mrs. Lewis. It has been awfully fine. Thank you for the smoke. You have been very hospitable, and I thank you. You are welcome to stop up and have a look around anytime. We have to be moving on now. It has been a real pleasure," Porter said as he approached the door.

As they reached the edge of the porch, Thomas turned. He bowed and tipped his hat. "Thank you, Ma'am. It was a real pleasure. Sir, I thank you for the smoke," Thomas said. He turned and followed Porter Martin to the buggy.

Diana untied his horse and the two men turned the buggy and disappeared over the hill and around the bend in the road. Porter waved his hat just as they disappeared out of sight.

"Come help with dinner," Agnus said. They all went back inside. The evening air was cold. Diana went to the pot hanging in the fireplace and stirred it. Josephine pulled the biscuits out of the stone fireplace wall. They were a little browner than usual, but still not burnt. Regina and Sofia were setting the table. Will had caught a couple of rabbits that day. With the provisions they had purchased at the general store, they were having biscuits and gravy. Meat gravy, too.

Will pulled up his stool. "Biscuits and red eyed gravy," he said. "Mmm."

They all sat down and began to fill their plates. Agnus poured some boiled coffee into Will's cup. Everyone chattered and laughed. This was a good night.

As the days went by, the weather became colder. The cracks in the walls had been filled in with mud and sod to keep the cold out. Will had prepared fur pelts all summer long, and Agnus had sewed several together to use to cover them as they slept at night. Agnus had also sewed pelts to make the girls new coats for the winter. The older coats had been patched and passed on to the smaller girls. They wrapped their feet in furs, binding them with leather strips to protect them while they did their outside chores. Josephine and her father had taken the long rifles and went hunting nearly every day. Recently, William had been preparing Diana to join them. She did not have a gun of her own, but she had practiced with a bow and sling. She was actually becoming very good with both. Her favorite was the sling. She found that it did not require re-loading, and could react much faster to rabbits that bolted from the underbrush. This meant that Regina and Sofia were left with the milking on the days when they went hunting.

The trips to town every other day seemed longer. The milk was nearly frozen at times when they delivered it to the general store.

It had been two years since they first encountered Mr. Martin and James Harris at the crossing. The house was up. It was a large two-story house complete with glass windows. James made it a habit to stop them when they crossed the stream and talk with Josephine. Josie was now fifteen. James was nearly twenty. At times, Diana had to nag Josephine to get her to part company with James.

This particular day, James had invited them to come look inside the house. Josie walked alongside of Buck as they went. James walked with her. As they approached the house, Diana noticed a hand pump just off to the left of the porch. "You have a well. Just like in town," Diana said as she ran her hand down the red pump handle.

James smiled. He poured some water from a bucket down the pump and began working the handle until water began to splash into the bucket. The girls watched carefully. "There's a pump in the kitchen as well," James said. The girls looked at one another.

James motioned them on into the house. Inside was an entrance room with hooks lining the walls for coats to hang on. To the left was a small room. "This is the parlor," James announced. He coaxed them on. To the right, wooden doors slid open to reveal a large room with tall windows that were concealed with shutters. A large fireplace took up the entire wall on the far side. The floors were smooth wooden floors. James approached the fireplace and put a couple of logs on the fire. To the right of the fireplace was a single wooden door. James opened the door. It led into a dining room. It too, had a fireplace that was blazing. The windows were protected by the wooden shutters here also. There was no furniture in any of the rooms as yet. They could hear Mr. Martin working upstairs. The girls were quiet as they went through the house.

Then James led them into the kitchen. Diana gasped. The windows were shuttered here as well, but the shutters have a small cross cut in the center to allow some light in. The fireplace was as large as the one in the formal, front room. There was a trough near a small back door with a pump in it. The trough was built so that when the water exited from the pump, it ran down hill into a hole that must have gone back into the well. Diana turned to look at Josephine. Josie was running her fingers across a large flat top stove that sat near the fireplace. It was a cook stove. Diana had seen pictures of them in the fliers Mrs. Hickman had at the general store. She went to stand near Josephine.

James began to explain how the stove worked. The round tops lifted off and wood could be inserted from the top, or a door opened on the front to put larger pieces of wood in. There was an oven, too. It was like a dream house.

James took the girls back toward the front of the house. There was a wooden staircase that went to the upper level of the house. Upstairs, the shutters were drawn back, allowing the light to fill the rooms. Mr. Martin was putting planks down on the floor in the first room. He turned and smiled when he saw the girls standing in the doorway. He stood up and stretched.

"Well, hello, ladies," he said. "Is James here giving you a tour?"

Josephine spoke for them. "Yes, Sir. This is the most beautiful house I have ever seen. It is even nicer than the houses in the picture books," Josie said.

"Well, thank you, Ma'am," Porter Martin said. He turned to the youngest of the girls, Regina, and pulled on her pigtails. "What do you think, little lady? Will Mrs. Martin be happy here?" he asked, teasing them.

"Yes, Sir! I am sure she will," Regina said.

"Well, we best be gettin on. Pappa will be watching for us, and I am sure he will worry if we tarry too long," Josephine, said looking up at James.

James smiled and looked over at Porter Martin. "I will just show them out and then I will be right back to help," James said.

"Good day to you, girls. Be sure to send my regards on to your parent, Porter said.

They said their goodbyes and went back down the stairs. They climbed into the cart and James led Buck back onto the trail. Rudy ran about sniffing in the brush alongside of them. They crossed the creek and soon the house was out of sight. The girls rode in silence until their own house came into view. They could not wait to report what they had just seen.

Josephine parked the cart just outside the barn, in its usual spot. Diana unhitched Buck and led him into the barn. Regina had already run to the house. She could not contain herself any longer. Josephine and Diana removed the harness from Buck and fed him some grain. Diana went to the stream for a bucket of water. There was a thin coat of ice forming on top of the water near the edges. She slapped at it with the wooden bucket. After filling the bucket, she carried the water back to the barn. Josephine was waiting for her. They went back to the two-wheeled cart and lifted the wooden barrel off. They carried it to the house. Once they were inside, they were met with excited conversation. Regina was describing everything they had seen at the house. Agnus was sitting on a stool with her hands in her lap. "A water pump right inside the kitchen you say?" she was saying. Martha had begun scrubbing out the wooden barrel. She listened as she worked. Ruth Ann seemed to listen intently; however, she did not know what a water pump was.

William was not there. He was off looking for one of the cows that Sofia and Martha could not find. Agnus asked Josephine to describe the house once again. She did not want to miss anything. Josie sat down on a stool and described everything as she recalled it. Diana broke in from time to time, with little tidbits of information that Josie had forgotten. Agnus just shook her head.

Finally, she stood up. She turned to the pot hanging in the fireplace. "Josephine, Diana, you go look for your Father. He might be needin' a hand with findin' that cow," she said.

Josephine and Diana both began to wrap their feet with the animal hides once again. They wrapped themselves with the furs and went out into the afternoon air once more.

When they reached the knob just before the woods, they split up. Diana rushed into the woods. She liked being in the forest. There was less wind here. It wasn't as cold. She looked about as she went. She headed for the clearing on the other side of the woods. That was a favorite spot for the cattle to graze. The wind blew over the top of that bank and sometimes there were patches of grass that were not covered. She thought that would be where to find any strays. As she went, she daydreamed of what it would be like to live in such a grand house as the one Mr. Martin was building. How much easier life would be then.

Soon, she reached the other edge of the forest. She looked in the direction of the bank. She saw her father coming in her direction. She called out. "Pappa! Pappa! Did you see any signs of her?" She waved her arms to get William's attention.

Will turned and walked in her direction. "We will be needing a couple of buckets. A mountain lion got her. It couldn't drag her off entirely and we may be able to salvage some of the meat. You run back to the house and get a couple of buckets. Watch as you go now. That mountain lion is out there somewheres. Just hope his belly is full," Will called to her from a distance.

Diana turned and ran. She felt her lungs burning from breathing in the cold air. She met Josephine just before she reached the clearing and the knob that led to the barnyard. They went to the house. Josephine got the other long rifle and Diana carried the two buckets. They went back into the woods and made their way back to William and the remains of one of their precious dairy cows. This would mean less milk to sell at the general store. They needed every drop of milk they could get to sell for the supplies they would need to get them through the winter. Diana had a heavy heart as she helped her father cut up pieces of the cow left by the mountain lion.

Once they had finished, Will and Diana each carried a bucket. In his other hand, Will carried his long rifle. Josephine carried her long rifle. They moved quickly and silently through the woods and back to the farm. Once inside, Will put the buckets on the table and began to cut the meat into smaller pieces. Agnus rinsed the meat and began to cook it right away. Dinner would be later tonight, but they were having beef. That was rare in this household.

As they worked, the girls reported their visit to Mr. Martin and what they saw. Will was silent. He worked away without any reaction at all. When they had told him about all there was to tell, he said, "Never thought I would see the day." That was it. The girls went to the barn and began to feed and tend to the remaining cows. Will told them to keep them in the corral tonight. Tomorrow, he would try to hunt down that mountain lion before it took another cow.

That night, Diana could not sleep. The things she had seen that day were pressing on her mind. How glorious it would be to live in a house like the one Mr. Martin was building. She prayed to God that such a day would come for her.

The next morning, William and Josephine took their long rifles and went hunting for the mountain lion. Diana was left behind to help with the remaining cattle and watch over the farm. They were all instructed to stay near the house. The day was long. The cattle were all in the small corral, which meant they could not graze. Diana went about finding food for them to eat. She pulled on some of the loose grass that grew close to the back of the house. She stopped every once in awhile to scan the tree line behind her for the mountain lion. She carried her bow and sling around her shoulder. Her father had warned her they would not be much help when it came to a mountain lion, however it did help to ease her nerves some.

Her hands were freezing, and they were becoming sore from pulling on the cold thick grass. She decided to go inside and warm them by the fireplace. She said a silent prayer that her father and Josie would return soon with news that they had killed the mountain lion and life could go on as it did before. Rudy walked at her side. He was also left behind to warn them of any danger.

Agnus smiled as Diana came into the kitchen. Rudy lay at the door. He knew he was not permitted any further into the house. Agnus had whipped him with the broom on many occasions. It was no longer necessary. He had learned his lesson. He moaned as he rested his head on his front paws.

"I have some leftover oats here. I have kept it warm. It will warm you from the inside." Agnus said as she placed a bowl on the table.

Diana pulled up a stool. She smiled up at her mother. "Thank you, Momma. It is a damp, cold day. I hope Pappa and Josie get that vermint. I hate the thoughts of keeping those cows locked in another day," she said. She began to eat her oats. Her mother was right. It did warm her from inside.

Ruth Ann pulled a stool close to Diana and sat down. "Diana, when you are done eating, would you tell me a made up story? You tell the best made up stories," she said.

Diana nodded and continued eating. Her mother turned to Ruth Ann and said, "Maybe she can tell you a story while we work on our dresses."

Diana did not feel much like sewing. Her hands had gotten so chapped from working out in the cold. At times, the cows even protested when she milked them. She smiled and finished her oats. He mother had heated up a small amount of milk for her to drink. Her father would protest. They sold every bit of milk they could spare. He would suggest she drink warm water to warm her insides. Diana rose from the table and washed out her bowl and tin cup. She smiled and nodded to her mother.

Martha had gotten the sewing kit out of the wooden box behind the door and placed one for each of them on the table. They all sat down and began to sew where they had left off the day before. Ruth Ann was practicing her sewing on a dishcloth her mother had made from remnants of a feed sack Agnus had used to make her last dress out of.

Diana cleared her throat and thought for a moment. Then she began her story. "Once upon a time in a little village in England, there lived two little girls named Martha and Ruth Ann." she started her story. She went on, making it up as she went. Everyone listened intently. Even Agnus had grown to enjoy her stories. Diana continued for some time. At times, she put her sewing down on her lap and watched their faces. It was really an excuse to give her aching fingers a break. Soon, they heard a wagon approaching.

Agnus rose and went to the door. Diana could not help but think to herself, "If we only had windows with those shutters on them, we would not have to open the door and allow the cold air to enter the house." She rose and went to the door as well. They all did. It was rare there was ever a wagon that came this far out. Unless, of course, someone was lost.

It was Porter Martin's wagon. James Harris was driving Porter's team. Josephine and William were riding in the wagon.

Agnus ran from the porch to meet them. "Will! Will, is everything all right?" she called as she ran.

James brought the team to a halt.

"Everything is fine, Agnus. We are all right. James here is just giving us a lift home, that's all," Will said as he climbed down from the wagon.

"Did you get the mountain lion, Pappa?" Diana called from the porch. She crossed her fingers and waited for her father's response.

"No. But James here got him. Killed him deader 'n a door nail, right behind that fine big house they are building," Will said.

Diana sighed. She was relieved. She watched as James helped Josephine down from the wagon. They stood there talking to one another, just beyond hearing distance. Diana watched as Josephine swayed back and forth. She was smiling. Diana flushed just watching them.

Will approached the porch. "James killed it early this afternoon right behind the house as I told you earlier. Good, clean shot, too. Porter Wagner took me through his new house and he showed me his sawmill, too. You should see it, Aggie. The darndest contraption I ever seen. Works mighty fine though. Cuts them logs nice and true. Leaves them boards nice and flat for building. I might even get some boards to put down on our floor," Will was saying. He was excited. His breath was freezing as he spoke. He turned toward the wagon and called out to James, "James! Come on in here and warm yourself before headin' back!" He waved his arms in the air.

James walked to the porch with Josephine. He stopped at the porch and said, "Thank you, Mr. Lewis, but I really need to be getting back. Uncle Porter wants to get as much work done as he can before dark. I really should be helping him. He is anxious to get Aunt Margaret here with us." He nodded to the ladies and said his goodbyes. He squeezed Josephine's hand and climbed back up onto the wagon. Then he drove the team back up over the knob and around the tree line until he was out of sight.

They all were inside before he had disappeared. All but Josephine. She stood on the porch until he was out of sight. When she came inside, her cheeks were red from the cold. She unwrapped the skins from her feet and legs. She put her fur coat on a hook near the door and went to the fireplace. She stood there silently for a moment and then turned to warm her backside. She looked at the faces all staring at her.

"What is it? What is wrong?" she asked.

They were all watching her. "That James Harris is a fine lookin' young man," Sofia teased.

Agnus interrupted. "Sofie, stop it. Josie is only fifteen. She has another year or two before she can start thinking of young men. You help me with dinner now," Agnus said. She glanced over at Will. He was smiling.

Josie stirred the stew in the pot. It was beef. "Momma, how old were you when you and Pappa got married?" she asked. She did not turn around.

Agnus had stopped what she was doing. She was looking at William. She cleared her throat and replied, "I believe I was sixteen. But I was almost seventeen."

"You didn't really know Pappa very long did you, Momma?" Sofia asked.

Agnus pursed her lips together tightly. She shook her head. She handed Sofia the bowls to put around the table. Will was cleaning his rifle. He pulled his stool closer to the fireplace and away from the table so they could set it for dinner. He had a dreamy look in his eye. He was thinking about what he had seen earlier at Porter Martin's house. The sawmill interested him very much. Porter had mentioned that after he got his house finished, he may be looking for some help at the sawmill. It would put food on the table. He was oblivious to the conversation going on behind him.

Josephine said, "I will be sixteen in four months, Momma. I think James Harris is a very nice man, and I think he would make a fine husband."

Agnus turned and stared right through the back of Josephine's head. She placed her hands on her hips and asked, "Josephine Lewis! Just what have you and that James Harris been talking about lately? Has he mentioned marriage to you?"

Josephine turned around to face her mother. "No, Momma. But I can tell he likes me fine," she said.

"Well, liken you fine isn't askin for your hand in marriage. You have to watch, girl. Some men will woe a girl into doing things that just ain't proper for a young lady to do. Then you don't see them no more!" Agnus said. Then she turned and poured water into a pitcher.

Josephine's face reddened. Tears welled up into her eyes. "Oh, Momma! What do you know about it?" she cried. She ran past them all to the ladder that led to the loft.

Will turned and looked at the faces behind him. "What is going on?" he asked.

"Josie's got a bow! Josie's got a bow!" Martha chanted.

"Martha! That will be enough!" Agnus said. "Sit down and eat!"

"What about Josie, Momma?" Ruth Ann asked.

"Josie will come eat when she is ready or she will go to sleep hungry tonight," Agnus huffed. She looked over at Will who was just pulling his stool to the table. He had a confused look on his face. He remained silent for it was obvious that Agnus was agitated about something.

Diana ate her dinner meal in silence. She could hear an occasional sob from the loft. After dinner, she left the clean up to Regina and Martha. She went to the barn with her father and Sofia. They pulled more grass for the cows. They were going to be hungry tonight. The three of them could not pull enough grass to fill them. It was too late to let them roam now. They would just have to wait until morning. They each knew that tomorrow's milking would not produce much. That meant little money in their pockets. No doubt, there would be another bill at the general store.

Diana washed up early for bed. She used the excuse that she wanted to get an early start tomorrow so the cows could get out to graze. She crawled up the ladder to the loft. She pulled the furs over her and rolled over toward her sister. Josephine had her back to Diana.

"Josie. Josie, are you awake?" Diana whispered. There was no response. She could be sleeping, but Diana knew her sister well enough to know she did not want to talk.

Soon, she heard Sofia crawling into her sleeping space. Diana lay there quietly.

"Josie. Josie, I know you are awake," Sofia whispered.

There was a moment of silence. Then Sofia whispered, "I think James is a very handsome young man. I think he like you mighty fine, too." There was another moment of silence. Then she concluded, "I hope you two get married and have lots of babies, but please don't go too far away. I want to come live with you."

Diana smiled to herself. She listened for more, but there was only silence. She fell asleep thinking how grand it would be if she and Sofia went to live with Josephine and James in a big house like the one Porter Martin was building. Diana dreamed of such a house. She wandered from room to room in her dream. It was exactly like the house Porter Martin had built.

The next morning started off with a bustle of activity in the kitchen. Josephine was quiet for the most part. She was still pouting. Sofia had cut herself with a sharp knife while cutting some pork bacon into strips. She was trying to slice it as thin as possible and her left thumb got in the way. Agnus had put a tourniquet on Sofia's arm. She had a wooden spoon through the knot and twisted it to stop the bleeding. Martha was wiping at it with a clean cloth. Diana went to her sister and held her around the shoulders. Sofia would moan every time Agnus took the pressure off, and the wound would start to bleed again.

Josephine wrapped herself in a fur and went to the stream for some fresh water. Soon, the bleeding had stopped and Diana and Agnus were cleaning up the mess. Sofia went to her parents' bed to lay down. Josephine arrived with a bucket of freezing water.

Now they would be shorthanded for the rest of the day. Diana and Josephine went to the barn and started the milking. Soon, Regina came out to help. She had finished her breakfast. Will came out also, allowing Diana and Josephine to go back inside to eat their breakfast. When they had finished, they went back out to wind up gathering the milking so they could take it to town. Will gave them some dried tobacco leaves to drop off at Porter Martins. He instructed Josephine that she was under no circumstances to allow Mrs. Hickman to know she had cash money on her. Will loaded the barrel onto the cart and Josephine took the reins. She eased Buck up over the knob and around the bend toward the shallow crossing in the stream. Regina and Diana steadied the barrel as they went. Rudy rode in the cart with them as usual. He was getting up there for years and did not run about as much as he used to. He had also become accustomed to stopping at Mr. Martin's. He allowed both James and Porter to approach the cart and even pat him.

It was a cold morning. It had started snowing earlier, and it was coming down quite heavily when they reached the Martin house. James ran out to greet them. Josephine gave him the tobacco. "Come on inside and warm yourself before you go on into town," James urged.

They could not resist. Porter paid Josephine with three gold coins. She put them deep into her skirt pocket. They huddled near the fireplace for a while. Diana kept urging Josephine to leave and get the milk into town before it froze. Josie could not seem to tear herself away from James. Finally, it was Porter who reminded James that if they got to it, they might just finish the house today. Josephine finally agreed to leave and they were on the road to town again.

Grace Hickman seemed in a good mood this morning. She tasted the cream, as she was accustomed to doing. Burt put the measuring stick into the milk. "Just under three gallons," he announced.

Grace smiled at the girls and said, "Oh, it is close enough. We will just say it is a full three gallons," she smiled and went to her ledger. After some writing, she announced, "That pays your father's debt and leaves you with sixty-five cents." She rang the register and handed Josephine the money. "Would you be needing anything today?" she asked smiling.

Josephine's eyes were opened wide. She could not speak. She only shook her head as she put the coins deep into her skirt pocket with the rest of the money.

Grace Hickman asked, "Have you, girls, been to visit your new neighbor? Mr. Martin I believe is his name?" Her teeth were so white.

The girls all three nodded their heads.

"I understand his house is nearly finished. Is that right?" she asked. She was leaning across the counter looking Josie eye to eye.

Again, all three of the girls nodded their heads. Josephine stepped back about three steps.

Grace went around the counter and stood in front of the girls. "What is it like inside?" she asked.

Regina seized the moment. Maybe Diana and Josephine were speechless, but she wasn't. Regina went on and on about the fine house Porter Martin was building and how just this morning he had mentioned that it may be completed this very day. Josie poked her in the ribs with her elbow, but this did not quiet Regina. She went on until she could think of no more to say.

Grace Hickman stood upright. She raised her eyebrows as she watched their faces. Finally, she went back around the counter. She took a deep breath and smiled at the three of them. "You tell your father not to expect my generosity next time. Once in a while, but we will not be making a habit of it," she said.

The girls smiled, "Thank you, Mrs. Hickman. You have a good day," Josephine said. They went back outside and crawled into the cart. Josie urged Buck back toward home.

When they came to the Martin house, there was no sign of James. Josephine strained her neck to watch behind them as they crossed the stream and went on down the narrow path toward home. Actually, Diana was thankful. The snow was beginning to drift by now and it would be wise of them to keep on going. If they stopped at the Martin house, who knows how long it would be before Diana could get Josephine out of there. They had taken long enough and she knew her father would be wondering what was keeping them.

When they arrived at the farm, Diana unhitched Buck. Josephine helped her to lift the wooden milk barrel off the cart and take it inside to be washed. Regina had taken Buck into the barn to remove the harness. Diana carried a wooden bucket to the stream to get some water for Buck. The stream was frozen over and there were about three inches of snow covering it. Finally, Diana gathered as much snow in the bucket as she could and carried the bucket back to the barn.

When they finally got inside the house, Agnus has made them a cup of sassafras root tea. Diana held the cup under her nose and breathed in the sweet aroma. There was no sugar or honey to sweeten the tea, but she did not mind. It warmed her hands as she held the tin cup. It warmed her stomach as she sipped it. She closed her eyes and enjoyed every sip of the tea. It was a treat, better than all the licorice drops. She opened her eyes to watch Josephine. She too was sipping her tea. She was quiet. Still pouting?

Diana looked over at her mother. "How is Sofia's hand?" she asked.

Agnus smiled and nodded her head. "She will be fine. It will likely be thumping for a day or two, but after that, she should be able to milk again. Provided she keeps it dry, that is," she said.

"Where is she?" Diana asked.

Agnus nodded in the direction of the loft. "She is nappin'. I reckon she has a weak stomach. All that blood got to her, I guess. She has been in bed nearly all day," she said.

Josephine drank the remainder of her tea and rose. She placed the cup on the sink board and grabbed up her furs. She bent down to tie the hide laces that secured the furs to her feet and leggings. "I better go fetch the cows. That snow is going to strand them out yonder if I don't," she said as she went for the door.

"I will be right out," Diana called to Josie. Her sister did not turn to acknowledge her statement. She went outside without a further word.

Diana placed her cup on the washboard and began binding her leather laces. She wrapped herself in her fur wrap and hurried outside. Rudy followed her. She went off the porch and toward the knob. There she could cut into the woods and over to the high bank. She expected to find a cow or two there.

She found some tracks in the forest and followed them. She was almost to the clearing when she heard Josephine calling to her from her left. She, too, had been following the tracks. They went to the clearing together. Sure enough, there were two cows grazing on a few blades of exposed grass protected by the slant of the bank. When the girls began to call to them, they looked up.

The cows knew the routine. They slowly made their way in the direction of the forest. They followed near the forest edge toward the farm. Occasionally, one or both would bawl. They were ready for their daily milking. Their bags swayed as they trudged the rough terrain. Once they reached the clearing on the other side, they were joined by another cow. That was three of them.

Once they cleared the knob and the barn was close, the cows went on alone. Josephine went to the back of the house near the stream while Diana went behind the barn and the pond where she gathered cattails when the weather was warmer. The reeds were still standing tall, only now they were frozen fast. Diana saw Jingles and her calf on the other side. Diana called to her. Jingles looked up and bawled. She did not come. That meant Diana would have to cross the stream up further and make her way back down. She was cold. She grew angry at the cow for ignoring her. Why couldn't she be as easygoing as the other three? Of course, Jingles did not need to be milked. She had a calf.

Diana crossed the stream by walking over a fallen tree. She hurried down to Jingles and her calf. She would have to herd them all the way to the shallowest part. There, the stream was frozen. She broke a branch from a small tree and slapped at the ground. Jingles lifted her head and moved slowly in the right direction. The calf struggled to get through the frozen high grass. Soon they had reached the clearing. To Diana's relief, the ice broke under Jingles weight and the calf followed her across. Diana went further downstream to where it was still frozen, and very cautiously, crossed by walking on the ice. It held under her weight. She breathed a sigh of relief as she jumped the last couple of feet onto the bank. She followed Jingles and her calf to the barn.

Between Josephine and Diana, they had seven cows accounted for. Diana was beginning to get very cold. Josephine was pulling her fur wrap close around her. She was also getting cold.

Diana motioned to Josephine that she was going back into the forest. Josephine nodded and pointed toward the knob. Diana thought that was strange. They had just come from that direction. All of the tracks led to the bank on the other side of the forest. Diana frowned and went on her way.

Once she was inside the forest, she turned and went to her left. There wasn't much for them to graze in this direction, but occasionally a cow or two would stray this way in search of fresh grass. Diana watched for tracks. She found them. She followed the tracks. They led to an area where several trees had fallen. This formed a natural corral. Three of the cows were standing there watching her as she approached. She went up behind them and slapped the stick on the fallen trees. The cattle turned and walked slowly back through the forest. She followed them to the barn.

Josephine had not returned as yet. Diana began to milk the cows, pouring the buckets of milk into the wooden barrel. Regina had already started and the two of them worked swiftly. Diana wanted to finish up and get back into the warm kitchen. By the time they had finished, William had joined them. He had been rabbit hunting again. They were having rabbit stew for dinner. Diana went inside. She removed her fur wraps and untied her leggings. She stood with her back to the fireplace. Regina had joined her. Josephine had not returned.

Will asked, "Which way did Josephine go?"

Diana nodded her head in the direction of the road. "She went over the knob, Pappa."

Agnus turned and looked at Will. "You better go find her, Will," she said.

Will nodded his head. He began to tie the pine branches to his feet. They would support his weight on top of the snow. Without sinking in the drifted snow, he could move more rapidly. He took his long rifle and went back outside.

When Diana had thawed out, she began to help her mother with dinner. Regina was kneading the dough for biscuits. Soon, the kitchen smelled of rabbit stew. They heard footsteps on the porch. The door opened and Josephine entered. William was right behind her. He glanced over at Agnus.

Josephine's cheeks were chapped. Her lips were stiff from the cold and she could barely talk. She unwrapped her leggings and stood in front of the fireplace.

"I think I will have to cut some fence posts this spring and start closing those cows in," William said. "I can't have you girls getting lost in the forest.

Who knows, there could be another mountain lion out there somewheres," he said. He kept glancing over at Agnus.

Josephine was quiet all through dinner. She helped with the clean up and then went right up to the bed in the loft. Diana and the others practiced their reading. Then they all gathered around the fireplace while their mother read from the Bible. Today's Bible lesson was about Joseph. He was placed in a well and sold off into slavery. Diana wondered if Joseph was a colored man. Soon, it was time for bed. Each of the girls kissed their parents good night and went to bed.

The next morning was a day of hunting. Diana had to stay behind and help Regina in the barn. They were shorthanded until Sofia's hand healed enough to milk and carry buckets. She was taking advantage of the situation, too. Diana was angry at her sister. Why couldn't she have done it in the summertime, when it wasn't so difficult? She wanted to go hunting with her father and Josephine. She carried her sling and bow with her when she went to the barn.

Diana had started shoveling the manure out of the barn two days ago. As cold as it was, the manure was warm down under the surface. If they didn't keep it shoveled out, the cows would be hitting their heads on the ceiling before long. Regina and Diana worked feverishly. Rudy had stayed behind with them. The girls talked as they worked. Soon, they had run out of subjects to talk about and fell silent as they worked.

Rudy's growling caught Diana's attention. He was facing the back of the barn. He went to the far wall and sniffed. He growled again and then barked. He turned and ran outside and around the barn. There was a commotion out back. Diana grabbed her bow and ran for the back of the barn. It was a wolf. Rudy and the wolf were locked together, biting, growling, and howling. The wolf was twice the size of Rudy. That did not stop the dog. He fought for all he was worth. Diana aimed her bow. She held fast, waiting for an opportunity to get in a clean shot. It did not come. She grabbed a stick and pounded on the wolf. It turned toward her. Rudy seized the opportunity and pounced on the wolf again, preventing it from attacking Diana. Regina stood back, screaming for her mother.

The wolf was too much for Rudy. He was down. He lay motionless. The wolf began to drag him, all the while snarling at Diana. She drew back her bow and sent an arrow into the wolf's left shoulder. It screeched and twisted about. Diana pulled back again. Another arrow hit the wolf, just a little further back. It sank deep into the rib cage. The wolf turned and began running for the woods. It did not get far. It fell. Diana ran to Rudy. He was panting and whining. She watched his rib cage rise and fall until it stopped. He was dead.

Diana rose and walked to the wolf. It too, was dead. She knelt down and began to skin it. Agnus had run out to where Regina was knelt over Rudy. They picked the dog up and carried it back to the house. Diana finished skinning the wolf and carried the hide to the porch. She went inside to wash the blood from her hands. She cried the whole time. Rudy was just like a member of the family.

"You go upstairs and lay down for awhile. I can handle this," Agnus said. Regina and Diana both went up the ladder and into the loft. They held each other and cried. Losing Rudy would affect them all.

After a while, Regina's breathing became slow and steady. She had cried herself to sleep. Diana could not sleep. She crawled back down the ladder. She dressed and went back to the barn. She would rather work than lay around, crying. Father and Josephine would be home soon.

Diana went out searching for the cows by herself. They were all standing at the edge for the forest today. Even Hughie was there. Diana approached cautiously. Hughie was unpredictable. Today, he snorted at her as she approached. She made a wide circle. She called to the cows as she went. They raised their heads, and started for the barn. Diana did not take her eyes off Hughie. Even when she was on her way back to the barn, she kept looking over her shoulder to make sure he was not charging her from behind.

Inside the barn, she began to milk the cows. She was about half through when Regina came out to help. Agnus had woke her and told her to help her sister. Diana could not help but think that they were all becoming lazy this winter. Even her own father seemed to find excuses to keep him out of the barn. It seemed nearly all of the work was on her shoulders these days.

After the milking, they carried the wooden barrel to the house. Agnus began to skim the cream from the top. She placed it into the butter churn. Martha began working the wooden handle. Agnus poured the leftover milk into a smaller wooden barrel and set it outside on the porch. She stopped, when she came back inside, and stared at the spot where Rudy used to lay by the door. She shook her head and went to the pot in the fireplace.

The noise on the porch told them that William and Josephine were back. The door opened. Will entered first. "Where did that wolf hide come from?" he asked.

Martha and Ruth Ann began chattering the whole story to him. Josephine and Will stood at the door motionless, listening to the tale of how Rudy saved them from the wolf. When they came to the part about Diana killing the wolf, William turned to look at his second oldest daughter. He removed his leggings and wraps. He untied the rabbit furs from around his head.

"That was a very brave thing you did, girl," he said.

Diana swallowed hard. Thinking about it caused her to choke up. "I just couldn't let him drag Rudy off and eat him, Pappa," she said.

They all were quiet at the dinner table that evening. Diana did not eat much. She would miss Rudy. William had mentioned they may get another dog, but it would never be the same as old Rudy. He was more like a member of the family. He would be missed by all of them.

After dinner, the girls all jumped in to help clean up. They gathered around the fireplace, taking part in their reading and writing lessons. Then Agnus read from the Bible.

The winter days dragged on. One day, on the way back from delivering their milk, James invited them to stop and warm themselves near the fireplace.

When they went inside, the fire was blazing. The room felt warm and inviting. Diana walked to the fireplace and turned with her back to the fire. There on the floor, lay a blond fur hide. "It's the mountain lion I killed," James explained. Diana ran her hand across it. It was so soft. She felt the thickness of it. It was the prettiest hide she had ever seen.

James was alone at the house. "Uncle Porter has gone to Philadelphia to collect Aunt Margaret. They are coming by stage. Thomas is coming by wagon. He is bringing their belongings and household furnishings," he explained. Then he grew quiet.

Diana looked over at James. He was looking at Josephine as he went on, "Then, Thomas and I are going to Philadelphia to run his sawmill there. We will be living at Uncle Porter's old house."

Diana looked over at Josephine. Her face was white. Her lip quivered. Diana thought she was going to cry. She continued to watch the two of them. They did not take their eyes from one another. After awhile, Diana urged them to leave. Regina was nearly as reluctant as Josephine. They had all grown quite fond of their moments within the big house.

Soon, they were all aboard the two-wheeled cart once again. They crossed the half-frozen stream and made their way on toward home. Regina sang as they went. Diana and Josephine both remained silent. Diana knew her sister's heart was breaking. Josephine had confessed her love for James to Diana. Now he was moving away.

When they got back to the farm, Josephine moved mechanically as they unhitched Buck and removed the wooden barrel. Will was off hunting somewhere. Agnus had baked corn bread. There was leftover stew in the iron pot that hung in the fireplace. There wasn't much, but with the corn bread, they would not go hungry. Josephine laid the few coins that Mrs. Hickman had given her on the washboard. Agnus wrapped them in a small rabbit hide and put them into her apron pocket.

At the dinner table that evening, Agnus kept watching Josephine. She knew something was wrong, but she could not put her finger on it. "How was the trip to town this morning?" Agnus asked.

"It was fine," Diana answered. She looked over at her sister and then at her mother. She smiled and said no more. That was when Regina started telling everything.

"We stopped at Porter Martin's house," Regina began. "He's in Philadelphia collectin his wife. They're comin by stage. James said Thomas is comin' by wagon so he can bring all their furniture. I can't wait to see what kind of furniture they have. That is such a fine house. I hope he comes callin' for us to go work for him. Can I work for him, Mamma? And, oh yes, I almost forgot. James and Thomas is goin to live in Philadelphia in Porter's old house so they kin run his sawmill."

Agnus looked over at Josephine. She now knew what was bothering her oldest daughter. William did not seem to catch on. He was more interested in the fact that Porter Martin was going to have two sawmills operating at the same time. "That man must have a pile of money hid somewheres," Will said.

After the dinner clean up, Josephine excused herself. She said she had a stomachache. She went up into the loft. Agnus placed the slates on the table and the girls began their studies. Will lit his pipe and sat by the fireplace. He stared at the flickering fire.

Then it was Bible reading time, and he turned his stool to face the rest of them as Agnus read.

When Diana crawled into the loft that night, she heard Josephine sobbing. She lay down close to her sister and put her arm over her. Josephine held Diana's hand. "What am I going to do, Diana?" Josephine whispered. "I can't live without him."

Diana swallowed hard and squeezed her sister tight. "I don't know, Josie. I don't know what to tell you to make the hurtin' stop," Diana replied.

They fell asleep holding one another.

The next morning was bitterly cold. Diana ate her boiled oats and drank a cup of warm milk. She went to the barn. They had been keeping the cows in the corral at night ever since the wolf attack. This made the milking much easier. Now, they only had to hunt down the cows once a day. Diana milked the cows, pouring the buckets of steaming milk into the wooden barrel. Josephine worked feverishly. She seemed to be in a hurry for some reason today.

When they had finished, Diana and Josephine carried the wooden barrel to the porch. Diana began to skim the cream off the top. Josephine went into the house. Soon, Will came outside carrying both long rifles.

"Diana, you are going hunting with me today. Josephine is feelin under the weather. Here, take this here long rifle of your sister's and come on," he said, holding the rifle out for her to take.

Diana had her sling slipped through her belt. She carried it with her at all times. She did not have her bow. It was in the house. "You won't be needin' your bow. This time, you will use the rifle," William said.

Once outside, Diana poured the black powder down the barrel of the Kentucky Long Rifle. She pushed the patched ball down the barrel and packed it with the ramrod. She pulled the hammer back, placed the blasting cap on the nipple, and returned the hammer to a half cocked position so the loaded rifle was safe to carry. Then she hurried to catch up with her father.

They walked through the forest silently. Occasionally, William would make a gesture with his hand, signaling her to stop or look in a certain direction. Diana followed his lead. She was ready. They walked for what seemed to be miles. At least it was warmer inside the forest. The trees broke the wind.

Diana whispered to her father. "Pappa, you hold the gun for me while I climb this here tree. Then you go on over yonder. I kin see better from up high," she said.

Will frowned and looked up into the tree. He nodded and waited for her to climb. When she had nestled herself into a safe spot, he handed the rifle up to her. He nodded at her and went on through the forest. Diana climbed higher into the tree so she could gaze through the forest. It was cooler up in the tree. She tried not to move about or make any noise.

Soon, something caught her eye. It was coming from her left. It was a doe. She was chewing on the bark of the trees. She chewed for a while and then moved closer. Diana held her breath and waited. Soon, the doe was within range. Diana moved very slowly so as not to alert the deer. She took aim. She held her breath again. She pulled the hammer back slowly and placed her finger on the trigger. She squeezed the trigger.

The gun fired. It kicked, nearly knocking her out of the tree. The doe was on the run. Diana dropped the gun out of the tree and climbed down. She took up the rifle and began running in the direction of the doe. She was breathing hard. The cold air was freezing her lungs.

There was a trail of blood. Diana followed the trail. Soon, she came to an area where the brush was thick. There was more blood. She saw the doe hiding under some overgrown brush. She began to pour more powder down the barrel of the rifle. She re-loaded the rifle and cocked the hammer into a firing position. The doe was watching her. Its big brown eyes seem to be pleading with her. She lowered the rifle.

A commotion over her shoulder told her that her father was coming toward her. She knew what she had to do. She drew the rifle to her shoulder and fired. The sound cracked through the forest like lightning. The doe lay dead.

Will was panting. "What is it? What did you get?" he asked, breathing hard.

Diana could not speak. She nodded in the direction of the doe. Will ran to it. "Good Lord, girl! We will eat good for better n a month!" he said, drawing his knife. Diana laid the rifle down and went to help her father gut the deer. Then they started preparing two poles to carry the carcass home.

It was a long trip home. Will stopped from time to time to allow them to catch their breath and rest their arms. Diana was small for a fourteen-year-old.

Soon, they were home. Will hung the deer from a tree in the yard and began to skin and butcher it. He told Diana she had earned the right to take it easy the rest of the day. She went inside and warmed herself near the fireplace.

Agnus was humming to herself as she heated a cup of warm milk for Diana.

"Where are Josephine and Sofia?" Diana asked.

Agnus stopped humming. "Sofia went to get some water at the stream. Josephine is in the barn I reckon," Agnus said.

Diana had just come from the barn. She knew Josephine was not there. She did not say anything. She drank her milk and warmed herself. She was proud of what she had done today.

After awhile, she began to wrap herself to go back outside. "I am goin to see if Josie needs any help fetchin the cows," she announced to her mother. She went back outside. Will was still working on butchering the deer. Regina and Martha had joined him. Diana went into the barn. Sofia was milking Prudy and Nelly. "Have you seen Josie?" Diana asked.

Sofia looked up at Diana and announced. "I haven't seen her in quite a spell," Sofia said.

Diana turned to leave. She called back as she went. "Ifin she comes back, you tell her to stay here." She began to head for the knob and forest's edge.

Once she made it to the top of the knob, she spotted small footprints in the snow. She followed them. They were not leading into the woods at all. They were following the cart trail that led to Porter Martin's house. Diana walked as quickly as she could. She had to find Josie and get her home before her father came looking for them. She was almost to the shallow crossing in the stream when she spotted Josie coming toward her. She was wrapped in the golden mountain lion fur.

"Josie! What are you thinkin? Mamma and Pappa are bound to know where you bin when they see that fur," Diana said.

Josie tossed her head. "I don't care, Diana! I don't care what anybody says! I'm fixin to go to Philly with James when he goes. I'm fixin to get out of here!" Josephine said as she trudged toward home. Diana had to hurry to keep up with her older sister.

"What are you sayin'? You know Pa is not goin to stand for that. He won't let you go. You're only fifteen." Diana tried to reason with her sister.

"I am almost sixteen. Mamma and Pappa were married when Mamma was sixteen. Besides, they will not be able to stop me. If they won't let me go with James, I will just run away!" Josephine said as she walked.

Diana decided not to argue with Josie. She knew her sister was in for enough of that when she reached the farm. Diana said a silent prayer. She was praying her father wouldn't take Josephine to the barn and whoop her hide for running off to see James.

They reached the porch. Josephine stood for a moment just outside the door. Diana caught up to her and stood by her side, watching her. Josephine took a deep breath and pushed the door open. They stepped inside together.

Agnus was at the fireplace. Will was sitting near her on his stool, smoking his pipe. Regina and Sofia were setting the table. Martha was braiding Ruth Ann's hair. They all looked up when the two sisters entered the room. Diana began to unwrap her leggings right away. She tried to keep her eyes lowered.

"Where have you two been?" Agnus asked.

Will stood up and approached Josephine. He took hold of the mountain lion hide and pulled it from around Josephine. He studied it for a while and then said through clenched teeth. "I know where they bin. This is the mountain lion hide that James Harris kilt. You girls been up to the Martin house."

Agnus went to stand at his side. "Not Diana. She just left a few minutes ago. She did not have time to git that far," she said.

"Then Josephine was up there. He gave this to you didn't he, girl?" Will asked, shaking Josie by the shoulders. "Answer your Pa!"

Josephine gulped. A soft gasp escaped her lips. She could not speak. She nodded her head, keeping her eyes lowered. Diana stood up. She was frightened for her sister. Will only used the whipping switch when they had done something very bad. Usually, it was something that put them in harm's way. He tried to impress upon them the seriousness of their actions. Diana was sure Josephine was about to be whooped.

William shook Josephine again. "What were the two of you doing up there in that house all alone?" he asked.

Josephine shook her head. "Nothin', Pappa. We were just talkin'," she whispered.

"You bin layin' with that James Harris? You tell me now, girl!" Will shouted.

Agnus touched his arm and said, "Will. The girls."

Will turned to look at the wide eyes staring at him. He turned back to Josephine. "You better tell me now and spare yourself a whoopin. I will deal with him in the morning," he said through clenched teeth.

Josephine found her voice. "He didn't do anything wrong. You leave him alone. He loves me and I love him. I am going with him when he goes to Philadelphia. We are goin to git married," she shouted at her father. She was crying now.

Will removed his hands from her shoulders. He stood up tall, puffing his chest out. "So, ya think so, do ya? Well, I will have a say in that! And I say you are too young!" Will said.

Josephine stepped back. She looked over at her mother. Her eyes were pleading with Agnus. "You married Mamma when she was just sixteen. I am almost sixteen," Josephine said.

Agnus stepped forward and said, "And look where it got me!" She gasped and threw her hands over her mouth. She looked over at Will. He did not return her gaze. She took a deep breath and said softly. "What I meant to say was we had hopes that you girls would have a better life n we have." Again, she looked at her husband. He continued to stare at Josephine.

Diana went to the fireplace to stand with the rest of her sisters. They huddled together. They were all frightened of what was taking place.

Will shoved the lion pelt back at Josephine. He said, "Wrap yourself in this and go to the barn!" He reached for his leg wraps and began to tie them on.

Josephine turned to her mother before going out the door. "Mamma, you said you wanted better for us girls. Well, what could be better n a big house in Philadelphia?" Josephine went outside. Agnus turned to look at the frightened faces that huddled together near the fireplace.

"Let's git this table set," she said. They broke away from one another and went back to their chores. No one spoke a word. They were all imagining what was taking place in the barn.

Soon, Josephine came inside crying. She went straight to the loft, carrying the mountain lion's hide with her. Will came in and sat down on a stool. He was quiet as he unwrapped his leggings. He took his pipe and went back to his spot near the fireplace.

Diana felt sick to her stomach. She was not hungry, even though they were having venison for dinner. She picked at her plate. They all did. After dinner, they cleaned up and sat down for their lessons. Agnus sat down at the table and announced, "There will be no lessons tonight. Lord knows no one will be able to concentrate no how." She started reading from the Bible. After about a minute, she closed the Bible and announced that it was bedtime.

Diana hurried up the ladder that led to the loft. Sofia was on her heels.

"Did Pa whoop you, Josie?" Sofia asked.

"Sofia!" Diana said. "Let her be."

Diana slid up close to Josephine and put her arm over her sister. Josephine lay there with her back to them. Diana could tell Josephine was not asleep because she was still sobbing. Diana stroked her hair. Sofia lay on her side, facing them. She had propped herself up on one elbow. After sometime, she gave up and put her head down. Soon, Sofia was snoring. Josephine was still sobbing.

Diana whispered in her ear. "Please, Josie. Please, don't go off to Philadelphia. I was hoping you would go to the Martin's with me to take care of Mrs. Martin. I don't want Sofia or Regina to help. Sofia will sit on her butt all day while I do all of the work, and Regina will drive us all crazy with her constant talking. Please, Josie. Don't leave me here. I need you," Diana begged her sister.

Josephine whispered between sobs. "I am sorry, Di. But nobody or nothing can stop me from goin' with James. We were meant to be together."

Diana closed her eyes tight. She took a deep breath. She tried to go to sleep, but sleep did not come for Josephine or Diana that night.

The next morning, Josephine did not go down to breakfast. Will dressed to go out. He went to the door. He turned toward Agnus and said, "She is not to go out today."

Agnus nodded. William went outside. Diana knew he was going to talk to James. She closed her eyes and took a deep breath. She ate her venison jerky and boiled oats. She could not taste anything. She wrapped her feet and legs, pulled her wraps about her, and went to the barn. As usual, Sofia stayed behind. Regina came out shortly to help with the milking.

"What is goin to happin to Josie? I think Pa will kill James Harris. Do you think he will kill Josie, too?" Regina asked.

Diana shook her head. "Pa ain't gonna kill nobody. He is just goin to talk to James. He is just tryin' to sort this whole mess out. That's all. Where do you come up with these ideas?" she said.

Finally, Sofia came shuffling her feet through the snow. No doubt, their mother told her she had to come help. She certainly wasn't about to do it on her own. Diana tried to avoid Sofia. It wasn't going to work.

"Ma's not sayin nothin this mornin. You know her and Pa talked about it last night after we went to bed. Do you think they are fixin to let Josie marry that James Harris?" Sofia asked.

"Who said he even asked her?" Regina asked.

Diana pretended not to hear. She worked feverishly. Soon, the milking was done. She left the two of them standing in the barn. She gathered up her bow and started for the back of the house.

"Diana. Where you goin?" Regina called.

"I'm going rabbit hunting," she called back over her shoulder.

Sofia called to her. "But we don't need any more meat. You know what Pa always said, "Don't ever take any more n you need.""

Diana waved her hands in the air and continued to trudge through the snow toward the stream. She wanted to be alone. She came to the downed tree and crossed the stream. She made her way into the forest. She walked along until she came to the area where she had found the cows amongst the fallen trees. She wiped the snow from one of the logs and sat down. The log was cold under her, but she did not mind. She just wanted to be alone with her thoughts.

After sometime of pondering over the events of the night before, Diana began practicing with her sling. She aimed at trees. She seldom missed her mark. When she grew bored with that, she began to wander further into the forest. Eventually, she came out near the snow bank on the other side of the forest. There stood Hughie. He looked up at her as she approached. To his right, all nine cows stood foraging for grass. Diana stopped. It was too early in the day to start herding them back to the barn. She began to back slowly into the forest, watching Hughie closely. He went back to grazing.

She worked her way further to the left. She eventually came out of the forest near the bend in the road. The shallow stream near the Martin house was just up a ways. She turned toward home. As she rounded the bend, she caught sight of a dark image in the snow. She walked slowly at first, for fear it was another wolf. Soon she was running toward it. It was her father.

She ran to him. "Pappa. Pappa. What happened? Did that James Harris hurt you?" she cried out.

Will was knelt on his knees. He was gripping his chest. He leaned into her as she knelt beside him. "Pappa, say something!" Diana cried. She began checking him for signs of an injury.

"My chest. I can't breathe," William said, gasping.

Diana looked about her. He was much too heavy for her to carry. She would have to go for help. Porter Martin's was the closest. She jumped to her feet. "I am going for help, Pappa!" She ran back toward the narrow crossing. She ran as fast as she could. She crossed the frozen ice and ran to the house. She pounded on the front door with both fists. "Help! Help me!" she cried with every strike of her fists on the door.

The door flew opened and James stood before her with an angry look on his face.

"What the hell?" he asked.

Diana was gasping, "It's Pappa. James you gotta come help him! He's down and I can't get him up. Please, James. Please won't you help me?" She was sobbing now.

James pulled her inside. He pulled his buffalo coat on and grabbed his pistol, sticking it inside his belt. "Lead the way!" he said, holding the door for her.

Diana started to run back to the stream. "Wait, Diana!" James called. "We will need a horse." He ran for the barn. Diana ran after him. James pulled two horses out of the barn. He bridled them both, but did not bother to put saddles on them. They mounted the horses, bareback.

Diana kicked her heels into the sides of the large horse and hung on. James followed her. They found William just as Diana had left him. He was still clutching his chest and moaning in pain. James helped Diana lift him up onto the back of a horse. James climbed on behind William and leaned him back against his chest. Diana climbed onto the other horse and they started for the Lewis farm.

When they got close, Diana rode on ahead, shouting all the way. Agnus and Regina came outside. Agnus rushed to them. James helped her get Will into the house and onto the bed. Agnus began to undress Will. James went to the fireplace. Sofia rushed up the ladder to the loft. Soon, Josephine and Sofia were coming into the kitchen.

"What happened?" Agnus called from the bedroom. "What did you do to him?"

Diana went to the door to the bedroom. "He didn't do nothing, Mamma. James helped me get Pappa home." Diana began to explain to the mother. "I found Pappa in the clearing just this side of the shallow crossin. He was down. I couldn't carry him. I ran to fetch James. He saved Pappa's life, Mamma." Tears were streaming down Agnus' cheeks. The sight of her mother so perplexed caused a chain reaction. Diana broke into tears.

She turned toward James and said, "Thank you, James."

James nodded. He turned to Josephine and said softly, "I have seen this before. It's called a heart attack. Most times, they don't make it, Josie. He needs a doctor real bad."

"What?" Diana asked. "There's no doctor here abouts that we know of. What will we do?" She turned to look back into the bedroom where her mother was wiping William's brow.

James went to the bedroom door and stood watching them. "I want to help, but I am afraid I do not know what to do," he said to Agnus.

"You did fine, James. Thank you," Agnus said. She knelt beside William and began praying.

James turned to Josephine. "I better go. My being here will probably just make it worse when he wakes," he said.

Josephine walked to the porch with James. Diana waited for him to mount his horse. She handed him the reins to the second horse. "Thank you so much

James. And, well, I am sorry for thinking you had done something to Pappa. That was wrong of me," she said.

James reached down and squeezed her hand. "It's all right, Diana. I understand. I hope it goes well for your father," he said. He took the reins and rode off toward home.

Josephine and Diana prepared dinner. They sent Regina to split some wood, and Martha and Sofia to herd the cows home. Agnus refused to leave William's side, not even long enough to eat a bite. Ruth Ann clung to her mother, sobbing.

After dinner, they left the clean up to Sofia and Martha. Josephine, Diana, and Regina did the milking. When they came back inside, they discovered that the evening meal's clean up was still not done. Josephine scolded Sofia for her laziness at this particular time. The two older sisters jumped in and finished the clean up. They sat quietly all through the night around the fireplace.

The next morning found all six of the girls huddled around the fireplace sleeping on the floor. Josephine was the first to stir. She went outside to gather some wood. Diana dressed and went to the stream for a couple buckets of water. They began to prepare breakfast. Agnus came out of the bedroom rubbing her shoulders. She went to the pot in the fireplace. The girls stood watching her. "There is not change this morning," Agnus said, without turning around. "You girls just go about your daily routine for today. We shall see where we are this evening."

"I will fetch a couple of extra buckets of water for you Mamma," Diana said. She dressed and went back outside.

They milked the cows and poured the milk into the wooden barrel. Usually, William would lift the barrel onto the cart, as it was too heavy for the girls. This morning, they placed the empty barrel inside the cart and carried the buckets from the barn to the cart. Regina stood inside the cart and lifted the buckets up, dumping their contents into the barrel. It took longer, but it was the only way. When they had finished, it was decided that Regina would stay behind with Agnus to look out for the girls and help. They knew Sofia would just sit on her behind with no one to prod her on. Also, Josephine did not want to listen to Regina's incessant chattering all the way to town.

They drove Buck up the narrow cart path and toward the narrow crossing. They drove right past Porter Martin's house. James stood on the porch and waved as they passed. They were nearly in sight of the town when James came riding up behind them.

"How is your father this morning?" he asked, riding alongside of the cart.

Josephine smiled. "There's no change, I'm afraid."

James frowned. "That is too bad," he replied. "I thought I might join you girls this morning. Perhaps I can be of some assistance," he said.

Josephine smiled. "That is mighty nice of you, James," she said.

They reached town. James went in the general store and stood at the counter while Mrs. Hickman and her sons measured the milk. "Is Sherman anywhere abouts?" he asked.

Grace smiled and called to her oldest son. "Willy, go fetch your Pa. Tell him that nice James Harris wants to see him," she smiled again at James.

Willy went through the curtained door that led to their living quarters. Soon, he emerged with Sherman Hickman right behind him. "What can I do for ya, Mr. Harris?" Sherman asked.

"Good morning, Mr. Hickman. I was wondering if you and your lovely wife, Grace, might see to it that these young ladies had everything they need to get them by for a spell. You see, Mr. Lewis has had a heart attack and they will be needing a few extra supplies. I know, you being the good neighbors that you are, you would want to help in any way possible," James said smiling.

Sherman began to scratch his chin. "Why, sure, Mr. Harris. Grace will gladly give them anything they need, and the boys will load it all onto the cart. What is that you say happened to Will?" Sherman asked.

"He had a heart attack last evening. It is my understanding that he is not well at all," James said.

Sherman continued to scratch his chin. "A heart attack you say. That is very bad news. I am very sorry to hear that. You tell your Ma, we will be glad to help in any way we can," he said to the girls.

Josephine nodded. "Thank you, Mr. Hickman," she said. She looked over at Grace who was glaring at her. "Thank you, Ma'am. I will tell Ma you send your best regards."

"What will you be needin?" Grace asked as she brushed past Josephine to get behind the counter. She took her pencil in her hand and paused over the ledger. Josephine swallowed hard. She thought for a moment. She knew that money would be very scarce until Pappa got better.

"This will go on my tab, Mrs. Hickman," James spoke up.

"Your tab, Mr. Harris? Why, that is very neighborly of you!" Mrs. Hickman said, straightening her hair.

James smiled and tipped his hat. "Yes, Ma'am! You see, where I come from a good neighbor does all he can to help those in need. You never know when you will be needing the favor returned," he said smiling.

Grace Hickman flushed. "Why, of course, Mr. Harris. I have always said that very thing. I think we could afford to be a little charitable ourselves. You needn't worry about this, Mr. Hickman and myself will take care of it." She nodded at Sherman. "Willy, get a couple of boxes for these lovely young ladies."

When they left the store, they had enough supplies to get them through a couple of weeks. Josephine knew that as soon as they left, Grace wrote every item they received into her ledger. They would worry about paying for it later.

James rode with them to the house. Before breaking away from them and going to the barn, he said, "You tell your Mother if she needs anything at all to send one of you girls after me."

"Thank you, James!" They called to him. They drove Buck on toward the farm. They were anxious to see how William was.

When they reached the house, Josephine pulled Buck to a halt near the porch. They unloaded the empty barrel onto the porch. Then they began carrying in the supplies.

Agnus met them at the door. "What is all of this?" she asked.

Josephine did not say anything. "It is supplies from Hickman's store, Mamma. James talked Grace Hickman into giving us some supplies until Pappa got back on his feet," Diana said.

Josephine went back outside. She climbed up onto the cart and drove Buck to the barn. "I better go unhitch Buck, Mamma. Sofia can tell you all about it," Diana said. She hurried out the door. Josephine was just pulling Buck to a halt near the barn. She jumped from the cart. Diana ran to help her unhitch Buck and led him into the barn. She removed his harness. Josephine remained silent.

Diana said, "Josie, that was a real nice thing James did for us. I think he would make a fine husband. I am sorry I asked you to stay with me. That was selfish of me. I think he would make a fine husband, just as I said."

Josephine swallowed hard. Diana thought she was going to cry. She nodded and replied, "Thank you, Diana. Thank you for tellin' me that."

They finished up and went back inside. Josephine was slower at removing her wraps. Diana had finished and was pouring a cup of warm milk for herself when Josephine sat down at the table. Agnus placed a cup in front of her.

"How is Pappa?" Diana asked, looking over her shoulder toward the bedroom where her father laid.

Agnus frowned and said, "He is not good, but he is alive. As long as he is alive, there is hope."

Diana took her cup and went into the bedroom. William lay there with his eyes closed. His chest heaved with every breath. His eyes were close. His bottom jaw was slack, leaving his mouth open, which caused slobber to run down the side of his cheek. Diana knelt onto her knees beside the bed. "Pappa, it is Diana. Don't worry, Pappa. I will see to it that everything gets done until you are better," she said. She squeezed her father's hand. Then she rose to her feet and went back into the kitchen.

When Agnus turned to stir the iron pot, Diana whispered to Josephine, "Josie, you should go say something to Pappa. Let him know you are not mad at him. It might help him get better."

Josephine looked at Diana. She frowned and got up from the table. Diana watched her as she went in the direction of the bedroom. She stopped at the door and watched her father lying in the bed. Then she went up the ladder to the loft.

Diana sighed. Josephine was still mad at her father, even with the threat of his dying. How could she be so stubborn? Diana finished her milk and carried her cup to the washboard.

"Mamma, did Regina split any wood this morning?' Diana asked her mother. Agnus nodded. She had her back to Diana. She wiped at her face. Diana knew her mother was crying. She went to Agnus and put her arms around her. "Don't worry, Momma. It will be all right." Agnus sobbed. After a minute, she seemed to recover.

Agnus said, "I'm goin' to sit with your Pa for a spell. Can you cover for me out here?"

Diana nodded. "Yes, Mamma. We can do our sewin' lessons. You go on in," she said.

The five daughters gathered around the fireplace with their dresses. "My dress is nearly finished," Regina said. Diana looked around. All of their dresses were close to being complete except for Sofia's. Diana watched Sofia as she sewed. After a few stitches, she would stare off into space. Her eyes glazed over. She had drifted into some fantasy world, leaving them all behind. Unfortunately, she was leaving her new dress unfinished, too. Diana shook her head.

Diana cleared her throat. Sofia continued to stare. Diana cleared her throat again, only louder. Finally, she said, "Sofia. Sofia!"

Sofia shook her head. She looked at Diana. "What?" she asked.

"You help Josephine get supper tonight so Mamma kin sit with Pa. Regina, Martha, and I will bring in the cows," Diana said.

Sofia frowned. She leaned over close to where Diana was sitting and said in a low voice so her mother could not hear, "You are not the boss of me, Diana!"

"You heard me. I kin whoop your hide any day of the week, and I will if you don't mind me. Mamma needs to stay with Pappa. You do as I say, or I will take you outside myself!" Diana said.

Sofia turned to walk away. She was pouting. Diana did not care if she had hurt Sofia's feelings. It seemed all of the work around there was put upon her shoulders. Lately, even Josephine had been spending most of her time lying up in the loft. Today, she had just had enough.

She put her sewing away. Regina and Martha joined her as she dressed to go outside. As they went across the front yard, between the house and barn, Diana called to them through the wind. "I saw all nine of them earlier on the other side of the woods." She pointed to show the way. "Just be careful, because Hughie is up there with them," she called.

The two sisters followed Diana into the forest. They followed fresh tracks to the opening where the bank was. The cows were no longer there. The tracks showed they had taken for the woods. They were seeking protection from the howling wind. Diana scanned the area for Hughie. She did not see him. They continued to follow the tracks.

Soon they came to an area where there were many young trees sprouting through the snow. Diana saw Hughie. He raised his head and snorted. She did not see the rest of the cows, so she motioned to her sisters to stay back. They made a wide circle around the bull. They found more tracks and followed them. They were leading to the barn. The three girls followed the tracks through the woods until they came to the clearing where they could see the farm again. All nine cows were making their way for the barn. Apparently, they wanted to get out of the wind.

Diana broke into a fast walk. Regina and Martha ran to keep up with her. They reached the barn right after the cows and started the milking. They began to pour the milk into the wooden barrel. Tomorrow, they did not have to make the trip into town. When they had finished, they went back inside.

Inside, Diana found her mother in the kitchen, preparing the evening meal. Josephine was outside, splitting wood for the fire. Sofia was sitting with her father. Diana went to the bedroom door and glared at her sister. Sofia stuck her tongue out at Diana and turned her back on her. Diana went back into the kitchen and said to Agnus. "I told Sofia to do that so you could sit with Pappa. You really should be the one in there, Mamma. Sofia is gettin' lazy. She needs to pull more of her own weight around here."

Agnus turned to Diana and smiled. She wiped her hands on her apron. She pulled Diana toward the table and motioned for her to sit down. Agnus sat down beside her. She smiled again and said, "I know it has been hard for you lately. You are workin' so hard. I am thankful to the good Lord that you are here. I don't think your Pappa is going to git any better, girl. I've bin prayin and prayin, but somethin tells me he will be with the Lord soon." Agnus took Diana's hand. She was choking up. "I thank ya for all your hardwork, Diana. I am afraid it is goin' to get harder and I truly am sorry. I don't think your Pa will be here much longer, as I said, and I told Josephine that she could go with James to Philadelphia. It is her chance for a better life, and I can't hold her back, even though I want to."

Diana's eyes widened. "Mamma, Pappa would not like that. He is against Josie even seein' James anymore."

Agnus nodded her head and kissed Diana's hand. "I know, Dear, but I talked to your Pappa about it all morning. I hope he heard me. I prayed about it, too. I just have to think of what is best for this family. Josephine has promised me that she will help all she can around here and not sneak off to see James, in return for our letting her go. I am allowing her to visit James, day after tomorrow, on your way back from Berlin. She can tell him the news then. You stay with her now. I don't want them spending too much time alone together. I am counting on you to step in for your Pa," Agnus said.

Diana thought for a moment. She sighed heavily and nodded her head. "I will do my best, Mamma."

Agnus hugged Diana. "That's my girl. I will have a strong talk with Sofia," she said.

Just then, the door opened and Regina and Martha came in. They stood at the door watching their mother and Diana sitting at the table. Agnus said, "You girls get undressed and help me out here." She rose from her stool and went back to the iron pot.

"Where are Sofia and Ruth Ann?" Regina asked.

Diana stood up. She said, "They are sittin' with Pappa. Thank you for helpin' me today. You both did really fine jobs. I appreciate the help." She looked over her shoulder toward her parents' bedroom. Sofia was still sitting with her back to the door.

Regina and Martha began untying their leggings. The door swung open and Josephine entered with her arms loaded down with wood. She was humming to herself. She dropped the wood near the fireplace and went back outside. Regina and Martha looked at one another. Then they looked at Diana and Agnus. Agnus smiled. Soon, Josephine entered once more with another arm load of wood. She dropped it near the fireplace also. She was still humming to herself. The sisters stood there watching her as she began to remove her fur wraps. She continued to hum. Diana looked over at her mother who was also watching. She turned her head to face Diana and smiled. Then she went back to stirring the iron pot.

Agnus was right about William going off to be with the Lord. The next day, he passed away. They all stood around his bed, crying. Agnus wiped her face on her apron and turned to Josephine, "Josie, you and Diana help me get him to the table. I will wash him down and prepare him for his buryin'," she said.

They lifted Will's partially stiff body and carried it to the table. Agnus sent the girls outside to dig a grave. "Dig it mighty deep. I don't want no wolf or coyote smelling him and diggin him back up," she said. The girls wailed and cried as they went outside. The ground was frozen and covered with nearly seven inches of snow.

Diana looked at Josephine and asked, "How are we ever goin to dig a grave with the ground bein' so hard?"

Josephine stood there for a moment. She said, "You wait here. I am goin to get James. He will know what to do." She turned and went in the direction of the barn.

Diana ran after her. "Josie, no! You promised Mamma you would stay away from James for now." She called out to her sister. The rest of the girls were following them into the barn. Josephine bridled Buck and climbed up onto the rail fence. She swung her leg over the horses back. "I will be right back!" Josephine said.

"Wait!" Diana called. "Take Martha with you. Mamma will be less likely to get riled if you have Martha with you," Diana said.

Josephine nodded. Diana held her hands out for Martha to step into. She lifted her younger sister high so she could straddle the horse. Josephine clicked her tongue and Buck began to walk. Josephine clicked her tongue several more times and Buck picked up the pace. Diana, Sofia, Regina, and Ruth Ann stood there watching them until they were out of sight.

Diana took the pick and a shovel and went behind the house. There stood a tall oak tree.

"This looks like a place that would please Pappa. What do you think?" she asked.

Ruth Ann clung to Sofia. They did not answer. They were still crying. "I will pick at the ground, and you, Sofia, will shovel it away." Diana said. She swung the pick a couple of times. To her surprise, Sofia did not complain or argue. She dug the shovel into the ground and began to clear the clumps of frozen ground. Diana swung the pick some more.

They had a hole about ankle deep when Josephine returned with James. He tied his horse at the front of the house. Regina ran to tell them where they were. James had brought a couple more picks and another shovel. He began digging right away. Josephine helped Diana dig at the ground with the picks. It seemed like it took nearly the whole day.

At last, they had a deep hole big enough to bury their father. They went inside to warm themselves.

To Diana's surprise, Agnus was not upset to see James there. She politely thanked him for his help. She had dressed William in his furs. He wore his rabbit skins tied around his ears and head, and his legs and feet were bound in his fur leggings. Agnus wrapped herself in furs and they carried William to the back of the house. They placed him in the grave. Josephine, Diana, and James shoveled dirt over top of his body. Agnus said a prayer and it was done.

"When the ground thaws, we will place a marker here," Agnus said. She turned to go into the house. "James, you are stayin for supper. You earned a home cooked meal. It is the least I could do for ya," she said as she went. Josephine looked up at James and smiled.

Diana hurried the girls along so James and Josephine could have a minute to themselves. She knew Josie wanted to tell James that her mother had decided to allow her to marry him and go off to Philadelphia.

"Let's gather up the cows and get the milkin' done. I could use some nice warm milk with my dinner," she said as they went toward the barn. Ruth Ann broke away from them and went into the house.

To Diana's surprise, the cows had come to the barn on their own. Regina and Sofia both helped her to milk them. Sofia was slow, but Diana did not complain. Her back hurt and her hands were blistered from using the pick. She imagined that Sofia was hurting, too. She worked harder today than she had in her whole life. "You did good today, Sofia. Thank you for the help," Diana said.

Sofia did not answer. She was sniffling. Diana knew her heart was breaking because they had just buried their father. Things would never be the same again.

That night, Diana lay in her bed and listened to the sounds within the house. There was coughing and sniffling. It seemed no one was sleeping. They all lay in their beds weeping over the loss of their beloved father. How were they going to survive? Will did most of the hunting and splitting of the wood. He relied on the girls to take care of the cows. Martha could be of more help, but she was only eight. Ruth Ann was just five. She could not be expected to help with the chores. There would be more money when Mr. Martin got back with his wife and two of them went to work for him. However, that meant less hands here on the farm. Diana tossed and turned. She was worrying herself into a sweat. She finally threw her arm over her eyes and tried not to think about it anymore. It was nearly morning when she fell asleep.

It was milk day. Agnus had breakfast ready for them when they got up. By the look on her face, it appeared as though she did not sleep all night either. She smiled, but remained quiet while they ate. "Regina, you go with Josie and Diana to cart the milk into Berlin this morning," she said. There was no sass or arguing. They were all too worn out to put up a fuss.

After breakfast, they went to the barn. Josie had taken Martha with her. She was teaching Martha the art of milking cows. They had finished all of the cows before Martha had finished her first one, but that was okay. She would catch on eventually. It was necessary for her to learn. It would become a matter of survival for them all. Someday, Ruth Ann would also be expected to help with the milking.

They poured the milk into the wooden barrel that was already loaded onto the two-wheeled cart. Josephine put the harness on Buck. They were soon ready to go. Agnus gave them some money wrapped in a rabbit hide. "You give this to Mrs. Hickman. You tell her to apply it to our bill." she said.

Josephine tucked the hide deep into her pocket and they started their journey into Berlin. They crossed the stream. The ice was thin this morning. It broke under Buck's feet. James was on the porch waiting for them. He waved as they went by, then he went back into the house. Diana knew he would have some warm coffee brewing for their return visit. It had become a ritual on the days they took the milk into town.

At the general store, Willy and Burt came to lift the wooden barrel off the cart. Burt smiled at Diana as they passed her. Diana had noticed his glances and smiles the last few times she was in town. She tried not to make eye contact with him, but she could not help herself.

"Burt, you measure the milk," Grace Hickman ordered after the barrel had been emptied. Burt put the stick down into the milk. Diana was standing next to Mrs. Hickman's milk barrel. She saw that the stick measured just under three gallons. She held her breath.

"It just over three gallons, Ma," Burt said, winking at Diana.

Diana felt her cheeks flushing. She watched Mrs. Hickman writing in the ledger. Josephine approached the counter and pulled the hide from her pocket.

"Mamma said to apply this to our bill," Josie said, opening the hide to reveal the coins.

Mrs. Hickman counted the change and wrote in the ledger without looking up at the girls.

"That still leaves a balance on your bill, young lady. You tell your mother, she still owes me for the last load of supplies," Grace Hickman said, peering over her glasses at Josephine.

"Yes, Ma'am," Josephine said. "She knows that was not enough to pay the full amount. She just wanted to pay what she could," Josephine said, looking at the floor.

"Well," Mrs. Hickman said, "your bill is almost ninety cents now. You be sure to tell your Ma, it is almost a dollar she owes us." She glared at Josephine, even though Josie would not make eye contact.

"Yes, Ma'am," Josephine said. They turned to go.

Mrs. Hickman called after them, "Wait a minute, girl. I heard a rumor a couple of days ago." She came around the counter. "I heard you were going to marry that James Harris and go off to Philadelphia. Is that true, girl?"

Josephine's cheeks flared. She tried not to smile. She lifted her head and faced Grace Hickman. "Yes, Ma'am. That would be a fact," she said. Diana felt her chest tighten.

"Well, aren't you the lucky one," Grace said, going around the counter again.

Josephine turned and went out the door to the cart. Diana and Regina followed her. Concetta was standing near Buck waiting on them. "Josephine, I am happy for you. James Harris is a very handsome man. Mamma said he was too old for me, so I am glad he chose you," she said. Josephine frowned and crawled up onto the cart. Diana smiled to herself. "You tell Sofia I asked about her," Concetta called as they drove away. Burt had joined his sister on the porch. As they were leaving, they heard Grace Hickman call out, "Burt! Where are you?" Diana looked back in his direction. He tipped his hat to her before disappearing into the store.

They road in silence for a while. Then Regina broke out in song. Josephine said, "Regina, will you please hush!" Regina fell silent.

Josephine turned back to look at Diana. "Burt Hickman has his eye on you, Di."

Diana shook her head. "Well, he can forget about me. I am only fourteen. I have other things to occupy my mind with right now. Like feeding this family and paying that darn bill off at the general store."

Josephine looked forward once again. Regina began humming to herself, softly. Soon, she was singing aloud once again. They rode along listening.

When they reached Porter Martin's house, they tied Buck out front. James met them at the door and invited them in. The house was warm. They had a custom of sitting around the fireplace in the kitchen. James had brewed fresh coffee, which they drank to warm themselves. It was hard to get Josephine to leave. These days weren't as bad, since she had promised her mother she would not dally, in return for permission to marry James.

James walked them back out and helped each of them up into the cart. "I am expecting Uncle Porter and Aunt Maggie any day now," he said. "You tell you Ma that he will be calling on her when he finds out about your Pa passing on," James said as they were leaving. They drove Buck on. By the time they had crossed the stream, Regina was singing again.

The next day was a clear day. The morning started off crisp and cold. The sky was clear blue with large white clouds. Diana went to the barn and began milking before the rest had finished eating their breakfast. Soon, Josephine, Regina, and lastly, Sofia joined in. Josephine and Diana had made plans to go hunting after they had finished the milking. Sofia was assigned the chore of splitting wood. Diana hoped she would not give them any trouble.

Josephine and Diana took the long rifles and went into the woods. Diana spoke softly as she explained how she had climbed the tree and waited until the deer came close enough for a clean shot. She wanted to try it again today. It was decided that they would split up and each pick a tree to climb on opposite sides of the woods.

Diana was nestled high in a tree. The wind blew the hair that hung down her back. She wished she had remembered to braid it. She sat there for what seemed like hours. She nearly fell asleep a time or two.

Soon, there was a loud crack that split the air. It was Josephine's rifle. Diana scrambled down the tree. She followed Josephine's footprints. She called out to her sister. "Josie! Josie don't shoot me, it's Diana!" she called as she went.

"Over here, Di!" Josephine called back.

Diana broke off into a run. She found Josephine standing over a small deer. "He ain't very big, but he will feed us for a couple of days," Josephine said. Diana said nothing as she helped her sister dress the deer. She knew in her heart that her father would not have shot a deer this small. However, she knew these were desperate times, and there were seven hungry mouths to be fed.

They cut two poles and strapped the deer to them. They each took an end and began to carry the deer back toward the house. Diana was grateful it was a small deer. If it had been an adult, they would not have been able to carry it. They rested a couple of times. Finally, they reached the clearing where they could see the farm. It was downhill all the way now. They crossed the clearing and made their way to the porch.

Agnus met them on the porch. She smiled and said, "Good work, girls. Your Pa would be proud of both of you." She went to the deer and ran her hand over its side. "You two go inside and get something hot to drink. I will take care of this. Send Sofia out to help me," Agnus said.

Diana and Josephine went inside. "Sofia. Mamma wants you to go out and help her," Josephine said.

Sofia sat at the table watching them as they undressed. "Sofia? Did you not hear what I said?" Josephine asked as she unwrapped her leggings.

Sofia rose slowly. She began to bundle herself up for the cold. "Mamma will have it done before you even get out there," Diana grumbled. Sofia paid her no mind. She continued to dress slowly. Finally, she went outside.

Diana turned to Josephine and said. "I know a reckoning is comin' between Sofia and me. I have about had all I can take of her laziness."

Josephine nodded and replied, "I do not know why Mamma puts up with it. Pappa would take her to the barn and whoop her legs with a switch."

Diana poured them each a cup of hot water. They sat at the table holding the cups in their hands to warm themselves. They sipped the water slowly. It wasn't much, but it was warm. Ruth Ann came to sit close to Josephine.

Josephine lifted her upon her lap. They sat there quietly for a time. Finally, Ruth Ann had fallen asleep. Josephine carried her into her parents' room and laid her on the bed. She covered her with a fur pelt and came back into the kitchen.

There was a commotion outside. The girls grabbed a fur wrap and went to the door. A buggy was coming down the muddy cart path. It was Porter Martin's buggy. Porter was driving the buggy and James sat next to him. They pulled up at the porch. Josephine ran down to the horses and tethered them to the post.

"Good day, ladies! Is your Mamma handy?" Porter asked.

Just then, Agnus appeared, wiping the blood from her hands. "I am here, Mr. Martin. Good day to you," she said.

Porter tipped his hat to Agnus. "You have my deepest condolences, Mrs. Lewis. James here, told me of your Mister's passing. I am very sorry. I am here to offer my services in any way I can," Porter said.

"Why don't you step inside out of this cold, Mr. Martin. You too, James," Agnus said.

They went inside. "I am afraid all I can offer you is a cup of warm water," Agnus said as she removed her fur wrap.

Porter waved his hand. He put his hat on the table and sat down on a stool. James sat down next to him. "We are fine. We don't need any nourishment, but I thank you for the offer just the same," Porter said.

The girls all huddled around the fireplace together, watching their guests. Agnus sat down on a stool across from Porter and James.

Porter took his pipe from his pocket. "Do you mind if I smoke?" he asked.

Agnus rose and came back with a skin full of William's tobacco. She handed it to Porter.

"Thank you, Ma'am," Porter said as he began to fill the pipe with the tobacco. "As I was saying before, I am very sorry to hear of Mr. Lewis's passing. I just arrived home today with Margaret. She would have come, too, but she is unable to, being in her current condition. She sends her condolences as well," Porter said as he lit the pipe. He puffed several times, exhaling the smoke. The familiar smell filled the air, reminding Diana of her father.

"Well," Porter continued. "This winter has been mighty harsh. It must be very difficult for you ladies here all alone with no man to look after you."

Agnus smiled and nodded. "It has been trying, that is true, but we are managing well enough," she said.

Porter smiled in return and went on, "Margaret and I have that big house up there. There is just the two of us, and James will be leaving us tomorrow. I understand he is taking your Josephine with him when he goes," Porter said, smiling over at Josephine.

Josephine's face blushed. She smiled at James. Agnus coughed and said, "I was not aware they were leaving so soon," she looked from Josephine to James.

"Yes, Ma'am." Porter said. "There is no minister here abouts, so I reckon they will have to get married in some town along the way. The stage stops at several along the way."

Agnus got up and walked to the washboard. She stood with her back to her guests. Diana knew it was to hide the tears streaming down her cheeks. She wiped her face with her apron and returned to the table. She cleared her throat and said, "I will have Josephine ready to go tomorrow. I think it would be proper of James to collect her and take her to town," she said.

"Yes, Ma'am." Porter said. "I was wondering if you would like to go see her off, I would be happy to take you all into town and bring you back."

Agnus looked over at the girls. She smiled and said, "I don't think we could all go. Someone will have to remain here and watch the place. I reckon I could say my good-byes in the morning, and the girls could all go ifin they want to."

The girls all smiled and nodded. They did not speak. It had been a custom that whenever there was a guest in the Lewis house, the children did not speak unless asked a direct question.

"Well, all right then. That brings me to my next question," Porter said. "I am here to offer you and your girls a home with Margaret and myself."

Diana closed her eyes. *Thank you, Lord, for delivering us*, she thought to herself.

Agnus raised her eyebrows. She was caught by surprise. Finally, after a moment of silence, she smiled and said, "Thank you very much, Mr. Martin, for your kind offer. That is very kind of you and Mrs. Martin to open your home up to us. I am afraid I must decline. We are fine. This is our home and we can manage. Thank you again, and please thank Mrs. Martin for us."

Diana's mouth dropped open. How could her mother do this to them? Her heart sank.

Porter puffed on his pipe a few times and said, "Mrs. Martin and myself have always wanted children. She was a teacher for many years while we lived in Philly. She misses the young ones. You would all be more than welcome in our home. You would not be taking advantage of us in no way as I need someone to help take care of Margaret during the day. That is a big house. I do wish you would reconsider, Mrs. Lewis."

Agnus smiled and said, "Thank you again, Mr. Martin, but this is where we belong. I will send a couple of my girls over every day to look after Mrs. Martin as we agreed earlier, but we will remain here."

Diana's heart felt like it was going to break. She fought back the tears. Josephine would be leaving. Martha was only eight years old. Sofia was worthless. That left just her and Regina to provide for the family. Regina had not yet mastered the long rifle. Diana fought the urge to protest. She gulped and remained silent. She clenched her fists tight until her arms ached.

Porter rose from his stool and took his hat in hand. He walked toward the door. James followed him. "Well, if you happen to change your mind, Mrs. Lewis, just send one of the girls up to the house. I would be more than happy to bring a wagon down to collect you all and your belongings. We can herd your cows up to our barn and you can still sell your milk to the general store. You don't have to change anything except where you lay your head at night. And as I said before, you are all very welcome in our house." He opened the door and stepped out onto the porch.

James turned to Agnus and said, "I will collect Josephine in the morning. I will bring the wagon and we can take as many of you that wants to go into town to wait on the stage."

Agnus nodded. "I'll have her ready for ya," she said.

They all went outside and stood on the porch until Porter and James drove the buggy back up the muddy cart trail. Agnus turned to them and said, "Diana, Regina, you help me finish this deer. Sofia and Martha, you start supper. Josephine, you get your belongings together. This will be our last night all together. Go on now!" she said. She wrapped her wrap around her and went to the left of the porch where she was cleaning the deer. Regina followed her.

Diana hugged Josephine, "I am so happy for you, Josie. I thought we would have more time." Josephine smiled. She was excited. Diana pulled her wrap around her and went outside to help her mother. The sun would be going down soon. They worked quickly. Diana was quiet. So was Agnus. Regina chattered on and on about Josephine riding a stage and getting married. Diana was too angry to speak. She was angry at her mother for not taking Porter Martin up on his invitation to live with him and Mrs. Martin in the big house.

Soon, they had finished. Diana stretched the hide and hung it from the tree that stood over her father's grave. She knelt down over William's unmarked grave and said, "Pappa, it is just not fair. I miss you so much." She wiped the tears from her eyes and went into the house to wash off.

Agnus was at the iron pot that hung over the fireplace. Martha had set the table. Sofia was sitting on a stool daydreaming. Regina was still rambling on about what was taking place tomorrow. "Can we all go to town to see Josie off tomorrow, Mamma?" she asked.

Agnus nodded. "Anyone who wants to go, can go," she said.

"Mamma, I think the place would be fine, iffin you wanted to see Josie off yourself," Martha said.

Agnus shook her head. "I'll say my good-byes in the morning. You all might just be in town all day waitin' on that there stage to come. I will watch things here." She was avoiding Diana's eyes. Diana watched her mother as she worked. She remained silent. She was still very angry. She knew her mother was aware of the burden she was putting on Diana's shoulders. How could she do this to her? Finally, Diana went up the ladder to the loft where Josephine was stuffing her things into the mountain lion's hide. She had sewed it to make a bag for her belongings, as soon as she received permission to go off with James.

Diana hugged her again. She began to cry. Josephine held her tight. She stroked her hair. "It will be all right, Di. Someday, you will meet a man and you will go off, too. I know the good Lord has someone very special in mind for you," Josephine said softly.

Diana said through her sobs, "I want to go with you, Josie."

Josephine smiled and said, "You know you can't leave Mamma and the girls. They need you, Di. James and me, we have to make a life for ourselves. This is where you belong for now."

Diana looked up at Josephine and said, "Why didn't Mamma take Mr. Martin up on his offer to live in that big house? How could she do this to me? Don't she know how hard it is for me to do everything? I hate it here. I just hate it. I am so mad at Mamma right now."

Josephine pulled Diana to her and held her tight. "I know it is hard for you, Di. I know. But you are the only one who can do it. Regina and Martha are too young, and Sofia is just plain lazy. You are the only one Mamma can count on," Josephine said softly.

Just then, Martha stuck her head up from the ladder. "Mamma said to come eat. Why are you crying, Diana? What are you crying for?" she asked.

Diana wiped her eyes. "Go on down, Martha. I am all right. I am just sad to see Josephine leaving us," she said. "You go on now. We are right behind you."

Martha disappeared. Diana could hear her as she reached the bottom. "Diana is cryin', Mamma. She is sad that Josie is leavin us."

Josephine reached the bottom first. Diana was right behind her. Agnus looked at the two of them and said, "Let's not make our last night together a sad memory. There will be no more crying tonight. We must all be happy for Josephine."

They sat around the table after dinner was over. They talked about things they remembered in the years past. There was no reading or writing lessons tonight. There was no Bible reading before bed. They all did join hands while Agnus said a prayer. The evening went quickly. Soon, they were all sent to bed. Diana and Josephine slept with their arms wrapped around each other that night. Sofia snored loudly and they chuckled about it. It was almost sunrise when they fell asleep.

The next morning, Agnus climbed the ladder and woke them. Sofia, Regina, and Diana went to the barn to do the milking. They poured the milk into the wooden barrel and went back inside to eat breakfast. Josephine sat at the table eating when they arrived back inside. After eating, they prepared to go to town. Diana hitched Buck to the cart and pulled it around to the front porch. Just then, James and Porter arrived in the buggy.

Josephine hugged her mother and climbed into the buggy between the two of them. Diana drove the cart with Ruth Ann sitting at her side. Regina and Sofia steadied the wooden barrel containing the milk as they followed the buggy back toward Berlin. Agnus stood on the porch waving as they went.

In town, James and Porter helped the girls with the barrel of milk. Grace Hickman was at her best this morning. She was polite and gracious. She gave the girls extra credit for their milk. Diana knew it was all an act to impress Mr. Martin. When the transaction was complete, they went back outside to wait for the stage.

Josephine and James went off by themselves. They were standing, hand in hand, speaking softly. Mr. Martin had bought some hard candy and he was entertaining the girls. Diana stood off by herself watching Josephine and James. She did not want to take her eyes off her sister. She did not want to forget what Josephine looked like. She concentrated on every detail of her sister's face and posture. Soon, she became aware of someone standing at her side. It was Burt Hickman.

"Hello, Diana," he said.

"Hello, Burt," Diana replied without taking her eyes off her sister.

"Josephine is a lucky girl. She is going off to the big city. I can only imagine the things that girl is goin to see," Burt said.

Diana blinked, but continued to watch her sister. "Mmm. I will miss her," Diana said.

"Well," Burt began, "someday you will get married, too. I know I can't wait until I can leave for the city. I want to travel and see everything. I like to read. A man came through here on the stage a while back and left a satchel full of books. I been readin' them. There is a whole other world out there. I want to see it. I was thinkin of bein' a preacher man, maybe."

Diana turned to look at Burt Hickman. "A preacher man?" she asked.

"Yep." He replied. "A preacher man. Now, Willy, he don't read no how. All he does is look at himself in the watering trough. He makes his muscles bulge and stares at himself. He sneaks out back and smokes Pa's pipe when nobody is watchin. Then he goes to the watering trough and poses like he is something special. Not me, though. I just want to be a preacher man. I want to get married and raise a family. Travel to all kinds of places preaching about the Bible. Would ya like to marry a preacher man, ya think?"Burt asked.

Diana's mouth dropped open. Burt Hickman did not look anything like what she thought a preacher man should look like. She never thought of him as being that pleasing to the eye either. She wasn't sure what to think at this moment. Was he proposing to her?

Diana turned back to look at Josephine. "I ain't lookin to get married no how, Burt. Ifin that is what your askin, you got the wrong girl." Then a thought came to her. She smiled and turned to face Burt. "However, Sofia, on the other hand, would make a fine preacher's wife. She is more lady like than I am. In fact, Sofia has always wanted to travel and see different places. She knows her Bible studies real good, too. I think she would make a fine preacher's wife." Diana said smiling up at Burt. She watched him as he shifted his gaze into Sofia's direction. He rubbed his jaw and studied her for a moment.

"Sofia is kind of young yet. I would have to wait for her to come of age before I could marry up with her. How old is she now, nine?" he asked.

Diana smiled. She said. "She is almost ten. You ain't ready to be no preacher yet anyhow. By the time you were all studied up on it and ready to take off, she would be old enough. Josephine is young and Mamma let her go because it was her chance for a better life. I am sure Mamma would let Sofia marry early. Ifin you were to promise her a better life, that is."

Burt shook his head. "I don't know, Diana. You are talking five, maybe six years. That is a long time."

Diana smiled and said, "Look at her, Burt. Sofia is the best lookin' one of all of us. She would be worth the wait. As pretty as she is now, just think how pretty she is going to be in five years. I think you would be a fool to overlook Sofia."

"Well, Regina is older. I wouldn't have to wait as long for her," Burt said, looking over at Regina.

Diana sighed and said. "No, you wouldn't, but I'm a tellin you, Sofia would make a better preacher's wife. Go on over there and talk to her yourself. You will see."

Burt frowned and looked back at Diana. "All right. I'll talk to her. Could you kind of soften her up for me? I don't know how she feels about me and I don't want to scare her off."

"I'll talk to her. You just go on over there and kind of get friendly with her," Diana said.

Burt turned and walked into the direction where Porter and the girls were gathered. Diana watched as he spoke to them. He started talking to Sofia. Diana watched as Sofia swayed from side to side. She did not even blush. Diana smiled.

Josephine and James came to stand by her side. She told Josephine what she had done. They got a laugh out of it. Just then, the stage pulled in. Diana began to cry. Josephine hugged her. They went to join Porter and the girls.

Porter and James talked to the stage driver. They loaded their belongings onto the top of the stage. They waited while the horses were fed and watered. They stood around about another hour until the horses were rested and Mrs. Hickman had fed the stage driver. Then Josephine and James got into the stage. There was another man inside going to Philadelphia as well. They said their goodbyes and Diana watched them leave until they were completely out of sight. They got into the two-wheeled cart and followed Porter's buggy back toward home.

They did not stop at the Martin house today. They had all been gone so long and they worried about their mother being home alone. They waved to Porter and crossed the shallow stream. Soon, the farm came into view. Smoke rose from the chimney. Diana knew they would be having venison for dinner. She pulled the cart up close to the house. She helped Ruth Ann down from the cart. Regina went to help her lift the wooden barrel down.

"Sofia! Sofia, come help with the barrel!" Regina called. Sofia stopped on the porch and turned to look at them. She slowly made her way back to the cart. They lifted the barrel down and set it on the porch.

Diana said to Sofia, "Go to the stream and get some water to wash the barrel out, Sofia. I will take Buck and the cart to the barn."

Sofia put her hands on her hips and said, "Why can't Regina do it? I'm cold and I want to go inside."

"We are all cold, Sofia. Go fetch some water to wash the barrel out," Diana said.

Sofia stomped off toward the creek that ran behind the house. Diana sighed and took hold of Buck's halter. She led him toward the barn. Regina began to unhitch the cart. Diana led Buck into the barn and gave him some grain. She patted his head and spoke softly to him. She did not feel like going into the house just yet. She wanted to be alone.

Her hand dropped to the sling that hung at her waist. "Regina, you tell Mamma I went hunting for awhile. I will be in soon," she said.

Regina called to her as she went, "Diana, we don't need any more meat. We still have venison. Why don't you come on in the house?"

Diana did not answer. She continued walking toward the woods. She found herself deep within the woods before she snapped out of her daze. She knew where she was. She was just beyond the spot where the fallen trees formed a natural three-sided corral. She leaned against a tree. There were plenty of thick brambles and underbrush around here. She went around kicking at it. Soon, a rabbit darted from its cover. Diana swung her sling in the air. With a flick of her wrist, the stone flew at the rabbit, striking it in the head. It lay motionless. Diana gathered it up by the feet and hung it from her waist. She continued kicking the brush piles and flushing more rabbits into the open. In a matter of two hours or more, she had four rabbits. She turned and started for home.

When she reached the back of the house, she knelt near the tree where her father was buried. She cleaned the rabbits and stretched their hides. She wiped the blood from her hands and went inside.

Agnus looked up at her from the table. "Diana. Where have you been?" she asked.

"I was rabbit huntin', Mamma. I thought maybe we could make fur caps and sell them to Mrs. Hickman at the store to help pay our bill," Diana said. She removed her outer garments and laid them in the corner, over top the wooden box where they kept their sewing.

Agnus rose and went to the iron pot. She dished a bowl of stew out and sat it on the table. "I never thought of that. Do you think she would pay for em?" Agnus asked.

Diana sat down. She looked up at her mother, "I don't know; why not. Maybe not too many at first. But it is worth a try," she said.

Sofia sighed. "That's a lot of biscuits n red eyed gravy. Pappa would have liked that."

"Yes, he would indeed," Agnus said. They all sat quietly while Diana ate her meal.

The days went by slowly for Diana. She missed Josephine so much. Sofia had taken a liking to Burt. At least she was taken with the idea of Burt's noticing her. It did not seem to make her any more active around the farm when it came to chores. Agnus had sent Sofia and Martha to the Martin house to help take care of Margaret.

Diana was disappointed. She had hoped she would be one of them chosen to work for the Martins. She had met Mrs. Martin. She was a very thin lady with long blonde hair, much like Diana's. The only difference was Diana's laid in long curls about her shoulders, whereas Mrs. Martins hung long and straight down her back.

Agnus had told Diana she needed her at the farm. Regina and Diana were the only two capable, of all the girls, to do the chores.

Soon, it was nearly two years since Josephine had left, and Diana was still missing her as much as she did a month after she watched her board the stage for Philadelphia. It was summer. Diana and Regina had been in the forest all morning chopping at a soft maple tree that was struck by lightning a week earlier. They took turns swinging the ax at the tree. Diana's hands were blistered and sore. Regina had wrapped hers in rabbit hides to protect them. Diana wished she had thought of that. She continued to work until her hands were bleeding. "We should take a break," Regina said.

"Takin' breaks won't get the job done," Diana said.

Regina leaned on the ax handle and watched Diana. "Why are you pushing so hard, Di? You never smile anymore. It used to be fun working with you. Now all you do is growl and bark at us like a dog," Regina said.

Diana stopped and straightened herself so she could see Regina when she spoke. "Pushin' is the onliest way of gettin anything done. There is so much work to do and you and me are the onliest ones to do it all. I am sorry if I am no fun to work with, but who is gonna feed and cut wood and milk cows and stretch hides, and fetch water, and all that we have been doing this past year?" Diana sighed and turned to look away. She did not want to start crying because she was afraid she would not be able to stop.

She wiped her face and turned to Regina. "You know what? You are right. It is hot and I am grumpy. Let's go to the creek and go for a swim," she said.

They ran until they came to the wide part of the stream that their father had dammed up. Here, the cattails grew. Diana waded in carefully at first, watching for snakes. Regina just jumped in. They swam for a while. Diana found herself laughing. They splashed and played. Then Diana called to Regina. "Okay, we have to get that tree down!"

They made their way to the shore and headed back for the forest once again. Regina began to sing. Diana decided not to stop her. Even though Regina could not carry a tune, Diana found pleasure in her singing. Regina shared the rabbit hides she had wrapped around her hands.

They went back to the house. The tree was down, but they would have to chop it into smaller pieces and load it onto the cart to get it back to the house. They found the cows and started them back to the barn on their way home. Hughie watched from a distance. They did the milking and poured the milk into the smaller wooden barrel that they used for themselves. Tomorrow would be the day for their milk run into Berlin.

They were heading for the house when they spotted Porter Martin's buggy coming down the dirt path with Sofia and Martha. He brought them home every afternoon about this time. Today, instead of dropping them off as was his custom, he tethered his horse and jumped up onto the porch.

"Is your Mamma handy?" he asked them as they stepped up onto the porch.

Diana nodded and said, "She's inside, Mr. Martin. Would you like to come in for a spell?"

"Don't mind if I do," he replied. He fanned himself with his hat as he entered.

It was hot inside the house. The fireplace was burning in order to heat the iron pot that contained their meal. Sofia and Martha sat down at the table. Diana and Regina stood by the fireplace in spite of the heat. Agnus stood at the end of the table facing Mr. Martin.

"Ma'am. Good evening to you. I don't mean to hold up your supper, but I need to speak with you about a matter concerning you and your girls' welfare," Porter said.

"Won't you have a seat, Mr. Martin?" Agnus asked.

Porter pulled a stool out and sat down at the table. He placed his hat on the table in front of him. "Well, Ma'am, as you know I have made frequent trips up to Philly lately. By the way, your daughter sends a letter for you. She is well. She has news, but I will let her tell you in her letter," he said. He reached into his vest and pulled out an envelope. He handed it to Agnus.

Agnus took the envelope and held it to her chest. "I will read it to the girls over supper," she said nodding at him. "Thank you, Mr. Martin. It was kind of you to bring this here letter to us."

"My pleasure, Ma'am," Porter said. "Well, as I was trying to explain….." He leaned back and took a breath. "I do not know if you are going to understand what I have to tell you, but if you don't, just say so and I will try to explain it.' He rubbed his nose and took another deep breath. "The news in Philly is about President Lincoln. He's in somewhat of a bind right now. I guess some of the states are in a big uproar over this slavery thing. Some people in pretty high places want to stop it all together. It has gotten so bad some of the states want to separate from the union. You see, all the southern states want to keep their slaves, and the northern states want to abolish slavery. So they are fightin back and forth, and well, I guess it looks like there is going to be a war. Now, I don't know how far up those confederate soldiers will be comin, but we aren't that far off. You and your girls should not be here by yourselves with no man to look out for you." He stopped and watched Agnus for a reaction.

"Why would they be comin after us? We don't have no slaves here, but we don't bother them down there that do," Agnus said.

"Well, Ma'am," Porter tried to explain, "Those soldier boys, they don't know that. They are just fightin." Again, he stopped and watched Agnus.

Agnus sat down on a stool at the far end of the table. She folded her hands in front of her. "You think we ain't safe here?" she asked.

"I don't rightly know, Ma'am. You may be, or you may not be. I just would feel a whole lot more comfortable if you came up to the house with us. We have hands there working at the sawmill and you would not be way off down here by yourselves. We could kind of watch out for you and your girls. Then maybe if this war doesn't last too long, you can come back," Porter said.

Agnus looked over at her girls. Their eyes were wide, their faces pale. She saw the fear in their faces. She looked at Diana. She was thin and overworked. Agnus stood up and rubbed her hands together. "All right, Mr. Martin. Just give us a couple of days to get ourselves gathered up and drive the cows up your way. How about day after tomorrow?" she asked.

"I will bring the wagon down day after tomorrow to collect you and the girls. My hands will help drive the cows up our way. We will leave your bull to roam, though. We don't want to mess with that one," Porter smiled. He stood up and bowed to the ladies. "I will see you ladies the day after tomorrow. Until then; enjoy your meal and your news from Josephine and James." Porter went through the open door and jumped off the porch. He placed his hat back onto his head and untied his horse. He climbed into his buggy and turned it around. He waved his hat as he drove off. They stood on the porch and watched him until he disappeared around the bend at the top of the knob.

Agnus shooed the girls back into the house. She told Regina and Martha to set the table. Diana poured the stew into the wooden bowls and placed them on the table. Soon, they were all seated around the table. Agnus opened the letter and read it aloud.

Josephine was very happy in Philly. They lived in Porter Martin's big red brick house. James worked at the sawmill alongside Thomas. She was worried because there were rumors of war. She hoped they would be safe. Porter had mentioned his plan to get them to move in with him. Then Agnus smiled. She covered her mouth and tears welled up in her eyes. Josephine was with child. The baby was due sometime in December. She closed the letter by saying she missed them all and wished they could come visit her sometime.

Sofia stood up and asked, "Mamma, does that mean Josie is going to have a baby?"

Agnus nodded and replied, "It would appear so." She held the letter close to her heart and smiled. She was going to be a grandmother. "I wish your Pa was here to hear this."

Diana closed her eyes. She was happy for Josephine. How strange life was. One day she was missing her sister and trying not to be angry with her for leaving Diana behind. She was breaking her back trying to keep food on the table, wood in the fire, and pay the outstanding bill at the general store. One visit from Porter Martin changed everything. She was so happy for her sister. She was happy and going to have a baby. How perfect life was for Josephine, and how happy Diana was for her older sister. It would appear that all their lives were turning for the better. They were going to Porter and Margaret Martin's house to live. Things were definitely going to be easier.

Diana did not know much about the war. She had an idea of what it meant. She did not understand how it applied to them, but she was grateful for having the opportunity to move into Porter's house.

That night she slept well. She was exhausted. Her mother had given her some butter to rub into her hands. She wrapped them in strips of clean cloth. They hurt, but Diana was so exhausted she slept soundly.

The next morning was milk day. They milked the cows and loaded it into the cart. They started off to Berlin. When they crossed the wide spot in the narrow stream, Diana could not help but think of how much shorter the run would be after tomorrow. She smiled as they passed the Martin house. Martha stood on the porch, waving at them as they went. This last year saw Martha grow at least two inches. She was going to be a tall, slim girl. Her dark hair had been tied up into a knot on top of her head. She wore an apron. Diana took a deep breath and smiled to herself.

When they reached the general store, Burt and Willy came to empty the wooden barrel. Burt smiled at Diana. Burt had not seen Sofia in a couple of weeks. It appeared he had turned his attention back to Diana. Once again, Burt exaggerated the measure of milk in the barrel. Grace Hickman wrote it in the ledger.

"Tell your Ma, this brings her bill down to eighty cents. I sold two of your rabbit fur hats. Do you want the money, or would you like to apply it to your bill?" Grace asked, peering at Diana over her glasses.

Diana cleared her throat. "Apply it to the bill, please," Diana said.

Grace smiled and wrote into the ledger. After a few minutes of her doing the math she said, "Now your bill is forty cents." Grace looked up at Diana. "You girls getting along all right out there?" she asked.

Regina could not contain herself any longer. "We are fine. We are moving in with the Martins tomorrow. Mr. Martin says it ain't safe with the war and all," she stopped for a breath. Diana put her hand over Regina's mouth to stop her from saying any more.

Grace Hickman came around the counter to stand in front of them. "So. You are going to move in with the Martin's. How nice for you. Things must be pretty bad out there at your place. How kind and merciful of the Martins to take you all in." Grace folded her hands. She tilted her head to one side. "Mr. Martin is a very charitable man, indeed."

Diana was angry. How vicious Mrs. Hickman was. She clenched her jaw tight to keep from saying anything. She knew she could not lose her temper. She smiled through clenched teeth. "Well, thank you, Ma'am. We really must get back. We have chores to do." She turned and shoved Regina toward the door. Ruth Ann had been riding along lately. She followed, looking up at Diana. She knew her sister was upset, but did not understand what had just happened. Diana helped her up into the cart. Regina climbed in behind her, pouting.

Grace Hickman had come outside as they were leaving. "Will you still be bringing milk into town?" she asked.

"Yes, Ma'am," Diana replied.

Burt untied Buck and handed Diana the reins. "Diana, I need to tell you something. Willy and me are joining the army. We are going off to fight in the war. I don't know how long I will be gone, but I can't wait that long for Sofia. I just don't have no feelins for her. She is pretty enough, but I was, well, I was wondering if I come back from the war, would you marry up with me?" Burt was speaking softly so his mother could not hear.

Grace Hickman turned to go back inside. She called over her shoulder, "Burt Hickman! You have chores to do. Stop lallygagging around and come help me stock these shelves!"

"Burt, I don't have them kind of feelins for you. I am sorry. I told you before, I ain't fixin' to hook up with anybody," Diana said.

"You will be staying with Porter Martin. Life will be different for you now. Maybe you will change your mind," Burt pleaded.

Diana shook her head. "Nothin' has changed. I just have more time to do what I want, and gettin married ain't what I want. I am sorry, Burt. I still think Sofia is the one you should be thinkin' about marrying."

Burt smiled and nodded. He stepped back from the cart. Diana clicked her tongue and Buck started off slowly through the town. They went back the way they came. Regina broke out in song. It hurt Diana's ears. Ruth Ann tried to sing along. Ruth Ann had a golden voice compared to Regina's. Even with Ruth Ann's soft voice, the song sounded horrible. Diana squinted her eyes and tried not to listen.

They waved at Martha once more as they passed on their way home. The sawmill was puffing smoke into the air. Diana could see Porter moving about in the distance. Edwin Morgan had been helping Porter on days when Zachariah Dillon did not need him at the feed mill. Porter had brought a couple more men with him when he returned from Philadelphia with Margaret. The railroad was planning on going clear to the west coast. Porter had plenty of work, plenty of lumber, and he paid well. He told Agnus he expected more help as time went on.

Buck crossed the stream and stopped. Regina and Ruth Ann jumped off the wagon. They waded in the cool water. They splashed and laughed. Diana did not feel like wading today. It was hot, but she was pouting herself. She was happy about moving in with the Wagners. Mrs. Hickman made it sound like they were destitute and had no options. Grace Hickman riled her. She tried not to show it and she hoped she pulled it off. Then there was Burt Hickman. He was losing interest in Sofia. He said he wanted to be a preacher man. Now he was going off to war. Nothing was easy anymore. Diana sat on the cart staring off into the distance. Finally, the squeals from Regina and Ruth Ann jolted her back to reality.

"Come on! Let's get Buck out of this sun," Diana called to them.

Regina helped Ruth Ann back into the wagon and climbed up after her. Diana clicked her tongue and Buck started for home.

That afternoon, Agnus had them wash everything down in the house. They would leave everything, except their personal belongings. They would be returning after this war was over. Diana tried not to sulk. She avoided eye contact with her mother. She was grateful that for once, Regina did not tell her mother about the incident with Grace Hickman. Diana thought that Regina suspected she may have told too much and possibly would get a tongue lashing from her mother.

They ate rabbit stew for dinner. Porter delivered Sofia and Martha just like clockwork. They all sat around the table talking. After cleaning up from dinner, they did their studies. Then Agnus read from the Bible and they went to bed.

It was a hot night. Diana had pocked a hole in the sod between the logs so she could peek out at the stars. She tossed and turned. It was a very warm night. She tried to remember back to the nights when they could see their breath. Finally, she fell asleep.

The next morning, they ate their breakfast early. Agnus cleaned out the iron pot. They washed the dishes and laid them upside down on the washboard. They would be there when they returned. They went around the house and stood over their father's grave. Diana and Agnus had made a wooden cross. Agnus had carved "W. Lewis, Husband," into the cross. They prayed and took turns telling William that they would return as soon as they could. Diana promised him she would visit often. Then Porter Martin came down the dry cart path with a wagon pulled by a two-horse team.

Each of the girls climbed in carrying a hide satchel with a change of clothes in it. Porter smiled and tipped his hat. "Good morning, ladies. What a fine day. Margaret is so excited to have you coming to our house. She is waiting on the front porch to greet you all," Porter said.

Agnus crawled up into the seat next to Porter. The girls piled into the back. Diana tied Buck to the back of the wagon, and Porter drove off, leaving Diana and Regina behind.

They went to the barn. They did not milk the cows. They took switches and began herding them in the direction of the Martin house. Soon, Edwin Morgan, who was better known as Stumpy, because of a limp, came toward them to help. He was riding one of Porter's horses. Together they got the cows to Porter's barn. There was a large fenced in corral. "Porter says to keep 'em penned up for a week or so. Then they will know this is their new home. It will be easier to keep track of 'em this way, too," Stumpy said.

Diana went to the house. Regina had run ahead. She was afraid she would be missing something. Diana took her time. She scanned the landscaping surrounding the large farm. She could smell the smoke in the air and hear the steam engine that powered the sawmill as it puffed and pounded in the background.

It was the first time Diana had seen the back of the house. There was a back door with a small wooden porch. There were two chairs on the porch and a broom. Just to the left of the porch was a small flower garden. A tall wooden archway had vines growing all over it. The archway led to a large vegetable garden. Diana went through the archway. It was beautiful. There were more vegetables here than Diana had ever seen in her entire life. She did not even know what some of them were. Off close to the house were two long rows of plants that had heart-shaped ret things growing close to the ground. She knelt down to inspect them. They were seedy little things. They left Diana's fingers stained red. Diana licked her fingers. It was a pleasant sweet taste. She would have to ask about these plants. She knew it had to be a fruit, but none like she had ever seen before.

Diana went around the front of the house. She went up the stone steps onto the porch. She knocked on the door. Martha opened the door laughing. "Come on in, Diana. You don't have to knock. You live here now." She stepped aside and motioned with her hand for Diana to enter. Diana took a deep breath. This is what she had been waiting for.

She heard voices in the kitchen. She followed Martha past the staircase and into the kitchen. Agnus was standing near the cook stove. Margaret was explaining how the whole thing worked. Agnus was in awe of the whole thing.

"See, Mamma. A pump and a cook stove. It's just like the magazines at the general store," Diana said.

"I ain't never cooked on anything like this before. All I ever had was an iron pot hanging in the fireplace," Agnus said, holding her left hand to her cheek.

Margaret smiled and wheeled her chair closer to Agnus. She said, "You will get used to it, Dear. It isn't hard at all. Why, even Miss Sofia and Miss Martha can cook on it, so I am quite sure you will master it in no time."

Martha went behind Margaret's chair and pushed it toward the dining room. "Miss Sofia, would you show your mother and sisters to their rooms? Then we will have tea in the dining room," Margaret said.

Sofia smiled. "Come with me, ladies." She said as she went for the hall between the kitchen and front door. The staircase was a wide set of stairs that curved near the top. It stopped, revealing a long hallway. There were three doors on the right and two doors on the left. The first door on the right was Porter and Margaret's room. Sofia went to the second door on the right. "This is your room, Mamma," she said, opening the door.

Agnus stepped into the room. There was a single bed along the far wall, with a window on each side of it. Next to the door was a tall dresser. To the right were a series of hooks for Agnus to hang her clothes on. There were far more hooks than she had dresses for. There was a small stand with a pitcher and bowl to wash with. The windows were open part way, and lace curtains blew back into the room. The entire room was larger than the main part of the log house Will had built for them. Agnus went to the bed and sat down. She smiled up at the girls. "I see what you mean. It truly is a fine house indeed," she said.

"Come along, ladies," Sofia teased. "The next room is for Martha, Ruth Ann, and me. We will be right next to Mamma." Sofia opened the door. This room had two larger beds in it. There was only one window. It, too, was open and the breeze blew the curtains back into the room. There were two dressers and a small wash stand with a pitcher and two bowls. There was another row of hooks on the wall. There was a picture hanging over the largest bed. It was a picture of a woman with a black dress on. She wore a large white collar that hung down long in front of her. She also wore a white bonnet on her head. She was stone faced and harsh looking. Ruth Ann stepped behind Sofia. "Who is that woman?" she asked.

"That is Miss Margaret's mother. I believe her name was Willamenna Graham. She was a school teacher, too," Sofia said.

"She looks scary to me," Ruth Ann said.

"Don't worry, Ruthie. She died a long time ago. She can't hurt nobody no how," Sofia said. "Now, come on." She motioned for them to exit the room.

They crossed the hall to the first door next to the stairs. Sofia opened the door. "This is Regina and Diana's room," she said.

Regina went to the bed and sat down, just as her mother had done. Diana walked around. There was one large bed in the room and two windows that were partially opened. There was a large dresser with a small mirror that pivoted on the very top. There was a washing station with one pitcher and bowl. Diana went to the window. It overlooked the garden behind the house. She could see the barn and the corral where the cows were penned in. If she leaned her face close to the window, she could see the sawmill to the far left. It was perfect. She sighed. She turned to look at her mother who had been watching her. Agnus was smiling. Diana smiled back.

"Now, let's go down and have that cup of tea Martha is brewing for us," Sofia said.

They went back down the stairs. Diana was sure Margaret knew they were coming: Their footsteps fell loudly on the wooden stairs. Margaret was sitting in her wheelchair at the end of the table facing the door where they entered the room. Martha was placing cups that rested on matching saucers around the table, one for each of them.

"Oh, my!" Agnus said. "It gives me the gitters to see my Martha handlin' such fine china. I don't think I ever ate or drank from anythin' this fine before," she said as she sat down.

"Oh, you will get used to it, my dear," Margaret said. "And don't worry if it gets broken here or there. It is, after all, just glass," she smiled at Agnus and motioned for Martha to pour the tea.

Agnus flushed. She took a sip of her tea. She returned the cup to the saucer and replied, "Mrs. Martin."

"Margaret, if you don't mind," Margaret interrupted.

Agnus smiled. "All right then. Margaret. I do not know how much the girls have told you about our way of life, but at our house, you would have got warm milk or hot water. And you would have been drinkin' out of an old, dinged up tin cup," Agnus said as she wrung her hands.

"I understand; may I call you Agnus?" Margaret asked.

Agnus nodded her head and smiled.

"Here we do not concern ourselves with such things. I know it appears differently; however, we believe in being comfortable. Fortunately for us, Porter has been successful and able to provide us with fine things. It was not always this way. We started out much like you and your girls. We are very happy that you are here. I do have one request to ask of you, though…," Margaret said.

Agnus took another sip of the tea. It was very pleasing to her taste buds. She could not speak so she nodded her head.

"I understand you were teaching the girls to read and write?" Margaret asked.

"Yes. I am afraid I am not a school teacher such as you are, Ma'am, but I tried to teach them what I knew," Agnus replied.

Margaret smiled and said, "Well, Agnus, I would like to teach the girls, and yourself, if you would be interested. I would like to teach them to read, write, grammar, arithmetic, spelling, and even a little social etiquette."

"Well, I think that all sounds pretty fine to me. I ain't sure I have much use for it myself, but it wouldn't do me no harm to learn. I got to tell you Mrs…, I mean Margaret, I don't know what that etiquette thing is, but I reckon it is somethin a lady should know. Else you wouldn't want to be teachin it to us," Agnus said.

Margaret smiled. "Etiquette means polite behavior in society," she explained.

Agnus flushed. She smiled and said, "I reckon we are a little rough around the edges. We ain't had no call to worry about manners and such before. It won't hurt us none to learn, though. I think it will help to keep our minds off this war situation. I will instruct my girls to pay mind to their lessons, Margaret. And I reckon I can give it a go, too." She finished her tea. "That is mighty fine tea!" she said.

Margaret smiled. "Martha, dear, would you mind pouring your mother another cup of tea? Then we shall begin a schedule and a list of duties for each of your girls," she said.

The chores that were assigned were simple ones. Everyone took a turn at cooking, everyone took a turn at cleaning. Each of them got two alternate days to themselves to do whatever they wanted. There was a large wooden clock in the dining room. When it struck one time, it was time for learning. Margaret would seat everyone around the dining room table. They started with reading. When the clock struck two times, they started writing and spelling. When the clock struck three times, they worked on arithmetic. When it struck four times, they were done for the day. They worked on their grammar and etiquette all day long.

The milking had to be done early in the morning. They made their usual trips into Berlin every other day, but it had to be done, and they were expected to be back before their studies. This was fine as the girls were usually up and moving about long before Margaret and Porter got out of bed.

It was no time at all before the store bill was paid. Mrs. Hickman was quite huffy about their milk deliveries now because she had to pay them money. It had been weeks since she had written anything in the ledger under the Lewis name. Willy and Burt were both gone off to war. Only Concetta remained to help around the store. Mrs. Hickman had asked Sofia if she would like to come work for her. Margaret told Agnus it would be her decision; however, she expressed her desire to keep Sofia at the Martin place so she could complete her studies. Mrs. Hickman was insulted by Sofia's rejection. Diana smiled all the way home that day.

On Diana's days to herself, she would take her bow and hike back to the farm. She visited with her father for a while and then went into the woods. She never came home empty handed. Porter showered her with compliments every time. Once she killed another deer and found she could not get it to the farm by herself. She hung it in a tree after she had gutted it and ran for the sawmill for help. Stumpy brought the wagon and they made it home before it got too ripe. The venison with the fresh vegetables from the garden were delicious. By now, Agnus had mastered the cook stove.

Diana had learned that the small red fruit in the garden were strawberries. Agnus made biscuits. They mashed the berries and poured them over the biscuits. It was Porter's favorite desert.

Every time Porter went to Philly, he would take one of the girls with him to visit Josephine and James. They returned with stories about how big Josie was and what a fine house she lived in. They raved about the city. Agnus sent letters to Josephine. She longed to see her herself. However, it would not be proper for her to accompany a married man to Philadelphia. So she relied on the stories her daughters brought back. She had her letters. She kept every one.

With Mrs. Hickman paying them for the milk now, Agnus could afford to buy fabric to make the girls proper dresses. They were beginning to look like proper little ladies. Agnus worried about how they would react to going back to the log house when the time came. Somehow, it seemed as though they did not belong there anymore. Yet she was determined to return when the time was right.

A year passed. Josephine had a boy, William James Harris. Josephine sent a letter telling her mother that when the war was over, she and James would bring William home to meet his family. Agnus did not understand all the fuss about the war. They had not seen any signs of war. It was always this rumor that hung over their heads. The men went off by themselves to talk about it. Her girls were growing to be such fine ladies. Agnus was very proud of all of them. Even she herself had changed drastically. Diana was seventeen now. Agnus was married and had two babies at that age. Yet Diana did not seem interested in getting married.

Diana came to stand near her mother. "Mamma, I was talking to Miss Margaret. She suggested that you and I go together with Mr. Martin when he goes to Philly next week. She said it may be our last chance to see Josephine for some time. Porter has told her that the war is coming closer. There were troops spotted moving south not far from here," Diana said.

Agnus turned and smiled. "I was under the impression that it wasn't proper for me to travel with Mr. Martin to Philadelphia," she said, turning to look out the window.

Diana smiled, "I know, Mamma. But she said it would be all right if we both went. I really don't think Miss Margaret cares what people have to say anyway. Anyone who knows the Martins know that they are devoted to one another. Porter is leaving next Tuesday. Mamma, would you go?" Diana watched her mother's facial expression.

Agnus turned her face toward Diana and smiled. She nodded her head as she said, "Of course, I will go. I miss my little girl so very much."

Diana hugged her mother. She knew her life had been turned upside down since they moved in with the Martins. She had become the housekeeper, cook, and personal assistant to Margaret Martin. The Martins had come to depend on Agnus and her girls. In return, they were fed and cared for as if they were family. Ruth Ann had become so fond of Porter that she sat on his lap in the evenings while he smoked his pipe. She stood at the door waiting for him to come in at the end of the day. He had become her father figure. Diana knew this bothered Agnus. She knew there were times when Agnus felt as if she were losing her girls to another family. In Diana's heart, she knew her mother had made the right decision when it came to moving in with the Martins.

Nobody's life had changed any more than Diana's. She still wandered off into the woods to hunt and be alone from time to time, but she had become a proper lady. She walked differently. Her grammar was better, and now she was studying hard to become a schoolteacher just like Miss Margaret had been. Miss Margaret even turned over the lessons to Diana in the afternoons. Miss Margaret had been trying to get Diana to give up her bow and sling, but Diana was just not ready to do that yet.

Today was a beautiful fall day. The leaves had begun to change. Metamorphosis was the term Margaret had used. Diana announced she was going for a walk. She crossed the stream by way of a small wooden bridge that Stumpy had made for them. She walked the old dirt cart path that led to the farm. Grass had grown high in the path, making it nearly invisible. Diana knew all too well where it was. She continued until she reached the knob that looked down on the farm. She quickened her pace.

The grass had grown up high all around the house that was once all dirt and mud. The barn had a hole in the sod roof. Some of the wooden railings that formed the small corral had fallen down. Diana stepped up onto the porch. The door had been propped shut with a board before they left to keep the vermin out. The board had since fallen over and the door was open. Diana stepped inside. The wooden bowls were still upside down on the washboard. All of the wooden spoons and utensils were still lined up near the wooden water bucket. There was a thick coat of dirt and dust covering everything.

Diana ran her hand over the wooden table that her father had made for them. It was dirty and dusty as well. The stools had been placed upside down on top of the table. One of them was on the floor. Diana picked it up and put it back in its designated place. She went to the fireplace. The iron pot had dried leaves in the bottom of it. She pulled them out and threw them into the fireplace.

Diana went to her parents' bedroom. The room was empty. Agnus had thrown out all of the straw bedding before they left. She took all of the hides with her. There was nothing in this room to indicate that anyone ever slept there. Diana turned and crawled up the ladder that led to the loft where she slept with Josephine and Sofia for the first fourteen, almost fifteen years of her life. It, too, was empty. There were no signs of anyone ever being up here as well. She went back down the ladder.

Diana went outside and propped the board back against the door to hold it shut again. She thought about getting a bucket of water and cleaning the place up, but she hoped they would never have to live here again. She went around the house to the big tree where her father was buried.

The grass was so high she had a hard time finding the marker. She began pulling the grass that grew over William's grave. She was beginning to work up a sweat. She heard a noise and stood upright, looking around. It was Hughie. He stood to her right, between the house and the woods. She watched him for a moment. He was watching her, too. Then he lowered his head and went back to grazing. Diana went back to pulling the grass. She stopped occasionally to see where he was. When she was satisfied with her work, she stood up right and stepped back toward the house. She made a wide circle around the house, avoiding Hughie. She went to the cattail pond. The grass was coarse and thick here. She watched the ground as she walked. She saw something slithering in the grass. It was a moccasin. She turned and went back toward the house.

Diana walked back to the knob and turned to look at the farm one more time before returning to the Martin house. Then she followed the trail she had made in the tall grass back to the wooden bridge. She stomped her feet on the bridge to remove the mud and dirt from her shoes. She smiled to herself and made her way to the house.

Porter had planted a grove of fruit trees to the right of the house. Diana went to it and inspected the trees. They were not big enough to bear fruit yet. She ran her hands over the leaves. They had already turned a bright yellow with brown edges. Some of the leaves had begun to fall already. Diana took a deep breath and went toward the house once again. Her stomach told her it was time for lunch. Then it would be time to study.

Once inside, she smelled the aroma of fresh bread. Her mother had been baking. Regina had set the table and Sofia was sitting near the fireplace. Martha came wheeling Miss Margaret into the kitchen. Ruth Ann was riding on her lap. Diana smiled. "You are getting a little too big to ride on Miss Margaret's lap, Ruthie," Diana said.

Margaret laughed. "I think it is my lap getting smaller," she said. "I seem to be losing weight these days, although I don't know why. Your mother is the best cook I have ever had the pleasure of having," Miss Margaret smiled.

Agnus turned and smiled at her. "You have been looking rather pale lately. Are you sure you feel all right?" she asked.

Margaret laughed and replied. "You ask me that nearly every day. Miss Lewis, I am fine. I think it is because I am unable to get any exercise. I know I am hungry enough. That bread smells divine."

Martha parked the wheelchair in Miss Margaret's spot. She went to help her mother. Diana began to wash her hands at the pump near the window. She dried them and began to slice a loaf of bread that sat on the cutting board. She looked over at Sofia. She had not turned to look at any of them. She sat with her back to them staring into the fireplace.

Diana asked, "Sofia, would you like to help?" Sofia did not acknowledge Diana.

Regina chanted, "Sofia misses her boy friend! Sofia misses her boy friend!"

"Regina!" Agnus said. "You help out here and keep still."

Diana looked around the room at the faces. "What boyfriend?" she asked.

Regina jumped at the opportunity to tell what she knew. "Oh, she misses Burt Hickman. He was Sofia's boyfriend. He went off to war and he ain't even written her a letter," Regina teased.

"Has not written her a letter. Not 'ain't'." Margaret Martin corrected Regina. She looked up at Agnus and smiled.

"Sofia is still too young to be thinking about a boyfriend. Be it Burt Hickman, or any other man," she placed a bowl of salad greens on the table.

Sofia turned to look at them. "Three more years. That is a long time, Mamma. All I do is work and learn my lessons. I want to go back to Philly again. I hate Berlin!" she pouted. "I want to go live with Josephine in the city."

Diana laughed. "Work? When did you do any work without being threatened? Most of the time you are just dead weight," Diana laughed again.

Agnus stepped between them. "Diana! That will be enough! You forget we are guests in this house. Have you forgotten your manners?" she spoke sternly.

Diana lowered her head. "I am sorry, Mamma. I apologize, Miss Margaret."

Sofia stomped out of the room, shouting over her shoulder, "I am not hungry!"

Diana helped her mother finish putting lunch on the table. They all ate quietly. After lunch, they cleared the table and everyone helped with the clean up. They were all anxious to get to the studies. They enjoyed learning. This was their favorite time of the day.

Before bed that night, they all gathered in Agnus's room. She read from her worn Bible just as she had done at the farmhouse. Usually, Ruth Ann fell asleep and had to be carried to her bed. This was their time together as a family. It was the only thing that did not change when they moved here.

Diana lay in her bed that night thinking about the day. She regretted not cleaning the old farmhouse before she left. Somehow, she imagined that it would jinx her and she would have to move back there. She never wanted to go back to that life again. She remembered her rift with Sofia. It embarrassed her mother to have her daughters arguing in front of Margaret Martin. Diana regretted that also. She did not want her mother to feel uncomfortable in this house. She did not want her mother to regret coming here. She remembered the look on Agnus's face when Margaret corrected Regina's grammar. It worried Diana. She had to find a way to make her mother happier here with the Martins. Perhaps the trip to visit Josephine would make Agnus happier. Diana went to sleep with Josephine on her mind.

It was another week and a half before Porter decided to go back to Philadelphia. Diana and her mother were dressed and packed early. They would accompany Porter to Berlin and wait until the stage came through. They packed light. They only had one change between them. Porter had told them he could only afford to be away for three days. It wasn't much time, but it was better than nothing.

Agnus had not been into Berlin in years. She hadn't left the house since Sofia was born. She was amazed at the changes. They were in the process of constructing a church on the other side of the general store. Diana supposed it was Grace Hickman's idea. Burt wanted to be a preacher, and she would do anything to keep him from leaving home again. Diana hoped the war would be over soon. She wanted Burt to come home safely. She had no interest in being a preacher's wife, but she liked Burt as a friend, and did not want any harm to come to him.

Grace Hickman put two chairs on the porch. Agnus sat down to wait for the stage. Porter went in the direction of the new church. Diana sat on the edge of the porch. Grace sat next to Agnus. Diana suspected that Grace Hickman longed for another female to talk to. She and her daughter, Concetta, were the only women in Berlin. Diana could tell that Grace was trying very hard not to insult Agnus. She needed a friend. Besides, any gossip she wished to receive or pass along could easily be done through Regina. Old Diarrhea Lips. Diana just sat on the porch with her back to the two women, listening to them talk.

It was hours before the stage arrived. There was no need to get excited. The horses were cared for and rested. Grace fed the stage driver. There were no passengers today, so there was no news from outside the general area. Porter came back to the general store and purchased some hard candy for the trip.

Soon, their bags were loaded on top of the stage and they were off in the direction of Philadelphia.

Porter fell asleep while the stage rocked to and fro. It was a bumpy ride. It was dusty. There were cloth flaps that hung over the stage windows on both sides. Diana tied them up so she and her mother could look out as they went. Porter told them they had two stops to make before they would reach their destination. Diana watched the scenery as they went. The trees were turning gold, orange, and red all along the hillsides. They rode through mountain trails and valleys. At times, there were rivers far below them that wound around deep gorges. Agnus gripped Diana's hand and closed her eyes.

The first stop was in a small town called Quincy. It was bigger than Berlin. They stopped at an inn. The horses were watered and put away. A fresh team was hitched to the stage. The innkeeper's wife gave the ladies a cup of tea and a slice of buttered bread. Porter was off somewhere with the stage driver. Soon, they were off again, winding through the Blue Mountain region. It would be hours before the next stop.

Diana found it hard to keep her eyes open. Porter was sleeping once again. Agnus had rested her head against the side of the coach. Diana watched as her mother's head bounced and swayed. Her eyes were closed, but Diana doubted that she would be able to sleep through such an ordeal. She watched the mountain scenery as they wound their way through the Blue Mountain Region. Here and there, she would see smoke rising above the trees. Diana tried to picture the log houses with the sod roofs, much like their own. Soon she had dozed off herself.

She woke to a mist hitting her in the face. It was raining. Diana untied the flaps that covered the windows. Still, Porter did not wake. Agnus sat up straight and looked around. "It is raining, Mamma," Diana whispered so as not to awaken Porter. Agnus wiped her eyes. She nodded and stared at her hands.

"I wonder how much longer the trip will be," Agnus whispered. Diana shrugged her shoulders.

"We should be coming to our next stop soon. The sun is beginning to go down," Diana said. She peeked out through the flap. It was raining harder now. A flash of lightning streaked across the sky. A loud boom of thunder woke Porter.

"Was that thunder?" he asked, sitting up straight.

"I do believe so," Agnus replied.

"That is not good. We may have to spend the night in Harrisburg," he said. He peered through the flaps. The rain blew in on him. He shook the water from his hands and wiped his face. "Yep. It looks like we will be spending the night in Harrisburg. Now, don't you ladies worry none. They have fine hotels, and I am always prepared for these things when I travel," he said, trying to reassure them.

Agnus was wringing her hands. "I hope we are not a burden to you, Mr. Martin," she said.

"Why, you are no burden at all. Don't you worry. We may spend the night in Harrisburg, but this stage driver knows he has a schedule to keep. He will get us to Philly as soon as the weather breaks," Porter said.

Diana was disappointed. That meant less time to spend with Josephine. She tried not to show her disappointment. She looked at her mother and smiled. "I wish I had brought some needle work to occupy my time," she said. Agnus smiled and squeezed her hand.

They rode along for a while longer. The rain was leaking through the openings in the window. It was getting cooler. Agnus had brought a fur wrap with her. It was one William had given her. She wrapped it around herself. Diana had a shawl. It was not very warm. Soon, Agnus draped her wrap around Diana's shoulders and the two of them huddled together close to keep warm. Diana draped her shawl over their laps.

It was becoming dark inside the coach. They heard noises that told them they were nearing Harrisburg. Soon, the coach pulled to a halt and they heard voices calling to the driver. He opened the door. Porter stepped outside. He held the door open. Diana was the first out. He held her hand and helped her down from the coach. Her mother was behind her. It had stopped raining. The storm had passed.

Agnus looked up at Porter and asked, "Will we be going on now that the rain has stopped?"

Porter turned his head to look in the direction of the stagecoach driver and the other men he was talking to. "I do not rightly know at this time, Ma'am. I will try to find out. You ladies step up there on the boardwalk out of all of this mud. I will get back with you as soon as I know something," he said. He held out his arm. Each of them took his arm as he escorted them up onto the wooden porch that stretched down through the city. There was an overhang. They stood close to the wall, away from the people who walked past them. Everyone looked them over as they passed. Some said a greeting of some kind, but mostly, they just stared. Diana did not like this town. There were too many people. Suddenly, she was grateful for the simplicity of Berlin.

"Have you ever seen so many people in one place before, Mamma?" Diana asked.

Agnus nodded. "Just once. When I was a little girl in England. I had all but forgotten it until now. I suppose I didn't miss it much. But I was very young then," she replied.

"Well, I am glad we live in Berlin and not in Harrisburg," Diana said. "Do you suppose Philadelphia will be like this?" she asked.

"Somehow, I believe so," Agnus said, without looking away from the people coming and going in front of them.

Diana heard music and voices. She looked across the street. SALOON was written on a glass window. There were many people coming and going from that building. She watched. It did not take long for her to realize that the men leaving the building were all drunk. She had seen her father drunk once. He was like a crazed heifer. Diana did not like seeing her father in such a state.

Now she was looking at a whole room full of drunken men. She thought she saw some women in there, too. Then Porter was standing in front of them.

"I hear the storm is over. The driver said we will be on our way soon. Would you ladies like some refreshments? They have a fine café here. We could get a bite to eat and some hot tea," Porter said.

Diana nodded her head. Agnus looked from Diana to Porter. "Not over there, I trust."

She said nodding in the direction of the saloon.

Porter laughed. He replied, "Oh, no, Ma'am! That is strictly for gentlemen. The café is right behind you here. It is a quiet place. It will be warm and dry. Come along. I will have a bite with you, if you Ladies don't mind."

Agnus and Diana followed Porter Martin into the café. There were two strange looking people clearing tables. Their hair was very black and shiny. It was braided down their backs, nearly to the back of their knees. Their skin had a yellow cast to it and their eyes were pulled tight making it appear as though they were squinting. Diana and Agnus both looked up at Porter.

Porter held the chairs for them as they sat down at a table. The very small woman came and stood before them. "The ladies would like a cup of hot tea, please," he said to the woman. She turned without a word and went into the kitchen.

Soon, she reappeared with a tea pot and three cups. "You like hot tea awso?" the small woman asked.

Porter smiled and nodded. "Would you ladies like anything to eat? Perhaps a bowl of hot soup?" he asked them.

"Hot soup sounds fine," Agnus said.

"We would like a bowl of hot soup, please," Porter said to the little woman.

"Yes. Hot soup," she said. Then she disappeared into the kitchen once again.

Porter smiled at Agnus. "They are Chinese. They were brought here to build the railroad. If it were day light, you would have seen it as we neared Harrisburg," he explained.

Agnus smiled. "What are Chinese? Where are they from?" Diana asked.

Porter smiled and said, "They are from China. It is a country half way around the world. They were brought over here by boat."

"Like the slaves?" Diana asked.

Porter cleared his throat. "Not quite. I believe they get paid. To be very honest with you, I do not know too much about them. They understand very little of our language. Just enough to get by. They all pretty much look like these two here. They all wear their hair in braids, they are all yellow skinned, with dark hair and slanted eyes. They work hard. They are clean. They eat different food from what we do, but you will like it," he said.

Just then, the small lady reappeared with their soup. "Soup," she said. She bowed to them and disappeared.

"She bowed to me," Diana said.

"They all do that," Porter said.

"This is a strange soup," Agnus said. "It looks like some kind of egg soup."

Porter smiled. "See what I mean. They have strange ways of cooking, but you will find it is very good," he said.

Agnus took a sip. "It is very good," she said.

Diana took a sip of the broth as well. It was very good. It was hot. It felt good to her stomach. "How much further, Mr. Martin, until we reach Josephine and James's house?" she asked.

Porter lifted his bowl and drank the broth as if it were a cup of tea. "About another two hours or more," he said.

Diana sighed. She smiled at him and continued to eat her soup. Soon, the driver stuck his head in the door and motioned to Porter. "It is time to go, ladies. There is an outhouse to the right out there if you need it. I will check to make sure it is empty and wait for you at the stage," he said.

They went to the door and waited until Porter had paid the small lady for the meal. Then he went ahead of them to the outhouse. He knocked on the door. It was empty. "I will be over here," he said. Agnus and Diana went inside. It was dark. When they had finished, they returned to the stagecoach where Porter and the driver were waiting. He helped them up into the coach and climbed in himself. Soon, the stage was rocking side to side and they were leaving Harrisburg. Diana was grateful they did not have to spend the night in that city. She felt more comfortable in small towns.

The rest of the trip was quiet. There was no scenery to look at. The skies were overcast. It was so dark inside the stage that Diana could not see Porter Martin sitting across from her. They did not talk. Diana and her mother shared the fur wrap once again. Soon, Diana heard Porter snoring. She giggled and Agnus squeezed her hand to quiet her. She pictured her mother smiling, too.

Soon, the stage pulled to a stop. Diana sat upright. By the sounds coming from Porter, he was sitting upright as well. He opened the door and helped the two ladies down from the coach. Diana looked around her. It was dark. There were lights here and there, but she could not see much of the city. They were at a livery stable. The stagecoach driver was unhitching the horses. A young boy threw their bags down to Porter. From time to time, he spit onto the ground, but said nothing. His hair was yellow, just like Diana's. He smiled at her and nodded.

Porter ushered them into the stable. The young boy hitched a horse to a buggy and they put their belongings inside and were off. Diana looked from left to right as they went down the street. It was dark and quiet. She guessed it was late and everything was closed. Soon, Porter brought the horse to a stop in front of a red brick house. There was a large porch with thick white pillars supporting a massive roof. He tethered his horse and lifted their bags from the buggy. They went up onto the porch. There was a small candle burning inside the window. The door flew open and there stood Josephine in her nightdress with a shawl wrapped around her. "Mamma!" she cried. Agnus hugged

Josephine. All three began to cry. James had joined them and helped Porter with the bags.

Josephine turned to Diana. "Oh, my, Diana, look at what a lady you are!" she said as she hugged her sister.

"How good it is to see the two of you!" Josie said. "Please, come in. Are you tired? I have rooms waiting for you."

"I am tired, but I don't want to go to bed just yet," Agnus said. "Let me look at you."

Josephine stepped back. Her long dark hair hung loose around her shoulders. Her green eyes were tearing with happiness. Her gown was white and hung to her feet. Her belly was large and round. "Josephine, I thought you had your baby?" Agnus asked. Then she put her hands over her mouth. "Josephine, your pregnant again!" she whispered.

Josephine smiled. James put his arm around her shoulders. Agnus looked from Josephine to James and back at Josephine again. "Another baby. How wonderful!" Agnus said.

Diana smiled. Her heart was pounding. What a wonderful surprise. Porter must have known. He did not want to spoil the surprise for Angus. Diana hugged her older sister.

"Come on into the kitchen and have a cup of tea," Josie said.

"Oh, please, no more tea. I will spend the night in the privy," Agnus said.

Josephine laughed. She pulled out a chair and sat down at the table. She motioned for them to join her. James stood behind Josie with his hands on her shoulders. He was smiling. Porter stood in the doorway.

"Josie, honey, I am going out to help Uncle Porter put the horse and buggy away," James said. He kissed Josephine on top of the head. The two men went through the kitchen door and out the front door.

"So, Diana," Josephine began. "Tell me, is there any special man in your life?"

Diana smiled and shook her head. "Not me. I have no interest in anyone," Diana replied.

"Not even Burt Hickman?" Josephine teased.

Diana flushed. "Regina," she said.

"Oh, yes. Regina told me all about it," Josephine said. Agnus was all ears. "She said you were trying to push Sofia off onto the poor man."

Diana looked over at her mother and lowered her head. "Sofia is just more his type. He went off to war. By the time he comes back, Sofia will be nearly old enough to marry. At least I hope so," Diana said smiling.

"You, scoundrel you!" Josephine laughed. Diana looked at her mother. Agnus was trying not to laugh.

"I am not sure Burt Hickman knows what he is in for," Agnus said.

Josephine went on. "Regina tells me he is really not all that taken with Sofia. She said any blind man could see he has eyes for you, Diana."

Diana shook her head. "Well, he can just look elsewhere. I am not interested in any man. I want to be a schoolteacher like Miss Margaret. Burt

Hickman wants to be a preacher and move to a big city. From what I have seen of big cities, I think I would be more comfortable in a small town," Diana said.

"Well, big cities do take some getting used to. I still have not adjusted to life here in Philadelphia. But little William keeps me busy enough. And with another baby on the way, I don't think I will have to worry about much of a social life. James and I are happy with the life we have right here together," Josephine said.

Agnus smiled. "It is a beautiful house you have here," she said.

"Oh, Mamma! Just wait until tomorrow. Wait until you meet little William!" Josephine said. Then she went on, "I fear I am keeping you up too late. I will show you to your rooms and we shall talk more in the morning. Come along, let me show you the way." Josephine rose and started through the kitchen door. She held it open while Agnus and Diana stepped through. Josephine closed the door behind them. She carried the candle and walked ahead of them. They were climbing the stairs.

At the top, she paused at a closed door. "This is your room, Mamma." She opened the door. There was a large posted bed with lace draped from the top. The bed had a lace coverlet over the top. There was a fire in the fireplace that had burnt down to soft embers. "James built a fire for you. We did not know how cold it was going to get tonight. This time of year, you never know," Josephine said. Agnus placed her bag and fur wrap on the bed. Josephine went to the fireplace and picked up a metal pan with a long wooden handle. "There are some hot coals in the bed warmer here, Mamma. Just wrap this around it and place it under the covers to keep the bed warm," Josephine said as she wrapped the pan with a small blanket. "There is one in your room as well, Diana.," she explained.

Josephine kissed her mother's cheek. "Good night, Mamma," she said.

She took Diana's hand and led her from the room. "Your room is right next door here. Oh, I am so glad you came. I enjoyed seeing the other girls, but I longed so much to see you and Mamma. I have missed you so much, Di," Josephine said. She opened the door and they stepped inside Diana's room. It was nearly a complete copy of her mother's room. There was a candle on the night stand. The fireplace burnt softly as it did in Agnus's room. There was a stepping stool beside the high bed for Diana to climb up onto the bed. There was a chamber pot with a lid on it at the foot of the bed, and a wash-stand between two windows. There was a large cabinet along the wall. Diana opened the doors. It was lined with hooks for her clothes. Why Porter and Margaret would ever want to leave this house was beyond Diana's wildest imagination. It was far grander than that beautiful new house they had near Berlin.

Diana turned to Josephine and smiled. "How divine," she said.

Josephine laughed. "I see Margaret has been teaching you well." She hugged her sister. "Don't be embarrassed. It just makes you even more beautiful than you already are," Josephine said. "Now you get some sleep and I will see you in the morning. Don't forget to use the bed warmer if you need it. James prepared them just for you and Mamma."

Josephine hugged Diana again, then left the room, closing the door behind her. Diana looked around the room. She climbed the small stepping stool and sat on the side of the bed. She had never slept in a room this elegant before. She opened her satchel and took out her nightdress. She climbed back down onto the floor and undressed. She realized her shoes were muddy from the rain they encountered earlier in the evening. She slipped them off. She undressed and put her nightgown on. She wrapped the small blanket around the bed warmer and shoved it down under the blankets. She crawled back up into the bed. The mattress was a feather mattress. She sank deep into the bed. It was warm and wonderful. Diana fell asleep quickly. She slept well. She dreamed of the days when she and Josephine walked the woods, looking for the cows. They were laughing and happy. William was there, too. Soon, the sun shining in the bedroom window awakened her.

Diana dressed quickly. She did not want to waste one moment of time while she was here with her sister. She hurried down the stairs. She heard voices behind the kitchen door. She pushed the door open slowly and peered through it. Josephine and Agnus sat at the table. Agnus was holding little William on her lap while Josephine was trying to get him to eat. He squirmed, turning his head from left to right. Diana laughed as she approached the table. Little William had dark hair which was not surprising, as both Josephine and James had dark hair. His eyes were green, just like his mother's and grandfather, William Lewis.

Diana pulled out a chair and sat down across from her mother. Josephine sighed. "It is useless. I am not going to get him to eat his breakfast. He is too curious about what is going on around him." She shook her head and pulled on little William's toes. She leaned close to him and kissed his forehead.

Agnus bounced her knee. Little Will laughed and tried to turn to look at her. Soon, he had his whole hand in his mouth. He was slobbering all down his arm. Josephine wiped at it with a washcloth. "He will eat when he gets hungry," Agnus said.

"How did you sleep?" Josephine asked Diana.

Diana smiled at the baby and replied, "Like a baby."

"Good," Josephine said. "Would you like some bacon and eggs?"

Diana rose from the table. "If you promise to let me help," she said.

"Sure. I welcome the help. I usually have it to do myself," Josephine said. She wiped little William's arm again. She pulled his hand out of his mouth and wiped his hand. "He is teething," Agnus said.

"Yes," Josephine began. "He gets pretty fussy at times. Sometimes, he even runs a fever. It must be terribly painful for the little fellow." She bent down and kissed his head again. He put his hands in the air. He wanted her to pick him up. He fussed and began to cry.

"Here, you take him and I will help Diana," Agnus said. She stood up and handed the baby to Josephine.

Josephine held Little William on her hip. She walked around the room until he stopped fussing. He watched the two strange women preparing breakfast in his mother's kitchen.

The whole kitchen smelled of bacon and eggs. Josephine had baked bread the day before, in anticipation of their arrival. Agnus was proud of her daughter. She was happy for her, too. She had a fine home with all of the modern conveniences. Agnus had made the right choice allowing Josephine to marry James. Agnus could not stop smiling.

"So, Mother, tell me how do you like living with the Martins?" Josephine asked.

Diana held her breath. Agnus paused and then smiled. "It was very kind of them to take us in. Mr. Martin said it was not safe for us to be alone because of the war. They say there were troops seen moving south not far from us, but I have seen no signs of war. I think we would have been just fine at home. The Martins have been very gracious, and they have such a grand house, but I think we would have done well at the home your father built for us," Agnus said. Then, as an afterthought, she said, "Only, we would not have gotten the education that Margaret has been kind enough to teach us." She smiled again and sat the plate of bacon on the table.

Diana followed by, setting the eggs on the table. She remained quiet. She just listened. It was as she had suspected. Her mother was indeed regretting moving in with the Martins.

Josephine put little William on the floor. He began to crawl about.

"James tells me the war is getting pretty bad just south of you. I am not so sure you would have been all that safe at the farm alone. It is just a matter of time until those Johnny Rebs make their way up to you. I really do worry about all of you." Josephine bent down to see where little William was.

"It's just that it has been a whole year since we left the farm. I really did not expect it to be this long," Agnus said. She put some bacon and eggs on a plate and passed it to Josephine. "What about James's breakfast?" she asked.

"James ate hours ago. He and Porter are working in the sawmill already. Thomas came after them at day break," Josephine said.

Diana poured them all a cup of tea and sat down to eat her own breakfast. She could feel little Will playing with her shoes. She remained quiet and listened to the conversation between her mother and older sister.

"The railroad is keeping them pretty busy. James said they have plans to take it all the way to the Pacific Ocean. I am not sure where that is but I know it has to be far. I would like to ride it someday. James said maybe after the war we can come to visit you on the train," Josephine said. She bent down again and picked up Little William once again. "Is there anything special you would like to see while you are here, Mamma?" Josie asked.

"I am seeing what I came to see," Agnus said. They all smiled and fussed over Little Will who had decided that he wanted some of his mother's eggs.

The day went by so quickly. They cleaned up from breakfast and Josephine rocked Little William to sleep. Then they prepared lunch for the men. All three of them came in and sat around the table. The women waited until they had finished and went back outside, and then they sat and had a quiet lunch together. It was Little William's crying that got them to move from their seats. Josephine went upstairs to get him, leaving Agnus and Diana in the kitchen. Diana was washing dishes in the dry sink when Josephine returned carrying the baby. The sun was shining in the window and it appeared to be a beautiful day.

"Why don't you two go for a walk in the sunshine while I sit with the baby?" Agnus suggested.

"Oh, Mamma! Are you sure? He can be quite a handful," Josephine said.

Agnus laughed. "Josephine, I raised six babies of my own. I think I can handle one little boy. Besides, I think the exercise would do you good."

Josephine looked over at Diana. "What do you say, Di? Would you like to go for a short walk?" she asked.

Diana smiled and nodded. "I would like that very much," she replied.

They wrapped shawls around themselves and went to the door. Little William began to cry and outstretched his arms to his mother. "He will be fine. You just go," Agnus said.

They closed the door behind them and could hear Little William crying as they stepped off the porch. They stood there for a moment and suddenly, the crying stopped. Josephine laughed, "I guess Mamma still has that magic touch," she said. They started walking.

They passed large red houses all up and down the street. They had white painted porches with beautiful gardens. Fine lace curtains hung in the windows. Some even had benches in front of them for people to sit on and rest. Diana tried to see everything there was to see. This was a busy neighborhood, but nothing like what she saw in Harrisburg.

"Now, this kind of city life I could get used to," she said to Josephine.

Josie laughed. "OH, you haven't seen anything yet. The further you go into the city the rowdier it gets," Josie said.

"Really?" Diana asked.

"Mmm," Josephine said, nodding her head.

Occasionally, a buggy passed them by. Everyone appeared to be so friendly.

"How is that Grace Hickman these days?" Josephine asked.

"Oh, ho," Diana laughed. "If anything, she has gotten worse. I really wish Regina would learn to keep her diarrhea mouth shut!" she said.

"What! Diarrhea mouth! Now, that fits perfect. Why didn't I ever think of that one? Wait until I tell James," Josephine said, laughing. Then they were both laughing. Josephine stopped and hugged her sister. "I miss you so much, Di," she said.

"I miss you too, Josie. More than you will ever know," Diana said.

"We better turn back now. Poor Mamma will be chewing her nails about now," Josephine said. They started back toward home.

The rest of their visit went by so quickly that Diana could not believe it. They stood on the porch holding each other and crying as they said goodbye.

James went with them to the stagecoach. They loaded their things and headed back toward Berlin. On the return trip, Diana got to see the railroad. It was quite simple. She did not see what the fuss was all about it. It was just two metal rails on the ground, bound by wooden ties, as Porter called them. She did not see a train. She was disappointed. She wanted to see what all the fuss was about. Perhaps, on their next trip.

They stopped in Harrisburg again. It was early in the day. They ate at the Chinese Diner again. The same little woman waited on them again. She smiled and bowed politely. They had soup again. When they had finished and were ready to go, they went to the outhouse again. This time, it was daylight. Diana held her breath. The outhouse was filthy. There were feces smeared all over the seats. It appeared as though none of the men in this town could control themselves when they peed, for it was all over the walls and the floor. Diana shuddered to think of the night they used this outhouse after dark. Agnus kept her head down. They did not speak of it. They returned to the stage without relieving themselves.

Porter fell asleep again as they rode through the hills. Soon, they were winding through the Blue Mountains again. They were making better time going back. Diana figured it was because the weather was clear. It was a warm day, too. She raised the cloth flaps on the coach and watched the scenery. It was early afternoon when they reached the inn at Quincy.

Again, the innkeeper's wife gave them a cup of tea and a slice of buttered bread. They hurried to the outhouse. Here it was clean. Diana sighed in relief when she stepped inside. Agnus stood outside the door and waited for her. Then they were back in the coach and homeward bound.

They pulled into Berlin just after sundown. Grace Hickman came to greet them. She invited them to dinner. Agnus graciously declined. They were anxious to get back to the Martin farm. Porter's buggy was at the feed mill. Zachariah Dillon helped him to hitch his horses to the buggy and Porter drove them home. He dropped them off at the house and went on to the barn to unhitch the horses.

Inside, they found the girls sitting around the kitchen table. They jumped up and ran to greet Agnus. They asked questions about Josephine and the baby. Regina had been reading from Agnus's Bible. Agnus took the Bible and tucked it under her arm. She inquired about Margaret.

Regina said, "Miss Margaret has taken to her bed as of yesterday. She does not have the strength to get up. Something is wrong with her, Mamma."

Agnus told the girls to stay downstairs. She went up to Miss Margaret's room. She was just coming back down the stairs when Porter came in from the barn. Agnus and Porter spoke softly in the hall. Then Porter went up the stairs. Agnus came back into the kitchen and sat down at the table.

"What is wrong with Miss Margaret, Mamma?" Diana asked.

"I don't rightly know, child. It appears as though she is very weak. She is as white as a ghost," Agnus said.

"We did everything the same as when you were here, Mamma. She just said she wasn't hungry and then she stopped eating. She is so thin. Regina and I bathed her this morning, but she did not want to be put into her chair today," Sofia said.

Agnus nodded her head. "Well, this is her home and we were brought here to look after her, not boss her. Mr. Martin will tell us if we are to do things differently. Right now, we should all go up for our Bible reading and get ready for bed. Tomorrow is another day," Agnus said.

After a few days, Miss Margaret seemed to get a little better. She still insisted on staying in her bed. They took her meals up to her. They sat and read to her. Diana had taken over the duties of their studies. She expected more whining from Regina and Sofia, but they were very co-operative. After their studies, it was her turn to cook the evening meal. Porter had butchered one of the cows that were getting too old to produce milk anymore. Diana was preparing a stew. Agnus had baked bread and made a pan of bread pudding. Diana hoped the smell from the kitchen would drift upstairs to Miss Margaret's room and entice her to eat dinner downstairs with the rest of them. The smell did drift up the stairs and into Miss Margaret's room. However, she requested a plate to be brought up to her. Porter took it upstairs. He ate his up there with her.

While pumping water from the small pitcher pump for the dishes, Diana looked out the back window at the barn and orchard. She could see the cows in the corral. There were three young ones. To the left, between the orchard and corral, stood Hughie. Diana had never known him to come this close to the house before. "How old do you reckon Hughie is, Mamma?" she asked Agnus.

Agnus was scraping the china plates so they could be washed. "I rightly don't know. He has to be getting up there pretty good," she replied.

"He is out back. I have never seen him this close to the house before," Diana said.

"Oh, I suppose he gets lonely sometimes, too. It has been over a year since the cows have been roaming about where he could get to them. Perhaps, he is lonely, perhaps he is curious. Maybe he just wonders what is so special about that corral," Agnus smiled.

Diana laughed. "I don't think that corral would hold old Hughie. He would knock it down in no time," she said. Then they changed the subject and began talking about Philadelphia. Agnus loved to talk about little William. She hoped she would see him again soon. The next time Porter went to Philly, it would be Regina and Martha's turn to go.

Two weeks later, Porter loaded up Regina and Martha and left for Philadelphia. Agnus had instructed them not to use the outhouse in Harrisburg. "Make sure you don't drink too much for you will have to hold it all the way to Philadelphia, after leaving Quincy," she instructed. The girls had promised they would obey her instructions. They left early on a Friday morning to go into Berlin and wait for the stagecoach.

Porter and the girls were gone for four days. Porter had a meeting with a railroad engineer. While they were gone, Sofia celebrated her thirteenth birthday. Agnus had made her a new dress. Diana had gone into Berlin a few days ago and ordered her a pair of store-bought shoes. They had not arrived in time for her birthday, so Diana put a picture of them in a homemade birthday card. Sofia was ecstatic. She danced around the room singing. She hugged Diana and thanked her over and over again. No one in this family had ever had a pair of store-bought shoes, straight from the store before. They did get hand-me-downs from years gone by, but mostly they were homemade shoes from leather hides.

When Porter and the girls returned on Tuesday, Porter brought the package with him. It had arrived on the same stage that returned them home. Sofia wore them around the house. Agnus warned her to wear them for short periods of time to break them in slowly. "Or else they will break you in," she warned.

By the time they went to bed that night, Sofia had blisters. She was not the only one hurting. Regina was quiet and dreamy eyed. She had met a young man while in Philly. His name was Dilbert Gordon. He worked for his father at a news printing shop in the city. He was quite taken with Regina. Apparently, Regina was quite taken with him. Sofia had written a letter to Agnus, telling her that he came from a very nice family. She also assured Agnus that Regina was chaperoned every time she was with Dilbert.

Over the next few weeks, Regina received several letters at a time with every stagecoach that came through Berlin. Regina mailed several in return. Sometimes, she wrote twice a day. Diana took Regina with her on her walks to the farm. They sat on the porch and talked for hours. Regina was definitely in love.

It was snowing. Diana was not ready for winter yet. She took her bow and went to the woods. Her sling hung always at her waist. She carried four round stones she found in the stream. She never knew what she would find. Sometimes it was just a rabbit or two. Sometimes a ground hog or a raccoon. If she were really lucky, she would get a deer. She did not like carrying the long rifle. She took it occasionally, but only so she did not lose her edge. Today, she went home with a red fox and two squirrels. Diana was going to send the red fox hide to Philadelphia with Porter on his next trip. It was for Josephine to wrap her new baby in when it arrived.

Miss Margaret was getting progressively worse. Porter cut his trips shorter. He had been going once a month. Recently he was going every six weeks or so. This next trip was Diana's turn again. Agnus said she could not, or would not, leave Miss Margaret. Diana would be going alone. They would be leaving in another two weeks.

Regina received eight letters from Dilbert. He had asked for her hand in marriage. He apologized for not coming for her himself, but with the war, the printing business was just too busy. His father could not spare him at this time. It was his hope that Regina would come to Philadelphia with Porter on his next trip and they would be married there.

Regina ran to her mother. She read the letter aloud for them all to hear. She begged Agnus to allow her to go. Agnus wrung her hands. She looked over at Porter and asked, "What should I do?"

Porter smiled and replied, "Ma'am. Regina is a lovely young woman. I cannot tell you what to do. She is your daughter," he said.

"Mamma, you allowed Josephine to go with James. She has a better life. I don't see how it is any different for me. I will be living right there in Philly where Josie lives. We will be living with Dilbert's family until we can afford a house of our own. Mamma, I will be sixteen soon. I am fifteen now, that is older than Josephine was when you let her go. Please, Mamma. Please, please, please," Regina begged. She went on so much that Agnus placed her hand over Regina's mouth to shut her up.

"Regina Lewis, would you please hush up so I can respond to your request?" Agnus asked. She lowered her hand and cupped Regina's face in her hands. "My pretty Regina. I don't know how we could survive here without you. The quiet alone would drive us all crazy. However, I think it is your life, and your happiness we are talking about. You should be the one to make the decision. If you want to go off to the big city and marry Dilbert Gordon, then I will not stop you," Agnus replied with a smile.

Regina jumped up and down. "Oh, Mamma! Thank you so much. I love you so much! I promise I will come visit. I promise, Mamma! Thank you! Thank you!"

"Just one question, Regina," Agnus said.

Regina stood still and waited. She held her breath.

"Has this Dilbert Gordon heard you sing?" Angus asked with a smile.

Everyone burst into laughter. Even Regina. "Oh, Mamma! I will miss you all so much!" She hugged Angus. Then she went around the room hugging her sisters.

Diana decided that she would allow Regina to go with Porter in her place. He did not offer to take them both. Diana supposed he wanted her to stay and help her mother look after Margaret.

That night as she lay in her bed, she could not help but think about the changes in her life; of all the circumstances that brought her to where she was now. It would soon be two years since they moved in with the Martins. Josephine was about to give birth to her second child. Regina was going to Philadelphia to marry a man in the printing business. Diana was not sure how it would work out with Regina living with his family. Regina took some getting used to. She was a hardworker. Diana and her mother would miss Regina very much. Diana knew Regina's mouth would be her biggest downfall. It was out of her hands now.

Sofia was pouting more than ever. She was so anxious to go somewhere, anywhere but here. Sofia was the prettiest of them all. She would make someone a beautiful wife—providing, of course, she had servants. Sofia was definitely not the housewife type. She was lazy. She was a dreamer. She was the most petite of them all. Her brunette hair hung in perfect curls about her face. Everything about Sofia was perfect. She was born for a better life. Diana tried to understand how her sister felt. There was no future for her in Berlin. There was no place for her to go at this time either. Burt Hickman was not the man for Sofia, even if he did become a preacher and traveled to another town. Diana could not see Sofia as a preacher's wife.

Then there was Martha. Martha was a carbon copy of Josephine. They both got their looks from William. Martha was a hardworker. She knew what to say and when to say it. She could hold her tongue even when angry, just like Josephine had done many times. She was quick to learn hunting and household skills. She was particular and precise. Diana would rely on Martha more now with Regina gone.

Ruth Ann was nine years old now. She had attached herself to Porter. She was a tomboy in every sense of the word. At times, she would sneak off to the sawmill to help the men. She had adjusted to living with the Martins better than any of them. Perhaps it was because she was so young. Diana knew this bothered her mother. She suspected that Agnus was in fear of losing her family to the Martins.

Then there was Agnus. She missed her husband. She missed her daughter who had moved away. Now Regina was leaving her, too. She knew her mother did not want Regina to go. She suspected that Agnus was afraid of Regina's adjustment to life with her new family. There was a strong possibility that Regina would return broken hearted. Agnus had lost control of her family. She was devoted to Margaret Martin. She was grateful for their hospitality, but yearned to move back into her own home once again. Diana knew that the only thing that kept them there was the fact that Agnus did not want to put that burden upon her girls. It was a hard life. Agnus had become such a fine lady as well. She was tall and very lean. Straight, erect posture. Her hair, when brushed at night, hung to the back of her knees. It was thin, with grey streaks at the temples. Her eyes were dark blue. She braided her hair at night and wrapped the braids close to her head. Diana pictured her mother as playing the piano or violin in high society. She smiled to herself and rolled over. It was with that picture in her mind that Diana fell asleep.

Porter and Regina caught the stage and went to Philadelphia. It had been a week and Porter had not returned. Margaret was worried. She had stopped eating. Diana saddles up one of Porter's horses and rode into Berlin. Grace Hickman was dusting the shelves.

"Good morning, Mrs. Hickman. Have you heard anything from the stage?" Diana asked as soon as she entered the store.

Grace tuned and shook her head. "Not a word. They've never bin this late before. I fear it has something to do with the war. Them dern Rebs. I ain't heard from my boys either," Grace said, fluttering about.

Diana sighed and said. "If you hear anything, would you send word out to the house? Miss Margaret is frantic. Mr. Martin was supposed to be gone only four days. He took Regina with him. We are all worried. I would be happy to pay for any inconvenience to you," Diana said.

Grace smiled and pushed the loose hair from her face. "Of course, Dear. You send my regards to your Ma and Miss Margaret. I'll let you know as soon as I hear anything," she said.

Diana left. She rode back to the farm. The skies were cloudy. Large snowflakes were falling fast. She had not ridden very far and the snow was blinding. She had no idea where the road to the Martins' was. Everything was totally white. She dismounted the horse and led it through the snow. At times, she felt the snow become deeper, and she knew she was off the path. Soon, it let up and she found herself far to the left of the path. She could see the sawmill and back side of the house. The wind was howling and she could hear horses. She could not tell which direction they were coming from. She could not see them. She jumped over the horse's back and swung her leg over him. She clicked her tongue and rode hard for the house.

She put the horse in the barn. She did not take the time to remove his bridle. She ran for the house. Agnus was at the stove cooking lunch.

"Mamma, I heard horses. I don't know if they are coming here, but there are quite a few of them!" Diana said, removing her wrap and peering out the window.

Agnus went to the window, too. "Which direction?" she asked.

"It was hard to tell. The wind was blowing and it sounded like it was coming from all directions," Diana said. Martha and Ruth Ann had joined them at the window. Sofia was upstairs with Miss Margaret.

They stood at the window looking in all directions. Agnus asked, "Did Mrs. Hickman have any news about the stagecoach?"

"No, Mamma. She said she would send word to us if she heard anything. She said she has seen no signs of the stage, and it is later than it has ever been," Diana said, without taking her eyes away from the window.

Soon, far to the left, just beyond the sawmill, a group of riders appeared. They seemed to be heading in the direction of the house. Sofia had heard them from upstairs and came running down. "Someone is coming!" she called out as she ran to the kitchen.

"Everyone sit down at the table and stay put," Agnus said. She removed her apron and went to the front door.

Outside, there was a group of confederate soldiers. Their uniforms were worn and dirty. The men were also dirty. The leader was a blond man with bright blue eyes. He approached Agnus without hesitation. Right behind him was an older man with all of his front, top teeth missing. Beside him stood a younger man with a patch over one eye. They stood near the porch while the leader approached Agnus.

"Well, good afternoon, Ma'am," he said, bowing with a smile. "Is your men folk handy?"

Agnus became very nervous. She wrung her hands. "They are off for the moment. They will be returning soon for their dinner," Agnus said.

"Dinner you say?" the leader asked. He turned to the men on their horses, about eight of them, and called out, "Did you hear that boys? They are serving dinner."

Agnus cleared her throat. She tried to hide her nervousness. "We weren't expecting company. We don't have enough for all of you," she said.

The leader turned again to the men on horses and said, "You boys can dismount. Take a look around," he said. Then he turned back to Agnus. "Well, now, we don't mind smaller portions, Ma'am." He brushed past her into the house. The two men standing near the porch approached her. They smiled and brushed past her also. Agnus gasped at the smell of them. They had not bathed in a very long time. They had mud on their boots. They did not bother to clean them off before entering the house.

The three men took their time going through the house. They looked in drawers. They appeared to be looking for something of value. Even though it was not her belongings they were violating, Agnus chose not to interfere. They made their way into the kitchen. The girls sat huddled around the table wide eyed and frightened.

"Well, look what we have here," the leader said. He tipped his hat and smiled at the girls. The older man walked up behind them and stood. He bent down and smelled Diana's hair. "They sure do smell pretty, Luke. I ain't been with a woman in a long time," he said. Diana pushed his hand away as he reached for her hair. She stood up. Her sisters joined her. They went to stand near Agnus in the corner.

The leader, Luke as they called him, went to the stove. He stirred the pot. "Mm. This smells mighty fine. Jakey, you check out the upstairs," he said to the younger man. Jakey went toward the stairs.

"There's only Miss Margaret up there," Agnus said. "She can't hurt anybody. She is bedridden."

"Now that is just where a woman should be. Huh, Luke?" The older, toothless man said laughing.

"Woman! You get some bowls and feed me and my men!" Luke said to Agnus.

Agnus hurried to the cupboard. "Come on, girls. Let's feed these men so they can be on their way," she said. The girls began to help their mother set the table.

Diana heard gunfire. It cut through her like a knife. She looked out the window. The soldiers that went to the barn were shooting the cows in the corral. She turned to the man sitting at the table. "Your men are shooting our cows," she said.

Luke laughed. "Yes, Ma'am. That is what they do. We will eat beef tonight. You girls will cook it up for us," he stared at Diana.

"You can't eat that much beef in a night. Why are they killing all of them?" Diana said planting her feet firmly.

"Because we aim to leave nothing behind that those Blue Coats can use," he said.

Agnus pulled at Diana's hand. She shook her head indicating that Diana was to be quiet and help feed these strangers so they could be on their way.

Diana heard shouting from the back of the house. She looked out the window in time to see three men running hard for the house. Right behind them was Hughie. He was gaining on them fast. Good old Hughie. Diana hoped he would plow right over them. She stood watching. Soon, there was a barrage of gunfire. Hughie went down hard. His legs kicked as he tried to get back up. More gunfire and he lay dead.

"They killed Hughie, Mamma," Diana whispered.

The younger man came back down the stairs. "Just an old woman up there. She ain't going nowheres," he said as he sat down at the table. They ate their stew. They ate fast. It had to have burnt their mouths, but they did not seem to mind. "Take some of this out to the boys," Luke instructed Sofia.

She gathered up some dishes. Luke lifted the pot and carried it out the front door. Agnus took the dishes from Sofia and said, "You stay in here." She followed Luke outside.

The older man was left alone in the kitchen with the girls. As Sofia was joining the rest of her sisters who were huddled in the corner, he grabbed her. "How about you and me taking a little trip upstairs? I ain't had me a woman in a long time. Specially a pretty little thing like you." He lifted Sofia over his shoulders and started up the stairs. She kicked and cried. He was about three steps up when, without giving it a second thought, Diana reached into her pocket for a smooth stone. She whipped her sling in the air and let the stone fly. It caught the older man right over his right ear. He dropped Sofia and they both fell down the stairs. He lay there dead.

Just then, Agnus and Luke came running into the house to see what all the commotion was. Diana rushed to Sofia and helped her up. "Go back to the kitchen. Keep your mouth shut!" she said softly to Sofia. She bent down placing her hand over the stone, while she inspected the older man. When she rose, she returned the stone to her pocket. The sling hung at her waist again. "It appears he caught his foot on her dress and fell," she said to Luke.

Luke went to the old man's body. "Jakey! You and Red get him out of here!" Luke said to the younger man.

A redheaded man with freckles came inside and they lifted the old man's body, carrying him outside. Luke walked up to Diana and bent down close to her face. "It appears as though he hit his head pretty hard," he said.

Diana looked him in the eye. "It appears so," she replied.

Just then, the younger man came running into the house. "The Blue Coats are headed this way! Wallace said he spotted a whole bunch of em. An' they is riding right for us. He says they is too many for us to fight. We better git. They must a heard the gunfire!" he shouted.

Luke turned and shoved Agnus toward the door. He grabbed Diana by the hair and pulled her along. "Come along, ladies. It's time to say good bye to your guests," he said. Diana fought him, but then gave up and followed along.

The soldiers were on their horses. Luke called to the younger man. "Jakey, you and Red burn the place!" he called.

"But the Blue Coats are coming!" Jakey protested.

"You heard me! Burn the damn place!" Luke commanded.

Jakey and Red went inside. They set fire to the curtains. Soon the entire place was in flames.

"Miss Margaret is in there!" Agnus called. "At least carry her outside!" she pleaded.

Luke shoved her to the ground. "Shut up, woman! Lest I throw you and your girls in there, too!" he said.

Jakey and Red mounted their horses. They were riding off behind the others. Luke went to Diana and grabbed her hair once again. "I'll be coming back, young lady!" he said. He went to his horse.

Diana reached into her pocket and pulled out a stone. She tugged her sling free and began to whip it in the air. She let the stone fly. It caught Luke in the back of the head. He fell from his horse. He tried to stand. He was unsteady. He staggered to gain hold of the horse's bridle again. Diana let another stone fly. It hit him right between the eyes. He dropped dead.

Jakey came riding toward them. He saw his leader dead on the ground. "Come on, Jakey! We got to git!" Red called to him. He turned his horse and they began to gallop off toward the orchard.

Agnus reached for Diana and pulled her close. She was sobbing. The Martin house was totally engulfed in flames. Agnus prayed that Margaret was already dead. She could not bear to think of her suffering in the flames and smoke that was destroying her home.

They heard horses approaching rapidly. Diana pulled away from Agnus and reached for her sling once more. It was the Union soldiers. They were riding hard toward them. Porter Martin was riding ahead of them at a full gallop. He pulled his horse to a halt.

Porter stood looking at the house. Then he looked around at the girls standing out front. His voice was cracking when he asked, "Where is Margaret?"

Agnus shook her head. She could not bring herself to say the words. Porter rolled his eyes back into his head and dropped to his knees. He let out a yell and began sobbing into his hands. Agnus went to him and put her hand on his shoulder.

A Union soldier who appeared to be someone in command, approached them. "What happened here?" he asked, nodding his head toward Luke's dead body.

Agnus responded between sobs. "They rode in here and shot all of the cattle. They were taking everything of any value. They tried to rape one of the girls. Thank God for Diana and her sling. When they heard you coming, they let out in a hurry, but not before they set fire to the house. They would not allow us to get Miss Margaret out." Agnus burst into tears again.

The soldier bent down and inspected Luke's lifeless body. He stood up. Looking at Diana, he asked. "Are you the little lady that did this?"

Diana nodded her head. Tears were streaming down her cheeks. "There was another one they laid out on the porch, but he burnt up in the fire," Martha said. "He was the one that was dragging Sofia up the stairs."

The soldier looked at the house and then back to Diana. "You're pretty good with that, sling you called it?" he asked.

Diana could only nod her head. She was beginning to shiver in the cold. The soldier went to her and removed his cape, draping it around her. "Corporal Kidder, get some blankets for these ladies!" he commanded. Another soldier began gathering blankets from the others and handed them to each of the girls.

"Which way did they ride?" Porter asked, standing up. It was obvious by the tracks in the snow. He turned to the soldier. "Lieutenant, I want to go after them," he said.

"How many were there, Ma'am?" the lieutenant asked Agnus.

"About nine all together, but thanks to Diana there is seven now. They rode past the orchard for the forest," Agnus said, pointing in that direction.

Porter turned to Agnus. "You and the girls go back to your house and wait for us there. We will be back." He mounted his horse. Then he asked the lieutenant, "Are you and your men coming with me?"

The lieutenant called out, "Corporal Kidder, you and two others stay here with these women. Escort them to wherever it is they want to go, for shelter. We will be back!" He mounted his horse and they rode off in the direction the Confederate soldiers had gone.

Diana pulled the blanket around her tighter. Her feet were freezing. All of their fur leggings and wraps were in the house. So was Diana's bow and arrows. The corporal came to her. "Ma'am, would you like to ride?" he asked.

They assisted Agnus and Ruth Ann onto one of the horses. Martha and Sofia onto another one, and Diana rode behind Corporal Kidder. The other two soldiers led the horses in the direction Agnus had instructed them. They were going back to the log cabin with the sod roof. Suddenly, Diana remembered the day she had visited the house last. She wished now that she had cleaned it. It was about fifteen minutes past the wide crossing in the stream.

The soldiers tethered the horses near the front porch. "This is your home?" The corporal asked. He looked around. It was obvious no one had lived here in a long time.

Agnus smiled, wiping her face once again. "This used to be our home. We have not been here in two years or so."

They dismounted and went upon the porch. The board that was leaning against the door to keep it shut had fallen over once again. The door was standing open. All eight of them went inside. Agnus sighed heavily. "Oh, my. This is going to take a lot of work," she said.

They all walked around inspecting the condition of the house. The corporal inspected the roof. "It does not seem to be leaking anywhere. We will go out and see if we can rustle up something to eat," he said.

Diana turned to face him. "There were about nine cows in the corral at the Martin farm. They shot them all. I think we can butcher them and get enough meat to feed ourselves and all of your fellow soldiers if we can get the meat down here." She went out onto the porch and looked over at the barn. "There was a two-wheeled cart parked near the barn. It may need a little work, but we could hitch two of your horses to it and haul the meat back here," she said.

"We will get right on it, Ma'am." Corporal Kidder said. He took the other two men and went towards the barn.

"Sofia, you and Diana go fetch some water from the stream. Martha, you and Ruth Ann fetch some wood for a fire. We will start scrubbing this place up and get ready to start cooking that beef when they return. We have a lot of mouths to feed today," Agnus said.

They busied themselves with cleaning the house. Soon, the fireplace was roaring and they were scrubbing everything down. It did not take long as the table, washboard, iron pot, and wooden bowls were all there was. Martha took the old broom and began to sweep. Diana went to the barn to gather some straw for them to sleep on. It was too old and molded, for them to use. They would have to sleep on the dirt floor.

Soon, the soldiers were back with a cart full of meat. They hung it high in the tree near the porch, to keep varmints from getting to it. Diana had requested they save the hides. She busied herself with cutting the sinew away from the hides in order to dry them. They would not be able to use them for a couple of days. Martha and Sofia finished helping Agnus with cutting the beef and putting it in the pot. They began helping Diana with the hides.

Sofia was quiet. Usually, she would be complaining. Diana knew the incident with the confederate soldier had rattled her pretty good. She reached over and covered Sofia's hand with her own. "Are you all right, Sofia?" she asked.

Sofia nodded and began to cry. "I was so frightened, Diana," she sobbed. Through her sobs, she asked, "Do you think Miss Margaret suffered in the fire?"

Tears streamed down Diana's cheeks. "I don't know for sure, but she was in such poor health, I like to think her heart could not take the stress, and died before the flames reached her," Diana said.

"I didn't hear any screaming," Sofia said. "Maybe you are right." She went back to scraping the hides.

Soon, they heard the soldiers returning from their chase. Porter was with them. "Are you ladies all right?" he asked.

Agnus nodded. "We are fine, Mr. Martin."

He sat down on one of the stools and laid his head on the table. "We got them. We killed every one of them dirty rebs."

Agnus placed her hand on his shoulder. "Mr. Martin, I am so sorry. We really did try to save Miss Margaret. They held us back until the flames were roaring too high and we could not get back inside." She was choking up. The lieutenant stood near the washboard, listening.

Porter raised his head. Looking at Agnus, he said, "Mrs. Lewis, no one blames ya. They were pretty bad men. You did what you could."

The lieutenant approached them. "Ma'am, they were bad, through and through. You are lucky we came by when we did. I have no doubt in my mind that they intended to kill all of you."

Agnus covered her hand with her mouth. Ruth Ann ran to Porter. "Diana wouldn't let them kill us. She killed them bad soldiers. She would have killed them all," Ruth Ann said.

The lieutenant looked over at Diana as she stood near the fireplace. "Ma'am, where did you learn to use that sling of yours?" he asked.

Diana blushed. "My Pappa showed me. The long rifle was always too heavy for me," she explained.

The lieutenant smiled. "Lieutenant Robert Shivley, at your service, Ma'am." He smiled and continued, "I don't know if I could have done it any better. But I know I could not have done it with a sling."

Diana smiled. Her hand automatically went to the sling that hung at her waist. Then she folded her hands in front of her.

"Lieutenant Shivley, I do not have enough bowls for all of your men, but I do have some beef simmering here for you to eat," Agnus said.

Lieutenant Shivley smiled. "Ma'am, we each have our own pan, spoon, and cup. It is part of our military issue. We will be fine. We can hold up in the barn tonight and tomorrow we will be on our way. We have orders to go to Fredericksburg, Virginia. We would like to stay, Ma'am, but we have orders, and we have to go," he said.

Agnus smiled and turned to face the lieutenant. "The barn will be crowded with your horses. It will be crowded in here as well, but I think we can fit you all in around the fireplace. At least you will have a warm place to sleep tonight. Please, lieutenant, it is the least I can do."

Porter raised his head to face Agnus, "I have a contract with the railroad. I need to get the sawmill fired up. I will stay up there in the barn. I will check in on you ladies from time to time. I reckon I will have to build another house." He rubbed his face with his hands.

Agnus spoke softly, "Mr. Martin, you are welcome to stay here with us. There is a loft we could put you up in."

Porter was shaking his head. Ruth Ann slid onto his lap. "Please, Mr. Martin. Stay here with us."

Porter smiled down at Ruth Ann. He rustled her hair and pulled her pigtails. "You are my little angel. Give me time to think on it," he said. He looked up at Agnus. "Thank you, Ma'am. People in Berlin will talk."

Agnus shook her head, "No more than they talked about our living at your house," she said.

Porter nodded. "You have a point there." His gaze shifted to the fireplace. He had a sad look about him. They knew his thoughts had gone back to his beloved Margaret.

Lieutenant Shilely turned back to Diana. "Miss Diana, is there anything we can do to help?" he asked.

Diana went toward the door. "We will need more wood cut. We have to get through the rest of this winter here. We will have no horse or cows. Food will be scarce but wood is our biggest need at the time. Could you have some of your men cut some for us?" she asked.

He smiled down at her. "Yes, Ma'am, that is the least we can do for you." He stepped outside and walked toward the barn.

Diana smiled to herself. She turned and took a deep breath. She felt warm inside. She had never felt this way before. She went back to scraping the hides.

Agnus, Sofia, and Martha worked on cooking dinner for all of them. Diana and Ruth Ann scraped hides. It was important that they had enough hides stretched and dried as soon as possible. They would need them to cover themselves at night. Also, it would be their protection from the elements when they went hunting and gathering wood. Unfortunately, they would not be taking milk to Berlin any more.

At dinner, the table was pushed against the wall to make more room for all of them inside the house. The wind howled outside. The snow blew against the front porch and under the door. The soldiers sat on the floor around the fire. They filled the entire room. The lieutenant sat near Diana. They talked about how the sling worked. Soon, they fell silent.

After a few moments, Diana asked, "Where are you from, Lieutenant?"

He smiled over at her. "I live in Boston, Ma'am. May I ask something of you?" he smiled.

Diana felt her cheeks flush. She stared at her feet. She nodded. "Would you mind calling me Robert? And may I call you Diana?"

Diana smiled. Soon, she laughed. She nodded as she said, "Yes, you may call me Diana, Robert."

"Thank you, Diana. You know, you are the prettiest little thing I have seen in a very long time. The girls back home are nothing like you. I can't picture any of them killing two bad scoundrels like you did. Your sister tells me you do all of the hunting. You're something pretty special, Diana Lewis," he said.

Diana felt her ears burning. She said, "I do what I have to for our survival. Mr. Martin has been very good to us, but before we moved in with him, we had to take care of ourselves. After Pappa died and my older sister moved away, there wasn't anyone else to look after us. I had to do what I could for our survival. I think any woman would do the same thing."

He laughed. "No, they wouldn't. Not any woman I know, anyway. You are really special," Robert said. Then he asked, "Diana, when this war is over, may I call on you?" he asked.

Diana swallowed hard. This was a surprise. She looked up at him. She blinked her eyes a couple of times and then smiled and nodded. She could not find words.

"I will write, too. However, I don't know if the letters will get to you. But I promise I will write. I am not going to forget you, Diana Lewis," Robert said.

Diana cleared her throat. "I don't think I will forget you either, Robert." She smiled up at him. In fact, she could not stop smiling.

That night, Diana did not sleep all night. She could not wait until morning. She was anxious to talk to Robert Shively again.

Morning came at last. Diana rose before the sun came up. She helped her mother prepare more beef for the soldiers. They rose and ate. They were all so polite and even helpful. They had a whole stack of wood cut and split. They stacked it near the porch. There was enough wood to get them through another two months or more. How different these soldiers were from the Confederate soldiers who invaded the Martin house.

Robert approached Diana after they ate. "Diana, when we caught up with those rebels yesterday, we caught four of their horses. Usually, we take them along with us. I think we could spare two of them. I really don't like leaving you here with nothing but a few sides of beef and some hides," he said.

Diana said, "Thank you so much, Robert. I don't want to get you in any trouble. Are you sure?"

"No trouble, Diana. The army can spare two horses, I am sure," Robert said, smiling.

They spent the rest of the morning walking around the farm. Diana was wrapped in his blanket. They talked about anything and everything they could think of just to stay within one another's company. Diana did not want him to leave. She had never felt this way about another person before. The time went too quickly. Soon, it was time for Robert to leave. His men were mounted and waiting. Diana handed Robert his blanket and smiled. She wrapped her arms about herself. "You better go inside, Diana. I promise I will write. I will be back as soon as this war is over. I promise," Robert said.

Diana smiled. She could not find words to respond. She just nodded.

Robert kissed her on the forehead and mounted his horse. He raised his hand in the air. The soldiers followed him as he went back toward the Martin farm. Diana stood watching them for as long as she could tolerate the cold. Then she went inside.

Agnus was scrubbing the iron pot. "Who thought we would be back here in our house again? It feels almost like we never left." She was smiling. Diana knew her mother was happy to be back in this little log cabin again. She knew her mother did not want anything bad to happen to Margaret or Porter's beautiful house. Agnus was in her own house and in control of her girls once again.

Diana smiled. She did not mind right now. She could only think of Robert Shively and how happy she was that he came into her life. He promised he would write her letters. She would write, too. Perhaps, the stage would come through soon and she could mail them. She hoped they would find him. She sat down at the table. Porter was sitting there with her mother and Ruth Ann. He had been talking. Diana had not noticed it until now.

"Regina made it to Philadelphia all right, Diana," Agnus said.

"Yes, Ma'am. Just like I said. We didn't have any trouble getting to Philly. We went the same route as we took with you and your Mamma," Porter said. "She is safe and sound."

Agnus tuned to Diana and said, "Mr. Martin was telling me about some trouble at the hotel in Quincy. You remember that nice Mrs. Anderson who gave us the buttered bread and tea?"

Diana nodded. "What kind of trouble?" she asked

Porter cleared his throat. "Some Confederate soldiers came through there, too. They were on their way to Gettysburg. Mr. Anderson and his wife poisoned them when they stopped for water. The bad thing was later, Mr. Anderson drank out of the bottle with the poison in it. Mrs. Anderson did not mark the bottle. He died." Porter shook his head.

"How did you come to meet up with the soldiers?" Diana asked.

"Those Johnny rebs hit the stage. They killed the driver and a passenger. We think it might have been the same bunch that burnt down the house. They stopped running the stage. Those boys went through here robbing and killing everyone they met. How they missed Berlin I will never know," Porter said.

Diana shook her head. "They were some pretty bad men. Why would they want to hurt people they don't even know? Are all Confederate soldiers like that?" she asked.

"Naw!" Porter said. "They were just bad men in soldiers' uniforms. They were like that before they joined the war is my guess."

Agnus asked, "Mr. Martin, is there any word on how much longer this war is going to last?"

"I wish I knew, Mrs. Lewis. It's gone way past what I expected already. President Lincoln was right out there on the front lines talking to the generals. He has guts, that President Lincoln does. The men look up to him. They will keep fighting if he asks them to." He shook his head. "I wish I had made it back sooner. They stopped the stage and I waited to ride with Lieutenant Shively. If I had just left and rode straight here, maybe I could have saved my Margaret." He hung his head and covered his face with his hands.

Agnus bowed her head and said, "Mr. Martin. You could not have stopped those men. They would have just killed both of you," she whispered.

"Maybe so. Maybe so, but life without Margaret is not any kind of life at all. Even with her disabilities, I loved every minute of my life with her," Porter said, looking up at Agnus.

"Well, as I said before, we have a loft above us here. We don't have any straw for it just yet, and you will have to sleep on the hard boards a couple of nights, but Diana and the girls should have those hides stretched and ready soon. At least, it is a warm place to lay your tired bones at the end of the day," Agnus said.

Porter smiled. "Thank you, Ma'am. That is mighty kind of you and your girls. I'll get to working on another house as soon as I fulfill my obligation to the railroad. Then you and your girls can come back up to the farm and live in a big house again," he said.

"Well, now, we are just fine here. Don't you fret none. We will be fine. You just get yourself straightened out. We will get through this somehow," Agnus said. She turned and went to the fireplace. She threw another log on the fire. Hot sparks and coals flew up. It was beginning to get warm in there, and the smell of simmering beef was in the air.

Sofia stepped up close to Diana and whispered in her ear, "Is that lieutenant coming back for you, Diana?"

Diana looked at her. She flushed. "He said he was, but the war is a funny thing. I hope he does," Diana said.

"Me, too, Di. You deserve someone nice and kind like that Lieutenant Robert Shively," Sofia said.

Diana stared into Sofia's eyes. That was a strange thing coming from Sofia's mouth. Diana would have expected her to whine about not having someone for herself to take her away, especially now that they were back in the cabin. Sofia wanted a better life. Better even than the life she had at the Martin's. She had gone backwards instead of forward. This new Sofia was confusing Diana.

Diana smiled at Sofia and reached for her hand. "Are you all right, Sofia?" she asked.

"Yes, Di. I'm all right," Sofia said. "I will be forever in your debt for saving me from that smelly old rebel soldier. I will work hard. I will cut wood and help you carry water and hunt. Whatever you need, I will do whatever I can," Sofia said.

Diana smiled. "We are in for a hard winter. I will appreciate every little bit of help I can get," she said to Sofia. They smiled at one another. No more words needed to be said.

The next couple of weeks went by quickly. Diana was so busy. There were no letters from Lieutenant Shively. Diana had made two trips to Berlin. Grace Hickman had been acting very strangely since she got word that Willy was killed in Spotsylvania. She had no word from Burt and was very worried. Sofia took the job at the general store, helping Mrs. Hickman. She enjoyed being there with her friend, Concetta. She promised Diana she would not tell Mrs. Hickman anymore than necessary. She was, after all, not Regina. Porter had driven her into town every morning in his buggy. He had become quiet, but it was understandable with the loss of his beloved Margaret. Also, he went from living in a fine big house to sleeping on the floor in the loft of a two room log cabin. He never complained.

One morning, Diana had wrapped herself in the hides of the cows and went hunting. The beef was beginning to disappear. They would need more meat. She found herself in familiar territory. She was in the spot where the fallen trees formed a three-sided corral. She sat down on one of the fallen trees and scanned the area around her.

Soon, without warning, she found herself crying uncontrollably. All the events of the past months came rushing at her. She had hoped to hear some word from Lieutenant Shively and there was none. There was no stage to take her letters. No way for his letters to come to her. Porter said he would take her letters to Philadelphia with him and mail them from there. He would be making the trip only once every couple of months now, as it was determined that travel was unsafe. The Confederate Army had moved into this territory. They were all on their guard.

The two long rifles were destroyed in the fire. Porter said he would purchase two more from Philly on his next trip. It was not safe for them to be there alone without any weapon. Diana's heart was not in the hunt today. She knew they needed the meat, but she just could not concentrate. She rose from her seat and began to walk back toward the house. She reached the clearing near the knob. She stopped and looked down at the farm. There was smoke coming from the chimney. She saw the big oak tree where her father was buried. She saw the stream that ran behind the house. She remembered seeing Hughie there the last time she visited the house before the rebels came.

Diana wiped the tears from her eyes. She started slowly for the house. Something caught her eye to her left. Without even thinking about it, she placed a stone in her sling and swung it over her head. She whipped her wrist and allowed the stone to fly at its target. She heard it strike. It was a squirrel. She got it. She ran to fetch it. At least it would be something. Usually it took two squirrels to feed all of them, but they still had a little beef left. This would get them through today. Tomorrow would be another day. Perhaps she would feel more like hunting tomorrow.

Diana went to the house. She skinned the squirrel of its hide and took it inside for her mother to put in the pot. She went to the stream for a fresh bucket of water. Martha was running after her. She, too, was carrying a bucket.

"Diana, would you teach me to use a sling?" she asked.

Diana nodded. "Sure thing, Martha. It is much easier than it looks."

"Can I go with you tomorrow?" Martha asked.

"Well, if Mamma can spare you tomorrow. That will just leave little Ruth Ann with Mamma to help her. We will ask her over dinner tonight. If she says you can go, it is all right with me," Diana said.

They carried the two buckets of water back to the house. "Remember when we used to go to the barn every morning in the freezing cold to mild the cows? And how we used to walk for, sometimes, miles to find them and bring them in at night?" Martha asked.

"Yes, I remember," Diana responded.

"I really miss the big house. I hate them rebels for what they did to Miss Margaret and that house. I hope they burn in hell. They even burned Mamma's Bible up," Martha said.

Diana remained quiet. She did not want to talk about any of this. She was afraid she would start crying again. She just remained quiet while Martha went on. Finally, Martha ran out of things to say and she quieted down as well.

It had been seven months since the rebels forced them to move back home. Diana had received no letters from Robert Shively. There had been a big battle in Gettysburg. Porter stopped going to Philadelphia. He continued his work at the sawmill. He had wood staked everywhere. The railroad had put everything on hold for the time being. They were having trouble with the Confederate Army also. Porter had started building his house. It was not as big as the one he built for Margaret, but it was way bigger than the log cabin they were living in at the moment.

Summer was upon them. Sofia was not working at the general store anymore. Grace Hickman did not need her as there was hardly anything there. There was no way for supplies to get through. Berlin had been very lucky. It was such a small town that the Confederate Army passed right by them several times without ever knowing of its existence.

Diana found herself killing more small critters and sharing them with the Hickmans, Stumpy, and Zachariah Dillon. It was becoming harder to find animals to kill. Apparently, the soldiers in the area were killing them, too. She did not stray too far from home for fear of running into a band of rebel soldiers. Once was enough. Porter told her they were not all bad, but she wasn't taking any chances.

The new Martin house was completed on the outside. Porter made better time with this house as he had Stumpy, Zachariah Dillon, Edwin Morgan, and Sherman Hickman to help him. There was nothing else for them to do. Porter had promised to pay them once the war was over and the railroad was up and running once more.

There was no glass for the windows. Porter put shutters on them, just as he had the first house. He said he would get glass later, once they were able to have supplies brought in. There were only three rooms downstairs, and three rooms upstairs. The inside was not complete yet.

The church in Berlin was not completed either. Porter had promised Mrs. Hickman that he would help to complete it after his own house was finished. He would donate the remaining lumber they needed. When Burt returned from the war, he would have his church.

Agnus seemed to be happy now that she was back in her own home. She knew it was trying on her girls to have to work so much harder. She thanked them often for all of their hardwork. She reminded them nearly every day that their father would be so proud of them.

Standing on the knob, looking down at the little farm with smoke coming out of the chimney, it looked almost exactly as it did the day they left for the Martin house nearly three years ago. The only difference was the area around the barn had grass growing where once the cattle had it eaten down to the bare earth. They still had the two horses that the soldiers had left them, but they seldom used them. There was no place to go. Porter used them around his sawmill, as the rebel soldiers shot his team when they slaughtered the cows.

Sofia had gotten over her ordeal with the rebels. She had drifted back into her old routine of sitting around, watching the rest of them do all of the work. For some reason, Diana could not figure out, Agnus tolerated it and expected the rest of them to do the same. This angered Diana very much. It was so hard to do everything as it was.

Ruth Ann was now eleven years old and capable of doing more, but there was so much to do. Porter supplied them with slab lumber from the mill to burn in the fireplace. That was a big help.

Diana had taught Martha to use the sling. She was not very accurate, but with a great deal of practice, she would get it. Stumpy had made Diana a new bow. He fashioned four arrows, which she carried in a leather pouch over her shoulder. She hadn't used them much, as there was very little wild life left in the area.

Diana prayed that Porter Martin would have his new house finished before winter. She knew he was not happy sleeping on hides up in the loft, but he never complained. The rest of them slept on hides in their mother's bedroom. It was crowded, but it was warmer in the winter months.

Diana found herself praying more these days. They needed so much. She prayed to be in the new Martin house before winter. She prayed for more food on the table at the end of every day. She prayed the war would be over soon. And she prayed to receive some word from Lieutenant Robert Shively. She prayed for his safety. Her heart ached so badly at times. She feared the worst.

She saw her mother carrying two buckets while she made her way to the stream behind the house. Diana began to walk back home. She had not killed anything for dinner. There would just be cattail bulbs and wild onions in the iron pot for dinner. She arrived at the house the same time as Agnus was returning with her water. Inside, Martha and Ruth Ann were cutting up the wild onions. Sofia was sitting on a stool, gazing down at her store bought shoes.

Agnus put the buckets on the washboard and looked up at Diana. Diana shook her head. Agnus smiled. She put her arm around Diana. "Tomorrow will be another day. It will get better. You will see," Agnus said.

She turned to Sofia and said, "Sofia, you go to the cattail pond and pull some roots so we can put them in the pot."

Sofia just sat there staring at her feet. "Sofia!" Diana shouted. "Did you hear what Mamma said? Go get some cattail roots for dinner!"

Sofia jumped from her stool and approached Diana. She stood nose to nose with her, glaring at her. She spoke through clenched teeth. "I don't have to take orders from you! You are not my boss! Shut up and leave me alone!" Sofia shouted at Diana.

Diana removed her bow. She was about to pounce on Sofia, when Agnus separated them

"That will be enough! I will not have this fighting in this house! I will go to the pond myself. And while I am gone, I do not want any bickering between the two of you. Is that understood?" Agnus shouted.

Diana turned away. She threw her hands in the air. "Yes, Mamma," she said.

Agnus grabbed a wooden bowl and went out the door. Diana glared at Sofia who had sat back down on her stool. Diana followed her mother outside. "I will get them, Mamma," she called after Agnus.

Agnus turned toward Diana. "No. I will get them myself. You have been hunting all morning." She turned and walked in the direction of the cattail pond.

Diana turned to go back into the house. She could not bear the thoughts of seeing Sofia sitting on her backside while the rest of them worked. She turned again and followed her mother to the pond. She ran to catch up.

"Mamma, why do you tolerate Sofia's laziness?" she asked when she caught up to Agnus.

"Diana, Sofia is different. That is all. She is just different from the rest of us. She has her own way of contributing. When things get really tough, she jumps right in there and does way more than her share. You can count on Sofia when times are really hard. You just have to be patient with her on her dreamy days. She is a daydreamer. Who really knows what is going on in that head of hers? Just give her some space. She is a little behind the rest of us when it comes to growing up," Agnus explained.

They had reached the pond. Agnus reached down and pulled her skirt up, tucking it into her waist. Diana did the same. They waded into the pond. They reached down into the water near the bottom to pull the cattails loose from the muddy bottom. They began tossing them up on the bank.

"But Mamma. Times are hard right now. We are all struggling just to survive. Even little Ruth Ann is doing more than Sofia. I just wish you would scold her more. I don't think Pappa would tolerate her laziness while the rest of us were working so hard," Diana said.

"Diana, your father understood Sofia more than you realize," Agnus said. She bent down, reaching deep into the murky water. Just then, she shrieked and stood upright. She pulled her arm from the water and held it high. "I've been bitten!" Agnus cried.

"What bit you Mamma? What was it? A moccasin?" Diana cried rushing to her mother. She looked about. There it was slithering away in the murky water. It was a water moccasin.

Oh, Mamma!" Diana cried.

She helped Agnus out of the water. She pulled the knife from the wooden bowl. "Look away, Mamma," she said to Agnus.

She tore a strip of fabric from her skirt and tied it around Agnus's arm. She cut the bite mark and began to suck the blood and poison from her arm. She spit each mouthful out onto the ground and sucked some more. Agnus moaned. She dropped to her knees onto the ground. Her face was white. After awhile, Diana helped her to her feet. "Come on, Mamma. I will help you to the house." Diana held her mother as they walked back toward the house. Diana started screaming, hoping one of the girls would hear her.

Soon, all three of her sisters were standing on the porch watching her. They knew something was wrong right away. The sun was beating down on them and Agnus was becoming very pale and sweaty. The girls ran to them.

"Someone run for Porter Martin. Mamma has been bitten by a water moccasin!" Diana called to them.

Sofia turned and ran toward the dirt path that led to Porter Martin's house. Martha and Ruth Ann walked beside Agnus, helping to support her. They got her inside and sat her at the table. Martha got her a tin cup of water to drink. Diana stretched her mother's arm across the table and inspected the bite mark.

The arm was swelling fast. She tried to suck some more of the poison out. The arm oozed blood some, but Diana knew she wasn't getting any more of the poison out, so she stopped.

"Ruth Ann, get Mamma a cool wet cloth for her head," Diana said.

Ruth Ann began to cry as she dipped a cloth in the bucket and wrung it out. She folded it and placed it on Agnus's forehead. Martha sat down beside her mother and supported her weight with her own body. "Mamma? How do you feel?" Martha asked.

Agnus smiled and patted Martha's hand. "I feel better, child," she said.

Diana knew by the look on her mother's face that she was not feeling better. She took hold of her mother's arm and inspected it once more. It was really beginning to swell. She lifted the arm and looked on the underside. There was a mark. It was a second bite. Agnus had been bitten twice. Diana had not seen this one. She went for a knife. She cut the second bite and began to suck on it. She spit. Again she sucked and spit. She was getting very little out. The arm was beginning to balloon. This was not working. Diana felt sick at her stomach.

"Mamma, why didn't you tell me you were bitten twice?" she cried.

Agnus shook her head. "It hurt so much, I did not know I was bitten twice," she said. Sweat was running down the sides of her face. Ruth Ann removed the washcloth and dipped it back into the bucket of cool water. She replaced it on her mother's forehead.

"We better get you to bed.," Diana said.

Martha and Diana each stood on both sides of Agnus. They helped her into the bedroom. Ruth Ann followed. She was sobbing softly.

"Ruth Ann, put some cool water in a bowl and bring it in the bedroom. Keep replacing the cloth on Mamma's forehead. We need to try to keep the fever down," Diana said. Ruth Ann ran for the kitchen.

Diana looked over at Martha. Martha was staring at her mother with eyes open wide. She was pale around the lips. Diana sighed. She did not know what else to do. She feared the worst. If only she had seen the second bite. She put her hands over her face. She did not want her younger sisters to see her crying.

There was a noise coming from outside. Ruth Ann ran into the bedroom. "Sofia is back with Porter Martin and Sherman Hickman!" she shouted.

Diana met them on the porch. "Mamma was bitten twice by a mud moccasin. Maybe two, I am not sure," she explained and Porter brushed past her and entered the house. "She is in the bedroom," Diana said.

Sherman stood in the doorway to the bedroom, watching. Porter bent over Agnus. He was inspecting the arm.

"I cut the first one and sucked the poison out. I did not know she was bitten twice. I didn't find the second bite until we were back to the house. I am afraid it was too late," Diana had tears streaming down her face.

Porter was knelt down on one knee. He looked up at Sherman Hickman and shook his head. Diana could not hold back the sobs. Martha and Ruth Ann had confused looks on their faces. Sofia stood to the right of Sherman Hickman with her mouth hanging open. Diana could not hold back.

She marched over to Sofia and struck her in the face. "This is all your fault! You should have gone for the cattail bulbs. You know that pond as well as I do. You know to watch for snakes!" Diana was crying.

Agnus moaned. "Diana, no. Don't." She cried.

Diana went to her mother's side. "Mamma, I don't know what to do. You have to get better. You have to Mamma." She sobbed.

Sofia was crying uncontrollably. This got Martha and Ruth Ann crying as well.

Porter stood up. "Well, at this point, all we can do is wait it out. She is a strong woman. She may survive. Just keep up with what you are doing. I don't know anything else we can do," Porter said.

"Ya want me to fetch Grace?" Mr. Hickman asked.

"Might be a good idea," Porter said.

"No." Diana spoke up. She knew her mother would not want that nosey, old Grace Hickman nosing about her home. "We can take care of her. Thank you just the same, but we will manage just fine."

Sherman looked from Agnus to Porter. Then from Porter to Diana. "Are ya sure? Your Mamma's a very sick woman. She is goin to get much worse before she gits better," he said.

Sofia wailed. She began to sob harder. She dropped to her knees, crying. Martha and Ruth Ann began to cry louder also. They clung to one another.

Diana stepped forward, "We can do it. Porter will be here tonight if we need him. There isn't anything that Mrs. Hickman could do that we can't. Thank you just the same," Diana said.

Porter walked to the front door with Sherman Hickman. "You go on back. I will stay here until Mrs. Lewis gets through the worst of it. You tell the rest of them to go on home. I will ride into town when I need you to come back to work," Porter replied.

Sherman nodded his head. "All right, Mr. Martin. Send one of em girls after me if ya need me." He turned to Diana. "I hope your Ma gits better, Missy." He threw his leg over his horses back and rode up toward the knob.

Diana went back inside. She went through the curtain that hung over the door to her mother's bedroom. Sofia, Martha, and Ruth Ann were all gathered around Agnus. Agnus's breathing was labored. She appeared to be sleeping. It was so hot in there.

Diana said, "Get back. Give her room to breathe. Sofia, get some more water. Bring the whole bucket in here. We need to keep her cool. Martha, get some more cloths. We will soak them in cool water and drape them over her. We need to keep her fever down. Ruth Ann, you help Martha rip some rags into strips," she commanded.

Porter knelt down over Agnus once more. He felt her forehead. "Mrs. Lewis. Can you hear me?" he asked.

Agnus did not respond. He looked up at Diana and shook his head. She had to look away.

The girls did everything just as they were instructed. Diana noticed that as long as she gave them something to do, they were not crying. Even Sofia worked diligently. Diana regretted her outburst and striking Sofia. She wished she could take it back. If her mother did not survive this, Sofia would feel to blame. Even though Diana felt she was partly to blame, she knew it was not entirely Sofia's fault.

Agnus seldom ever went for water or gathered cattails. The girls had always done it before. Agnus was not aware of the snakes around the pond area. She was trying to keep the peace between Sofia and Diana. Diana vowed to herself that she would never quarrel with Sofia over her laziness again. She only wished she could take it all back. It was as much her fault that her mother was at the pond as it was Sofia's. The guilt she felt was overwhelming. Tears ran down Diana's cheeks freely. She tried not to let the others see.

Porter went to the fireplace and peered into the iron pot. There were just a few wild onions cut up in some water, simmering in the pot. "I think I will go see if I can rustle up something to eat," he said. He went outside.

Diana hung her head. She had been out all morning and saw not one critter. She knew Porter was not going to find any fresh meat for the pot.

She sat down beside her mother. Martha and Ruth Ann delivered the strips of cloth. Sofia arrived with a bucket of cool water from the stream. They all sat around Agnus, dipping the cloths in the bucket and laying them over Agnus's pale, sweating body.

Soon, Porter arrived with a few crawdads. He cleaned them and placed them into the pot.

Porter slept just outside the bedroom door that night. He had brought his hides down from the loft. He told Diana, "If there is any change, you wake me."

The girls gathered around their mother. They continued to dip the cloth strips in the bucket of water and drape them over Agnus to keep her cool. One by one, they all drifted off to sleep, except for Diana. She watched her mother closely. Agnus was breathing harder. It sounded as though she were struggling for every breath. Diana wiped her face with a cool cloth. Agnus's tongue was swelling and beginning to protrude out the side of her mouth. She had saliva foaming from her mouth. It was obvious that her throat was swelling shut. Diana woke Porter.

He quietly entered the room, stepping over the sleeping girls. He inspected Agnus. He stood upright and looked at Diana. He shook his head and whispered, "It won't be long now. There is nothin we can do, child."

Diana began to sob. She watched her mother as she struggled for air. Soon, there was a gargling sound and Agnus stopped breathing. Diana put her hands over her face and sobbed. Porter reached over and placed his hand on her shoulder.

Diana looked up at him and asked, "Would you help me carry her to the table? I don't want the others to wake and find her like this."

Porter nodded. They lifted her and carried her to the table. Diana began to wash her and prepare her for burial the same way she had watched her mother prepare her father. "I will dig a grave next to your father," Porter said. He went outside.

Diana had finished preparing Agnus. Porter was still digging. She could hear him out there. She thought about going out to help him, but could not seem to leave her mother. She pulled a stool close to the table and sat down. She rested her head on her mother's lifeless body.

Soon, the digging stopped and Porter returned. "It will be sun up soon," he announced.

"Will you help me wrap her in a hide so the girls won't see how bad she looks? I don't want them to remember Mamma this way," she asked Porter.

He nodded. He collected two cowhides from where he had been sleeping. They lifted Agnus and placed one under her body. The other they draped over her.

Diana heard a noise and turned to find Martha standing in the doorway to the bedroom. Martha ran to the table. She threw herself over Agnus's body and cried. This woke the others. They were all gathered around the table crying their hearts out. Diana could take it no longer. She went out onto the porch for some air.

The sun was coming up. It was one of the most beautiful sunrises Diana had ever seen. She turned and went inside. "Sofia, Martha, and Ruth Ann, come out here. I want to show you something," she called to her sisters.

The girls went out onto the porch. Diana pointed to the rising sun. "Look. Look how beautiful the sunrise is. It's Mamma's spirit. She's telling us she is happy. She is with Pappa. She is sending us a sign that she is okay," Diana said.

The girls stopped crying. They stood there watching the sun come up. Porter had joined them on the porch. They stood there until the sun was completely up and shining brightly.

"Mamma is happy. She is with Pappa and Miss Margaret," Ruth Ann said.

Tears were forming in Porter's eyes. He put his arm around Ruth Ann.

They carried Agnus to her grave and gently placed her in it. Porter began to shovel the dirt over her. They all began crying once again. Soon, it was done. Ruth Ann and Martha went to gather flowers. Sofia went to the oak tree and leaned against it, staring at the grave. Diana approached her. She put her arm around Sofia. They stood there quietly for a few moments.

Sofia looked up at Diana. Through her sobs, she said. "I am so sorry. It should have been me, just like you said. It was all my fault. I am so very sorry, Diana."

Diana hugged Sofia. She was also crying. She said, "I should not have blamed you, Sofia. Mamma did not go to the pond because of you. She went because I was arguing with you. She didn't want us to argue. I am just as much to blame. And if I had seen the second bite, I may have been able to get the poison out before it went up her arm."

They stood by the oak tree holding one another and crying. Soon, Sofia pulled back and said. "Diana, let's not argue anymore. Let's do it for Mamma and Pappa."

Diana nodded her head and hugged Sofia. "That would make them both very happy, Sofia. I am sure of it."

After awhile, Diana released Sofia and said, "I better go see what I can find for us to eat."

Sofia followed Diana back into the house without saying anything.

Diana could not help but think how things were going to get even harder yet for her. How was she ever going to take care of all of them alone out here? She tried to push it out of her mind, but it kept creeping back.

Porter had left. He went to Berlin to report to the others what had happened. He told Diana he would return by sundown. He rode off leaving her with the other horse. It was the one they called Buckley. It was named by Ruth Ann. Buck had been shot by the rebel soldiers. It was only fitting that one of the soldiers' horses took his place. So Buckley had become the girls' favorite of the two horses Lieutenant Shively had left with them.

Martha told Diana she was going hunting. She did not want to eat breakfast. Diana smiled at her. Martha knew there was nothing for them to eat, anyway. She took her sling and went toward the woods.

Diana turned to Sofia. "Sofia, do you think you can keep an eye on things around here while I go hunting, too? We can't go all day without anything to eat."

Sofia nodded. "I will clean the iron pot out and have everything ready. I will keep a close eye on Ruth Ann," Sofia said.

Ruth Ann spoke up, "And we will watch out for any rebel soldiers, Diana."

Diana bent over and looked Ruth Ann in the eye. "If any rebel soldier come this way, you and Sofia run for the woods. Don't you stay in this house alone," she commanded.

"We will, Diana. I promise. Because they will just burn the house down like they did Porter Martin's house," Ruth Ann said.

Diana smiled and nodded her head. She went outside and mounted Buckley. She would have to travel away from the area to hunt today. There was bound to be some kind of wild life somewhere out there. She rode off in the direction of the dammed pond where her mother was bitten by the water moccasin.

She crossed the stream just down from the dam. She rode in the same direction that Lieutenant Robert Shively and his soldier went. Diana had been this way a couple of times, but not very far. The forest was very dense here and she was always afraid of getting lost. She had watched her father go this way many times. Perhaps, this is the direction she needed to go to find some wild life.

Diana bent tree limbs as she went, marking her way so she could find her way home. She rode for what seemed a long time. Every once in a while, she would stop to allow Buckley to graze. She would stand quietly with her bow in hand, waiting and watching for some kind of movement. The forest was quiet. It was hot already, and it was still early in the day. Diana heard a chirping sound. She knew it was a squirrel, but she could not see it. She stood silently, watching. She missed it. At least she knew there was something here to hunt.

She mounted Buckley once more and rode deeper into the forest. The trees seemed to be taller here. She was moving north west. The forest was beginning to get thicker. There were many grape vines clinging to the trees. Diana stood on Buckley's back and picked some wild grapes. They were sour, but they were food. She ate some and put some in a leather pouch that hung over Buckley's back.

The sun was directly overhead. It was noon. Diana turned directly west, carefully marking her trail. She kicked up leaves that lay on the forest floor to help mark her way. She piled sticks and rocks to mark every turn she made.

Soon, she tethered Buckley to a tree and moved away from him to listen for movement. She decided to climb a tree. She wedged herself firmly in the tree and scouted the area.

There was movement to her right. It was an opossum. She hated opossum, but it was food. She drew back her bow. She let go and an arrow flew in that direction. The opossum squirmed and flipped about. Then it lay still. She scrambled down the tree and went to gather it up. She removed the arrow and hung the bleeding opossum over Buckley's back. He tossed his head about some. Diana figured he did not like opossum either. She spoke softly to him and stroked his nose and jaw line. She took hold of his halter and began to lead him back the direction they had come.

Diana could smell peppermint. She found a grove of wild peppermint growing in a clearing. She began to gather the leaves. They made good tea. It was better than drinking warm water. She was very pleased with herself. She mounted Buckley once again and started home.

Diana heard bees. Bees meant honey. Honey, unfortunately meant stings and possibly bears. She looked about carefully. She followed the sound until she came to an apple tree where the bees had a hive. There was honey here. She dismounted. All around her on the forest floor were deer tracks. There was wild life here after all. The deer had been eating the apples that had fallen from the tree. Diana inspected the apples. They were pretty bad, but if she gathered enough of them, they could cut the bad parts off and make some applesauce. She filled the leather pouch, which had the grapes in it, to the top. She could barely get it closed. She tethered Buckley away from the bees.

Diana clenched her left fist tight. She took a deep breath and reached into the hive, very slowly. She pulled out a handful of honey. That was enough. Never take more than you need. She did not get stung. She went back to Buckley. She pushed the soft honey down into the pouch over top of the apples. She decided to head home before a bear came along. She led the horse away from the area singing as she went. She did not want to surprise a bear. When she thought she was far enough away, she mounted the horse and began her trip home.

She lost her way just once. It took awhile, but she found her pile of stones and the bent tree limbs that marked her trail. Soon, she was in the clearing near the dammed cattail pond. She began to cry once again as she crossed the stream. As she approached the house, she regained control of herself.

Ruth Ann rushed out onto the porch as she dismounted. She handed her youngest sister the pouch. "Here are some treats for us. Tell Sofia to make some peppermint tea. I will clean this opossum. Has Martha returned yet?" Diana asked.

"Not yet. What do you have in here?" Ruth Ann asked as she began to inspect the contents of the pouch. "Oh, boy! Honey!"

Diana laughed. "Tell Sofia that is to sweeten the tea."

Diana carried the opossum to the spot near the side of the porch where she cleaned all of her kills. She skinned it and laid the skins on a pile of rocks. She cut the opossum into pieces for the iron pot. Ruth Ann had brought her a fresh bucket of water to wash it in. She then brought her a wooden bowl to collect the pieces. Once Diana had finished, Ruth Ann took it inside for Sofia to cook. Diana washed herself in the remaining water. Then she went inside and began to peel and cut up the apples. She went outside to a spot they used for cooking when the weather was warm.

There was a ring of stones. Diana piled wood into the center and started a fire. She had another iron pot that they rescued from Porter Martin's house fire. She put the apples in the pot and added a small amount of water.

Diana stood up straight, stretching her back. She looked at the sky. The sun was to her right. Martha should be home by now. She went inside the cabin. Sofia was stirring the iron pot.

"Ruth Ann, would you be able to keep an eye on the apple sauce? Martha should have returned home by now. I need to go look for her," Diana said.

Sofia turned to look at Diana. "Do you think she is all right?" she asked.

Diana nodded. "I am sure she is. Perhaps, she got something big. I'll take Buckley and go look for her. That is, if Ruth Ann can watch the apple sauce," she said.

"I can watch it Diana.," Ruth Ann said. She followed Diana outside to the fire.

Diana stirred the pot. "You have to stir it often, Ruthie. If you don't, it will stick to the bottom of the pot. Once it is smooth and sort of creamy like, you can take it off of the fire and let it cool. It should not take very long, so you really have to watch it close," she explained.

"I can do it, Di," Ruth Ann said.

Diana smiled and went for the barn. She led Buckley out near the wooden fence. She climbed up onto the fence and swung her leg over his back. She rode into the direction of the knob. That was the direction she had watched Martha go when she left that morning.

Diana rode through the forest. She looked for signs of disturbed leaves and other markings that Martha had passed this way. She called out to her sister and then listened for a reply. There was none. She continued on.

After awhile, Diana came to the other side of the forest where the high bank was. This was where the cows used to find grass in winter. She stopped and looked around. She heard gunfire. Heavy gunfire. A lump came up into her throat. "Martha!" she called in her panic.

"Diana. Shh... I'm over here...." Martha called out softly.

Diana saw Martha crouched near the bottom of the bank. Diana dismounted Buckley and led him in that direction. She squatted down next to her sister. "What are you doing?" Diana asked.

Martha nodded in the direction of the gunfire and said, "They are fighting over there. I think the Union soldiers are fighting some Johnny rebs. I was afraid to move so I just hid here."

Diana raised her head above the bank and looked around. The gunfire was far off. "I don't think they can see us from there, Martha. I think it is safe to go back to the house. I think we need to get back home and warn the others, just in case they come our way. Come on, we can ride Buckley," she said.

Diana helped Martha up onto Buckley's back. She led him into the woods until she came to a fallen tree. She climbed on top of it. It elevated her high enough that she could mount the horse's back behind her sister. They rode back to the farm.

Ruth Ann was waving at them as they approached the house. "Look, Diana, the applesauce is done. I did not let it stick to the bottom," she said.

Diana smiled and turned to Martha. "Martha, go hitch Buckley to the cart. I will get Sofia. We are going to Porter Martin's," she said.

Martha led Buckley toward the barn. Diana went inside. Ruth Ann followed her, confused.

Diana found Sofia stirring the peppermint tea to dissolve the honey. Diana went to the iron pot and lifted it off the fire. She carried it to the table. Sofia stood there, watching Diana. "What are you doing? That is not done yet," Sofia asked.

Diana sighed and spoke calmly. "There are soldiers fighting on the far side of the forest. They may or may not come this way, but if they do, we need to get out of here. Martha is getting the cart ready. We can load all of this into the cart and go up to Porter Martin's. We don't want to be here by ourselves. We will not be able to protect ourselves."

Sofia went white. "Oh, Diana! Not again! I will help you get this in the cart. We have to hurry!" She began to rush about the kitchen collecting the wooden bowls and tin cups.

Diana turned to Ruth Ann. "Ruthie, you collect the hides. We may have to sleep at Mr. Martin's tonight. Get everything you think we might need into the cart. Tell Martha to help you when she gets finished."

Ruth Ann went into the bedroom and began dragging the hides out onto the porch. "Don't forget to get the hides in the loft, Ruthie," Sofia called to her.

They worked hurriedly until they had stripped everything they needed from the log cabin and loaded it into the cart. Diana crawled up into the driver's seat and clicked her tongue. Buckley obeyed her command and began to pull the cart.

Sofia was trembling. They rode in silence. Diana listened for the sounds of gunfire or horses approaching. Soon, they reached the wide shallow crossing near the Martin house. She could hear pounding sounds coming from inside the house. They pulled Buckley to a halt near the front of the house.

"Wait here. I'll get the men to help us unload the cart," Diana said as she jumped down from the cart.

"No way! I am not waiting out here," Sofia said. Diana did not argue with her. Sofia was frightened. The memory of the smelly Confederate soldier would be forever in her mind. They all went inside.

Zachariah Dillon met them at the door. Ruth Ann brushed past him. She was searching for Porter. He had become her father figure. "What's wrong?" Zachariah asked.

"There are soldiers fighting on the other side of the forest. We heard gunfire, lots of it, while we were hunting," Diana explained.

Sofia sighed and leaned against the wall. She looked as though she were going to faint. Diana put her arm around her waist to support her. Zachariah turned and went toward the pounding sounds. Soon, he returned with Stumpy, Sherman Hickman, and Porter Martin.

"Where exactly was the gunfire?" Porter asked.

"It was back on the other side of the forest. Northeast of here. It must be a far piece, because you can't hear it from here or at the farm. But they are there all right. It was a lot of gunfire. Sounded like a big battle to me. It wasn't just a few men shooting, Mr. Martin. The whole ground was vibrating," Diana explained.

Sherman Hickman spoke up. "I better get back to town. Grace and Concetta are there alone. Old Marcus is at the stables, but he won't be good for much. He can barely see anymore." He went out onto the porch.

Porter followed him. "Wait, Sherman! I was thinking it might be a good idea if all of us went into town and stayed for a spell. There is safety in numbers and all of that," Porter said.

Zachariah said, "I will go saddle up the horses and bring them around." He jumped off the porch and ran toward the barn.

Porter went about closing the house up. He closed the shutters and bolted the back door from inside. They were all mounted and ready to leave soon. Diana followed behind the men as they went to Berlin. They were all quiet, listening for the sounds of gunfire that might be coming closer.

When they pulled up in front of the Hickman's general store, Concetta ran to greet them. Grace was close on her heels. Diana's heart sank. The thoughts of staying at the Hickman's weighed heavy on her mind. She did not care much for Grace Hickman. She wished no ill to come to her. She knew that she would have to be on her guard the entire time they were there. She warned her sisters that they were not to offer any information to the nosey Mrs. Hickman.

Grace welcomed them inside. Diana figured it was because they had brought food with them. They were told they could put their hides on the floor in the store. The girls could sleep in the boys' room upstairs. They would have to sleep two to a bed, and the beds were small, but at least they would have some privacy. The girls politely thanked Mrs. Hickman and went to inspect their rooms.

Diana assumed that the rooms were exactly as Willy and Burt had left them. It must have been hard for Grace to allow them to sleep in here. She looked at the two small single beds.

They had store-bought mattresses on them. There were two quilts covering the beds and feather pillows. It was just like her room at Porter Martin's house before the rebel soldiers burnt it to the ground. Sofia flopped down on the bed. A cloud of dust rose into the air. The boys had been gone for almost four years. They would have to shake the dust out of the bed before they slept in it. There was one glass window that overlooked the front street. Diana could see Buckley still hitched to the two-wheeled cart down front.

"I'm going to take Buckley to the stables. You three dust this room out. Be quiet as not to alarm Mrs. Hickman. It may embarrass her. I will be right back," Diana said.

She went down the enclosed stairwell. It was narrow. At the bottom, she found Grace Hickman and Concetta putting the iron pot with the opossum in it, on the wood stove to finish cooking it. "Is this all the meat ya got? It ain't gonna go far," she said, inspecting the contents of the pot.

"Most of the wild life has disappeared, Mrs. Hickman. I reckon it is because of the war. Soldiers are probably killing everything they can get their hands on. They have a lot of mouths to feed," she explained.

Grace nodded her head and put her hands on her hips. "Well, we will just have to make it do," she said.

Diana went outside. She untied Buckley and led him to the stables. The men were inside discussing what they would do if the battle came this way. Diana stood back and listened. Porter looked up and saw her standing there.

"Diana. I will unhitch Buckley for ya. You needn't worry yourself or the others about that shootin'. It's off a far piece. I think we'll be safe here," Porter said. He took hold of Buckley's halter and led him inside. Stumpy went to help him unhitch the two-wheeled cart. Diana stood looking around the stables. It appeared to be nearly vacant. Some of the equipment had dust and cobwebs covering it. It had been over two years since the stage came through Berlin.

"Mr. Martin, we will be needing more food. What I brought is not going to feed us all. We might make it stretch for tonight, but we are all going to wake up hungry tomorrow morning. I was thinking I would go hunting first thing in the morning. I saw some deer tracks a couple of miles into the forest to the west of the farm. I would like very much for someone to go with me, though. I don't really want to risk running into a band of hooligans," she said.

Porter stood there rubbing his chin. "I think you should leave it to us menfolk, Miss Diana. It should be our job to put food on the table, anyhow," he said.

Diana shook her head. "I beg to differ with you, Mr. Martin. I think it is more important that the men protect the women. Besides, I am probably the best hunter you have at the moment. I just want someone to go along with me. That is all I ask," she said, standing directly in front of Porter.

He looked around the stable at the faces of the men there. She was right about being the best hunter amongst them. There really was no one besides himself that was capable of going with her. He was not sure if any of them were capable of protecting the women either. He continued to rub his jaw.

He smiled at Diana and said, "Miss Diana, I'll be ready at sunrise. I would be happy to escort such a lovely lady as yourself on your hunting expedition," Porter said.

Diana nodded and turned to go back to the general store. She would leave the men to their planning and plotting. She wanted no part of any kind of conflict with the Confederate army anyway. She hoped it would not come to that.

Inside the store, she found Mrs. Hickman, Concetta, and Sofia working on the dinner. Martha and Ruth Ann were out back searching for any over-looked vegetable that may still be growing in Mrs. Hickman's garden.

Mrs. Hickman handed her a stack of china dishes to put around the table. Diana handled them carefully. Sofia went out back to pump some water. It was almost dinnertime. Diana felt her stomach growling. She had not eaten anything since she came across the grapes earlier that morning.

Dinner was quiet. It appeared everyone was listening for gunfire or some signs of soldiers approaching. It weighed heavily on all of their minds. When they had finished, the men retreated out to the front porch. There was a breeze blowing there. They could smoke their pipes and talk of things only men knew about. Diana helped clean up. She noticed a Bible resting on a stand near the window in the kitchen. She remembered her mother's Bible.

After dinner, Diana asked Grace, "Mrs. Hickman, would you mind if I read your Bible to the girls tonight before we go to bed?"

Grace wiped her hands on her apron. She looked over at her Bible, and back at Diana. "I suppose it would do us all good. Would ya mind readin' aloud to us all?"

"Of course. I would love to," Diana said.

Ruth Ann said, "Diana wants to be a school teacher like Miss Margaret."

Grace looked at Diana and smiled. "Well, now. How nice. Just where were ya plannin' on gettin' pupils to teach, Miss Diana Lewis?" Grace asked.

Diana felt her face turning red. "Well, obviously, I would have to move to another location. That is unless, Berlin acquires more settlers," Diana said.

Mrs. Hickman straightened herself. "Hmph! I reckon that is a possibility. My Burt wants to be a preacher man. He was plannin' on movin' elsewheres, too. I was buildin him that church out yonder in hopes that he would settle right here in Berlin. Ifin he did, he would no doubt have children, and I would want my grandchildren to be educated," she said, standing erect and tall. She towered over Diana. Then after a moment, she smiled and put her hand on Diana's shoulder. "Of course, he would need to marry someone local first," she said, smiling.

Diana looked over at Sofia. She had been listening to every word they were saying. She had a smile on her face. Diana smiled at her sister and nodded as she said, "That is correct. He would need a wife."

Sofia smiled back at Diana. Concetta spoke up, "Mother, Burt had his eye on Sofia before he left. She was too young then, but she is fifteen now."

Mrs. Hickman turned to look at Sofia. She looked her up and down. Even though she was sweaty and ruffled around the edges, she was still beautiful. Grace Hickman must have liked what she saw. "Yes. Sofia, Dear. You are charmin', indeed. You would be perfect for my Burt," she said smiling.

Diana sighed a sigh of relief. Thank goodness, she was off the hook! Grace Hickman deserved Sofia for a daughter-in-law. Diana only hoped Burt would come home safe and sound. She also hoped that he would turn his attention away from her and toward her sister, Sofia.

That night, they all settled out on the porch for some air. Grace had given Diana a kerosene lamp to read by. Diana read from the Bible until her eyes were becoming too heavy. Then they decided to retire for the night. Porter had told her he would be waiting for her in the morning. Diana slept soundly.

The next morning, Diana was up and dressed before the sun was up. She went out onto the porch and listened. She heard no sounds of gunfire. Porter came from the stables leading two of his horses. The rest of them were still sleeping. They moved about quietly so as not to wake them. They rode in the direction of the Lewis farm.

As they passed the Martin farm, Porter rose up in the saddle and looked around. Everything was just as he had left it. They continued on. Soon, they were at the Lewis farm. It, too, was as it was when the girls packed up and left. They rode past the cattail pond and into the deepest part of the forest. Diana found the trail she had marked the last time she was there. They followed the trail until they came to the apple tree. Porter dropped down and inspected the footprints that were all over the ground.

"Looks like they were here just a while ago. The bite marks in these apples are fresh. They aren't even tuning brown yet," he whispered. Diana motioned to Porter that she was going up a tree.

She found a tree further to the left and climbed it. Porter went the other direction. She climbed halfway up the tree and settled herself securely between two limbs. She pulled her bow from her shoulder and got an arrow ready. She quietly waited.

Before too long, a doe came into view. It had a young one with it. Diana frowned. She did not move. She did not really want to kill them. She looked around. There to her far left stood a big buck. He had a big rack on his head. He had been rubbing some of the felt from his antlers. Diana drew back her arrow and froze. The buck raised his head high. He was looking around. Diana aimed for a spot right behind the neck and shoulder. She let the arrow go. It flew through the air. It struck the buck right where she had aimed for. He turned and ran. The doe and fawn ran, too, only in the opposite direction. Diana began to climb down the tree. Just then, she heard Porter Martin's gun crack through the air. She ran in the direction the buck had gone. She followed the blood trail until she found it lying dead on the forest floor. She knelt down and began to disembowel the deer. She said a silent prayer that there were no Confederate soldiers in the area to hear Porter's gunshot.

She worked on the deer feverishly. Soon, Porter came leading the two horse. He had missed the deer. "You are really good with that thing," he said. "I forgot how good you were."

Porter helped her tie the deer to one of the horses. They walked back toward the apple tree. "I will get us some honey and peppermint. We will have more tea with our dinner," Diana said.

Again, she made a tight fist with her left hand. She reached her right hand into the beehive and pulled out a handful of honey. Porter had taken the horses way ahead to where she told him the peppermint grew. She would meet him there, if none of the bees chased her.

They filled pouches full of peppermint and wild onions. Diana found an area that had sponge-like mushrooms growing around a fallen log. They picked as many as they could find. They moved silently, listening for sounds of the war. There was none. They headed back toward the Lewis farm and on into Berlin.

As they rounded the bend and came into the clearing that overlooked Berlin, they spotted a group of horses tied in front of the general store. There were about seven horses in all. Porter and Diana stopped and watched. Soon they saw two Union Soldiers come out onto the porch. Porter motioned for them to continue on. They rode a little faster as they approached the store.

The soldiers stopped and watched them as they approached. The soldiers that were inside joined them. They waited until Diana and Porter pulled their horses to a stop. Diana dismounted and stood below them looking up. "Were you the soldiers that were fighting over that way yesterday?" she asked pointing in the direction they heard the gunshots the day before.

One very tall soldier nodded his head. "Yes, Ma'am. We ran into a band of renegade soldiers who jumped us in the woods. They apparently didn't know the war is over," he said.

"What? The war is over?" Porter asked stepping up onto the porch. Diana followed him.

"Yes, Sir. Lee surrendered to Grant weeks ago. I guess you didn't know, either." He smiled at Porter. His gaze kept drifting to the deer hanging over Porter's horse's back. He looked back at Porter and smiled again.

"The war is finally over," Porter said softly to himself. "And we won the war!" he said turning to Diana smiling. "We won the war!" he said again louder. He lifted Diana and swung her around. He set her back down on the ground. "Well, that is the best news I have heard in a long time," Porter said, turning back to the soldier.

Diana stepped closer to the soldier. "Do you know of a Lieutenant Robert Shively?" she asked.

The soldier looked at the other soldiers standing on the porch. They were all gathering around now. One of the other soldiers spoke up. "I've heard of a Captain Branden Shively. But I never heard of no Lieutenant Robert Shively," he said.

The tall soldier said, "Sorry, Ma'am. Was he some relative of yours?" he asked.

Diana felt her heart pounding. Her face was beginning to turn red. She smiled and said, "No. No. No relative. Just someone I met a while back. He promised to write, and I reckon he did not have the opportunity to do so."

"Oh, Ma'am, don't feel bad. Lots of us soldiers wrote many letters. We just had no way of mailing them. I'm taking my letters home with me," he said, smiling.

Diana smiled and nodded her head. "I understand," she said.

"That's a nice deer you have there. Pretty good size one, too," the tall soldier said.

Porter put his arm around Diana's shoulders and said, "This little lady here got him. She is a hell of a shot with a bow. And a sling. My, oh, my, you should see what she can do with a sling. Why, she killed two rebel soldiers with her sling about a year ago!" Porter bragged.

The tall soldier frowned. Then he smiled. "We could have used you on the front lines, little lady," he teased. Diana was still flushed.

"Well, Sir, we have a lot of hungry soldiers that sure could use that deer you have there. We cannot pay you for it, but they would be mighty grateful," the tall soldier said.

"We can't give him to you," Diana said without thinking. Then she smiled and apologized. "I am very sorry. We appreciate all that you have been through for our sakes. It's not that we don't want to give him to you; it's just that we are starving. You must understand that. There has been no stage or wagon train to bring supplies in here for so long. Our food is all gone. It is so hard to find wild game. We were lucky to find this one. And we had to go so far to find him," she explained.

The soldier looked down at his feet. He was quiet for a while. Then he looked at the other soldiers who were shaking their heads. Fear was gripping Diana. She felt certain they were just going to take the deer and there would be no way of stopping them.

The soldier sighed and said. "That is a big deer. I am sure he would feed a lot of people. I think he would feed all of us and have some leftover for you too," he said.

Diana knew they would not be able to stop them from taking the deer if they really wanted to. She looked over at Porter. "It is your kill, Missy," he said.

Diana turned to the soldier. She nodded and said, "I suppose it is the least we can do for all of you, after what you have been through. We will share."

The soldier smiled. "Thank you, Ma'am. I promise we will take no more than we have to."

The soldiers removed the deer from Porter's horse. They began to cut at it. "Please, Sir, save the hide. We need it for the winter months ahead," Diana called to them.

"Yes, Ma'am. We understand," one of the soldiers called back.

"Where are you boys headed now?" Porter asked.

"We are headed to Harrisburg and then to Philadelphia," the tall soldier said.

Porter asked. "Would you mind if I tagged along? I have a place in Philly. I could get some supplies and bring it back here to these nice folks."

The tall soldiers sighed and smiled. "It is all right with me, Sir, but my commanding officer will have the last say on the matter," he said.

Porter smiled. "Well, let's get this buck butchered and go ask him, shall we?"

Diana went inside. Everyone was in Grace Hickman's kitchen. They were all sitting around the table. Grace was sitting with her head bowed. "What is it?" Diana asked.

Martha said, "There is still no word from Burt. The soldiers told us that he was in a battle in Antietum. There were many casualties on both sides there. It was a pretty bloody battle."

Diana went to stand near Grace Hickman. She put her hand on the woman's shoulder. "I am sorry, Mrs. Hickman. Perhaps he made it. I, for one, would not give up hope," Diana said.

Diana turned to Sofia. She was sitting in a chair near the window crying. "Sofia, don't worry. Don't think the worst. Burt may return. Come help me with the deer meat. We are going to have a big dinner tonight to celebrate the end of the war. Come on now. Cheer up," Diana urged Sofia until she rose from the chair and followed Diana outside onto the porch.

The men had skinned the deer and cut a large part of the shoulder off for them. They were preparing to leave. Porter was returning from the stables with a fresh horse. He was packed and ready to leave with the soldiers. He turned to Diana and Stumpy who were standing near the porch.

"I will be back as soon as I get some supplies. Just hang in there for a week or so. If you girls want to go to my place to stay you can. I will be back as soon as I can," Porter said.

Diana nodded. "We will be at our place, Mr. Martin. It is safe now and your place isn't finished yet. We will be watching for you to return. Have a safe trip and give Josephine and Regina our love," she said.

Ruth Ann ran from the porch to Porter. "Please, Mr. Martin, take me with you," she begged.

Porter pulled on her pigtails. "Naw! Little Angel. I need you to stay here and wait for me. I will be back. I promise," he said. He bent down and kissed Ruth Ann on top of the head. He swung his leg over his horse and followed the soldiers to the east where they said the rest of their column was waiting.

Diana went back inside. The girls had taken over Mrs. Hickman's kitchen. She was still sitting at the table holding her head. They prepared the venison and applesauce. It felt good to be cooking on a wood stove again. It brought back memories of Margaret Martin's kitchen and the happy times they had there. Connie was boiling the peppermint tealeaves to make tea. Before too long, Grace had joined them. "It smells so good in here," Grace said.

Dinner that evening was delicious. There was nothing left. "Porter don't know what he missed," Marcus said.

They went to the porch once more. They watched the sun go down. Diana read from the Bible again, by the light of the oil lamp. They all went to bed with their bellies full and smiles on their faces. All, that is, except for Grace Hickman.

The next morning, the girls loaded the two-wheeled cart with their belongings and hitched Buckley to it. They were going back to the cabin. Grace begged them to stay in town until Porter returned. Sofia tried to convince Diana to stay also.

"We will be fine at the cabin. There isn't much to fear now that the war is over," Diana defended her decision.

"But there may still be some raiders out there that don't know the war is over. Just like the ones that were fightin' two days ago," Grace pleaded.

"I really feel confident that it will be fine. We will keep our eyes and ears open, and we will come this way if there is any sign of danger. I promise," Diana said.

They piled into the cart and headed back toward their home. Sofia sulked.

As they approached the Martin house, Sofia asked, "Can we stay at Mr. Martin's house?"

Diana tuned in her seat and said, "Sofia, his house isn't finished. Our place will do until he gets back. When he returns, he is going to want to work on the inside. It will be difficult with us trying to cook and move around in there. We will just stay at home until it is done. Then we will have a family meeting and take a vote on whether we move in with Porter Martin or stay in the cabin."

"What do you mean a vote? What is there to vote on? We all want to move into the Martin house!" Sofia whined.

Diana sighed. She said, "I know. You are right. I just think that it is important that we all take part in any decision when it comes to our future. I am just saying that no one of us will make the decisions for all of us. Do you understand what I am saying?"

It was quiet for a while. "I think that is a good idea. We will put it to a vote. I suppose the majority will decide," Sofia said.

Martha spoke up, "I think that is a good idea."

They rode for a while longer and then Sofia began to sing. Soon they were all singing. The little log cabin came into view as they reached the knob and clearing. They stopped singing. Diana stopped Buckley at the porch. They all began to unload the cart, and carry everything inside.

Diana announced, "I am going hunting. You unhitch Buckley, Martha. I will be back when I find something."

Martha called to her. "Diana, Wait for me. I want to go with you. There is safety in numbers, remember?"

Diana stopped and turned to face Martha. "All right. I will help you. We can take Buckley with us. Who knows, we may find another deer."

They led Buckley to the corral. They unhitched the cart and led him to the stream behind the house. They allowed him to stop to drink before they went any further. Then they crossed the stream and turned left toward the cattail pond. They talked as they went. As they approached the cattail pond, they fell silent. They did not speak again until they were in the forest.

Diana again looked for her markings. As she found them, she was careful to bend more branches and make the trail more distinguished. They whispered whenever it was necessary to speak. They moved even deeper into the forest than Diana had ever been before. They heard a squirrel chirping high in the trees. They strained their necks looking up for it. Martha pointed.

It was a flying squirrel. It was leaping from tree to tree. Diana removed her bow from her shoulder and took hold of an arrow. She was ready. They stood still for a time. It was too high for Diana to get it right now. They would have to be patient and wait for it to come into range. It was moving away from them. Diana moved as quietly as possible in the same direction. She knew the squirrel knew they were there. It felt safe high in the trees. She continued to wait.

Diana felt her shoulders aching. She had been holding the bow taunt for too long. She slacked the tension and rolled her head around. She moved closer, trying to keep her eye on the squirrel. Suddenly, he disappeared. She looked from tree to tree. Where was he? He must have gone into a hole in one of the trees. She listened. It was quiet.

Martha had moved closer to her. She was also looking for signs of the squirrel. She looked at Diana and shook her head. Diana waved her hand at Martha and they began to move on. They would have to give up on the squirrel. They continued moving through the forest quietly. Diana motioned to Martha that she was going to climb a tree. Martha nodded.

Diana went up a maple tree. She nestled herself securely between the limbs and scouted the area. She knew it could be hours before anything came along. She watched Martha as she moved about below. She was kicking at the brush.

Diana looked about. As far as she could see was still and quiet. Then she heard Martha's sling whistling in the air. She had chased a rabbit from the underbrush. Martha let the stone fly. It struck the rabbit. It made a little squeal when the stone struck it. It lay kicking for a moment and then it laid still. Martha looked up at Diana. She was smiling. Diana smiled back. Martha had mastered the sling. She had been practicing and it paid off. They would have rabbit for dinner.

Diana sat for a while longer. It was still quiet. Her stomach was growling. They had not eaten since the night before. She was beginning to cramp from being wedged in the tree. She decided to climb back down. As she was descending, she once again heard Martha's sling whistling in the air. He jumped to the ground just as Martha let go of the stone. It was another rabbit.

Martha lifted the two lifeless rabbits into the air. Diana rushed to her side. "Martha! You are really good with that. You may even be better than me. I am so proud of you. We will eat rabbit today and again tonight." Martha was smiling. She was proud of herself. She had killed two rabbits. Diana, who had been the main source of food lately had not killed anything. They hung the rabbits over Buckley's back and climbed on him. They rode together back toward home. When they came to the bee tree, Diana instructed Martha to keep Buckley way back while she got the honey.

Diana made a tight fist with her left hand, and reached into the hive with her right hand. She pulled out some more honey. It was getting low and she knew that there would not be any more this year. She slowly turned and walked away. The bees landed on her. She kept her left arm tight. She continued to move away from the nest. Soon, the bees left. She went toward where Martha and Buckley were waiting.

"How did you do that? How is it you were not stung?" Martha asked.

Diana scraped the honey into the pouch. She looked back at the tree and said, "Pappa showed me. He said if you make a real tight fist with your left hand and hold it really tight, the bees will not be able to sting you. I watched him do that many times. I was stung a couple of times, but not enough to worry about," she smiled.

Martha shook her head. "Well, I trust anything Pappa says, and I just witnessed it with my own eyes, but I think I will leave the honey collecting to you. I don't think I want to try it," she said, shaking her head again.

Diana laughed. "That is okay. The honey is gone for this year anyway. Besides that, you got dinner and supper today. Now, let me show you where the peppermint grows. We will have more tea tonight," she said.

They continued back toward the marked trail. They stopped and began to pick the peppermint. "I think I might try to pull some cattail bulbs when we get back home," Diana said.

Martha stood upright and said, "Oh, no, Diana. I don't want you to. I don't want any of us in that pond again. Please, don't. Mamma would not want you to."

Diana shook her head. "Mamma was bitten because she was not familiar with the pond. She was not watching for snakes. She was talking to me and she was distracted. We need the food. I think it will be okay. Also, I was thinking about something else. Remember the grove of fruit trees Porter Martin planted to the right of the barn? Well, they may be producing this year. After we drop all of this off, I thought I would ride Buckley up that way and take a look around," she said.

Martha went back to picking the peppermint. They put their pickings in the pouch with the honey and climbed back onto Buckley. They rode back toward home. They talked as they went. Diana felt like a big weight had been lifted from her shoulders. The war was finally over. She wondered where Lieutenant Robert Shively was. Did he survive? She prayed he had. He said he would call on her. When?

They came to the cattail pond. Martha held Buckley by the halter. She scanned the area for snakes. She saw none.

Diana pulled her skirt between her legs and fastened it at her waist. She peered into the green murky water. She wadded in slowly. She continued to watch her surroundings as she reached deep into the water, feeling for the bottom. She began to pull cattails up and tossed them onto the bank. She stopped when she had collected about six of them. Then she climbed onto the bank. She went over to Martha and pulled the pouch from Buckley's back. She reached down and took hold of a knife she kept strapped to her leg. She cut the tops off the cattails and put the bulbs into the pouch. They led Buckley back to the porch.

"You take these inside. You skin the rabbits while I ride up to the Martin's orchard. I will be right back," Diana said. She climbed onto the porch. Then she swung her leg over Buckley and rode off. She could hear the squeals behind her. The girls had seen the rabbits. They knew they would all eat soon.

Diana approached the Martin farm slowly. She scanned the entire area. It appeared to be quiet. She rode to the barn. There were still signs in the fenced in area, where all of the livestock had been slaughtered. It was a year ago. She dismounted Buckley and put him in the corral. She put the pouch over her shoulder. She patted Buckley and spoke softly to him. He was familiar with this area. Porter had brought him here many times. She turned to walk toward the orchard. She walked among the trees. They were still young and fairly small. There were two pears on one of the pear trees. They were still fairly green. The apple trees had yellow apples on them. Some had fallen to the ground. She picked them up and placed them in the pouch. The red apples were not as plentiful. They were bigger, but not as many of them. She collected all she could.

She stood facing the back of the Martin house. She remembered the day she discovered the garden. She walked closer to the new house. It too, had a back porch. It was about the same size as the previous one. The wooden archway was still there. There were grapes hanging from the vines. Diana stuffed them into the pouch. She walked through the archway and into the garden. It was just weeds. It needed re-plowed and sewed. She found the strawberry plants growing near the house. All but a few of them had been destroyed by the fire. She picked two strawberries and ate them. She was very hungry.

She went around front and into the house. The sounds of her footsteps on the wooden floor echoed in the empty house. There was no sitting room. No parlor. The living room was smaller. There was just one window. There was no glass, but the shutters were closed and secured. There was a large fireplace on the far wall. The entire wall was made of stone. There was a hearth that protruded out from the fireplace. Diana closed her eyes and tried to imagine a fire blazing, throwing heat out into the room. She went into the kitchen.

The kitchen had a fireplace as well. It too had a stone hearth. There were drying racks hanging from the ceiling all around it. There was a hole cut into the wall where Porter had planned on placing another wood stove to cook on. She went through the door into the hall. She turned and went up the narrow stairway to the second floor. There were three small bedrooms up here. Diana smiled. Porter had told her there were going to be just two bedrooms. The rooms were a lot smaller than the ones in the last house. There was room for two beds and a dresser, but it would be cramped. She turned and went back down the steps. She went out the front door and closed it behind her, being careful to make sure it was latched tightly. She walked toward the sawmill.

Porter Martin would be firing up the mill once again now that the war was over. The railroad would want its lumber and more, no doubt. Diana looked around and turned to go back for Buckley. She heard a noise. She reached for her sling.

The noise was coming from under a stack of boards piled to the left of the railroads lumber. Diana kicked at the stack. The noise stopped. She kicked it again. She carefully lifted the boards and squatted down to look under them. She saw movement. Four shining eyes peered at her. She lifted the board. The smell of rotting flesh hit her and took her breath.

There were two small starving puppies staring up at her. They were lying amongst a litter of dead puppies. They had starved to death by the looks of them. Diana lifted the two and held them in her arms. They were too weak to fight her. She carried them to the barn. She pulled some grapes from her pouch and held them under the puppies' noses. They licked at them, but they were too weak to eat. Grapes were not good puppy food anyway. Diana climbed onto Buckley's back. Holding the puppies close to her, she rode back toward the house.

Ruth Ann rushed to meet her. Diana handed her the puppies. She put the pouch on the porch and led Buckley to the barn. She tied him behind the barn, where the grass was tall and he could get to the stream. Then she went back inside the house.

Sofia was going through the pouch. "Apples and grapes! Oh, Diana! Thank you. We will have a good dinner today. Are we supposed to eat those puppies, too?" she asked.

Ruth Ann jumped to her feet and stood her ground in front of Diana. "No, Diana! We are not eating these puppies!" she cried.

Diana smiled and shook her head. "No, Ruthie. We are not eating those puppies. There was a whole litter of them under a woodpile. The rest of them have already starved to death. I thought maybe we could find enough scraps to feed them. They may make good hunting dogs."

Martha picked one up. "They are pretty weak. They may not make it," she said, looking over at Ruth Ann.

"I will feed them, Di. I will take care of them. Maybe we can save them," Ruth Ann said.

"Okay, Ruthie. That will be your job," Diana said. "Now let's get this rabbit going. I am hungry."

They all pitched in. Ruth Ann took a small piece of rabbit meat and broke it in two. She gave one piece to each of the puppies. They nearly took her fingers off getting the meat down.

Martha made peppermint tea. Sofia cooked the rabbit. Diana went outside and began cooking the apples down into applesauce on the outside fire.

That night, they spread the hides onto the floor in what used to be their parent's bedroom. They had all been sleeping in there since Agnus had died. Porter Martin had been sleeping in the loft. Or in the winter months, he slept near the fireplace, keeping the fire from going out during the nights. Diana could not sleep. They had a good day. They had eaten well. She wondered how the Hickmans and the rest of them in town were doing. She knew they would not have enough food to go around to all of them. The men were just going to have to go out hunting themselves. Still it nagged at her. She was doing the best she could to provide for them. So much had been asked of her these past five years. She was now twenty years old and still not married. Yet, she had an entire household depending upon her. She heard the puppies whining. They were nestled between Ruth Ann and Martha. They had eaten well today, too. Diana hoped they would survive, for it would break Ruth Ann's heart. She had lost so much already. Losing one or both of the puppies would really be just too much. Diana hoped Porter Martin would return soon. She was anxious to hear from Josephine and Regina. She knew Josie had to have had her second baby by now. Perhaps, even more. It had been over two years now. Maybe the stage would be running again and Porter would take them with him on his trips back to Philadelphia. Diana heard the birds chirping outside. She knew it was morning. She had not slept all night. She rose and went into the kitchen.

Diana took the water bucket and went to the stream for water. When she returned, she found the two puppies playing under the table. They were still very thin, but much stronger. They were both long legged, which told Diana they were some sort of hound. They were both black with brown noses, and they had spots over their eyes. They each had four brown stockings on their legs. Their ears hung long. Their markings were so similar that Diana could not tell them apart. She reached down and played with them for a while. Then she went to the pot and swung it back over the fire. It was time for breakfast.

One by one, the girls came into the kitchen, with Sofia being the last. Diana had breakfast nearly ready. The smell of food cooking filled the entire room. Martha put the bowls on the table and Ruth Ann began to divide the grapes up between them. Sofia sat on her stool watching.

Diana wanted to say something to her so badly, but she held her tongue. She had promised herself she would not argue with Sofia again. As difficult as it was to restrain herself, she did so. She did, however, give Sofia a look every now and again. It did no good. It was what Agnus had called, one of her dreamy days.

They ate their breakfast. Ruth Ann fed the puppies a few scraps. There was not much to give them. They would not be able to eat much anyway. They were still not ready for that.

"How can you tell them apart?" Diana asked Ruth Ann.

Ruth Ann picked one of the pups up and held it high in the air. "See here? This one has a brown spot on the inside of his leg right here," she said, pointing to the puppy's back leg. "I will call him Brownie. The other one is Blackie," Ruth Ann said.

Diana smiled and nodded. "I see that now. Those are nice names, too. Very fitting," she said to Ruth Ann.

Diana rose and went out onto the porch. She looked up at the sky. The clouds were dark. She could hear thunder far off in the distance. There was a storm coming. That meant no hunting today. She went back inside.

"There is a storm coming. We won't be able to hunt. Will there be enough apples leftover for us to eat today?" she asked Sofia.

Sofia just sat staring at the table. "Sofia!" Diana called out to her. Martha and Ruth Ann stood watching Sofia. She looked up with a blank stare on her face.

"What?" she asked.

Diana sighed. "There is a storm coming. Will there be enough apples leftover to get us through the day?" she asked again.

Sofia shrugged her shoulders. "I don't know," she said.

Diana turned to face the door. She clenched her teeth hard. Then she went outside. She stood on the porch watching the sky. Martha and Ruth Ann had joined her.

Diana turned to Martha, "Martha, Sofia is having one of her dreamy days. She will be of no use to any of us. I need you to stay here and watch over the place. I am going out for a while. I will not be long. I hope the storm will get some critters moving," she said. He patted Martha on the back. "I will leave Buckley here. Is that okay with you?"

Martha nodded her head. "Just hurry. It is really going to break loose soon," Martha said.

Diana nodded and jumped off the porch. She adjusted her bow and headed for the knob on a hard run. When she reached the edge of the forest, she slowed down to catch her breath. She walked slowly, watching for any sign of life.

It was beginning to rain. It was a light sprinkle. Diana headed for the thickest part of the woods. She made her way beyond the spot where the trees formed a three-sided corral. She continued on. She was approaching the area where they had heard the soldiers fighting. She quickened her pace. It was raining harder now.

Diana tried not to make any noise. She looked about as she moved. She was becoming soaked through and through. Her hair was pasted to her head and face. Her skirt was becoming heavy and clung to her legs as she walked. She tripped over something. She stood up and looked down at the ground. It was a dead Confederate soldier. No doubt he had been overlooked when they buried the dead from the battle. He was decomposing. Diana stared at the body for a few moments. She did not realize how far she had traveled. The rain was beginning to pound harder. The thunder shook the forest. A crack of lightning flashed through the sky. Diana knew it was not safe in the forest. She turned and ran back the way she had come.

She stopped to catch her breath. Her feet slid in the wet undergrowth of the forest. She held onto trees as she made her way back. She looked around her to get her bearings. There to her right were four wild turkeys huddled under a thorny shrub. Diana removed her bow from her shoulder. She took hold of an arrow. It was slippery in her hand. She drew back. It was hard to concentrate with the rain beating at her face. She blinked several times. She let go of the arrow and it flew in the direction in which she had aimed. The turkeys squawked and fluttered about. They scattered in all different directions. One was flopping about on the ground. It was hit, but not dead. Diana drew back another arrow. She let it fly. It too struck the turkey. It continued to flop. She drew her knife from her leather strap that bound it to her leg. She ran to the turkey. She began to cut at the turkey's neck. He fought her until finally he laid dead. She looked at the blood that was running from her hands and arms. The rain was washing it away. She saw the scratches on her arms from the turkey fighting for its life. She pulled the two arrows from the bird and began to drag it toward home. The storm continued to pound at her. Sometimes the lightning struck very close. One strike hit a tree somewhere close by.

The turkey was heavy. Diana had to rest. She leaned against a tree to catch her breath. She knew she had at least another mile to go before she reached the knob. She picked up the turkey and started walking again. Soon, the thunder and lightning stopped. But the rain continued to pound down on her and the forest floor. The fallen trees were slippery and slimy as she crawled over them, dragging the bird that was nearly as big as she was.

She was nearly exhausted when she finally reached the knob. She looked down at the farm below them. There was no smoke coming from the chimney. She sighed and began her descent down the hill to the farm. She could see the stream that ran behind the house. It was high. Diana made it to the porch. She laid the turkey down and tried to rest.

Soon, the pups were out there tearing at the turkey. Diana lifted it high above them and called out. "Ruth Ann! Come get your pups."

Ruth Ann came out onto the porch. "Diana is back! She has killed something. Something very big!" Ruth Ann called back into the house.

The girls gathered around the turkey. "This will feed us for days," Martha said. "How far did you have to go to find it?"

Diana sat down on a stool inside the cabin. She was out of breath. She shivered. "I was really out there. I don't know exactly how far away I was, maybe three miles or more. I stumbled over a dead Confederate soldier," she began to dry herself off. "I think he was killed in that battle we heard the other day."

Diana went to the fireplace. She began to build a fire. "Why isn't there a fire going?" she asked, turning to Sofia.

Martha spoke up, "I was going to build one, but Sofia said it was too humid in here from the storm. So I didn't."

Diana sighed. She continued to build the fire. She had a small flame flickering. She began to pile dried leaves on it that they kept in the hide near the wall. It was burning higher now. She put some wood on it. "I have to get out of these wet clothes. You girls start taking the feathers off that bird." She went to the curtained doorway and turned around. Martha and Ruth Ann had started pulling feathers. Sofia sat on a stool near the open door, staring out at the falling rain.

Diana put her hands on her hips and stared at Sofia. Martha and Ruth Ann paused for a moment looking at her. Then they continued plucking feathers. They remained quiet. Sofia did not notice them watching her. Diana finally threw her hands in the air and went through the curtain calling back as she went, "Anyone who does not contribute to cooking that bird, does not get to eat any of it!"

When she had changed into dry cloths, she emerged through the curtain once again to find things just as they were. She went over to Sofia and stood looking down at her. Sofia still continued to stare out at the rain. Diana kicked the stool hard. Sofia went sprawling on the floor. She jumped up and shouted at Diana. "Why did you do that?"

Diana stood nose to nose with Sofia. She shouted, "Everyone is working hard around here, with the exception of you. Get some water boiling so we can scald that bird! Do something, anything, to help. No work, no eat!"

Sofia lunged at Diana. They were both rolling around on the floor. Diana was five years older than Sofia. She was stronger, even though she was still exhausted from her hunting ordeal. They struggled pulling hair, and scratching one another. Finally, Diana managed to straddle Sofia and hold her hands down. Sofia kicked until she was tired and finally lay still. "Are you going to help?" Diana asked. Sofia nodded, but did not say anything.

Diana let her up. Sofia brushed herself off. She went to the fireplace and swung the iron pot over the flames. She poured water into the pot. She straightened up and turned to face Diana. "I want to go stay with the Hickmans until Burt comes back. I want to work for Mrs. Hickman. I don't want to stay here anymore. The stage will be running again soon, and Grace will need me in the store," Sofia pouted.

Diana nodded. "Yes. You are right. The stage will be running soon. Tomorrow morning I will take you into Berlin myself. For the rest of today, you will pull your share of the weight around here or you will sleep in the barn tonight without any supper," Diana said.

Sofia turned away from Diana. She stood facing the fireplace for a moment. Then she went to the table and began to help her two younger sisters pull feathers from the turkey. She kept her head down. No one said anything. They all worked in silence. The water was boiling. The heat in the cabin was stifling. They would eat outside on the porch tonight.

The next morning, Diana had taken Sofia into Berlin to stay with Grace Hickman at the store. Grace told her she could not pay her yet, but she could work for her room and board. Sofia was okay with that. Diana returned home. They had enough turkey leftover to last them a couple of days.

It had been almost three weeks since Porter Martin left with the soldiers. He returned just as he had promised. Thomas was with him. They brought letters from Josephine and Regina. Diana sat Martha and Ruth Ann down and read the letters aloud to them.

Josephine had three children now, and was pregnant with her fourth. Two boys and a girl. William was now three years of age. James Porter was two and Agnus Diana was a year old. Josephine's next baby was due in November. She begged them all to write and let her know all the news from home. She was grateful the war was over. She hoped they would be able to visit on one of Porter's trips to Philadelphia. She said she was very busy with the children and did not see Regina much. However, she did know that they no longer lived with Dilbert's family. They had moved above the printing shop. She said she would send more letters home with Porter, begging them to do the same.

Regina wrote that she had one daughter, Margaret Agnus Gordon. She was now two years old. Regina had a difficult time with the pregnancy and they were not sure if she would be able to have any more children. She was happy and concerned for their safety, as Porter had told them about the incident with the Confederate soldiers. She also asked for them to make an effort to come visit her, as she could not travel with a small child.

The three of them returned letters whenever Porter made his trips to Philadelphia. The days passed quickly.

Porter finished his house, and once again, they packed up the two-wheeled cart and moved into the Martin's new home. It did not take long for them to settle into the lifestyle that they lost at the hands of the Confederate Army.

Porter finished the church, just as he had promised. They all had their doubts that Burt would return at this point. It had been too long. But Grace refused to give up hope.

The stagecoach was up and running again. Travelers came to town with stories of news from other parts of the country. Some even traveled from across the ocean to a new life.

Porter and Stumpy were currently working on a small, one room structure to the right of the church. Porter would not divulge the purpose of this building. It was to be a surprise. Porter told the girls it was expected to be done by the end of summer. Stumpy continued working on the building while Porter made his trips to Philadelphia. It was a matter of curiosity to the whole town.

There was another family that settled next to Marcus O'Harah's house. They built a small two-room house. It was a man from Pittsburgh who said he passed through this region during the war. His name was Herbert Faulk. His wife was a short slender woman with dark skin and very black hair. She was part Shawnee Indian. Her Christian name was Alda. They had three children, Thelma, who was seven years of age, Beatrice, who was five, and Wayne who was just four.

As Diana rode into town, she stopped and looked down at the town. It was growing. She smiled. This was her world. She used to dream of leaving this town and moving to a big city like her sisters, Josephine and Regina. Now, she was comfortable here. She wondered if her dreams would ever be fulfilled. She used to dream of a life with Robert Shively. The war was over. She did not receive any letter from him. She feared he had been killed. Diana sighed. She now dreamed of someday being a schoolteacher. For now, she would have to settle for being a spinster who lived with her two sisters, in the home of a generous neighbor. She fought back the tears as she rode on toward the small town of Berlin.

She rode up to the general store. She dismounted and tethered Buckley to the hitching post. She climbed up onto the wooden porch. She heard voices inside the general store. One was her sister, Sofia. She went through the door and stood back, listening.

"You can't expect the shelves to stock themselves, Sofia. You can't get anything done lying on your bed upstairs all morning. You are here to help. Remember our agreement? You would work for your keep," Grace Hickman was saying.

Diana sighed. Sofia was apparently having one of her dreamy days. Diana sighed and stepped on into the room. Grace caught sight of her and coughed. "Well, look who is here. How nice to see you, Diana Lewis. I was just having a talk with your sister here. She seems to be neglecting her duties. I am afraid she may have to move back home with you. Well, I mean, back to the Martin house, as he has been generous enough to provide a home for you girls." Grace was arching her back and raising her nose into the air. Diana could not help but think Grace had the nostrils of a horse. She fought back a smile at the very thought.

Diana took a step closer. She smiled politely. She looked at Sofia. "What do you have to say for yourself, Sofia?" Diana asked.

Sofia lowered her head. "I will work harder, Mrs. Hickman. I really like being here. I get to meet the travelers on the stage, moving through the area. I will work harder. I would like another chance, please," Sofia pleaded.

Grace stared at Sofia. "Well, Concetta enjoys your company. She would pout and carry on if I sent you away. I will agree to give you one more chance." She smoothed her hair and walked around the counter. "What can I get for you, Miss Lewis?" she asked as if the previous conversation never happened.

Diana smiled. "Mr. Martin and Thomas are due back any day now. I would like some flour, yeast, and sugar," she said. She shifted her gaze to Sofia.

Sofia's face was red. She had turned her back to Diana and was dusting the bottom shelf near the potbelly stove.

"Baking a cake, are we?" Grace asked. She began placing the items on the counter. "Are we celebrating something?"

"Just preparing a nice meal for them," Diana said.

Sofia turned to glance at her older sister. She was still the most beautiful of all William and Agnus Lewis's children. Diana remembered her previous thoughts before she rode into town. How disappointing it must be for Sofia. She certainly must feel trapped in this town. Diana would talk to Porter about possibly taking Sofia to Philly with him sometime soon.

She turned to exit the store. Then she stopped and turned to her sister. "Sofia," she said. Sophia turned and smiled. "You are welcome to come visit us anytime you want," Diana said.

Sofia nodded and went back to dusting the shelves. She was obviously embarrassed.

Diana carried her items outside to the saddlebags that hung over Buckley's back. Zachariah Dillon was approaching the store. He stopped and tipped his hat to her. "Miss Lewis. When is Porter due back?" he asked.

Diana stepped closer to him. She smiled. "He should be arriving on the next stage," she said politely.

"Well, we have a problem," he said. He looked back at the stable. He replaced his hat and turned to face Diana once again. "When I went to the stable this morning, I discovered something. Well, more like someone," he stammered.

"Someone? What do you mean?" Diana asked.

"There's a Negro woman and four younguns sleepin' in the straw. They don't know where they came from. She said they was just walkin. They got cold and hid in the stable for the night," Zachariah said. "I don't know what to do with them. She said she has nowheres to go."

Diana frowned and said, "Show me, Zachariah."

He turned back toward the stable and began walking. Diana followed him. Diana remembered the last time she was in the stable. Everything was covered with cobwebs and white dust. It was different now. The tools hung along the walls. They were clean and showed signs of use. There was a new harness hanging on the stall that Zachariah had been working on. He led her around the corner to where a pile of loose hay was stacked taller than Diana. There stood the Negro woman and her four children. She was thin, obviously under fed. The children huddled around her. They all looked half-starved.

Diana approached them slowly. She smiled and held out her hand. She reached down, taking hold of the woman's hand. She shook it, and released her grip. She said, "Hello. My name is Diana Lewis. May I ask what is your name?"

The woman looked at Zachariah and then to Diana. She spoke softly when she said, "My name is Tilly."

"Tilly what?" Zachariah asked.

She looked over at him and shrugged. "Just Tilly," she said.

"Well, Tilly," Diana began, "where are you from?"

"We is from that way," she said pointing. "Masser says, we is free and hast to go. We just started walkin. We is cold and hungry."

Diana turned to Zachariah. "Could we get them something to eat, Zachariah?" she asked.

He nodded and turned, leaving the stables. Diana turned back to the Negro woman. She smiled and asked, "Tilly, are these your children?"

Tilly shook her head. "This n is," she said, pointing to a girl approximately eight or nine years of age. She was wearing a dress that hung like a rag on her thin frame. "This is my Gilda." Tilly said. "These here uns was Annie's younguns. She died a couple of days ago. This is Hoppy, Homer, and Percy." She pointed to each of them as she said their names.

Diana tried to guess their ages. The oldest was around seven and the two younger ones looked like they were somewhere around five and six. Diana sighed. "What are we going to do with you, Miss Tilly?" she asked.

"We will move on, Ma'am. We is just cold. We meant no harm," Tilly said.

Diana shook her head. "No, Tilly. I cannot allow you to take these little ones without having something to eat," she said smiling.

"We is mighty hungry, Ma'am," Tilly said.

Zachariah returned with a loaf of bread and a jug of milk. Tilly's eyes opened wide. The children began to make soft noises. Diana offered it to Tilly. "You eat this and stay right here. Don't leave, Tilly. I have to go home, but I will be right back," she said.

She turned to Zachariah and said, "Zachariah, would you keep them here until I get back? I may take them off your hands."

He nodded and said, "Porter Martin ain't going to like you takin' no Negro and her younguns into his house, Miss Diana."

Diana had reached Buckley. She untied him and turned to face Zachariah. "You don't know Porter Martin very well, Zachariah. I don't recall saying anything about moving them into Mr. Marin's house. I would never do such a thing without his permission. Just keep your eye on them for now. I will be back soon." She retied Buckley and stepped up onto the porch. She stuck her head through the door to the general store and called to Sofia.

"Sofia, we are having a family meeting at the house when I get there. Would you like to come out with me?" Diana called.

Sofia stopped stocking the shelves and turned to look at Grace Hickman. She looked back at Diana and shook her head. "No," was all she said.

Diana went back to Buckley and climbed up into the saddle. She turned him facing home, and rode off.

She rode right up to the back porch of the Martin house. She removed the saddlebags and carried them inside. Martha was at the stove. Ruth Ann was on the floor crocheting a rag rug. She rose when Diana entered the room. "Oh, yes! We will surprise Mr. Martin and Thomas," Ruth Ann said, smiling.

Diana placed the items on the table. She said, "We need to have a family meeting."

"What about? Is Sofia all right? What is wrong?" Martha asked.

"Come sit down, you two," Diana said. She waited until they both had sat down at the table. She took a deep breath and began, "There is a woman and four children in town. They walked in last night and slept in the stables. They are without a home. They are half starved."

Martha interrupted, "Diana, we can't just bring them here. Porter has been so good to us. I know he would want to help them, but that is for him to decide. We can't make those kind of decisions without his permission," she said.

"You are right, Martha," Diana said. "I wasn't thinking of bringing them here. I was thinking about taking them to our cabin. It is just sitting there empty. I think Mamma and Pappa would want us to do this."

Ruth Ann stood up and asked, "But Diana, what if we need to go back there again? What if Mr. Martin's house burns down again?"

Diana smiled and said, "It isn't likely to happen again, Ruthie. Besides, there are four little children with nowhere to sleep tonight. They are half starved, and with winter coming, they will likely freeze to death. What kind of Christians would we be to have a cabin with a fireplace sitting there empty, and not offer it to them? I am not saying we are going to give it to them. Mamma and Pappa are buried there. I just thought, perhaps, we could let them stay there for as long as we were not using it."

Martha and Ruth Ann sat there staring at Diana for a time. Then Martha spoke up, saying, "I think it is a kind and Christian thing to do. It is what

Porter and Margaret Martin did for us. I think it would be only proper for us to do the same for this woman and her children."

"Martha is right. I think we should do it," Ruth Ann said.

"Good," Diana said. "I will hitch up the wagon and go into town after them."

"We want to come along," Ruth Ann said. She looked over at Martha who was nodding her head.

"Okay. You get ready and I will bring the wagon down to collect you," Diana said. She went out the back door and led Buckley in the direction of the barn.

Porter had purchased four more horses since the war was over. He used them to pull timber back to the sawmill. He also bought two milking cows and three crates of chickens. Diana turned Buckley loose in the corral and hitched two of Porter's large draft horses to the wagon. She climbed up into the driver's seat and drove the team toward the back door. Martha and Ruth Ann climbed up into the back of the wagon.

The ride into town was quiet. The leaves had begun to turn. Shades of yellow and orange scattered the landscape. The sun was warm, but Diana knew that when the sun went down tonight it would be cold. She arrived back in Berlin to find Zachariah, along with Sherman and Grace Hickman waiting for her at the entrance to the stables.

Sherman took hold of the horses halter and waited for the girls to get down from the wagon. It was not yet noon. The sounds of Stumpy pounding away at the one room structure could be heard, echoing through the hills that surrounded them.

"Miss Diana," Sherman was saying. "Surely, you ain't thinkin' on taking these people to Porter Martin's place?"

Diana smiled and shook her head. "No, Mr. Hickman. I am not. I am taking them to our cabin," she explained.

Grace Hickman stepped forward. "You have given Mr. Martin enough mouths to feed young lady. You need to let this woman and her children be. We should send them on outta here. You got no call takin' them in. We are a growin' town. We don't want to be attracting this sort." She was fidgeting.

Diana noticed Concetta and Sofia standing on the porch of the general store, watching them. She walked up to Grace Hickman. Martha and Ruth Ann were standing behind her. Diana smiled and as politely as she could said, "Mrs. Hickman, your sons went off to fight a war so these people could be free to live wherever they chose. Your Willy died for them to have such a right. Possibly even Burt. Why would you want to deny this woman and her children the very right your sons died for?" she said softly.

Grace turned white. "Hmph!" she said. She turned and marched back toward the store. She was mumbling to herself as she went.

"Miss Lewis. How is Porter Martin going to feed you all this winter? That is a lot to ask of the man," Sherman explained.

Diana stood directly in front of Sherman Hickman. She looked up at him and said, "Now, Mr. Hickman, you know that Martha and I do all of the hunting to feed us. I do believe that there were many a night that you yourself, would have gone hungry if it were not for Martha and I supplying you with meat for your table. Now, if you will excuse me, I really need to get them to the cabin and settled in before the end of the day." She turned and went inside the stables. They all followed behind her.

Tilly and the children were waiting right where she had left them. Martha whispered from behind Diana, "Di, you did not tell us they were Negroes."

"They are people, Martha. Just like Thomas," Diana said. Then she smiled at Tilly and said, "Tilly these are my sisters, Martha and Ruth Ann. We want you to come with us. We have a place for you and the children to stay. It is warm there. You come along with us now."

Tilly shook her head, "Don't want to be no trouble, Ma'am. Me and the younguns can just move on. I heard that lady out there. These people don't want us here," Tilly said.

"It is not their decision to make, Tilly. Winter is coming and you and the children need to find a place to stay for the winter. If you want to move on in the spring, you can do so. For now, you need to come with us. You need to think of the children," Diana explained.

Tilly and the children followed Diana and her sisters outside. They climbed up into the back of the wagon. Diana drove off, leaving Sherman and Zachariah standing there watching them as they left. They rode for a while in silence. Then Ruth Ann began to sing. After a while, Tilly began to hum along. The children smiled. When they came to the Martin house, Diana turned in her seat and said to Tilly. "This is where we live, Tilly. If you need anything, you come here to find us. This cart path will lead you right to us."

Tilly raised herself up, peering at the Martin house as they crossed the stream. "Is you my new Masser?" she asked.

Diana laughed. "Oh, no, Tilly. There are no masters here. You are free. Free to come and go as you please. Come spring, if you are not happy in your new home, you are free to leave. I just ask that you stay here for the winter. You will be safe and warm here," she said.

They began to sing again. Tilly seemed to relax some. Diana turned to Martha and said, "Martha, after we get them settled, we will go back to Mr. Martin's and gather a load of slabs. They will need some firewood to keep them warm tonight."

Martha nodded her head as she continued to sing along with Ruth Ann. Soon, they had rounded the tree line that followed the cart trail and reached the knob from which the farm could be seen. "This is your new home," Martha said aloud.

Tilly stretched her neck to see the place. Once again, Diana found that the grass had grown up around the porch and barn. The plank that propped the door shut had fallen over again and the door was standing open. They stopped at the porch. They all went inside.

The wooden bucket was upside down on the washboard. The wooden bowls were stacked upside down also, right where they had been left. Tilly went to the iron pot that hung over the fireplace. She pulled the dried leaves from the bottom.

"I am going for some slabs to build a fire. Martha, you come help. Ruth Ann, you show them around. Fetch a bucket of water from the stream and make sure you warn them about the snakes in the cattail pond. We will be back directly," Diana said as she went out onto the porch. "It will be dark by the time we get settled back at the house. We have that cake to bake tonight."

Diana and Martha headed back toward the Martin house. Along the way, a rabbit darted across the trail ahead of them. It hid in a group of bramble bushes along the side of the road. Martha jumped from the wagon and began kicking and tugging at the bushes. The rabbit darted into the clearing, headed for the forest. Martha had her sling in her hand. She let the stone fly. It caught the rabbit along the side of the head. It fell dead. Martha ran to retrieve the rabbit. She held it high over her head by the back legs. "They will have meat tonight!" she called to Diana as she returned to the wagon.

Diana pulled the wagon to a halt near the slab pile at the sawmill. "Martha, run down to the orchard and gather some apples. I will get this started," she said.

Martha ran toward the orchard. Soon, she returned with her skirt full of apples and pears. "The bees are awful today. I hope I didn't bring any with me on these pears," Martha said. She placed the fruit in the wagon and started helping Diana toss slabs into the back of the wagon. Once they were satisfied with the load, they climbed up onto the wagon and headed back toward the log cabin. Blackie and Brownie ran alongside of them as they went.

Tilly had a small fire started in the fireplace when they arrived back at the cabin. Diana and Martha tossed the slabs off the wagon onto the porch. Ruth Ann took the fruit and rabbit inside. She explained to Tilly that it was to feed her family for this evening and tomorrow. Once everything had been unloaded from the wagon, Diana told Tilly they would return tomorrow afternoon. "Do you know how to cook over a fireplace, Tilly?" Diana asked.

"Yes, Ma'am. I cook over open fire on Masser's plantation," Tilly replied.

"Where was that plantation?" Martha asked.

"I don't rightly know, Ma'am. We walked for many days. We just followed the road," Tilly said.

Diana sighed. "Well, Tilly, you and your children settle in here. When you skin that rabbit, you save the hide. You will need all the hides you can get for the coming winter months. Do you know how to skin animals?" Diana asked.

"Yes, Ma'am," Tilly said.

Diana and her sisters went back outside. The sun was beginning to go down. They climbed back onto the wagon. Blackie and Brownie jumped up next to Ruth Ann. They headed up the hill toward the knob. Martha turned and looked behind her. "I think we did the right thing, Di," she said.

"I wish we had taken the time to visit Mamma and Pappa's graves," Diana said.

"I did. I showed the children where they were buried. Hoppy said she would put flowers on their graves for us," Ruth Ann said. Diana smiled to herself.

They reached the house and put the team back into the barn just before dark. All three of them took part in the feeding. Martha milked the two cows. She carried the fresh buckets of milk toward the back door. Just to the right, they saw a rider approaching. As he approached, they recognized him. It was Porter Martin. Behind him, Thomas appeared in the dusk, driving a wagon.

Martha sat the milk on the porch and joined her sisters as they ran to meet Mr. Martin. He dismounted his horse and tethered it to the hitching post near the porch. Ruth Ann hugged him.

"Hey, there. How's my little angel doin'?" Porter asked.

They all proceeded to talk at once. They were telling him about Tilly and the children. Soon, Thomas drew the team to a halt next to Porter's horse.

Thomas got down from the wagon. Ruth Ann ran to him and threw her arms around him. Thomas laughed. "Miss Ruth Ann, you grew a whole foot since last I saw you!" Thomas teased.

They went inside. Diana began to build a fire in the fireplace. Thomas took over and had a warm fire roaring very quickly. They went to the kitchen and started a fire in the wood stove. They had not eaten since breakfast. Diana put a pot of oats in a pan that was still sitting on the table from that morning. Soon, the water was boiling. It was not the meal they had planned for Porter's return. They did not get the cake baked. Tomorrow was another day. They would have a feast.

They sat, talking until late. Porter brought letters from Josephine and Regina. Diana promised to read them aloud to her sisters before bed. Porter and Thomas agreed to visit Tilly in the morning. Ruth Ann was going with them. Diana and Martha would go hunting early, and hopefully, they would come home with enough for both households. Soon they all went upstairs to bed. Diana gave her room to Thomas for the night. She went into the other bedroom with her two sisters and opened the wax seal on the letters. They all sat on the bed as she read.

Josephine was preparing for her next baby. Her son, James Porter, had been sick. There was some kind of influenza going around. She was trying not to go out at all until it had passed. She said she had not seen or heard from Regina in over a month. She missed seeing people, but the safety of her children had to come first. She did not have much news. Porter had told her what the surprise was he had been working on. She was very excited to hear from them about it. She could not reveal what it was, but wanted them to know she was happy about it.

Diana put the letter in her lap and looked at her sisters. "What could it be? Do you suppose Porter is building a house for us in town?" Diana asked.

Ruth Ann asked, "Do you think he doesn't want us here? I don't want to move into town. Do you think he will let me stay here?"

Diana put her hand on Ruth Ann's shoulder as she spoke. "Ruthie, we aren't sure he has built a house for us to live in. It is only one room. I am not sure. He may feel we are safer in town while he is away, but then, his house would be sitting empty. I don't know. I think we should wait and see what it is first. It would be rude to reject his gift. Let's just take it a day at a time."

Martha said, "Maybe if we try really hard, he will change his mind and he will want to keep us here. We could all work harder to please him."

Diana sighed. "We don't know that it is a place for us to live. Again, I think we should wait and see."

Diana opened Regina's letter and read it to her sisters. It basically said the same thing as Josie's letter had said. They were fine. They were all healthy even though there was an influenza going around. Dilbert had to hire two men to help in the printing shop. His father had a stroke and was not able to leave the house anymore. The business was growing, and they had started printing different things now besides just the paper reporting on the war. They had printed many fliers announcing the assassination of President Lincoln. She begged them to write soon and send their letters back with Porter on his next trip to Philadelphia.

"President Lincoln was assassinated? When did that happen? Will there be another war?" Martha asked.

Diana sat for a moment thinking. Then she said, "We will have to talk to Mr. Martin about this tomorrow. He will know about it. For now, we need to go to bed. Tomorrow is going to be a busy day for all of us."

The next morning the girls had breakfast on the table when Porter arrived downstairs. They were all nearly done when he decided to go upstairs to waken Thomas. It was not like Thomas to sleep so late. Porter went up the stairs. Diana watched him as he climbed the stairs. He moved slowly. Porter's age was catching up to him. He was either working at the sawmill, on his knees building another house, building one for someone else, or he was riding or driving a wagon on the long trips back and forth to Philadelphia. He disappeared at the top of the stairs.

When he came back down, he had a worried look on his face. He stood at the end of the table and said, "Thomas has the influenza. I don't want you girls goin' anywheres near him, or that room. I will take food to him. This is most likely the same sickness that was goin around in Philly. It lasts about three days. Thomas is healthy, so he will surely survive it. Just keep away from him. Do you girls understand?"

All three of them nodded their heads. Porter sat back down at the table to finish his coffee. "If you fix him a bowl of oats, I will take it up to him before I head on down to the cabin to see these folks you were tellin me about," Porter said.

Diana nodded and began to fix Thomas a bowl of oats. Martha asked, "Mr. Martin, what is the influenza?"

Porter put his cup down and said. "It is a sickness. There are different kinds. This one lasts about three days or so. You just get mighty sick on the insides. Some of the older folks or young ones are too weak and die. But that ain't gonna happen to Thomas. He is strong and healthy. But I don't want any of you girls catching it."

Diana sat the bowl down on the table. She got a tray from the cupboard and began placing the bowl and spoon on it. Porter took the tray and climbed the stairs once again. He returned and sat back down. "Now, you girls just go about your day as you had planned. Don't give Thomas another thought. Come dinnertime, I will take another tray up. I am goin to visit this family stayin' at the cabin. I will check on him when I get back before I go into town."

"Wait, Mr. Martin," Diana said. "Regina wrote that President Lincoln had been assassinated. What happened? Was it the rebels?"

Porter slid his chair back. He shook his head and said, "Naw. It weren't like that. Just one rebel that wasn't happy with the way things went, I reckon. His name was John Booth. He was an actor. He shot Lincoln. They ain't captured him as yet, I don't recollect. At least not as of when we left Philly. They are huntin' for him though."

"Will there be another war?" Ruth Ann asked.

"There is always going to be unhappy people somewheres wantin' to start a war over something or another. But for now, I think we have had a belly full of war. I don't rightly see people takin' up there guns again for sometime in this part of the country," Porter said. He stood up and turned to go out the back door. He turned before leaving and said, "Now, you girls mind me. Stay out of Thomas's room. Just go about your business. I'll stop on my way back through to town and check on him."

Diana began to clear the table. Martha pumped some water and put it on the stove to wash the dishes. Porter pulled his buggy down toward the house. Ruth Ann ran out to join him. She was going to ride along. Diana and Martha finished the chores and took up their bows and slings, walking back behind the orchard toward the woods.

It was after lunch when they returned. They had two rabbits, a squirrel, and a ground hog. They'd seen a wild boar, but could not get a good shot at it. Diana cleaned one of the rabbits and the squirrel. Martha had saddled up Buckley and was taking the ground hog and the other rabbit to the cabin for Tilly and the children.

Diana worked over dinner. She had the cake in the oven when Martha returned. She reported that everything was fine at the cabin. They seemed to be settled in and were very grateful for the food. Porter must have been back and checked on Thomas already. They had missed him while they were out hunting. Martha went to the orchard. There wasn't much left out there. Today was a sunny, but crisp day. Winter would be upon them soon.

The next three days went by quickly. Thomas had recovered. He was weak, but was up and moving around. He was working in the sawmill with Porter. Porter announced that the surprise in town was complete and would be taking them to town with him that afternoon. The girls were excited and curious. The morning hours seemed to drag. Finally, the wagon was waiting on them out front. They all piled in and Porter began to drive them towards town.

When they rounded the bend that revealed the small town of Berlin, the girls all began to chatter. They were trying to guess what the building could be. Ruth Ann asked, "Is that a house for us to live in, Mr. Martin?" Diana and Martha held their breath.

Porter laughed. "I thought you were happy living at my place," he said.

"We are!" All three girls said at once. Then Martha spoke up. "We don't want to live anywhere else."

Porter pulled the wagon to a halt in front of the little building. "Good to know, cause I like havin' you gals around," Porter said.

They jumped down from the wagon. Porter held the door open for them and one by one, they entered the building. Diana knew right away what the surprise was. It was a schoolhouse. She turned to Porter and smiled. "Thank you so much, Mr. Martin," she said with tears in her eyes.

"You are welcome, child. I promised my Margaret that someday, I would build this here schoolhouse for ya. We knew how much you wanted to be a schoolteacher. There aren't many children here right now, but there is enough. They all need to learn to read and write. And, well, Berlin just ain't done growin' yet," Porter said.

Diana walked around the room. The back wall was one large chalkboard. There were chalk and erasers placed on a small ledge at the base of the board. There were rows of bench seats with small tables stretching across the front of them. There were small slates placed along the table. There was a pot bellied stove in the corner. Just in front of the chalkboard was a mahogany desk. It was the grandest looking desk Diana had ever seen. She ran her hand across the top of it. There was a matching mahogany chair sitting behind the desk. Diana looked up at Porter and smiled.

"That there is a gift from Josephine and James. It came all the way from Philadelphia. They sent this, too," Porter said as he opened the top drawer. He pulled out a bell with a long wooden handle.

Diana laughed. "What a wonderful surprise!" she said.

"When is school going to start, Diana?" Ruth Ann asked.

"We will pass the word around today. It will start tomorrow," Diana said.

"Thomas and I will bring a load of wood into town later. You will need a fire in that pot bellied stove. It is going to get mighty chilly in here," Porter said.

"I want to go door to door and let everyone know that school will start tomorrow morning," Diana said.

Porter nodded. They went back outside. "There is a pump out back and the two out houses—one for the ladies and one for the gents. Just like the big school in Philadelphia," Porter said.

They walked around back. Diana smiled. It was the greatest surprise she could have imagined. She hugged Porter and then Thomas. "Don't forget

Stumpy. He worked mighty hard on this building while I was out of town. We wanted to have it finished weeks ago, but didn't make it. Had to wait for me to get the stove, chalkboard, and desk here by wagon. Was some trick keepin' it a surprise, too," Porter said, smiling.

Diana ran up the street to the general store. She ran inside. Sofia and Concetta were looking through a big catalog that rested on the counter.

"Porter Martin has built us a schoolhouse! School will start tomorrow morning. You are welcome to join us!" Diana said, panting from the excitement.

"We will be working here at the store," Concetta said. She looked over at Sofia.

Sofia nodded. "I have to work here. Besides, I already know how to read and write. I have been learning arithmetic, too," she said.

"Well, if you want to join us, you can," Diana said. She turned and ran on down the street. She ran to Herbert Faulk's little house. His wife was in the garden.

"Good day, Mrs. Faulk. Porter Martin has built us a schoolhouse. School will start tomorrow morning. Your children are welcome to come. I will be teaching them to read, write and also some arithmetic," Diana said.

Alda Faulk smiled up at Diana. "How do I know what time to send them?" she asked, speaking very slowly. Her English was broken. Diana imagined it was a form of both English and Shawnee Indian.

"I will ring a bell when I get there. I will ring it again when school commences. There will be time for lunch and a recess afterward, for them to get some exercise. Then I will ring the bell when it is time for them to go home," Diana said, planning it all in her head as she spoke.

Alda nodded and said. "Our Thelma is seven. She will be there. Our other two are too small for school right yet."

Diana smiled and nodded. "I understand. School will be there waiting for them when they get old enough." She smiled and waved as she left. Alda Faulk went back to gleaning her garden.

She walked back toward the school. She thought to herself. There would be Martha, Ruth Ann, and Thelma Faulk. She had three students. Martha and Ruth Ann knew way more than Thelma Faulk. Diana would have to work on her pretty hard to help her to catch up. Then she thought of Tilly's children. She could pick them up in the morning and bring them to school with her. They were all of school age with the exception of the smallest boy, Percy. She would take a ride out there before going home.

Diana told Porter her plan. He thought it was a good idea. He told her that down south, the slaves were mostly forbidden to learn to read and write. Diana had already started working out a plan in her head.

They rode back to the house in the wagon. Porter hitched up the buggy so Martha and Diana could go visit Tilly. Ruth Ann wanted to stay behind and help Porter in the sawmill. Martha put the rabbit and squirrel in the back of the buggy and they started down the old familiar cart trail to the cabin.

Martha hummed to herself as they went. Diana's thoughts went back to the many times they had rode the two-wheeled cart back and forth over this trail, taking the milk to the general store in Berlin. She could almost see her mother cooking at the fireplace and her father sitting on his stool near the fireplace smoking his old stone pipe. Diana thought she could smell the tobacco.

Soon, they had reached the knob that overlooked the small farm. There was smoke coming from the fireplace. Diana smiled to herself as they approached. All of the children came out onto the porch as they pulled the buggy to a halt near the hitching post. Martha pulled the large basket from the back of the buggy that contained the carcasses of the rabbit and squirrel.

Tilly came out to greet them. They went inside. There was some kind of greens cooking in the iron pot. Diana was not familiar with them. The wooden bowls were turned upside down on the table where each of them apparently had sat that morning eating their breakfast. Martha gave Tilly the basket.

"Thank you, ladies," Tilly said. She held the carcasses up for the children to see. They all smiled but remained quiet.

"Miss Tilly, Porter Martin has built us a school in town. I will be teaching classes starting tomorrow morning. I would like to teach your children. I realize that Percy is too small, but the other three are certainly old enough. I would be happy to pick them up in the morning and take them into town with me. I will bring them back home after school," Diana explained.

Tilly stood there staring at Diana. At first, Diana thought she did not understand a word she had said. Perhaps she spoke too fast in all of her excitement. Tilly rubbed her hands together. She had a frightened look on her face.

Tilly said. "We don't want no trouble, Miss Diana. We is fine. We is mighty pleased with the home you give us. We don't want to be no bother to nobody."

Diana sat down on a stool. She placed her hands on the table and folded them in front of her. "Miss Tilly. You are no trouble. The world is changing. These are new times we are living in. These children need to be educated so they can go out into the world and be somebody very special some day. I would be so very grateful to be a part of that. Let me teach them," she said.

Tilly sat down across from her. The children huddled together over near the fireplace. Diana could not help but remember that it was the very same spot that she and her sisters huddled together whenever they had a visitor.

"In town you say?" Tilly asked.

Diana nodded her head. "Yes, in town. There will be my two sisters, and one other little girl there," she explained.

"But, the law says," Tilly began.

Diana reached across the table and took Tilly's hand. She said, "Forget the law. That was an old law. That was for slaves. There are no more slaves, Tilly. You are free. You are allowed to go to school now."

Tilly watched Diana closely. Diana knew she was finding it difficult to believe what she was hearing. Finally, Diana stood up and said. "Tilly, I would not ask you to do anything that would put you and your children in danger.

Look where you are. I will be here in the morning. If you want your children to learn to read and write, you have them ready." Diana went to the door. Martha was standing there waiting for her. They collected the empty basket and left. Diana felt all of their eyes watching them as they rode out of sight. She said a silent prayer that they would be ready tomorrow.

That night, Diana found it difficult to sleep. She was too excited. She rose just before sun up. She went downstairs and began to prepare breakfast. She had prepared two slices of bread and butter for her lunch. Then as an after-thought, she stuffed a whole loaf of bread into a rabbit skin pouch. It was likely that someone would forget to bring a lunch.

Martha came down early also. She, too, was excited. They were talking softly when Porter and Thomas came down. Ruth Ann was last to arrive at the table. She was not her bubbly self this morning. Diana thought maybe she was nervous about going to school. When everyone had finished breakfast, Martha began pumping water to put on the stove to do the dishes. Ruth Ann sat at the table, quiet.

"You need to go comb your hair and get ready to leave, Ruthie," Diana said.

Ruth Ann stood up. She made a dash for the back door. She stood at the end of the porch, vomiting over the side. Diana and Martha both went to her side. Ruth Ann was pale. She was trembling. She leaned over onto Martha.

"I think she has the influenza," Martha said.

They helped her up the stairs and into her room. Once she was tucked into bed, she closed her eyes and began to moan. She clutched at her stomach.

"We can't leave her like this," Diana said.

Martha went downstairs and returned with a pan of cold water. She began to wipe Ruth Ann's face. She turned to Diana, "You go to school today. I will stay with Ruth Ann," she said to Diana.

Diana sighed. She thought for a moment and then said, "If you need me, you come for me. Try not to expose yourself anymore than you have to. Ruth Ann just hugged Thomas and she got sick. I reckon it is passed on by contact, so you make sure you wash your hands, arms, and face every time you touch her. Try not to breathe the same air. Stay out of this room as much as possible. I will only teach for half a day today."

Martha nodded her head. Diana patted Ruth Ann's arm. "I will be back soon, honey. You just rest," she said. Then she turned and left the room.

Diana went to the kitchen. The water was boiling on the stove. She poured it into the dishpan and saved some for the washbowl. She added some cold water to cool it down some. She scrubbed her hands, arms, and face. Then she turned her attention to cleaning up the kitchen.

Martha came back downstairs and helped her clean up. Once they had finished, Diana took the rabbit skin pouch and headed out the back door toward the barn. Porter had a horse hitched to one of the smaller wagons. She climbed up onto it and clicked her tongue. She headed for the shallow crossing and the old cart trail that led to the cabin.

Her mind drifted as she drove the wagon down the bumpy trail that led to her old homestead. She had given up on Robert Shively. She was convinced that he was a man of his word, which led her to the conclusion that he was dead. She was now twenty-one years of age. She had hoped to be married and have children by this time.

Her mind went to Ruth Ann. She was so child like, even at fourteen years of age. She adored Porter Martin, and was more like his child. She prayed that Ruthie would be all right. She was healthy. Porter said the healthy ones survived this influenza. Diana said a prayer as she rode along. She prayed that her baby sister would come through this.

When she reached the tree line that formed a bend in the trail, she perked up. Soon, she was at the top of the knob and looking down onto the farm below. There, on the porch stood Tilly and all four of her children. She smiled. They were waiting for her. She felt relieved. She drove the wagon up to the porch and stopped.

"Good morning," Diana called to them.

"Mornin', Ma'am," Tilly said.

Diana jumped down from the wagon. "I am so glad to see you all are going to school this morning," she said as she approached the porch.

Tilly nodded and waited for Diana to come up onto the porch. Diana looked at the children. Their clothes were tattered and old. But they had been washed and patched. They wore no shoes, but they were scrubbed and had their hair combed. Diana smiled at them. "Come along. We don't want the teacher to be late for school now, do we?" she asked.

The three oldest children followed her to the wagon. Percy clung to Tilly's skirt. Diana called to Tilly as she climbed into the driver's seat. "They will be home shortly after lunch time today. I am only teaching for half a day this week. My sister is sick, and I need to be at home. I will bring them home and tomorrow I will be back about the same time to collect them once again."

Tilly nodded and waved as Diana turned the horse around and headed back up the trail to the knob. She stood on the porch, watching until they were out of sight.

The children were silent all the way to town. Diana would ask them questions and they would nod or shake their heads. They appeared to be frightened. She tried to assure them that they would be safe with her and would be returned home right after lunch.

She pulled the team to a halt just outside of the school. She asked Hoppy to fetch a pail of water for the horse. She entered the schoolhouse. Standing just inside the door, she looked around. She could not help but smile. Soon, the children had gathered around the door. She invited them to come inside. Diana showed them their seats and explained what the slates were for. She stepped outside and rang the bell. She began to build a fire in the potbelly stove.

It wasn't long until little Thelma Faulk arrived at the door. Diana invited her inside and showed her to her seat. She gave Homer the school bell and asked him to go outside and ring it. He smiled.

Diana spent most of the morning acquainting the children with each other. She wrote her name on the board and told them they were to call her Miss Lewis. She explained that they would have school classes for half a day for the first week. After that, they would have school until two hours after lunch. She asked each child to stand and tell the class something about themselves.

Hoppy was the eldest, so she went first. "My name is Hoppy. I lived on a plantation with mys Mamma. We picked cotton for the Masser. They was bunches of us that worked for Masser. Then one day, Masser says we is free and has to leave. We started walkin'. Miss Annie and her younuns walked with us. Miss Annie got sick and died. Now I has a sisser and two brothers. We live in a fine house that Miss Lewis took us to. I ain't never bin to school before. I like it mighty fine though." Then Hoppy sat down.

Diana smiled. "That was very good, Hoppy. Now it is Gilda's turn."

Gilda stood up. She looked like she was going to cry. "My name's Gilda. My Mamma, Annie died and I lives wit Hoppy." Then she sat down.

Diana smiled and cleared her throat. She asked, "How old are you, Gilda?"

Gilda shrugged her shoulders. Diana smiled, "Well, I would guess that you are somewhere around eight years old. We will declare tomorrow your birthday. We will have a little party tomorrow and celebrate Gilda's eighth birthday. Would you like that, Gilda?"

Gilda shrugged her shoulders once again. Diana knew it was going to be difficult to get this child to open up to her. She straightened her back and said, "Thelma, I believe you are next."

Thelma Faulk stood up. She raised her nose into the air and said, "My name is Thelma Faulk. I already had my birthday. I am seven years old. My daddy fought in the war. He was on the side that won. My Mamma is part Shawnee Indian, so that makes me part Indian, too. We moved here 'cause it was a small town. Daddy says people don't take too kindly to us 'cause we are half breeds. He wants us to be educated, though." Thelma sat back down.

Diana smiled. "That was very nice, Thelma. Welcome to Berlin. We are happy to have you in our town and happy to have you in our new school." Then she pointed to Homer. "Homer, I believe you are next."

Homer stood up. "I is Homer. I live wit Tilly and Hoppy and Gilda and Percy. He ain't her on account of he is too little. I is the onliest boy in this here school," he said. Then he sat down.

Diana smiled. She said to Homer, "Yes, you are the only boy in this school. You will be a very valuable student indeed. You will have the duty of ringing the bell. But only when I tell you to, understand?"

"Yes, Ma'am," Homer said.

Diana put more wood into the potbelly stove. She went to the blackboard and began to write the alphabet on it. She turned to the class and said, "Now.

We are going to start learning the letters of the alphabet. It is easier if we put them into a little song."

The morning went quickly. Diana gave Homer instructions to ring the bell, dismissing the class. She banked the fire and closed the schoolhouse. She broke the bread into pieces and passed it around to all of the children. Then she loaded them up into the wagon and left the schoolhouse. She took Thelma home. She waited until the little girl was inside the house and then headed out of town.

The air wasn't much warmer than it was that morning. She pulled her shawl around her tight. She would have to throw some hides in the wagon for tomorrow. Soon, the snow would be blowing. She would talk to Porter Martin about making some sort of cover for the wagon, to protect the children. She crossed the stream at the wide, shallow spot. There was smoke coming from the chimney at Porter Martin's house. She was anxious to get back.

Soon, she reached the log cabin. Tilly came out onto the porch to meet them. Diana waited until the children were on the porch. She called from the wagon. "We had a good day today, Tilly. I will be back for them tomorrow, same time. Bye now!" She waved and turned the wagon around. They stood on the porch once again and waited until she was out of sight.

Diana reached the Martin house. Her hands and feet were cold. She drove to the barn and unhitched the horses. She could hear the engine from the sawmill. She ran to the back porch as quickly as she could. She found Martha in the kitchen. She was baking bread.

"How is Ruthie?" Diana asked.

Martha wiped the flour from her hands and said, "She isn't very good. She sure is throwing up a lot. She was pale this morning, but now she is aglow with a fever. I don't recall seeing Thomas like that."

Diana frowned. "We didn't see Thomas after Mr. Martin took him to his room. Maybe he was like that, too. I better go look at her," Diana said as she removed her shawl and went up the stairs.

Ruth Ann was asleep. She was panting softly. She was glowing red, just as Martha had said she was. Diana touched her cheek. It was hot. Ruth Ann moaned and opened her eyes. "Diana, I thought you was Mamma," Ruth Ann said.

Diana smiled and said, "Shh. Just rest now. I will be back to check on you soon."

Ruth Ann closed her eyes again. Diana waited a few moments until she was sure her little sister was sleeping once again, and then she quietly left the room. She went back downstairs.

Diana washed in the washbowl and then tossed the water out the back door. She went to the stove. Martha had a pot of stew cooking in a large pot.

Martha asked, "How did she look to you?"

Diana frowned and shook her head. "Not very good, I'm afraid. Has Porter been in?"

Martha shook her head and said, "No. He usually stays out until sundown. He seldom comes in until it is suppertime. Do you think we should go fetch him?"

Diana paced the room. She was wringing her hands. The pictures of her mother's dying face kept flashing in her mind. "I don't know. I hate to disturb him, but I am really worried. I don't recall seeing anyone that sick before, except...." She could not finish her sentence. She continued to pace.

"You know Porter dotes on her so. I think he would want to know. He may even know something we could do to help her get better faster," Martha said.

Diana reached for her shawl. "You are right, Martha. I am going to the mill. I will be right back to help you with the bread." She wrapped the shawl around her and went out the back door. She walked to the sawmill. The wind was blowing and the clouds were becoming dark. Soon, the snow would be flying.

As Diana approached the mill, she could smell the sawdust. She saw the two crosscut saws moving back and forth, cutting the logs. The smell of the engine puffing smoke into the air filled her lungs the closer she got. Stumpy saw her coming and shouted to Porter. He turned, motioning for Thomas to take over. He went to meet her.

"Miss Diana, what brings you out here? How was your first day at school?" he shouted as he approached her.

Diana nodded. "It was fine, thank you, Mr. Martin. I'm afraid I need your help. It is Ruth Ann!" she shouted in order for him to hear her.

"Ruthie? What is it?" Porter asked.

"I think she has the influenza. She is terribly ill. I was wondering if there is something we should be doing for her. She can't keep anything down and she has a fever," Diana said. She was speaking to his back, for Porter Martin was already heading toward the house. Diana had to run to catch up with him.

They reached the back door. Usually, Porter always removed his boots before entering the house. This time, he did not. He went inside. Diana was right behind him. He nodded at Martha as he entered and looked around.

"She is upstairs in bed," Martha said.

Porter went straight for the stairs. Both Martha and Diana followed him.

He entered the bedroom and knelt next to the bed. He touched Ruth Ann's forehead and shook his head. "She has it mighty bad," he whispered. He stood up and faced the girls. "Remember how you kept the cool, wet, cloths on your Mamma's forehead? Well, that is what I want you to do for little Ruthie. Just give her a sip of water whenever you can get it down her. No more than a sip. Try to give her a sip as often as possible. She needs the cool water on her insides, but not enough to make her retch it back up." He turned toward the door. "Try not to expose yourselves anymore than you have to. I will shut the mill down early and come give you a hand with her." Porter went back down the stairs.

Diana went to the kitchen. She pulled a rag from the cupboard that they used to dry the dishes. She began to rip it into strips. She kept her back to Martha, who was pumping a pan of cold water. Diana could remember all too well how they had layered her mother with cool, wet, strips of cloth to reduce the fever. She also remembered the outcome. Tears were stinging her eyes. She wiped her face and turned to go back up the stairs. Martha stopped her.

"Diana. Let me take care of Ruthie. You stay away. You have to think of the schoolchildren. You don't want to carry anything to them that could hurt them. I will stay home and take care of Ruth Ann," Martha said.

Diana did not want to put this burden upon her sister. She knew that Martha was speaking the truth. She felt a lump come up into her throat, preventing her from speaking. All she could do was nod her head. She placed the strips of cloth into the pan of cold water. She went to the basin and began to wash her hands, arms, and face. Martha went up the stairs.

Diana worked on the bread. She tried to occupy her mind. Pictures of her mother's foaming mouth and swollen tongue kept haunting her. She prayed over and over again for her baby sister. They had been left in her care. Ruth Ann had to pull through this.

That afternoon, Porter and Thomas came to the house early. Porter told the girls that from what he had seen in Philadelphia, you could only catch the influenza once. They had decided that for everyone's safety, Thomas should nurse Ruth Ann back to health. Diana wasn't so sure. After all, they had already been exposed. Porter assured her that it was the best thing to do right now. After sometime of listening to reason, Diana gave in. Martha scrubbed herself down. They explained to Porter how they had washed themselves after every exposure and urged him to do the same. He did.

The next morning, Diana rose and went downstairs to prepare breakfast. She found Porter Martin at the stove. He smiled. Martha was coming in the back door from milking the cows.

"How is Ruth Ann?" Diana asked.

Martha smiled and said, "Mr. Martin said she is still sick, but much better than she was yesterday. Thomas thinks the worst is over."

Diana sighed a sigh of relief. "You go on to school this morning. Thomas is going to sit with her all day. Stumpy and I can get along without him for another day or two," Porter said.

Diana sat down at the table. She put her hands over her face and began to cry. Martha sat the bucket down and went to her sister's side. Porter went to her also. He put his hand on her shoulder. "There now, Miss Diana. I knew you were thinkin' about your Mamma. My little angel is goin to come through this all right. Don't you fret none," Porter soothed.

"I am going hunting this morning, Di. I am taking Mr. Martin with me. I will show him where we saw that wild boar. I'll be back before lunchtime. If anything goes wrong, I will come into town for you," Martha said.

Diana nodded as she wiped her face. "I am only teaching for half a day all week. I will be home about the same time as I was yesterday," she said. She pushed her chair back and went to the washbasin. She dipped her hands into the cold water and splashed her face.

Porter was at the stove again. "Look here. I made us all flapjacks for breakfast," he said over his shoulder.

Martha winked at Diana and said, "They sure smell good, Mr. Martin."

Diana went to the cupboard and began to set the table. "Is Thomas coming down?" she asked.

Porter said. "Oh, he will be down after you girls are out of the house. We know he can't catch that influenza, but we ain't sure if he can carry it."

They sat at the table eating their breakfast. When they had finished, Diana began to wrap a loaf of bread and stuffed it into the rabbit skin pouch.

Porter went to his saddlebag hanging on a nail by the back door. "I almost forgot. I got this for your first day of school and just plum forgot all about it," he said reaching into the bag and pulling out a canvas pouch about the size of his fist. It was secured by a drawstring. He handed it to Diana. She looked inside. It was hard candy. She smiled.

"Thank you, Mr. Martin. The children will really like this," Diana said.

She went for her shawl. "Oh, by the way. I was wondering, with winter coming, is there some sort of covering we could put on the wagon to protect the children from bad weather?" she asked.

Porter frowned and thought on it for a minute. "Give me a day or two. I will come up with something. Now, let me hitch up the wagon for you while you get yourself ready to go."

Porter grabbed his poncho and threw it over his head as he was going out the back door. Diana cracked the door and watched him go. She could see his freezing breath as he walked toward the barn. "I think I will throw some extra hides in the wagon this morning. It looks like it is going to be a cold one," she said as she went into the front room. There by the fireplace was a wooden trunk where they stored their hides. She pulled out as many as she could carry.

"I will help you carry all of this to the wagon," Martha said.

They went outside. The frost was heavy upon the ground. Martha rode in the back of the wagon as far as the house. She jumped out and waved at Diana as she went toward the shallow crossing in the stream and turned left, following the old cart trail that led to the cabin.

Once again, she found Tilly and all four children standing on the porch waiting for her. They all had smiles on their faces. The children climbed up into the wagon and Diana headed back up the knob and back toward Berlin.

The children rode quietly. They were well-behaved children. Mostly shy, Diana assumed. Who knows what their previous lives were like as slaves? Diana had heard stories of abuse and torture at the hands of cruel plantation owners. She had also heard stories of compassion and kindness at the hands of others.

As she drove the horse onward, her mind drifted back to her baby sister. She had so hoped that Martha and Ruth Ann would share in her teaching the smaller ones. They were both so much more educated. They would have been a big help. She thought of poor Ruthie lying in her sick bed. Porter said she was doing better. That was good news. Perhaps, she would be on her feet by tomorrow. Thomas seemed to recuperate quickly. He was big and strong. Ruth Ann was small and frail, but other than that, she was healthy.

Then there was dear Martha. She had taken on so many responsibilities. She was seventeen already. She, too, was nearly past the marrying age. She was a good hunter. Even better with the sling than Diana was. She was not very good with the bow, however. She could shoot the rifle as well as Josephine could, but much like Diana, she was on the small side and the rifle was cumbersome for her to carry any distance.

Diana could not help but see so much of herself in Martha. What would she ever do without her? What would any of them do without her? She made a mental note to tell Martha how much she appreciated all of the hardwork Martha had done for them.

The school was in sight. Diana smiled. Her hands were beginning to get cold holding on the reins. The fire would feel very good, once she got it going.

Diana gave the bell to Homer. He proudly stepped outside and began ringing it. She began to build a fire in the potbelly stove. Once it was blazing, she went to the door and told Homer to stop ringing the bell. Before long, Thelma Faulk arrived. Homer went out and rang the bell once more. It was time to start classes.

They worked on their alphabet song. Soon, they had caught on and were singing joyfully. Then Diana began touching each letter she had written on the board as they sang. They worked on letter association all morning. Diana announced that the studies were done for the day. She asked that they practice their songs after they got home. Then she said it was time to celebrate Gilda's birthday. She passed around slices of bread and two pieces of hard candy. "One piece for now, and one piece for later," she announced. She gave Thelma two extra pieces to share with her sister and brother. She gave Hoppy two extra pieces to share with Percy and Tilly.

Then it was time to load up in the wagon and Diana would take them home. She said to Thelma, as she dropped her off. "You tell your mother, I will stop in the morning to pick you up on my way to the school. It will be too cold for you to walk through town to the schoolhouse. I don't mind, as long as you are all ready when I get here."

Thelma agreed to relay the message and thanked Diana for the candy. She ran to the house, just as Alda Faulk came to the door. She waved at Diana as she pulled away.

Diana dropped the three children off at the cabin and reminded Hoppy to share the candy. She was anxious to get back to Porter Martin's house. As she cleared the knob, it began to snow. It was light. It was a reminder of what was to come. Diana sighed and blew into her hands. She rested the reins between her knees and tucked her hands inside her shawl. The horse knew the way home. He moved faster. He knew he would be fed and watered when he reached the barn. Diana did not try to hold him back. She was cold. She was anxious to see how her sister was doing. And she wondered if Porter and Martha had killed a wild boar.

Porter had built a shed for curing meat. He called it a smokehouse. He said the meat would last longer without spoiling. He had also built another stone building back into the ground. He called it the springhouse. He said they could store a bucket of milk a whole day or two inside the springhouse.

Now, the Martin house was in sight. The horse crossed the shallow spot in the stream and went right for the barn without any urging from Diana. Once they reached the barn, she unhitched the horse. There was a bucket of water sitting there waiting for them. Diana smiled. Martha thought of everything. She gave the horse a handful of grain and some loose hay. Then she pulled her shawl around her head and walked toward the back door, to the house.

Martha was in the kitchen rolling out a flat mass of dough. She was making noodles. "Hello there, Miss Lewis. How was school today?" she teased.

"Aren't you in a good mood today. It was fine, thank you for asking," Diana said as she hung up her shawl. She went to the stove and peered into the pot. "What are you cooking?"

Martha pushed a few strands of loose hair from her eyes with the back of her hand. "Rabbit," she said. "We did not see any sign of boar. Porter took one of the rabbits to Tilly. I hope the wild game holds out this winter. Feeding two families may become a problem," Martha said.

Diana frowned. She stood near the fireplace to warm herself. She asked, "How is Ruth Ann?"

Martha looked over at Diana and smiled. "Thomas said she is much better. The fever has passed and she is sitting up some in the bed. He says she has a bad cough, though."

"This cold weather certainly won't help any. It is good to hear she is coming along," Diana said. She pulled a chair over to the fireplace and propped her feet up toward the fire to warm them. "I have been meaning to tell you, Martha. I really appreciate the way you have been working around here. You have handled this household every bit as well as Mamma did. Your hunting is better than mine. I just want you to know that I don't know what I would do without you," Diana said, staring into the fire.

Martha smiled and wiped her hands. "Thank you, Diana. I have to say that filling your shoes is quite difficult. I have been trying. You took over when Pappa died and cared for all of us. Then when Mamma passed away, we all would have died if it weren't for you. I have tried to help you as much as I could. It is good to hear such a compliment coming from you," Martha said, pouring two cups of tea. She handed one to Diana.

Diana smiled as she took the cup. She held it in her hands to warm herself. "Thank you, Martha. I think you have done very well. I could not have done it any better."

Martha sat down on a chair next to Diana. Smiling, she said, "Speaking of working, have you seen Sofia lately?"

Diana laughed. She said, "Not lately. I invited her to school, but she said she had to work at the store. She should be pretty busy there. The stage is due to go through today or tomorrow. There will be some supplies for the store and Grace Hickman will be cracking the old whip. Of course, I imagine it would take a whip to get Sofia to move, especially on her dreamy days."

"Do you miss her, Diana?" Martha asked.

"Oh, yes. I really do. Sometimes I regret fighting with her, and I wish I could take it all back just to have her here with us again. Then other days, I am grateful that she is gone. Besides, Sofia is happier in town where she can see the people on the stage. Hopefully, someday, she will meet a nice man and get married. I just hope he is someone who likes working inside as well as outside. We both know that Sofia is not going to amount to much when it comes to taking care of a houseful of kids," Diana said, watching the flames flicker in the fireplace.

Martha stood up. She went into the living room and came back with an arm full of fabric. It was all colors and designs. She smiled as she showed it to Diana. "Mr. Martin purchased this for us on his last trip to Philly. He said he forgot all about his purchases because he was so busy trying to get the school-house finished."

Diana felt the cotton fabric. "What pretty dresses they will make."

"Yes, indeed. That brings me to something else I wanted to talk to you about. Once Ruth Ann is on her feet again, she can help you with teaching at the school. I was thinking about dressmaking. I could sew dresses and sell them. What do you think? Mr. Martin said they have dress shops all over in Philadelphia," Martha said.

Diana looked up at Martha. "Dress shops? You mean someone makes dresses for other people?" she asked.

Martha smiled and said, "Mm hum. Ladies go to the shop and get measured. Then when the dress is finished, they go pick it up and pay for it. Men, too. He told me he had a pair of trousers and a jacket made by a woman in Philadelphia once. He wore them when he and Miss Margaret got married."

Diana shook her head, "Well, I'll be. I never heard of such a thing. Do you think there are enough people in Berlin to support such a business?" she asked.

"I don't know. It sure is growing. And if I get too busy, I could get Miss Tilly to help me. Did you see how small the stitches were on those patches? She is a very good seamstress," Martha said.

Diana smiled and nodded. "Well, I don't know how it will go over in Berlin. But I do know this town is growing. And one thing is certain, if anyone can make it work, you can. If I can do anything to help, I certainly would be happy to do so."

Martha carried the fabric back into the living room. She returned and sat back down next to Diana. They chatted until they had drunk their tea. Then they both began working on preparing the evening meal.

The next morning, Thomas announced that they could see Ruth Ann. She was propped up in her bed. Her face was pale and her lips appeared white. Martha had taken her a cup of sassafras tea. She was weak and trembled as she held the cup. The worst had passed. The girls sat on each side of the bed. Thomas went to the mill to help Porter Martin. Diana told Ruth Ann all about the school and how they had a birthday party for Gilda. Ruth Ann rested her head on the pillow. She smiled.

"I can't wait to go to school with you, Di," Ruth Ann said.

"You will get there soon enough. Don't be too anxious, because it is getting mighty cold out there. Did you see the snow yesterday?" Diana asked.

Ruth Ann shook her head. She began to cough and Martha took the cup of tea from her hands. She coughed hard and the veins on her forehead stood out. Diana frowned. She knew Ruth Ann would not be going to the schoolhouse anytime soon.

Martha said, "You go on to school, Di. I will stay with her. We will see you this afternoon."

Diana stood up. She bent over and kissed the top of Ruth Ann's head. "I'll be home before you know it. Just stay in your warm bed and think of me freezing out there driving that wagon back from Berlin. That should make you feel better," she said teasing.

Ruth Ann smiled. She began coughing once again. She nodded and waved to her sister. Diana went down the stairs. She wrapped in her shawl and a heavy beef hide. She went for the wagon. Again, Porter had the horse hitched to the wagon. This would be her last trip in this week. Tomorrow was Saturday. She had taught the children the days of the week. They knew that Saturday and Sunday were days that they did not go to school. She began her morning journey to the cabin.

The children had all been working very hard on their studies. On occasion, Alda Faulk would show up and sit in the back listening. Today, Diana thought she would ask her to join in the class participation. Diana stopped at their small house to pick up Thelma. Alda stood in the door waving as they were about to leave.

Diana cleared her throat and asked, "Mrs. Faulk, if you want to join in Thelma's studies, you are more than welcome. Would you like to come to school with us this morning?"

Instantly, she regretted it. Mrs. Faulk's face turned red. She looked to the ground and shook her head. "I have too much work to do here," she said.

Diana was embarrassed. She feared that Mrs. Faulk may never appear in her classroom again. "Well, if you change your mind," Diana began. "You are always welcome." She turned the wagon toward the school and left.

That day, they began talking about the upcoming holiday. It would be Christmas in another week or two. Diana told them the Bible story of the birth of Christ. They listened intently. They were each told to make some little homemade gift for the secret person whose name they drew from a straw hat. They were excited. Diana told Homer to ring the bell signifying school was over for the day. They climbed up into the wagon and Diana proceeded to take Thelma home.

She asked the children to wait in the wagon while she made some purchases at the general store. The stage was pulled up out front. There were two passengers standing on the porch.

The one gentleman was dressed in tight legged pants that came down low over his boots. He had lace cuffs on his shirt and a lace bib that protruded out the opening in his velvet jacket. He wore a small round topped hat with a very small rim. Diana thought it certainly was not designed to protect him from the rain and sun. He carried a black cane with a silver handle. It appeared as though there was no need for it, for he walked just fine. He tipped his hat and bowed to her as she passed.

The second man wore brown wool pants with a black wool jacket. He wore a hat just like the one Porter Martin wore. He smiled as she passed him, and said, "Good afternoon, Ma'am."

Diana smiled and replied, "Good afternoon, Sir." She went inside the store.

Grace Hickman was behind the counter. She seemed to ignore Diana. Concetta and Sofia stood at the end of the counter watching the two strangers.

Diana coughed. Grace looked at her. "Yes, yes. What do you need?" she said.

Diana handed her the list. Grace read it and passed it to Concetta. She lowered her voice and said, "The stage has something wrong with it. These gentlemen are waiting on Zachariah to fix it," Grace said.

Diana turned to look at the two gentlemen. The one in the brown wool pants had stepped inside the store and was looking out the window in the direction of the church. "That is a very nice church you have there. It is of great size for a town this small," he said.

Grace smiled and came around the counter. She went to stand beside the man. Looking out at the church, she said, "Why, yes, indeed. However, this town is growin'. We hope to fill it someday," she said, smiling at the stranger.

He nodded and asked, "Do you have a preacher in town?"

Grace smiled again. She shook her head and replied. "Not at the moment. My son, Burt, wanted to be a preacher. He went off to fight in the war gainst the South. It is waitin for him when he returns."

The stranger studied Grace for a moment. Diana knew he was thinking that Burt should have returned by now. However, he was too polite to say the words. He smiled and reached out to take her hand as he said, "Ma'am, my name is Jonathan Gilbert. Pastor Jonathan Gilbert. I have been traveling in search of such a town that may need a preacher. I feel the Lord has brought me to this place. I would be more than happy to stay and minister to you good people until your son returns."

Grace flushed. "Why, Parson Gilbert. How kind of you. We do not have many people here. This may not be a big enough town for what you have in mind," she said.

The parson looked back out the window at the church. He smiled and said, "Oh, I think it is the perfect town. Again, I must tell you I feel strongly that the Lord has brought me here for a purpose. I must have your permission first, Ma'am."

Grace looked around the room. She smiled and said, "Why, of course, Parson Gilbert. How could I deny the will of God?" she said looking at Diana.

Just then, Sherman Hickman stuck his head through the door. "Grace, the stage has a cracked axle. Zachariah and Stumpy are going to have to build a new one. It may take a day or two. These gentleman will have to stay in Willy and Burt's room until it is finished," he said.

Grace smiled. "Well, of course. Mr. Gilbert here will be staying on. We may have to come up with a more permanent arrangement for him," Grace said.

Sherman shifted his gaze to the parson. He nodded and turned to leave. Grace turned to Sofia and said, "Sofia, you need to move your things into Concetta's room. Tidy up the room so these gentlemen will be comfortable. Connie, you start preparing something for dinner."

Sofia smiled at the parson and ran up the stairs. Diana could not remember a time when she saw Sofia run so fast except the time she ran for Porter Martin when their mother had been bitten by the water moccasins.

The fancy dressed gentleman entered the store. He was waving a lace handkerchief about as he spoke. "Madame, my name is Gwain Brewster. At your service," he said with a bow. "I am an actor from London, England," he spoke with a thick accent. "I am on my way to New York where I am to meet a troop of actors and actresses. From there, we are headed for Saint Louis. May I ask, how long will we be held up here?" He was a strange man. So strange that Diana wondered if he was indeed a man at all. He reminded her of Porter Martin's big red rooster.

Grace Hickman smiled. "Well, Mr. Brewster, they will have to build a new axle and then put it on the stage. I reckon it will be a couple of days. Mr. Dillon and Mr. Morgan are very good at that kind of thing. It shouldn't take any longer than necessary," she said.

The fancy actor rolled his eyes up into his head. "Very well. I suppose I could put up with the inconvenience for a day or two. I do hope it isn't any longer. Would you happen to have a bath?"

Grace was fluttering about. "Of course. I will have a couple men carry it up to your room and we will heat some water for ya. It may take an hour or so. I will show you to your room as soon as Sofia is finished up there," Grace said.

She happened to notice Diana standing at the counter. "Oh, Miss Lewis. Here is the supplies you asked for. Will there be anything else?" Grace asked.

"That will be all," Diana said. She pulled some change from her purse.

Grace wrote in her ledger and then announced. "That will be forty cents."

Diana paid her and began collecting the items from the counter.

"Here, allow me," the parson said as he helped her carry the items outside to her wagon. He studied the children in the back huddled under the cowhides to keep warm. He placed the items into the wagon and went back upon the porch to watch her leave.

Diana heard Grace Hickman say as she was leaving, "That is Diana Lewis. She is the schoolteacher. Her school is right next to the church."

Diana drove the horse and wagon on out of town. She was anxious to get home. She had news to tell Martha and Ruth Ann.

She dropped the children off at the cabin. She reminded Tilly that they did not have school on Saturday and Sunday, but she would be back on Monday for the children, as she usually did. She also reminded them that starting Monday, they would have school for a full day and would be getting home later. They waved and stood on the porch watching her leave until she was out of sight.

She hurried about unhitching the horse. Once again, there was a full bucket of water sitting inside the barn for her to give the horse. There was a thin layer of ice covering the top. She fed him a handful of grain and some loose hay. Then she collected the hides from the wagon and carried them to the back door. Martha opened the door for her and held it until she was inside. She had been waiting for her.

"Where have you been? I was beginning to get worried," Martha asked as she took the hides from Diana, setting them on a chair. She poured a cup of tea and sat a chair next to the fire for Diana to sit down and warm herself.

"I got held up in town. I stopped at the general store for some things. I forgot them. They are still in the wagon," Diana said, pulling her shoes off and propping her feet up to the fire. She sipped the tea. Then she said, "The stage is broke down. They have to build a new axle. There are two passengers staying at the Hickman's. One is the fanciest man I have ever seen. He says he is an actor headed to New York to meet some other actors. Then he is going to Saint Louis. You have to see this man! Martha, I can't describe him to you. You would not believe me. He looks like a woman." Diana began to laugh. Martha was smiling.

Diana went on. "Then, there is another man. He is a preacher. Pastor Jonathan Gilbert. He is going to stay on and preach at the church. We have a minister at the church now. I don't know where he is going to stay. Sofia has moved into Concetta's room. She may have to move back home, I don't know. What a day this has been. I can't wait to tell Ruth Ann."

Martha listened intently to Diana as she told her about the two strangers staying in town. She smiled and nodded her head as she listened. Finally, they began preparing for dinner.

Diana rushed upstairs to visit with Ruth Ann and tell her all about her day in town. Ruth Ann smiled as she listened. She would have a coughing spell now and then. Diana would wait patiently for the cough to subside, and then continue on with her story.

Ruth Ann said, "I can't wait to get to town to see them."

Diana took her small hand. "Oh, honey, the stage will be gone before you are able to go to town. I am sure of it. But you will soon be up and able to go to church and meet the new parson. He seemed really nice. I hope he stays on here. Berlin needs someone to preach the word of God in that nice church Porter Martin built. It is too fine a building to just sit there," Diana said.

Over dinner, Diana found herself repeating the tale for the third time to Porter Martin and Thomas. They listened intently and smiled from time to time. They spoke of the theater in Philadelphia. Porter said that actors were a strange lot. He was never really comfortable around them. Then, in conclusion, he admitted that he knew very few of them personally. He had only seen them a couple of times.

Saturday morning was sunny, but very cold. Diana went hunting with her bow. She wondered far back behind the orchard. She climbed a tree and looked around for as far as she could see. Nearly all of the leaves had fallen from the trees by now. The wind cut through the forest and blew at her rabbit skin hat. She had to secure it tightly a couple of times to keep it from blowing off. It had been a long time since she went hunting alone. She enjoyed the quiet time. Her mind wondered to different things.

Diana was nearing the Martin farm after hours of walking through the woods. She had killed a pheasant and one small quail. She carried them to the back porch. Martha came outside to help her to pull the feathers off. It was still early in the day. They were working intently and chatting when they heard a horse coming up the road. They both walked around to the front of the house. It was Pastor Gilbert.

"Good morning, ladies!" he called. He tipped his hat to them.

"Good morning," the sisters said together.

"I hope I have not come at an awkward moment," he said.

"No, not at all," Martha said.

"Well, I was calling on everyone in the area. I am preaching the word of God tomorrow morning at the church. Services will begin around nine o'clock. I would be mighty happy to see as many faces there as possible," Parson Gilbert said.

Diana smiled. "It would be our pleasure, Parson. I will stay home with our sister who is ill. My sister, Martha, has not been to town in sometime. I think it would do her good to make the trip in for services tomorrow," Diana said.

Martha looked at Diana and asked, "Are you sure, Diana?"

"Of course, I am sure. The trip would do you good. You have been working so hard," Diana said.

The preacher dismounted his horse. "You say you have a sister that is ill?" he asked.

"Yes, Sir. Ruth Ann. She is our younger sister. She is just getting over the influenza," Martha explained.

The parson removed his hat. "She is over it though?"

"Yes, Sir," Diana said.

"If you don't mind, I would like to visit with her. Perhaps I could say a prayer for her," the Parson said.

"Oh, Sir! That would be very kind of you," Diana said.

"Follow us," Martha said, leading the way into the house.

They went up the stairs to Ruth Ann's room. Diana waited in the hall with the preacher, while Martha prepared Ruth Ann for her visitor. Soon, she returned and motioned for him to enter.

"Good morning, Miss Lewis," the parson said taking her hand. "Allow me to introduce myself. I am Jonathan Gilbert. I have been blessed with permission to be the new preacher in Berlin. We are having our first Sunday service tomorrow morning. I was making calls and these two young ladies have informed me that you have been ill. I hope you don't mind my intrusion."

Ruth Ann smiled. She began to cough. They all waited patiently for the cough to subside. "I am so sorry," she said. She began to cough again.

"Please, don't apologize, Miss," the parson said. "I was wondering if I might say a prayer for you."

Ruth Ann smiled. Her voice was weak. She found that talking only brought on the cough, so she nodded her head, giving the parson permission to pray.

He knelt on his knees next to her bed. Holding her hand, he began, "Dear Father in Heaven, please smile down on this young lady and bless her with good health. Release her from her suffering. Bless this household and those who live in it. In the name of our Savior, Jesus Christ, we pray. Amen"

"Amen," Martha and Diana echoed.

Parson Gilbert rose and stood over Ruth Ann. He wore the same clothes he had on yesterday. "Thank you, ladies. I do hope to see you for services tomorrow," he said. Diana led him back down the stairs. They went back outside. He was just mounting his horse when Martha joined them.

"Are you going on to Tilly's?" Martha asked.

"Tilly? Who is this Tilly you speak of?" Parson Gilbert asked.

"Tilly lives at the end of this little trail here. She is a Negro woman with four little children," Martha said.

Diana watched his expression. No doubt, Grace Hickman had warned him about bringing the Negroes into town.

He smiled and said. "Why, of course. The children riding in your wagon yesterday. You say they live at the end of this cart trail?"

Diana nodded. "Tilly may be uncomfortable having a stranger approach her and the children way out there all alone. Perhaps I should ride out with you. She knows me," she said.

"That may be a good idea," Parson Gilbert said.

"I will go saddle up a horse and meet you back here," Diana said. She went toward the barn. Martha stood there on the porch, watching her go. She said to the Parson. "Diana will need a wrap. It is cold out here." She turned and went inside.

Soon, Diana returned on horseback. Martha handed her a wrap. "I'll make a pot of tea to warm you when you get back," Martha said.

"Thank you, Martha. We won't be long," Diana said.

Diana clicked her tongue and guided the horse toward the shallow crossing. The parson followed. Diana began explaining to him about the time the rebel soldiers burned Porter's house. She pointed in the direction of where Martha and she had heard the fighting off in a distance. Parson Gilbert rode beside her, listening intently.

"How long have you lived around here?" he asked.

"We were all born in this cabin down here, where Tilly and her children live," she said, pointing to the cabin that had just come into view. "Mamma and Pappa are buried behind the cabin under that big oak tree."

They rode on down the hill to the cabin. Smoke floated from the chimney. They tied their horses to the hitching post. Parson Gilbert waited near the horses while Diana went to the door. Before she could knock, it swung open and Tilly stood there with all four children gathered around her.

"Is it a school day, Miss Diana?" Tilly asked.

Diana smiled and shook her head. "No, Tilly. It is Saturday. I want you to meet our new parson. He will be preaching Sunday services at the church to-morrow. He came all the way here to invite you and your children to church tomorrow," Diana said. She turned toward the preacher and he approached the porch. He did not climb up onto it.

Tilly watched the man. Her gaze shifted to Diana. Diana nodded her approval. Tilly opened the door wide, motioning them inside.

Diana entered and the Parson was right behind her. Diana looked around. There were all sorts of greens hanging around the fireplace. There were tree bark shavings in the corner. Other than that, the room looked exactly as it did when the Lewis's lived there. The children huddled near the fireplace. Diana pulled out a stool and the Parson did the same.

"Miss Tilly, is it?" he asked.

Tilly nodded her head. She looked over at her children and then back to the parson.

"Miss Tilly, I understand you are new to these parts. So am I. I am staying with the Hickman's in Berlin. Have you ever been to a church service before?" Parson Gilbert asked.

Tilly shook her head. She looked from Diana to the parson.

"Do you know about God, Tilly?" he asked.

Again, Tilly shook her head.

The parson sighed. He looked over at Diana and smiled.

Diana reached for Tilly's hand and said, "Church services are like school, Tilly. Only, it is for every one of all ages. Instead of learning to read and write, you learn about God and Jesus."

"I has heard of Jesus," Tilly said.

"Good. That is good," the Parson said. He smiled, looking back and forth from Tilly to Diana. "I will be teaching about Jesus. We will say prayers and sing songs. I would really like it if you and your children could come," he said.

Tilly looked at Diana. "I don't know, Sir. It is mighty cold and that is a far piece to walk with the younguns," Tilly said.

Diana smiled. What was she getting herself into? "I will send my sister, Martha, for you in the morning, if you want to go. It will be about the same time as school."

Tilly was watching Diana. "You want I should go, Miss Diana?"

Diana patted Tilly's hand. "I cannot make that decision for you and your family, Tilly. I will do everything in my power to help you get there, if you want to go. But whether you go or not is your decision."

Diana was aware of the parson fidgeting. He coughed. She did not look his way. "Do you have a religion of your own, Tilly?" she asked.

"No, Ma'am," Tilly said.

"Then it is up to you. Should I send Martha for you and the children?" Diana asked.

Tilly looked over at her children. She turned back to Diana and nodded her head. "Yes, Ma'am. We will be waitin' for her in the morning," Tilly said.

Diana stood up. "Good. You are doing the right thing, Tilly," she said as she moved to the door.

"Ma'am, may I pray with you and the children?" the Parson asked.

Tilly looked at Diana with a confused expression on her face. Diana smiled. She stepped back, away from the door. "To pray, Tilly, you fold you hands, bow your head, and close your eyes, like this. The preacher will do all of the talking."

Tilly looked over at the children and motioned for them to stand. They folded their hands and bowed their heads. They waited patiently. Then, the parson said a short prayer. When the prayer was concluded, he looked at Diana. Tilly and the children still stood in their spots with their heads bowed.

Diana spoke softly. "Tilly, you can look up now. When the preacher says, 'Amen,' the prayer is over."

Tilly looked embarrassed. Diana took her hand. "It is all right, Tilly."

They went back to the door once again. They said their good-byes and mounted their horses. They rode back toward Porter Martin's house. Diana thought about warning the parson against Grace Hickman's dislike of Tilly and her children living in the area. She decided to wait and see what happened.

When they reached the Martin house, Diana invited the parson in for a cup of tea before he went back to town. He declined. He said he wanted to work on his sermon for tomorrow morning. He rode on as Diana went to the barn. She removed the saddle and bridle from Buckley and went to the house. Martha had a cup of tea waiting for her, just as she had promised. She had a chair pulled to the fireplace. It had become a routine. Diana made a mental note to do the same for Martha tomorrow when she returned from church.

The next morning, Martha and Diana worked together on breakfast. Martha had been working on a new dress, which was completed. She had her hair piled on top of her head. She looked lovely. Porter and Thomas were preparing to go to church also. They sat together at breakfast talking about the changes in the area over the years. It was decided that after church, they would bring Tilly and her children home with them for a big dinner. Diana would work on it while they were gone.

They were all smiles and the mood was light as they prepared to leave. It was snowing. Porter went to the barn. Soon, he pulled the wagon up next to the porch and called to them all. Diana went to the door to wave good-bye. She gasped. Porter had built a small wagon that looked very much like a house on wheels. It had a closed in seat with a small slotted hole where the reins went through. There was a window in the front. There was a door in the back. Porter opened the door. There were two bench seats that ran along the length of the wagon. It was entirely closed in. Porter smiled. He had a team of two horses that pulled the wagon.

"What do you think, Miss Diana?" Porter called to her. She jumped from the porch into the snow. She ran to the back of the wagon and climbed up inside. She was squealing with delight. "Oh, Mr. Martin! This is perfect!" she said.

Porter smiled. "I'll let you know how it handles when we get back." He tipped his hat to her. Martha and Thomas climbed inside.

"It is kind of like a big square stagecoach.," Martha called out to Diana.

Diana went back up onto the porch and watched them as they left. She went back inside. She could not stop smiling.

Diana made a cup of tea and took it up to Ruth Ann. She helped her to sit up. Ruth Ann seemed to be better this morning. Diana was still worried because it seemed to be taking so much longer for Ruth Ann to get better than it did for Thomas. Her cough was not going away.

Ruth Ann sipped her tea. Diana sat and talked with her. She told her about Tilly and the children going to church, the new wagon Porter had built for her, and how excited she was that Porter was bringing Tilly and the children to dinner.

"I want to go down," Ruth Ann said.

Diana smiled. "I am not so sure that is a good idea, Ruthie. You are so weak. And your cough is still pretty bad," Diana said.

"Well, what if we give it a try? What if I go down and talk to you while you prepare dinner? I am so tired of staring at these walls, Di," Ruth Ann said.

Diana thought about it for a moment. "All right. I will help you down the stairs. You can sit near the fireplace and have a cup of tea. If you get tired, you tell me. I don't want to wait until you are too weak to get back up the stairs. I can't carry you, Ruthie," she said.

Diana helped Ruth Ann sit up in the bed. She swung her legs over the side. Ruth Ann began to cough. They waited for the cough to stop. Diana supported Ruth Ann as they made their way to the stairs. They descended the stairs one at a time. Ruth Ann clung to the railing. When they reached the bottom of the stairs, they slowly made their way into the kitchen. Diana sat Ruth Ann on a chair next to the fireplace. She made a cup of sassafras tea and sat it on another chair next to her sister. Diana began preparing dinner. They talked while she worked.

Soon, Ruth Ann began coughing. She coughed hard. She fell onto the floor on her hands and knees. She coughed so hard the veins on her forehead were swelling. Diana knelt at her side and held her. Finally, it stopped.

Ruth Ann was crying. "Oh, Di. I peed myself. I am so sorry. I need to go back upstairs. I wanted to spend more time down here. I am so sorry," she sobbed. She began to cough again.

Diana held her tight until the cough stopped. "It is okay, Ruthie. I will clean you up. Come on. Help me get you up. We will get you bathed and back in bed."

Diana supported Ruth Ann once again. They slowly made their way back up the stairs. Diana put clean sheets on the bed and bathed Ruth Ann. She put a clean gown on her and tucked her in. She brushed Ruth Ann's hair. "There. You look lovely. You are all prepared for visitors. Now, take a nap and get some rest. You will not want to be drowsy when our guests arrive," Diana said. She left the room and went back downstairs to the kitchen. She cleaned up the mess and went back to preparing dinner.

Diana heard the wagon coming. She rushed to the front room and opened the shutters to look out. It was Porter and the wagon house. She closed the shutters and wrapped in a cowhide that draped over a chair. She went out onto the porch. She waved at them.

Thomas opened the back of the wagon and one by one, the children jumped down. Tilly was the last to exit. She looked around, squinting from the bright snow. Thomas held her hand as she climbed up onto the porch.

"Come in. Welcome to our home!" Porter was saying to Tilly.

Inside, the children clung to Tilly. When she moved, they all moved with her. Diana fought back laughter. "Come into the kitchen. I have dinner all prepared. You can put you wraps near the fireplace so they will be nice and warm when you are ready to leave," Diana said.

They dropped their wraps in a pile near the fireplace and followed Diana into the kitchen.

Porter said, "I am going to put the horses in the barn. I will be right back."

He went out the front door. Diana could hear the team pulling the wagon house around the house to the barn.

"I will go help, Mr. Martin," Thomas said. He went out the back door.

Diana turned to Tilly and the children. "Please, sit down. You are our guests."

Tilly sat down on a chair. The children continued to cling to her. Diana smiled and asked, "What did you think of the church service, Tilly?"

Tilly smiled. "It was mighty fine, Miss Lewis."

"What about you, Homer? What did you think about church?" Diana asked.

Homer nodded. "It was fine, Miss Lewis. It were different than school. Preacher man rung the bell," he said.

Diana laughed. "Well, I will speak to Parson Gilbert about possibly allowing you to ring the bell."

Hoppy spoke softly. "Preacher man says God made his son, Jesus Christ. He helped God and they made everythin'. He says they made a man named Adam. He says we can't see God, but we kin see everythin' he made. He even made the snow."

Diana nodded her head and said, "That is right, Hoppy. God made everything on earth."

"Miss Lewis, what is earth?" Hoppy asked.

Diana thought for a moment. This was really going to be challenging. She smiled. "I think we will learn about earth in school. There is so much to learn. Do you like going to school?" she asked.

The children were all nodding their heads. "They is learnin so much," Tilly said. "Every day they come home tellin' me bout what they learnt."

"Good," Diana said. "That is good."

Just then, Thomas and Porter came in the back door. Porter said as he was removing his boots, "It is really comin' down out there. We may have to dig the wagon out after dinner."

"Well," Diana began, "dinner is ready. If Martha will help pour the coffee, we can all eat now."

They gathered around the table. Martha assigned the seats. The children were reluctant to move away from Tilly. Once they were all seated, Porter said a prayer. He thanked the Lord that they were blessed with Tilly and her children as guests in their home. After the prayer, they raised their heads to find Tilly staring at him wide eyed.

"What is it, Tilly? What is wrong?" Diana asked.

She shook her head. "We ain't never bin no guests before. Guests are special," she said.

"That is right, Tilly. Guests are special. You and your children are our special guests today," Martha said, smiling.

Tilly shook her head. Porter began to pass the food around the table. Homer was piling food upon his plate. Tilly reached over and touched his hand. She shook her head. He began to put some of the food back. Porter laughed. "Aw! Go on, boy. Eat as much as you want," he said.

After dinner, Tilly helped Martha and Diana clean up. She seemed right at home in the kitchen. She told them that she helped clean up after dinner at the plantation. She did not do any cooking, though.

Porter took the children upstairs to visit with Ruth Ann. Thomas joined them. After everything was cleaned up, Thomas said he would hitch up the wagon house and take them home. He would build Tilly a fire before he left to come back. Martha wrapped some leftovers up and handed them to Tilly.

Diana reminded them that tomorrow was another school day and they would need to pack a lunch because they would have a full day of school. Then they were gone. Porter was still upstairs with Ruth Ann. He was reading to her. He had bought a book at the general store. It was some story about a boy who lived along a river.

Once Diana and Martha were alone in the kitchen, Diana motioned for her sister to sit down next to her by the fire. "You have to tell me all about the services," Diana said.

Martha smiled and began. 'Well, first off, you should have seen Grace Hickman's face when Mr. Martin pulled the wagon house up to the church. Then when Tilly and her children climbed out, I thought the old girl was going to faint. She ran right to the parson and started whispering in his ear. He smiled and said something to her that she obviously did not like. She sat right there in the front row while he preached his sermon. I could not see her face, but you can bet she was giving him the old evil eye." Martha laughed. Diana could not help but smile.

"Go on. Did you see the fancy man? Was he in church?" Diana asked.

Martha nodded and replied. "Oh, he was there all right. You were right. I am not sure he is a man either. He sure is a sissy, if he is. He sat way in the back. Tilly and her children sat back by the door. Mr. Martin tried to get them to move up closer, but she wouldn't do it. He thought it was better to wait until she was more comfortable with being around all of those people. She was really nervous, Diana."

Diana stood up. She walked around behind Martha. Then she returned to her chair.

Martha continued. "Sofia sat right up front with Mrs. Hickman and Concetta. She just said hello. That was all. You would think she was a total stranger or something. If I get a chance to see her again, I am really going to give her a piece of my mind. She thinks she is better than we are or something." Martha was becoming angry.

Diana covered her hand with her own and said, "Never mind Sofia. She has problems of her own. We should pity her, Martha."

Martha frowned. "Pity her! She needs another good whooping like the one you gave her the day before you took her to live with the Hickman's," she said.

Diana smiled and looked at her sister. "I think that is her problem. I think she hasn't forgotten that day and she is still pouting about it."

"Well, good!" Martha said.

The two sisters sat there laughing for a time. Then they began to talk about the new dress that Martha had made. It was very pretty. Diana told Martha she thought she had a good chance of making the dress shop work.

Martha said, "Mr. Martin told me he would build me a dress shop. I don't know if I am ready for that just yet. I think I need to establish myself first."

Diana agreed. Besides, "Someone needs to be here with Ruth Ann until she gets better," she said. She explained to Martha about bringing Ruthie down for a while earlier in the day.

Martha nodded her head and said, "I tried that one day, too. The very same thing happened. I suppose I should have warned you about that."

They sat for a short time discussing Ruth Ann's condition and then decided it was time to turn in. Tomorrow was a school day.

It had been three days since the stage broke down in Berlin. Zachariah and Stumpy had it repaired, and it pulled out taking the fancy actor from London, England, with it. Concetta had taking a liking to the fancy man and all of his far away stories. She had locked herself in her room. She was crying and throwing a tantrum.

Sofia had been spending more time with the preacher. He had moved in with Marcus O'Hara. Marcus was nearly totally blind by now, and found the preacher to be most helpful. He sat quietly while the preacher read from the Bible and practiced his sermons on him.

Diana had been driving the wagon house back and forth to school. They all were much warmer inside the enclosure. Diana found that it was too heavy and had to watch exactly where she crossed the rough spots in the road. It took two horses to pull it, which left Mr. Martin short one horse for pulling logs. He told her not to fret none. He had been meaning to pick up another team anyway. She knew he was just being kind.

One morning in particular, the snow was too deep for the wagon. Thomas had gone back to Philadelphia to work with James. Porter rode one of his large draft horses to the cabin and told Tilly there would not be any school that day. He also checked to make sure she was stocked up on wood. She still had a pot of stew hanging over the fireplace. He returned home to reassure Diana that they were safe and well stocked.

Diana spent the day helping Martha sew another dress. This one was for Ruth Ann.

Some days Ruth Ann's cough was not so bad, and others it appeared to be getting worse. She was almost skin and bone. She was blonde, like Diana, with bright blue eyes. Her face was always porcelain like with rosy cheeks. Now she was pale. Her cheekbones protruded and her temples sunk in. She had dark circles under her eyes. Porter spent more and more time in her room reading to her. Diana could tell he was worried.

Martha put another log on the fire. They heard footsteps on the front porch. "Who could it be, in this weather?" Martha asked Diana.

She went to the door. Diana stood back watching.

It was a tall gentleman. He had ice around his mustache. He tipped his hat. With chattering teeth, he asked. "Miss Diana Lewis?"

Martha turned to Diana. She came forward. "I am Miss Diana Lewis."

"Ma'am. I am sorry, but I am half frozen. May I come in, please?" he asked.

Diana thought she recognized something faintly familiar in the man. She stepped aside and invited him in. Martha pulled a chair close to the fireplace in the living room. He sat down. Diana handed him one of the cowhide wraps to pull around him.

"I will make a cup of tea," Martha said and she disappeared into the kitchen.

Diana stood there watching this familiar stranger. What was it about him that was so familiar? She could not put her finger on it. He was shivering from the cold. He had a heavy coat that should have kept him warm, but it was soaked through. Diana stepped forward. She smiled and said. "Sir, if I may, your coat is soaked through. If we get you out of those wet clothes, I believe you will warm up faster."

He looked down at himself and then back up at Diana. "Yes, Ma'am. I believe you are right. I did not realize I was this wet. My apologies, Ma'am," he said.

He was so polite. Diana helped him pull his heavy fur coat off. His shirt was wet as well. She said nothing about it. He wrapped the hide around himself and pulled his chair closer to the fire. Martha arrived with a cup of hot tea. He wrapped his hands around it to warm them.

"I will take your horse to the barn," Martha said.

She disappeared into the kitchen only to re-appear wearing a heavy wrap and furs tied to her feet and legs. She went out the front door, closing it behind her. Diana stood watching the man for a moment. She hung his coat over the broom handle and propped it against the stone fireplace.

He looked up at her and smiled. "It took some searching to find you, Miss Lewis. Pardon me. I forgot to introduce myself. My name is Brandon Shively. I'm from Boston. My brother was Lieutenant Robert Shively."

Diana gasped. She clasped her hands over her mouth. "Robert?" she asked.

"I am sorry, Ma'am. My brother, Robert, was killed in a battle in Fredericksburg, Virginia. He had all of these letters on him." He fumbled through his shirt and then said, "They are in my saddle bag. I am sorry. I was cold, I forgot to take them out. Then I was not sure I was at the right place," he explained.

So Robert did write. Diana felt her eyes filling with tears.

The man went on. "They sent all of his letters home to Mother. She had all of these letters he had written to a Diana Lewis in Berlin, Pennsylvania. Frankly, Ma'am, we did not know where Berlin, Pennsylvania was."

Martha arrived through the kitchen door. Porter Martin was with her. They came into the front room. Porter tipped his hat and said, "Hello. I am Porter Martin. This is my place. May I ask what brings you here looking for Miss Lewis? She is my ward."

The gentleman smiled and said. "Yes, Sir. My name is Brandon Shively. My brother was Lieutenant Robert Shively."

Porter rubbed his head. "Yes, I remember Lieutenant Shively. He was my escort from Philly. He helped me hunt down that band of rebels who killed my wife, Margaret. How is the lieutenant?" Porter asked.

Brandon shook his head. "He was killed in Fredericksburg, Sir. I was just telling Miss Lewis."

Porter frowned and said, "Oh, I am so sorry. He was your brother, you say?"

"Yes, Sir," Brandon said.

"I believe he did tell me he had a brother who was a captain in the army. That was you?" Porter asked.

"Yes, Sir," Brandon replied.

"Captain Shively, you were saying?" Diana urged.

Brandon turned his attention back to Diana. "Yes, Ma'am. As I was saying, there were all of these letters addressed to a Diana Lewis. We had no idea who you were or where to send them. Mother put them away. We were hoping to find someone who served alongside of Robert, who might remember passing through Berlin. Then Mother became ill. Before she passed away, she asked me to try to find you and deliver the letters to you. She said Robert came to her in a dream and begged her to do this," he explained.

He approached Porter who was standing there, holding his military saddlebags. Porter turned them over to Brandon. He retrieved the letters. He handed them to Diana. She leafed through them.

"I am sorry, Ma'am. It was necessary to open them and read through them for some sort of clue as to who you were, and where we could find you. I apologize for the intrusion of your privacy. Were it not necessary, I would not have done so," Brandon said.

Diana nodded. She clutched the letters to her chest and smiled at Brandon. "Thank you. I've waited for so long for his letters to arrive. Somehow, I knew he did not survive the war. At least I know he did write and I have these letters to remember him by," Diana said. Tears were forming in her eyes.

"Yes, Ma'am. I was happy to do this for my brother," Brandon said.

Porter coughed and said, "Excuse me, Captain, but you will not be going anywhere today. I think we will find room for you here and you are welcome to stay as long as you like," he said.

Martha spoke softly to Diana, "We could move back in with Ruthie, and he could have our room."

Diana nodded, still clutching the letters to her chest.

"Oh, Ma'am, I do not want to drive you out," Brandon said.

"You are not driving us out. My sister is ill. She is in the room next door to the one you will be staying in. There is room for us in there. It is no imposition, really," Diana said.

"Yes, Ma'am. Thank you very much. I am sorry to hear that your sister is ill," Brandon said.

"Well, Captain Shively, I have to get back out to the sawmill. We are short-handed today. You warm up and dry off. These little ladies will take good care of you," Porter said. He nodded and turned to go back outside.

Martha smiled and said. "Mr. Shively, what should we call you? Captain?"

"Brandon will do, Ma'am," he said.

"Okay, Brandon, I am Martha and this is Diana, whom you know already. Our other sister is Ruth Ann. You needn't be so formal, Brandon. Welcome to our home," Martha smiled.

Brandon smiled and nodded. "Yes, Ma'am, I mean Martha."

Martha looked up at Diana. Then she smiled at Brandon and said, "Why don't you come into the kitchen and warm up over another cup of tea. Then I will get something hot into you," she said, pointing to the kitchen.

Brandon nodded and followed Martha into the kitchen. "I will go upstairs and move our things into Ruthie's room." Diana called to them. She ran for the stairs. She could not wait to get alone so she could read her letters.

Alone in the room, she closed the door and went to the bed. She sat down. There were eight letters in all. They had been opened, just as Brandon said. She began reading. She did not stop until each letter had been read. She tried to stack the letters in the order she thought they had been written. Then she busied herself with carrying their belongings into Ruth Ann's room.

She sat near Ruthie's bed. She explained all of the morning's events to her baby sister. Ruthie said she was glad they would be sharing her room. She would not be as lonely. Diana kissed Ruth Ann's pale forehead and went downstairs to the kitchen.

Brandon was sitting at the table, eating some leftover stew. He smiled. Diana smiled in return. When he had scraped his bowl clean, he stood up.

"Thank you very much. I can't tell you the last time I ate such a good meal. If you don't mind, I will change into dryer clothes and go out to give Mr. Martin a hand. He said he was shorthanded. It is the least I can do for his hospitality," Brandon said.

Diana smiled. She handed Brandon his saddlebag. "I'll show you to your room," she said.

He turned to Martha and nodded his head. "Thank you, Martha," he said. Then he followed Diana up the stairs.

It was another three days before the snow stopped and settled enough for them to go into town. Porter told Diana he was not sure she should take the wagon house down that rough cart trail to collect the children. He had put a set of runners under it to form a sleigh-like wagon. He told her he would drive it for her. He would collect them after school and drive it back. Brandon suggested that Porter allow him to do that for him. He wanted to see the cabin that he read about in his brother's letters. Porter agreed.

Brandon brought the wagon house around. He had a team of four horses pulling the heavy contraption. Diana crawled into the back. She pointed Brandon in the right direction. They moved along quite smoothly. Diana was surprised at how smooth the ride was. She had a stack of hides inside for the children.

When they reached the knob that overlooked the farm, she began to describe the buildings to Brandon. "There is the barn where Robert's horses stayed. All of his men slept on the floor around the fireplace, right there in that cabin. They were in rows. It was quite impressive to see. They were all very polite. They cut wood for us. We were very grateful to them," she said.

Brandon said. "I remember reading about it in one of Robert's letters. He said you killed two of those Confederate rebels with a sling. He said you were the most amazing woman he had ever met."

Diana's face flushed. She smiled. She could not find the words. The letters she read seemed to bring Robert back to her. It was hard for her to except the fact that he was gone.

After a moment, Brandon pulled the team to a halt near the porch. The door opened and Tilly and all four children stepped out onto the snow-covered porch.

"Those children aren't wearing any shoes," Brandon said.

"Yes. That is why I make this trip twice a day. I can't allow them to make such a journey barefooted," Diana said.

"I agree," Brandon said.

The children piled into the back of the wagon house. They wrapped themselves in the hides. Brandon urged the team around in a circle and back up the way they came. They passed the Martin house again and went into Berlin.

Diana pointed the Faulk's little house out to Brandon. He pulled up in front of it. Alda walked Thelma to the back of the wagon. She waved to Diana and went back inside.

At the schoolhouse, Brandon tied the team. He went inside with them. Homer rang the bell. Brandon built a fire for Diana. Then he promised to come back into town for her around two o'clock. He pulled a pocket watch from his pocket and noted the time. Diana watched him leave. She was glad he was there. She would miss him when he left.

Diana spent the day recapping what they had learned. The students had been practicing their alphabet while they were off. They had celebrated Christmas during the storm. Diana promised that they would do it next year. It would be even a bigger celebration. Maybe they could include their families.

At lunch, she shared her loaf of bread with them. Thelma had a lunch, but Tilly's children did not. Hoppy said, "We only eat onest a day, Miss Lewis."

Diana gave them an extra slice of bread. She had buttered it heavily. She would have to bring something for them every day. She rested her head in her hands as they ate. It seemed that she was getting in deeper and deeper. She had hoped that Martha and Ruth Ann would be able to help her. It appeared now that everything was on her shoulders. She would have to plan ahead and come up with something to get through this school year. She needed a schedule. She would do that tonight before she went to bed.

After lunch, Homer rang the bell again. They resumed their studies.

Diana was explaining how snowflakes were formed, when she saw the wagon house coming down the road. She told the students to put their things away and prepare to leave. Homer rang the bell one last time before they went to the wagon. Diana locked up the school and climbed inside.

Brandon drove the team to the Faulk house. He climbed out the back of the wagon and carried Thelma through the snow to her mother, who was waiting at the door. Alda Fauld stared at the stranger carrying her daughter.

"Brandon Shively, Ma'am. I am assisting Miss Lewis," he explained. He turned and went back to the wagon house. He climbed inside and pulled the door shut behind him. Then they went toward home.

As they went toward the cabin, Diana and the children sang their alphabet song. Brandon joined in. The children laughed. They liked this tall dark stranger. So did Diana.

When they reached the cabin, Brandon carried Hoppy in one arm and Gilda in the other. He put them down just inside the door to the cabin. Homer walked. Diana followed.

Diana introduced him to Tilly. "Tilly, this gentleman is Brandon Shively. He is staying at Mr. Martin's house. He is helping us get to and from school while the weather is so bad."

Tilly nodded at Brandon. She said nothing. Brandon looked around the room. He shook his head.

"Pardon me, Miss Tilly. My brother and his soldiers slept in this room once. I was just trying to imagine all of them sleeping on the floor here," Brandon said.

Tilly looked at Diana. Diana smiled and said, "We pushed the table against that wall, and it opened up the room some. It was cramped, but they did it. We slept through there," she said, pointing. There is a loft up there, where Mr. Martin slept," Diana said.

"Homer sleeps up there. The girls and me, we sleeps in there," Tilly said.

Gilda went to stand next to Brandon. She took his hand. He smiled down at her. He reached down for her, lifting her over his head to sit on his shoulders. Her head nearly touched the ceiling. She squealed with delight. Tilly looked up at Gilda and smiled. She was becoming more comfortable with the strange man.

"Well, we have to get home. How are you for food, Tilly?" Diana asked.

Tilly nodded and pointed to the iron pot. Diana looked at it. It appeared to be tree bark floating in boiling water. "What is that?" Diana asked.

"Soup," Tilly said.

Diana looked back into the pot. "What kind of soup?"

Tilly shrugged her shoulders. "Just soup," she said.

Diana looked up at Brandon. She smiled and said. "Well, I will try to get out and hunt us something to add to it," she said. She walked toward the door.

Brandon put Gilda down and followed her. He jumped from the porch and lifted Diana in his arms, carrying her to the wagon. She shrieked with surprise and the children laughed. He climbed into the wagon behind her and took the reins. He turned the team and headed back to the Martin house.

He dropped Diana off at the front door. He went on to the barn. Diana was still blushing when she went inside. Martha met her at the door. She took Diana's wrap and draped it over the chair near the fireplace in the front room. Diana followed her to the kitchen. The two chairs were next to the fire with two cups of sassafras tea. Diana smiled.

"How was your day?" Martha asked.

Diana smiled. "It was great! Really. The kids have been keeping up with their studies. They are progressing so much better than I expected. However, they need so much more than I can provide. Tilly's children only eat once a day. They were having tree bark soup for supper. How am I ever going to take care of them and teach them, too? I fear I may have bitten off more than I can chew," Diana said.

She sipped her tea and stared into the fireplace. Martha sighed. "I could try to go hunting. Maybe if Ruth Ann takes a nap I can get away for awhile," Martha said.

Diana shook her head. "I am not so sure you should leave her. How is she doing today?"

Martha frowned and turned to face Diana as she replied. "She isn't getting better, Di. She is just wasting away. I don't know what else to do for her. Her cough is terrible. I think she might have broken a rib while coughing. She is in a lot of pain around the rib area."

"Oh, no. What does Mr. Martin say?" Diana asked.

Martha said, "He just shakes his head. I know he is worried. He treats her like she is still a little girl. It don't hurt nothing, but he is hurting, too. I know he hates seeing her like this."

"Well, I am going up to see her for a little while. I will be right back to help with supper," Diana said. She set the teacup on the table and went up the stairs. She cracked the door, peeking inside. Ruth Ann turned her head and smiled. Diana went on into the room.

Diana pulled a chair close to the bed. She sat down. Ruth Ann began to cough. Tears rolled down her cheeks. She cried out in pain, holding her ribs as she coughed. Tears rolled down Diana face. She felt so helpless. She put her hand on Ruth Ann's shoulder. "Try not to talk. I want to tell you about our day. You just stay still," Diana said.

She told Ruth Ann about the wagon runners Porter Martin built so they could move through the snow. She talked about their studies and how the children have taken to Brandon Shively. She blushed and told Ruth Ann how he carried her to the wagon. Ruth Ann was sweating. Diana dipped a cloth in the washbowl. She dabbed it on Ruth Ann's face. She kissed her sister and sat quietly until Ruth Ann had fallen to sleep again. She tiptoed back out of the room, and down the stairs to the kitchen.

She helped Martha with supper. Soon, the sun was going down. Porter Martin came in the back door. He was alone.

"Where is Brandon Shively?" Diana asked.

Porter smiled and winked at Martha. "He went huntin' about two hours ago. He said he would be back around dark. I expect to see him wanderin' in here any time," Porter said.

He removed his boots and coat, placing them near the back door. He went to the washbowl. "I am going up to check on my little angel," he said. He went toward the stairs.

Martha and Diana were putting supper on the table when he came back down. His face was white. He looked at them with tears in his eyes.

"What is it?" Diana asked.

"Oh, no," Martha said. "Oh, no, no."

Diana dropped herself onto a chair, staring at Porter Martin.

"She is gone," he said. "My little angel went to heaven."

Martha was sobbing. Diana rose and held her in her arms. Just then, Brandon Shively came in the back door, holding up four rabbits. One look at the them, and he laid them near the fireplace. He began to remove his coat. "What has happened?" he asked.

Diana looked up at him and said. "Ruth Ann has passed away."

Brandon sighed. "Oh, no. I am so sorry. I really am." He went to the girls and put his arms around them. They both sobbed into his shoulder. He looked up at Porter Martin. He was lowering himself onto a chair. Tears were streaming down his cheeks.

Diana and Martha broke away from Brandon and went upstairs. After awhile, they came back down. Diana asked, "Could we bury her next to Mamma and Pappa?"

Porter nodded and then said, "Yes, but with all of this snow, I am not sure we can do it right away."

Brandon said, "I will do it. Shoveling snow, shoveling dirt, it is all the same to me. Just show me where you want to bury her and I will do all of the digging."

Porter rose and said, "You girls get her ready. I'll take Brandon here and we will go to the cabin. We will dig the grave and come back for her." He began to pull his boots on. He slipped into his coat and hat. Brandon followed him out the back door. Soon, Diana heard two horses riding off toward the cabin.

Diana and Martha carried Ruth Ann down to the kitchen. They laid her on the table. Martha began washing her down. Diana brushed her hair and closed her eyes. Martha got one of her new dresses out of the wooden chest and they dressed her. When they had finished, they pulled up a chair on each side of her, and sat down. It was dark outside.

"What about Sofia?" Martha asked.

"It is too late. By the time we get to Berlin, she will be in bed. I will tell her in the morning when I go into town. She can't do anything anyway," Diana said.

They continued to sit there in silence for another couple of hours. Martha rose occasionally to put more wood on the fire. Soon, they heard the horses coming back.

Porter came in the back door. He was panting. "Brandon's gone for the wagon house. We have a grave dug right next to your Ma," he said. He went to the table and looked down at Ruth Ann. He began to sob. "First my Miss Margaret and now, my little angel," he said through his sobs.

Brandon came in the back door and lifted Ruth Ann's body. Diana held the door for him as he carried her outside. Martha handed her a cowhide wrap and they followed him to the wagon house. Porter pulled the door closed behind them and helped the ladies into the wagon. Then he climbed in and they rode to the cabin for the third time that day.

Tilly and the children were standing on the porch. Brandon drove the wagon to the back of the cabin, pulling up to a stop under the oak tree. He and Porter removed Ruth Ann and placed her gently into the grave. The girls huddled close to one another while Porter and Brandon filled in the grave. Porter said a prayer and they left.

By the time they reached the house, it was very late. Brandon took the rabbits outside to the smoke house. He was still out there when Diana and Martha went to bed. They could hear Porter Martin in his room sobbing and moving about. Diana and Martha both slept holding one another all night. Finally, the sun shining in the window woke them.

Diana jumped up. She would be late picking up the children for school. She dressed and washed her face. Brushing her hair, she let it hang loose as she ran down the stairs. In the kitchen, she found Brandon frying eggs. "Good morning. I wasn't sure if you would be conducting classes today, but I thought I would fix breakfast just in case," he said smiling. "I am so very sorry, Diana."

"Thank you, Brandon. I was going to school. I have to go to town and tell my sister, Sofia, anyway," she said.

"I will get the horses hitched to the wagon," he said. He began putting his coat on, when Martha came into the kitchen.

"I could smell breakfast. It smells good. Are you going to school now?" Martha asked.

"Yes," Diana said. "It will help me keep my mind off of things here. I am worried about Mr. Martin. You look after him today. Okay?"

"I will," Martha said.

Brandon pulled the wagon up to the back door. Diana went out and climbed up into it. As they drove toward the cabin, Diana recalled the night before. The feeling of déjà vu overcame her. Tears streamed down her face. The sun was shining this morning. She covered her eyes with the wrap.

Soon, they had reached the cabin. Brandon got out and went to the door. He presented Tilly with two rabbits and then carried Hoppy and Gilda to the wagon. Homer waded through the snow. When Brandon opened the back door to allow the children to enter, Diana saw the tracks in the snow that the wagon had made the night before. Brandon climbed in after the children and went back to the driver's seat. It was a quiet ride into town.

Brandon picked Thelma up at her house. He drove to the general store. "I will build a fire at the schoolhouse, and then I will come back for you," he said. He lifted Diana down from the wagon and placed her onto the porch. Grace Hickman was standing in the door watching them.

"Well, isn't he the gentleman. He was a soldier, I hear," Grace said. She was trying to pump Diana for information.

Diana brushed past Grace and went inside. "Is Sofia here? I need to talk to her," Diana said.

Grace sighed and batted her eyes. "Oh, Sofia. Yes, well she normally isn't down at this time," she said. She went to the stairs and yelled up to Sofia. "Sofia! Sofia, get up! You have company. Sofia!"

"I'm coming. I'm coming. Who is it?" Sofia called back.

Diana could hear her footsteps on the wooden stairs. She reached the bottom of the stairs. She was still in her nightgown, with a shawl wrapped around her. Her brown hair was messed and hung loose around her shoulders. She stopped when she saw Diana standing by the potbelly stove.

"Di. What do you want? I was just getting dressed," Sofia lied.

Diana took a deep breath and swallowed hard. She stepped closer to Sofia. "Ruth Ann died last night, Sofia," she said.

Sofia's lips quivered. She blinked as the tears formed in her eyes. "From what?" she asked.

"Sofia," Diana began. "You knew she was sick. She has been sick for a long time. I begged you to come out and see her. You were always too busy here at the store. Now, she is gone. We buried her late in the night last night, right next to Mamma."

Sofia turned her back on Diana. "I have been so busy. I really did mean to get out there. I just never found the time. I am so sorry, Diana." Sofia began to cry. Diana went to her and put her arms around her. Sofia threw her arms around Diana's neck and sobbed into her shoulder. Diana heard the wagon house pull up out front. Brandon came into the store.

Upon seeing the girls, he said, "Perhaps, we should cancel classes for today," he said.

Diana looked back at him and shook her head. "No. We will be fine." She pulled away from Sofia. "Are you all right?" she asked.

Sofia nodded her head. "Yes. I am fine. You go now. I have to get dressed." She stepped back and watched Diana as she went outside.

Grace followed her out onto the porch. "I am so very sorry, Miss Lewis," she said.

Brandon lifted Diana from the porch and carried her to the wagon. He climbed inside and tipped his hat to Grace, before pulling the door shut. He drove toward the schoolhouse.

Brandon opened the door and carried Diana inside the school. He put her down near the stove.

"You really don't have to do that," Diana said, blushing.

"It is my pleasure," he said. "I will be back for you at two." Then he winked at the children and left.

It was already getting warm enough inside the building for them to remove their coats and wraps. Diana began by asking, "Who remembers what we learned yesterday about snowflakes?" Homer raised his hand. He looked around and saw that Thelma and Hoppy had their hands raised, too. He began waving his hand high in the air. Diana smiled. "Homer. What do you remember?" she asked.

The day went more quickly than Diana had anticipated. She had brought slices of bread again. Today, she had sprinkled sugar over the butter. The children liked that. It wasn't really nice enough for them to go outside during recess so they played games inside. Soon, she heard the wagon house approaching. She began to bank the fire. Homer rang the bell. Class was dismissed for the day. Tomorrow was Saturday. They would not be back for three days.

Brandon took Thelma home. Diana reminded her that there would be no school until Monday. Then they headed for the cabin. The children were singing the alphabet. Diana knew they were trying to cheer her up. She sang along and smiled. It made the children happy. Brandon sang along, too.

When they arrived at Porter Martin's house, Brandon dropped Diana off at the back door. When she entered, she noticed Mr. Martin's boots and coat were on the chair next to the door. The kitchen was empty. Diana removed her outer garments and went into the front room. Martha was sitting near the fireplace. She looked up at Diana. She had been crying. Diana went to her.

"I am so sorry, Diana. I did not hear you coming. I just can't snap out if it," Martha said.

Diana held her in her arms. She, too, was crying. "It is all right, Martha. We did everything in our power to save her," Diana said through her sobs.

Martha said, "Mr. Martin is upstairs. He is preparing to leave tomorrow for Philadelphia. He said he is going to be gone for a month or more. Something about the railroad. He is so brokenhearted, Diana. The preacher was here earlier today. I know he was trying to help, but he just upset Mr. Martin even more."

Diana shook her head. She was not quite sure how to respond. She heard footsteps coming down the stairs. She looked up in time to see Porter Martin come into the front room. He went to the fireplace and tossed another log on the fire. He stood gazing at the flickering flames.

Diana straightened up. She watched him for a moment. Then she asked, "Mr. Martin. Martha tells me you are going to Philadelphia in the morning? You are going to be gone for some time, she says. May I ask when you will be back?"

Porter stood up and faced the girls. "I will be gone for better n four weeks, I reckon. I need to talk to the railroad people. They ain't bin payin me lately. I thought I might spend some time with James and Thomas. When I come back, I am bringing a wagonload of supplies to build a couple of houses in town. I need windows and such. It will take some time to gather up some of those things. I just feel that I need to get away from here for awhile," he said. He went to Diana and putting his hand on her shoulder, he said, "This place has too many memories. First, my beloved Margaret, and now my little angel. I just need a change of scenery. Don't you fret none, Miss Diana. I am going to ask Brandon to stay on and look after you, girls, and the sawmill. He knows his way around out there pretty good. He is a good lad. Every bit as capable as our James. I trust him," Porter concluded.

Diana smiled and nodded. She could not bring herself to say anything.

Martha stood up and announced that she was going to begin preparing dinner. Diana followed her to the kitchen, leaving Mr. Martin alone with his thoughts.

Brandon came in the back door. He removed his outer garments and asked, "Is Porter in here?"

"Yes," Martha said. "He is in the front room"

Brandon nodded to the sisters and went into the front room. Diana and Martha continued preparing supper. They were having pheasant gravy over biscuits.

Dinner was rather quiet. They all were still mourning over their loss of Ruth Ann. Diana felt so guilty. She felt as though she had let them all down somehow. It was her place to look after them all. She had promised both her parents that she would take care of her sisters. Now the youngest had died. Diana was helpless to prevent it. It made her feel vulnerable. She had been so preoccupied with teaching her students.

Porter turned in early. He was going to town with Brandon in the morning. He was taking the stage to Philadelphia. Brandon sat next to the fire in the front room, staring at the flickering flames, while the girls cleaned up the kitchen. When they had finished, they joined him by the fire.

Martha was sewing another dress. Diana picked up a loom and began doing her needlepoint. The room was quiet. It was Martha who broke the silence. "Mr. Martin said he was going to ask you to stay on, Brandon."

Brandon looked over at her and nodded his head. "Yes, Ma'am. I mean, Martha. Yes, he did ask me to stay on. He has been teaching me all about the sawmill business. I really like helping out. I am not sure I am ready to go off on my own just yet. Porter seems to think I am ready. I just hope I don't let him down. He has been very good to me," Brandon said.

"Do you have somewhere else you need to be?" Diana asked.

"Well, I was going to study to become a lawyer," Brandon began. "Then when Mother asked me to look you up, Diana, I put that on hold. It had always been my dream. Now, I look back on it, and it isn't all that important anymore. Being here and helping Porter to build up that little town, and then helping you with the children, it just seems my priorities have changed." He was smiling at Diana. She smiled back.

Martha asked, "Do you think you might like to stay on here in this small town? We would certainly love to have you."

Brandon was still smiling at Diana. "Yes, I think I might like to stay here. I feel I have a strong connection here."

Martha smiled without looking up from her sewing. Diana felt her cheeks flush as she went back to her needlepoint. After a while, she stood up and stretched her back. "I need to turn in. I want to get up early and fix Mr. Martin a special breakfast in the morning." She put the needlepoint back in the wooden chest and said, "Good night."

"Good night.," Both Martha and Brandon said. Martha was already putting her sewing away. She would be following Diana up to bed. It would not be proper for her to sit up alone with Brandon without a chaperone.

The next morning, Diana was up early. Martha moaned and rolled over. Diana slipped into her dress and brushed her hair. She braided it in a long braid that hung down her back. Then she tiptoed down the stairs.

There was a fire in the front room. She went into the kitchen to find Brandon at the wood stove making coffee. "Good morning, Diana," he said.

"Good morning. I thought I would be the first one up this morning," Diana said.

Brandon laughed. He held the coffee pot up in the air. "Coffee?" he asked.

Diana smiled and said, "I will wait for breakfast." She went to the cupboard and pulled down the crock that contained the flour. "How do pancakes sound?" she asked.

"Sounds terrific," Branded responded. "What are your plans for today?" he asked.

"I was going hunting after I finished cleaning up after breakfast. I have not been out hunting in a while. I always did enjoy being out there in the fresh air," Diana said as she was putting her ingredients in a large bowl.

"If you could wait until I get back from town, I would like to go with you," Brandon said.

Diana stopped mixing and looked up at him. "Of course. But when I go, it is not unusual for me to be gone nearly all day. Are you prepared for that?" she asked, smiling.

"I think I can handle it," Brandon said.

Diana teased. "Well, you better be, because I am not going to carry you home," she smiled.

Brandon smiled back at her. Just then, Porter Martin came into the kitchen. "I smell coffee," he said, smiling. He looked at Diana and back at Brandon. "Did I interrupt something?" he asked.

Diana flushed. Brandon shook his head. "No. Diana was just teasing me." He winked at Diana, and she quickly looked away.

Martha came into the kitchen. "I smell coffee," she said. They all laughed. "What?" she asked.

"It's nothing," Diana said. "We all seem to be smelling the coffee this morning."

"It smells really good," Martha said, looking at the faces in the kitchen. "What are you making there, Di? Pancakes?"

"Yes. That is Mr. Martin's favorite. I thought we would send him off with a full belly. Then, perhaps he will hurry back to us," Diana said.

Porter looked up at Diana and smiled. "I will always come back, Miss Diana. This is my home. This is where my Margaret and my little angel are. I will always come back until the day I go to join them," Porter said.

"Well, I hope that won't be for a very long time," Diana said.

Martha went to Porter and hugged him as he sat in his chair. "We love you, Mr. Martin," she said.

Porter looked up at Martha. He had tears in his eyes. He cleared his throat and said, "You, girls, are my only family now. I love you too. Now, how long before those pancakes are ready?" He was embarrassed.

After breakfast, Porter went upstairs to pack his bag. Brandon went to the barn to hitch up the buggy. He pulled up to the front door. Diana and Martha walked out onto the porch. They watched Porter climb into the buggy. He waved to them as Brandon pulled it around and went toward Berlin.

The sisters went back inside. Martha put another log on the fire in the front room. Diana went directly to the kitchen to begin cleaning up. Martha joined her. Diana began to hum as she worked. Martha smiled. "Aren't we in a good mood this morning?" she asked.

Diana smiled and replied. "I am going hunting after I finish cleaning up in here. You know I haven't been out there in some time. I miss it."

"Oh, Di. I can handle this. You go ahead and go. Get out there early," Martha said.

Diana looked over at Martha and said, "Oh, no, Martha. I have to wait for Brandon to get back. He is going with me."

"Oh, I see. It isn't the hunting that has you feeling so gay after all. It is the company," Martha teased.

Diana flushed. "Martha, I was so relieved to hear him say he was happy here, and he thought he might stay. I hope it doesn't show."

Martha laughed again. "Oh, it shows all right. On both of your faces. I think he has very strong feelings for you, Diana."

"Do you really think so?" Diana asked.

Martha nodded her head. They both began singing as they worked in the kitchen. When they had finished, Martha began pumping water to put on the stove. She was going to do the washing. Diana started helping her. She went upstairs to strip the beds. When she came back down, she strung a line across the kitchen to hang the laundry on. They were nearly finished when they saw the buggy coming back to the barn.

"You go get ready. I can finish this," Martha said.

Diana began to wrap her legs and feet with the smaller hides they had collected. She put her wrap around her and tied it at the waist. She smiled at Martha as she stepped outside the back door. She met Brandon coming from the barn leading two horses.

They walked behind the orchard, into the forest. They continued walking silently for some way. Then they separated, keeping one another in sight. Diana climbed a tree. Brandon watched her as she went about half way up a sugar maple. He looked around until he found a tree he could climb. He followed her lead. They waved to one another and wedged themselves in tight so they could free their hands. Brandon had a rifle. Diana had a bow.

They sat there for some time. The horses were tied just within sight. It was quiet. Soon, they heard a rustling in the underbrush. It was a deer. Diana drew her bow. Brandon took aim, but hesitated. Diana let the bow go and the arrow struck the deer. It turned and bolted. Brandon pulled the trigger and the gun cracked loudly, echoing through the forest. They both began to scramble down from their trees. They ran in the direction the deer had gone. They found it lying on the ground. It was dead. Diana pulled her buck knife from her strap that was tied to her leg. She cut the deer. Once they were finished with the deer, Brandon went for the horses. He lifted the deer over the back of Buckley and tied it securely. They started back toward the house.

The wind blew softly. The trees swayed to and fro. The air was feeling warmer. "Spring will be here soon," Brandon said softly. Diana nodded and remained silent. As they were just about at the forest edge, they heard another noise to their right. It was a wild boar. It had stopped and was looking right at them. It turned to run. Brandon pulled his rifle to his shoulder and fired. The boar squealed. Brandon ran toward it. Diana held the horses. She heard the gun go off again. She waited.

"I got it!" Brandon called. Diana led the horses in the direction of his voice. She found him kneeling over the boar. "He is a big one!" Brandon said. He pulled his knife and gutted the boar. "We will have bacon when Porter gets back."

They started again for the house. Once they reached the smoke house, they carried their kills inside and hung them. Diana began to skin the deer. Brandon was working on the pig. They worked together.

Diana asked, "Could we take some of this to Tilly?"

Brandon looked up at her and smiled. "Of course," he said. "We will have some dinner and then I will load up the wagon. Do we need the hides?"

Diana thought for a moment. "We could always use the hides, but they need them more," she said. It was decided. They finished up and went into the house.

The kitchen was a mass of linens hanging from the line that stretched back and forth across it. Martha sat by the fire. She was drinking a cup of tea. She looked up at them as they entered. "Did you get anything?" she asked.

"Oh, yes! We got a deer and a boar," Diana said.

Martha stood up. "Oh, very good! What will it be for supper?"

Diana smiled as she poured two cups of tea. She handed one to Brandon. "I think we should let Brandon decide. He did most of the work today."

Brandon laughed. "It doesn't matter what we have. You girls would make an old shoe taste good," he said.

They drank their tea. After warming up, Diana turned to Martha and said, "We are taking some of the meat to Tilly. Do you have anything you want to send along?"

Martha nodded. She went into the front room and returned with a dress. "This is for Tilly. Tell her it is for church," Martha said.

Diana held the dress up. "Oh, Martha! This is very nice. She will be so happy. I would be happy to wear such a dress myself," Diana said.

"Good," Martha said, "because I am nearly finished with one almost like it for you."

Diana hugged Martha. "Thank you, Martha!" she said.

Martha smiled and nodded her head as she said, "You are welcome, Diana."

Diana began to wrap up again to go back outside. Brandon went to the smoke house for some meat to put in the wagon. Diana wrapped the dress in the same paper the fabric came wrapped in when Porter brought it from Philadelphia. She smiled at Martha. "When I get back, I will help you make up the beds and iron the clothes."

Martha waved her on. "It gives me something to do," she said, smiling.

Diana climbed up into the wagon alongside Brandon. He turned the horse toward the shallow crossing. The ice had melted. The water was clear. Spring was on its way. There was just a light ground cover of snow that covered the ground. The wheels of the wagon left muddy tracks as they made their way to the cabin. Hoppy met them at the door, followed by the rest of them.

Tilly smiled at the sight of them. She invited them in. Brandon carried the meat into the kitchen. Tilly stood smiling, with her hands over her mouth. "Misser Shively! You is too good to us. Thank you so much!" she said.

Brandon smiled. "You are very welcome, Tilly."

Diana held out the dress that was wrapped in paper. "Martha sent you a present, Tilly."

Tilly took the gift. She unwrapped it and held the dress up. Her eyes opened wide in surprise.

"It is to wear to church tomorrow, Tilly," Diana explained.

Tilly sighed as tears filled her eyes. "I ain't never had a new dress all my own afore. It is a pretty un too. You be sure to thank Miss Martha for Tilly," she said.

The children all felt the fabric. Tilly held it up to her and showed them. "I will look like a grand lady at church tomarra!" Tilly said.

"Yes, you will, indeed. I can't wait to see you in it," Brandon said. "You be ready in the morning. I will pick you up, and we will go to church in style."

"Don't forget dinner, too," Diana said.

"Mr. Martin has been so good to us," Tilly said.

Diana said. "Mr. Martin is going to be in Philadelphia for a while. But we will carry on as usual until he gets back."

"Mr. Martin will be missed," Tilly said.

Brandon and Diana went back outside and climbed up into the wagon. They followed the muddy tracks back to the shallow stream. As they crossed, Brandon asked, "I have to go back into Berlin to the store. Would you like to ride along?"

Diana smiled. "I really should help Martha with the washing. I would like to go with you, though. I suppose I could make it up to Martha when I get back," she said.

"I think maybe we could pick up something at the store for her. We will look around for something really special. I ordered something, and it should have come in on the stage. I would like to see if it made it," Brandon said.

Diana smiled. "All right. I would love to accompany you to town," she said.

Brandon continued past the Martin house and on toward Berlin. The sun was nearly blinding against the white snow. Diana pulled her bonnet down over her eyes to shield herself from the glare.

As they approached the town, Diana heard the familiar sound of pounding. There was another building being built across the street from the general store. "What are they building now?" she asked.

"That is to be a dress shop for Martha. Over there is another building. It is to be the blacksmith's shop. Porter said he was bringing a blacksmith from Quincy to settle here. They already have one in Quincy. He is hoping this town will grow to be even bigger than Quincy. Grace and Sherman may have to build a bigger general store. Porter wants to build a hotel for the visitors that come by stage. He is building it right beside Martha's dress shop. That is coming next," Brandon said.

Diana smiled. "I am not so sure I want it to grow bigger than Quincy. In fact, I am not so sure I want it to grow at all. I kind of like it the way it is," Diana said, looking around.

"Diana, you need pupils for your school. Growing is a good thing. Sometimes, changes have a way of making us feel anxious and unnerved. But in the end, it all works out," Brandon said, smiling at her. He pulled the wagon up to the general store. He climbed out and helped Diana down.

Grace Hickman met them at the door. "Good morning, Miss Lewis. Good morning, Mr. Shively. How are you this morning? Did you come for your crate?" she asked.

Brandon nodded. "Yes, Ma'am," he said.

"Sherman! Sherman, Mr. Shively is here to collect his crate. Sherman! Do you hear me?" Grace called out.

Sherman appeared through the curtain. "Hello, Mr. Shively. I have your crate out front. It was too heavy to bring inside. I'll get Stumpy to help us load it into the back of the buggy," Sherman said. He disappeared out the front door. Diana walked around the store looking at the new items Grace had stocked. She fingered through some fabric. It was not as nice as the fabric Mr. Martin brought from Philadelphia, but it was good cotton. The prints were all small, but neat. She pulled a bright purple bolt of fabric from the pile, and placed it on the counter.

"I will need some thread too, please," she said to Grace Hickman.

Grace turned and placed a spool of thread on the counter. She was looking at Diana over her glasses. "I hear your sister is quite the seamstress. I may have her make a dress or two for Concetta and me. Perhaps we could work out some sort of trade for goods from the store," Grace said.

Diana smiled. "That is business you will have to take up with Martha," she said.

Grace had a disappointed look on her face. "She doesn't come to town much, that sister of yours. She was always nursing your sick sister. I hear that Mr. Martin is building a shop for her. I suppose we will be seein' more of her around town now that your sister has passed away," Grace said.

Diana looked up at Grace and frowned. She did not respond to the remarks. She continued to look around. Soon, Brandon came back inside and announced that he was loaded and ready to leave.

Diana turned to Grace Hickman and said, "Tell Sofia I am sorry I missed her."

Grace cleared her throat, and said. "Sofia, yes, well she is off somewhere with that preacher. They have been spending a lot of time together these days."

Diana detected a note of hostility in Grace's voice. She suspected that Grace was pouting because she expected Sofia to wait for Burt to return. She smiled and nodded at Mrs. Hickman before leaving the store.

Stumpy rode his horse behind them to the farm. He was going to help Brandon unload the crate. Diana wondered what was inside, but since Brandon did not offer any information, she decided not to mention it. She knew she would find out soon enough.

They arrived at the Martin house. Brandon drove to the back door. He helped Diana down. Stumpy helped Brandon lift the crate next to the back door. Diana went inside and removed her wrap. She gave Martha the fabric. Martha was excited. She said she was going to make Hoppy a dress from it, and if there was enough fabric, she would make one for Gilda, too. Diana was glad she had purchased the fabric. She decided not to mention the dress shop to Martha. It may be a surprise from Mr. Martin, much the same as the schoolhouse was a surprise for Diana.

She heard banging at the back door. She opened it. Brandon and Stumpy carried a large copper bathtub into the kitchen. "Where would you ladies like your bath?" he asked.

Martha squealed with delight. "A bath! Oh, Brandon! A real bath!" she said.

Diana was speechless. Suddenly, she realized they were waiting for instructions. She said, "This is the warmest room in the house. I suppose you could put it over there," she said, pointing to the corner next to the fireplace. They carried it over to the corner. Brandon looked to her for her approval.

Diana nodded and said, "That is perfect. Thank you so much. I do not know what to say." Then she turned to Stumpy. "Thank you so much, Stumpy, for riding out here and helping Mr. Shively bring this in. Could I get you something? Perhaps a cup of coffee and a slice of toast?"

"What is this Mr Shively?" Brandon teased.

Diana blushed again. Stumpy smiled and tipped his hat. "That would be real nice of you Ma'am," he said.

Diana began to prepare Stumpy's toast. Martha poured him a cup of coffee. "I apologize for the laundry, Mr. Morgan," Martha said.

Stumpy looked up and smiled. "Ma'am, you might as well call me Stumpy. Everyone else does. I take no offence by it. To tell you the truth, I am so used to it, I don't hardly notice it at all anymore," Stumpy said.

Martha smiled. "You have been very good to us, Stumpy. Mr. Martin relies on you very much. We are very grateful to you," she said.

Stumpy took a sip of his hot coffee and replied. "Thank you for sayin' so, Miss Martha. But to tell you the truth, there isn't much need for me in town. Just on the days when the stage is comin' in. Sherman calls on me sometimes when he has some heavy liftin' to do, but he don't pay me nothin'. Mr. Martin pays me to work in the mill. He is easy to work for, too." Then he leaned over and said softly, "And I don't have to put up with that snooty old Mrs. Hickman when I am out here."

They all laughed. "Well, we will keep that amongst us," Diana said.

Brandon and Stumpy left. They were putting the team and wagon away. Then they would be working in the mill for the rest of the day. Diana helped Martha put the sheets back on the beds and they began to iron their dresses for church tomorrow. The time went quickly. The girls were in better spirits. Tonight, they would take a bath in a real bathtub.

After dinner that evening, they pumped water to fill the tub. It was decided that Martha would have the first bath, as she did most of the work that day. Diana followed, and Brandon was last. They emptied the tub. Diana rinsed it out and polished it until the copper looked new again. She stepped back to look upon it. It was the grandest tub she had ever seen.

They went to bed early. Tomorrow was Sunday. They would collect Tilly and the children, then go to church. After church, they would have a dinner at the Martin house, all together. It had become a tradition. Diana fell asleep with thoughts of Robert Shively. At times, she tried to recall Robert, but Brandon's face kept coming to mind. She wondered what Robert would think about her feelings for his brother. It was with those thoughts that she finally fell asleep.

The next morning, they were up, dressed, and eating breakfast early. They were anxious to go to church. It was a social day for them. It was the only day Martha left the house. That would be changing soon. Diana was anxious to see Tilly in her new dress. They loaded up the wagon house with wraps, and were on their way.

Tilly and the children were waiting. The dress Martha had made for Tilly was a perfect fit. She had her hair in tight braids pulled around her head and fastened at the top. The children were scrubbed and they wore clean clothes. They piled into the wagon house and were off toward Berlin. "Soon, we will have to put this away for the summer," Brandon called back to them.

Diana smiled. She loved the summer. She looked over at Tilly. She was smiling. She could not stop running her hands over her new dress. She smiled all the way to town.

When they arrived at the church, Brandon helped them each down out of the wagon house. They entered the church. They filed down the aisles to the front of the church. Tilly followed them. She was not sitting in the back today.

Inside the church, Grace and Sherman Hickman sat in the front pew on the left with Concetta and Sofia. Zachariah Dillon, Marcus O'Hara, and Stumpy sat in the front pew on the right. Diana, Martha, and Brandon sat down in the second pew on the right. Tilly and her four children sat directly behind them. Diana noticed Grace Hickman turn and look at them. The look of shock came over her face to see Tilly and her children sitting near the front of the church. Diana tried her best not to smile. She nodded at Grace and folded her hands in her lap.

Parson Gilbert smiled down at all of them. They began to sing, "What a friend we have in Jesus." Tilly and her children did not know the hymn. They stood silently until the singing stopped. Parson Gilbert said a prayer and everyone sat down. Again, Grace Hickman turned, giving Tilly a dirty look. Parson Gilbert began his sermon. He preached about the love for thy brother. He told the story of Cain and Abel. They sat, listening intently. Then they rose to sing another song. Parson Gilbert said one final prayer and walked to the back of the church where he greeted everyone as they exited the church.

Tilly and her children were the last to leave. Brandon stood outside talking to Sherman and Marcus O'Hara. Grace approached Diana and Martha who were waiting to speak with Sofia.

"I do not believe it is proper for the Negroes to be here at all, but if they must come to church, would you please ask them to sit in the back?" Grace said, fidgeting with her hat.

"I will not. And neither will Martha," Diana said. "Tilly and her children are no less children of God than any of us."

Grace turned and marched toward the preacher. Diana knew she was going to give him a good piece of her mind. She was watching him as Grace began whispering in his ear. Soon, she marched off toward the general store. It was apparent that she did not like his response. Diana smiled at the parson. He nodded in her direction.

Diana approached Sofia, who was standing next to the parson. "Sofia, I missed you at the store yesterday. I was hoping for a chance to speak with you," Diana said.

Sofia smiled politely and said, "Grace told me Brandon bought you a bathtub. That was very nice of him."

Diana smiled. "Yes, it was. We all used it last night." She noticed that Sofia was watching Tilly and her children as they climbed into the wagon house.

Diana said, "Sofia, I do hope you do not share Grace Hickman's animosity toward Tilly and the children."

Sofia looked at Diana. Shaking her head, she replied. "I do not. They are welcome in the house of God."

Diana smiled. There was something about Sofia today. Something reserved. "Sofia, I would like to invite you to Mr. Martin's house for dinner today. Won't you come? It would be so nice to have the whole family together at the table again," Diana asked.

"Jonathan and I have no plans as I know of," Sofia said with her nose in the air.

Diana sighed. She tried to restrain from slapping Sofia. She was becoming very agitated. She smiled and said, "Please, invite Jonathan to dinner also. We would be pleased to have him."

Sofia looked Diana in the eye and announced. "Jonathan and I are getting married soon. Porter Martin is going to build us a house. Just so you know."

"Well, how nice, Sofia. I am very happy for you. Please know that I am most sincere. This is very good news. Dinner today will be a celebration. Now, you really must come. We will make it a special celebration in your honor," Diana said.

Sofia studied Diana's face. She frowned. "You are not angry?" she asked.

"Why would I be angry, Sofia? I have always wanted the best for you. You must know that I never meant to turn you away. You were the one who wanted to leave. Those were very difficult times for all of us. They are over now. Through all that has happened to us, we are still a family. We love you, Sofia," Diana said. She reached for Sofia's hand.

Sofia looked at Diana with tears in her eyes. "Thank you, Diana. I am so sorry. Please, I don't want to be angry anymore. I want us to be sisters again," she cried.

Diana embraced Sofia. She said, "We were always sisters, Sofia."

Sofia pulled away, "Please, come with me. I want to ask Jonathan about dinner." She pulled Diana by the hand. They went to Jonathan, who was speaking with Brandon.

Sofia took Jonathan's hand, "Jonathan, Diana has invited us to dinner today. I told her about our upcoming marriage, and she wants to celebrate it today. Could we go?" she asked.

Jonathan laughed. "Of course, we could go. It would be my pleasure." He smiled at Diana.

"Well, in that case, I better get these ladies home so they can start on dinner. I will see you there later, Parson," Brandon said.

They piled into the wagon house and headed toward the Martin farm.

Tilly helped Martha and Diana prepare the meal. It was decided that they would have ham for dinner. Tilly sang as she worked. She was right at home in the Martin kitchen. Diana and Martha proceeded to teach her the hymns that were sung in church. The children gathered around the fireplace listening. Soon they were all singing happily.

Sofia and Jonathan arrived before dinner was prepared. Sofia began to help in the kitchen and Brandon took Jonathan to the mill to show him around. It was a wonderful day. Diana did not tell Martha the news of Sofia's upcoming marriage. She allowed Sofia to tell her. Martha was ecstatic. She pulled Sofia into the front room and began going through her bolts of fabric. It was decided that Martha would make Sofia a wedding dress. It was like old times.

When they sat to eat dinner, the kitchen was full. Tilly and three of her children filled one side of the table. Brandon and Parson Gilbert sat at the ends. Sofia, Martha, Diana, and Hoppy sat on the other side. Blessing was said. Diana felt happy. She looked around the table. The only one missing was Porter Martin. This was a happy day indeed. She wished he could have been there to celebrate with them. She hoped that he knew he was missed.

After dinner, Brandon and Jonathan retired into the front room to smoke by the fire. The girls cleared the table and washed the dishes. Diana wrapped some of the leftovers and placed them in a basket for Tilly to take home. Tomorrow was a school day. She set aside some extra ham to make sandwiches for the children. The girls poured a cup of tea for themselves and sat around the table. Homer climbed inside the bathtub and fell asleep. The little girls played on the floor in front of the fire.

It was sometime before Jonathan announced that they should be heading back to town. Sofia promised that they would be back. She hugged Martha and Diana before leaving. Diana and Martha stood on the front porch waving at them as they rode their horses back to Berlin.

Brandon went to the barn. He was going to hitch up the wagon house and bring it to the back door for Tilly and the children. They were preparing to leave. Tilly woke Homer who was still sleeping in the bath tub.

Martha said to Diana, "You ride along with Brandon, Di. I am tired. I think I will go up and read my Bible for awhile."

Diana smiled and pulled her wrap around her. She hugged Martha. "Thank you," she whispered in her ear. She climbed into the back of the wagon house. They sang all the way to the log cabin. Diana had a happy heart. There was nothing that could happen to make this an even more perfect day. Or so she thought.

They dropped Tilly and the children off. Brandon went inside and started a fire for them. He helped Homer bring in enough wood to get them through the night and most of the next day. Then Diana and Brandon got back into the wagon house and headed back to Porter Martin's house.

After they breached the knob and rounded the bend, Brandon said to Diana. "I was pleased to hear about Sofia's engagement to the parson. They seem to be happy."

Diana smiled. "Yes, they do. Sofia is a beautiful young woman. I was so worried that she would never find the right man in a small town like Berlin. But she has, and they seem to be very happy indeed," she replied.

Brandon looked at Diana. "What about you, Diana? Are you happy?" he asked.

"Oh, yes, I am!" she said, smiling up at him.

Brandon was quiet for a time. Then he asked, "Diana, do you still have feelings for Robert?"

"Robert?" she asked. "I think I will always remember Robert, Brandon. There really wasn't all that much between us. I had hopes that there would be, but when I think about it, he just promised to write and said he would call on me after the war. We really did not know each other that well. We were only together for a day and a night," she said. Then she blushed. "By a night I did not mean to imply that we were together all night. He slept with his men and me with my sisters, I mean."

Brandon laughed. "I know what you mean." He laughed again. Then he asked, "Do you suppose you could have feelings for me? Would it be presumptuous of me to expect more of our relationship?" he asked.

Diana looked up at him. Her mouth was hanging open. She said, "I do not know what to say. I mean, Brandon, I am not sure what you are asking of me."

Brandon stopped the horses. He reached for Diana and she yielded to his embrace. They kissed tenderly. "I love you, Diana. Robert was right. You are an amazing woman. I can see that. I can't imagine life without you. I am asking you to marry me. Be my wife, Diana. Share in my life," Brandon said, looking down at her.

Diana felt herself melting into his arms. She opened her eyes and gazed up at him. She smiled and said. "I love you, too, Brandon. I have loved you since the moment I met you. I will always love you. And, yes, I will be your wife. I would be happy to be your wife."

They kissed again, long and tenderly. The horses were becoming restless, standing in the night. Brandon pulled away from Diana and urged them on. "As soon as Porter Martin gets back, we will announce our engagement," he said.

Diana reached out and touched his arm. "Oh, Brandon. Please, can't we wait until after Sofia and Jonathan get married? I do not want to take anything from her. She is so happy. Would you mind terribly?" she asked.

Brandon looked over at her and smiled. "My Diana. Always thinking of others first. If that is what you want. However, I do not want to wait too long."

Diana said, "I promise. I want to tell Martha, but only Martha. She will need to make my dress. Then as soon as Sofia is married, we can announce it to the world."

They held each other all the way back to Porter Martin's house. Brandon dropped Diana off at the back door. He took the team on to the barn. Diana went into the kitchen. It was quiet. She put a log on the fire and went upstairs. Martha was asleep. Diana felt disappointed. She wanted so much to tell her sister the news. It would have to keep until after school tomorrow. She could not sleep that night. She was the happiest she had ever been in her entire life.

The next morning was a rainy morning. March winds blew across the open fields. The daffodils were popping up near the edge of the forest. Spring was here. Diana sang as she prepared breakfast.

Martha laughed. "You are in a gay mood this morning," she said.

Diana nodded and continued to sing. Brandon came downstairs. He entered the kitchen with a smile on his face. All through breakfast, he stole looks at Diana. They smiled at one another. Then Brandon went to get the wagon house. It was time to go to school. Diana proceeded to pack a basket with ham and bread for the children's lunches.

"Okay. I can't stand it anymore," Martha said. "Did I miss something?" she asked.

Diana looked back at her from the window, where she was watching for Brandon. "Oh, Martha. I was going to tell you after I got home from school, but I can't wait any longer. Brandon proposed to me last night. We are going to get married. You need to make two wedding dresses," she blurted out excitedly.

Martha rushed to Diana's side. She took Diana's hands and squeezing them tightly, she said. "Oh, Di! How wonderful! I just knew it was coming. A blind person could see the two of you love each other. I am so very happy for you. When? When? Tell me when."

Diana laughed. Brandon was pulling up at the back door. "Not until after Sofia's wedding. Please don't say anything to anyone. Not yet. I must go. He is waiting. Please, Martha, I will explain later." She kissed her sister on the cheek and rushed out the back door.

Martha watched her go. She went to the front room and watched until they were out of sight.

Diana smiled up at Brandon. He looked down upon her face, smiling back at her. They rode on toward the cabin. The daffodils were up but, had not bloomed yet. It would not be long.

Tilly and the children were waiting. They piled into the wagon house and chattered on for some time as they went the familiar trail to Berlin. Diana did not hear a word they were saying. She could not stop smiling. Soon, they reached the Faulk house. Thelma came out. Diana made room for her in the wagon house, and Brandon drove the team on. They were, at last, at the school.

Brandon held the door for the children. He built a fire while Homer rang the bell. Diana erased the blackboard. Brandon said good-bye to the children and left.

Diana printed a sentence on the blackboard. "Who wants to read first this morning?" she asked. All of the children raised their hands. "Gilda, you go first. Then I want you to come up and write a sentence of your own." Gilda had a nervous look on her face. "It's all right, Gilda. If you get it wrong, we will just make it right. Someone else will read your sentence and then they will write one of their own. So forth, and so on, until everyone has a turn," Diana explained.

It had started to rain. The sky was dark, making it even darker inside the school. Diana lit candles. It wasn't long before it began to thunder and lightning. Gilda shrieked each time the lightning flashed and the thunder boomed. Diana thought it was a good time to explain some good things about thunder and lightning.

"Thunderstorms nourish the earth. It feeds the plants and stirs them from their long winter's nap," Diana was saying, when she saw Brandon coming down the hill toward the school. He had removed the planks that formed the runners and replaced them with wheels. Diana banked the fire in the stove and asked Hoppy to erase the board. Homer stood inside the door and rang the bell. Brandon pulled close to the door and helped the children inside the wagon house.

"The creek is getting pretty high. It has been pouring all day. I haven't gotten anything done at the mill. I worked on the wagon all day," he said to Diana as he loaded the children in the back.

They dropped Thelma off and started for the cabin. By the time they reached the shallow crossing, it was not shallow at all. The water was flowing rapidly. Brandon hesitated before urging the team onward, across the stream.

When they reached the knob, they could see that the stream has risen behind the cabin. It was almost up to the three graves under the large oak tree. Diana gasped. Brandon reached for her hand. "Don't worry, Diana. It will stop soon and the water will recede," he said.

"I do not recall a time when the water was ever up that high before," Diana said.

They unloaded the children and left right away. Brandon wanted to make sure he could get back across the stream. It finally stopped storming, leaving them to deal with a light drizzle. The stream was still rushing rapidly when they reached it. Brandon hesitated again before crossing. They made it safely. He looked at Diana and shook his head once they reached the other side. He dropped her off at the back door and urged the team toward the barn.

Martha was waiting for her. She had a pot of tea prepared. Two chairs were sitting near the fireplace. Diana removed her wrap and sat down. She was fairly dry, but chilled.

"Diana, I have been waiting all day for you to return. I want to know more about our conversation this morning. Hurry, please, before Brandon comes in," Martha said.

Diana smiled. "Well, Brandon asked me to marry him, as I have already told you. And, of course, I said yes," Diana said smiling at her sister. "We decided to wait until after Sofia's wedding. It is going to be our little secret. I do not want to take any of the excitement away from Sofia. She deserves to have her special time. Mine will come. That is why I have asked you not to say anything to anyone just yet," Diana explained.

Martha listened intently and nodded. "All right. I understand. Diana, you have always put everyone else before yourself. Even when we were small children. You deserve to have something really special. I am going to make you the most beautiful wedding dress anyone has ever had," Martha said.

Just then, Brandon came in the back door. Martha poured him a cup of tea. He stood next to the fireplace to take the chill off himself. Diana announced that they would begin preparing dinner. He moved into the front room to smoke his pipe.

The days went by, and spring was upon them. Leaves were beginning to open up on the trees. Martha had finished Sofia's wedding dress. It was beautiful. Sofia was very happy with it.

A man arrived on the stage from Massachusetts. He was a British captain of the navy. He was a friend of Pastor Gilbert. He was going to perform the wedding ceremony. Porter had returned. He had three wagons of supplies. Once again, Thomas returned with him. He shared the bedroom with Brandon.

The day of the wedding arrived. The whole town was at the church. Porter Martin was to give Sofia away. Concetta had picked fresh flowers so Sofia would have a bouquet to carry down the aisle. Sofia never looked more beautiful.

It was a warm day. Diana fanned herself in the church. She noticed that Concetta had a shawl pulled around her. Diana wondered how she could tolerate such heat. When they all stood up, as Sofia came down the aisle, she saw why. Concetta's belly protruded under her dress in a mound. She was pregnant. Concetta noticed that Diana was looking at her. She adjusted her shawl and lowered her head. Diana tried not to stare. She looked over at Sofia and held her gaze there. Throughout the ceremony, Concetta stole a look Diana's way, from time to time.

After the ceremony, Grace whispered to Concetta. They seem to argue some and Concetta rushed toward the general store in tears. Grace fluttered about like a peacock. She fussed over Sofia as if she were her mother. Sofia was so happy, she did not notice. Diana waited for the right opportunity to get Sofia to herself.

"Tell me, Sofia, where are you and the parson going to live?" Diana asked.

Sofia smiled. "With Marcus. That is, until Porter Martin gets our house finished. He brought the windows back with him, so it should not be long now. Just wait until you see it, Diana. It has two bedrooms. Jonathan and I are going to have lots of children. We are going to fill your schoolhouse," she said, laughing.

Diana laughed, too. Martha joined them. They talked about what a beautiful dress Martha had made for Sofia. Then Martha asked.

"Sofia, I could not help but notice, well, Concetta, she is pregnant. She looks like she will be due in a couple of months.," Martha said.

Sofia leaned close and whispered, "It was that actor. That dreadful Gwain Brewster. He promised Connie he would come back for her. She believed him. Grace is trying to hide it from the town. Although I do not know what she thinks she is going to do when the baby comes."

They all looked in Grace Hickman's direction. She caught sight of their gazes and flushed. She puffed herself up and marched straight for them.

"Well, well. Look here. All three of the Lewis girls. That is something you don't see often. Tell me, when are you two old maids going to get married?" she seethed.

Martha's face reddened. Diana looked Grace in the eye and smiled. She said nothing. After all, her mother had always told her there was no excuse for rudeness. Rude people were to be pitied.

"What are you now, Diana? Twenty-five?" Grace asked. "A little late for marriage now, don't you think? Of course, there is always that Brandon Shively. I suppose if you hurry, you might have a couple of children before it is too late."

Diana felt a lump come up into her throat. She struggled to maintain her composure. She smiled at Grace and replied. "I am twenty-four years old, Mrs. Hickman." She decided not to say anymore for fear she may lose control.

Grace turned to Martha. "And what about you, Dear? How old are you now?"

Martha looked over at Diana. Her face was still red. Then she drew in a deep breath and said. "I am one year younger than Concetta, Mrs. Hickman."

Grace blinked. She was speechless. She threw her nose into the air and marched toward the general store.

The three sisters began to chuckle. Soon, Jonathan and the British Naval captain, Oliver Broderick, joined them. Sofia introduced the captain to her sisters.

Diana invited them all to the Martin house for dinner. It was agreed that they would celebrate the wedding there. They hurried back to the house to begin preparing the meal. Tilly and her children helped. They were having a ham dinner.

After dinner, Porter went upstairs and returned with his fiddle. Stumpy played his banjo. They formed a large circle around Sofia and Parson Gilbert and watched them dance.

Soon, they were all dancing. Brandon and Diana twirled around the room several times. Soon, Sofia and Jonathan were dancing beside them.

"When do you think the next wedding will be?" Sofia called to Diana.

Diana flushed. Brandon threw his head back. "Soon. Very soon," he said.

Sofia's mouth dropped open. "Oh, my! Di, I had no idea!"

Diana smiled at Sofia. "Let us just enjoy this one for now," she said.

Brandon and Diana began to twirl their way further around the room. Zachariah danced with Martha and Thomas danced with Hoppy. Tilly danced with Homer while Gilda and Percy swung each other around in circles. Everyone was laughing and having a good time. Sherman Hickman banged a spoon against a pan. Grace said Concetta had a headache and she was staying home with her. She wasn't missed much. Diana was grateful that Grace Hickman was not at the house. She would not be able to relax, wondering whether she might be nosing about. They were having a good time without her.

Soon, the sun began to go down. Thomas took Tilly and her children home. The townspeople left to go back to Berlin. The stage would be coming in tomorrow. The captain and Thomas would be leaving, and everything would be normal again, with the exception of the newlyweds living with Marcus O'Hara. It would be Saturday. There was no school.

Brandon helped the girls put the kitchen back in order. Porter had gone to bed. He had drunk too much; he was most likely passed out on his bed by now. Martha excused herself and went upstairs. Brandon and Diana were alone.

Brandon took Diana's hand and pulled her over near the fireplace. Blackie and Brownie were sleeping on the floor. He opened the door and chased them outside. He took her hand once more and pulled her to him. "I am so sorry, Diana. I hope I did not let the cat out of the bag tonight. I mean, I know you wanted to wait to tell everyone, but I just couldn't keep it to myself any longer. I don't want to wait much longer either," he said.

"Oh, Brandon," she said looking up into his eyes. "We have so many plans to make. Where will we live?" she asked.

Brandon smiled. "I have been talking to Porter. He wants us to stay here. He said he would build us a house not far from here. Between here and Berlin. What do you think?" he asked.

Diana pondered for a moment on what Brandon had just told her. "Does Porter want us to leave? Couldn't we just stay here? I like it here," she said.

Brandon smiled. "Oh, Diana. You certainly don't like change much do you? Well, as a matter of fact, he did ask me to stay on here. The house was just an option to make sure I did not take you back to Boston."

"I like it here, Brandon. This is my real home. I have always wanted to live here. I know it gets crowded at times, but that is what I like about it most of all. I like the closeness of a family. I was always surrounded with a big family. Then Josie left and Mamma and Pappa died. Then Regina left. Then...." Brandon stopped Diana by putting his finger over her lips.

"Shh. I understand, Diana. We will have a big family of our own, someday. If you want to stay here, we will. If we outgrow this house, which I intend on doing, we will build another house." Brandon kissed her.

Diana melted into his arms. "Oh, Brandon, I really must go upstairs. It isn't proper for us to be down here alone. Soon, we will have all the time in the world to be together," she said. He kissed her again.

"You go on up. I will take care of the fireplaces. Thomas will be coming back soon. I will wait and help him put the horses away," Brandon said.

Diana smiled. She kissed Brandon tenderly on the cheek. She went up the stairs, smiling. She could hear Martha breathing steadily. She had fallen asleep quickly. Diana knew she was exhausted from the day. She undressed and slipped into her nightdress. She crawled into what used to be Ruth Ann's bed. She lay there for a long time. She heard Thomas arrive. She heard Brandon go out the back door. Then she fell asleep.

Sunday morning was a busy morning. Porter had a bad headache, he was not going to church. He moped around until breakfast was over. Then he decided that it was not proper to miss church because of his drinking the night before, so he dressed quickly and rode along to collect Tilly and the children. This morning, the sun shone brightly. It was a warm morning, so Porter decided they would take an open wagon to church. He put some wooden crates in the back of the wagon to serve as seats. It was a beautiful morning for a ride to church.

Once they arrived in town, they gathered outside to greet one another as each person arrived. Grace and Sherman Hickman arrived just before the parson went inside. Concetta walked behind them. She did not wear a shawl. Apparently, there was no use in trying to hide it anymore. The whole town knew anyway. This morning, Sofia sat next to Porter Martin. Grace seemed insulted and kept to herself. Diana figured that was a good thing.

The parson began with a prayer. They all joined in singing a hymn. Then the parson thanked everyone for their contribution to his wedding and the reception which followed at the Martin home. His sermon was about the love God has for his people. He emphasized the fact that he loved all people regardless of color. From where Diana sat, she could see Grace Hickman's neck turning a bright red. They sang another hymn and finished with a prayer. The preacher met them all at the door as they filed out into the spring morning air.

Grace was rather quiet. She politely spoke to each of them, avoiding Martha. Martha looked over at Diana and smiled as Grace walked right by her with her nose in the air. Tilly was all smiles. They piled into the wagon and began their journey toward the Martin house. It was Sunday, a day of family and friends around Porter Martin's kitchen table.

Another two weeks went by. Porter had taken Martha into town and showed her around her new dress shop. It was attached to a small three-room house. Martha was pleased with the shop, but in her heart, she did not want to leave the Martin house. Porter said, "Now, Miss Martha, I do not want you to think you are not welcome in my home, for you certainly are. This is, more or less, just so you are not sittin' in that little shop all day. You have your kitchen to fix yourself somethin' to eat, and if you happen to work late, well, you have a place to sleep," he announced with a smile. This seemed to please Martha. She was still welcome at Porter Martin's home.

As the days went by, Diana found herself spending a lot of time at that dress shop. Martha fitted her, measuring every inch of Diana for her wedding dress. Porter had brought her some more fabric from Philadelphia. Some of it was very fancy silk and lace. Martha was going to use it for Diana's dress; however, Diana was not permitted to see the dress until it was finished.

The new blacksmith had settled in. He was a delightful man. He was the biggest man Diana had ever seen. He was taller than Porter Martin and built like a brick wall. His arms were larger than Diana's waist. His name was Carver Wilks. He had light hair, not quite as light as Diana's. He had green eyes that seemed to sparkle in the light. He was very soft spoken, and rather shy. He worked hard and kept to himself. He moved into the new home that Porter Martin had built for him. He worked feverishly in his shop and built his own iron fence that went around the front. He planted a little vegetable garden and flowers. Diana found him very intriguing. She was not the only one, for her sister Martha watched his every move when he was within sight. As the days went by, Martha began to spend more and more time in town.

It was late May. There was a cool day now and then, but summer was on its way. Diana and Brandon had decided it was time for the wedding. They would be married right after the Sunday services, while everyone was already at the church. Martha would have everything at her shop to dress Diana and prepare her to walk down the aisle.

The stage was coming in today. Porter said there was a present on the stage for Diana and Brandon. Diana was excited. This was the day she had been waiting for.

The morning went like every other morning. Diana found it hard to concentrate on preparing breakfast. Martha sang as she made a pot of coffee. Porter Martin came down the steps slowly. He was growing older. All of the strain he had bestowed upon his body over the years was catching up to him. He walked about half bent over. Diana went to him, kissing him on the cheek after he sat down at the table. Brandon was just coming in the back door. He was outside feeding the livestock and the dogs. The dogs were trying to slip in the door as he entered. He put his leg out, blocking their entrance and closed the door quickly.

Diana looked up at him and smiled. "They are getting lazy. We feed them too much," she said.

Brandon removed his hat. It was warm enough that he did not require a coat. "It sure is a nice day for a wedding," he said, winking at her.

Diana pulled a chair out and motioned for him to sit down. Then she sat down next to him. "When we go after Tilly and the children, I would like a few extra minutes to visit Mamma, Pappa, and Ruth Ann, if you don't mind," she said.

Brandon smiled and squeezed her hand. Porter led them in a prayer. They ate their breakfast with a light conversation. Porter continued to tease Diana. She smiled as she looked around the table. These were the people she loved most in the world. This was a very happy day for her. She was beginning it as Diana Lewis, the second oldest daughter of Agnus and William Lewis. She would end the day as Diana Shively, the wife of Brandon Shively from Boston. It was a special day indeed.

After breakfast, Porter and Brandon went to the barn, while Diana and Martha cleaned up the kitchen. They had noodles drying on a board. They were preparing for the feast and party that would follow the wedding. They finished in the kitchen and went upstairs to prepare for church.

Porter had the wagon hitched up and ready to leave by the time the girls were ready. Brandon had the smaller buggy hitched as well. Diana and Brandon would travel alone in the buggy. First, they were going to the cabin, so Diana could visit the grave site. They were soon on their way. Porter and Martha followed in the wagon.

It was such a beautiful day. Diana could not stop smiling. She rode quietly, reflecting on all of the times she rode in the back of the two-wheeled cart to Berlin. Josephine would drive. Diana and either Regina or Sofia would steady the milk barrel, and Rudy would either run beside them or ride along. Those were hard times. They were also happy times.

Soon, they stopped at the cabin. Tilly and the children came out onto the porch. Brandon helped Diana down from the buggy. They were just going around the house, when Porter pulled the wagon up next to the buggy. They all went to the gravesite. There were fresh wild flowers on the graves. Diana looked over at Tilly. She smiled and nodded. Diana smiled and went to Tilly, kissing her on the cheek. "Thank you, Tilly," she said.

Porter said a prayer over the graves. Diana stared at the wooden crosses, three in a row. Then she said, "Mamma, Pappa, today is my wedding day. I would give anything if you all could be there with me today. Ruthie, we all miss you so much. We will be thinking of you all today." A tear swelled up into her eyes. Martha went to her side. She put her arm around Diana's waist.

"Di, they will be there. They will always be there, no matter where we go," Martha said. Diana put her head on Martha's shoulder and wiped her eyes. She smiled and blew her nose. Brandon reached for her hand.

Porter said, "We must be going. I have a surprise waiting at the general store I need to collect before church."

Martha took Hoppy and Gilda by the hand. Homer took Tilly's hand and Porter carried Percy. They piled into the wagon while Brandon and Diana got into the buggy. They were on their way to church.

Once they reached the church, Brandon and Diana went inside. Brandon sat on the inside of the pew, which was unusual. He smiled over at Diana. Martha and Porter sat behind them, with Porter holding Percy on his lap. Tilly, Hoppy, and Homer sat in the third row.

On the other side, Grace, Sherman, and a very pregnant Concetta sat in the front row. Sofia, who had gained a considerable amount of weight, sat in the second row with Zachariah and Marcus O'Hara. In the third row sat Stumpy and Carver Wilks. In the back, Herbert and Alda Faulk sat with their three children.

Jonathan Gilbert stood at the pulpit. He was silent as he looked down on his congregation. There was a stir at the back of the church. Everyone turned to see Regina walking down the aisle. She walked up to the pew where Diana was sitting. "Is this seat taken?" she asked.

Diana jumped up. "Regina! What are you doing here?" she asked, throwing her arms around her sister.

"Porter brought me here for the wedding. Josie could not leave the children. Maggy is staying with Delbert's mother. I can't stay long, but I wanted to be here for your wedding. You have no idea how hard it was to keep my presence a secret until today," Regina said.

Suddenly, Diana became aware of all the eyes upon them. She sat down, pulling Regina by the hand until she sat close by her side. She put her head on Regina's shoulder and whispered. "I am so happy you are here. It is the best gift of all."

Parson Gilbert preached about Abraham and his love for his wife. Diana found it very difficult to concentrate on the sermon. Soon, they were singing a hymn and then saying a prayer.

Martha pulled Diana by the hand. Sofia, Martha, Regina, and Diana went to the dress shop. They began to dress Diana. Concetta and Grace began to decorate the church. Brandon paced back and forth outside, while the men gathered to jeer him and smoke their pipes.

Diana's dress was white. It was a soft silk with a lace cascade about the neck, shoulders waist, and down the back. While they were positioning the veil over her head, Sofia went for the buggy. They helped Diana up into the buggy. Porter was urging Brandon inside the church so he would not see Diana approaching. The girls walked next to the buggy as Martha drove it to the hitching post outside the church. They all helped Diana down and worked to adjust her dress and veil. Porter was standing at the door. He had four bouquets in his hand. He handed one to each of the girls.

Sofia walked down the aisle first. Brandon was standing there with the preacher. She stepped to her left and turned facing the door. Grace and Concetta sang a hymn. Regina and Martha were the next to walk down the aisle. They stepped into the front pew on the right and turned to face the door. All eyes were on the door. Porter and Diana came down the aisle. Both of them were smiling. Diana's eyes were fixed on Brandon. He was finding it hard to breath. Diana was the most beautiful woman he had ever seen. He smiled at her. Porter took Brandon's hand and placed Diana's hand in it. Then he went to the pew on the right, standing next to Regina and Martha.

Parson Gilbert said a prayer. Then they began repeating their vows. It was a beautiful ceremony. Diana trembled when Parson Gilbert told Brandon to kiss his bride. Then he introduced Mr. and Mrs. Brandon Shively to the congregation. There was an eruption of applause. Brandon scooped Diana up into his arms and carried her to the back door. They stood there greeting the congregation as they exited the church.

When everyone was outside, Brandon lifted his bride into the buggy. He climbed in beside her. Porter announced, "Everyone, there will be food and festivities at the farm." He climbed into the wagon. There was a procession that followed the buggy to the Porter Martin house.

At the house, the women placed food around the table. They all ate joyfully. It was a wonderful celebration. When they had finished eating, the table was slid over near the wall. The musical instruments were brought out. They all began dancing. Diana and Brandon were placed in the center of a circle, and they danced around them. The children danced, too. It was the happiest day of Diana's life.

As the sun fell in the sky, the guests, one by one, left. Porter took Tilly and the children home. The girls went upstairs. Brandon carried Diana to his room. Diana could hear her sisters giggling in the next room. She secretly wished she could join them. It had been so long since she saw Regina. She was nervous. It was her wedding night. Brandon sat her on the bed. He helped her remove her veil. Then he took her in his arms, kissing her tenderly. She kissed him back. They fell back onto the bed. Somehow, the nervousness seemed to disappear. This was Brandon. He was the most tender man Diana had ever met. She loved him and he loved her. He would never hurt her. The rest of the world seemed to disappear. The sounds of Regina and Martha's giggles seemed to fade in the night, as Diana yielded to the touch of her new husband.

Diana rolled over. The sun was shining in the window. It was going to be another beautiful day. She looked up into Brandon's eyes. He had been watching her. She smiled. He kissed her. They made love again.

The kitchen was buzzing with activity when they finally came down. Sofia had ridden out to have breakfast with them. Porter was sitting next to the window, smoking his pipe. Martha was sweeping the floor of the remnants from the night before. Regina and Sofia sat at the table drinking a cup of tea.

"Good morning," everyone chimed as Diana and Brandon entered the kitchen.

"Sit down right here," Sofia said, pointing to two chairs beside them. The girls all began preparing breakfast. Porter came to the table to join them.

"I am takin' Regina back to Philadelphia today. Miss Martha is goin with me. You two will have the house to yourselves for about a week. School is out for the summer, so all you need to worry about is feedin' the livestock. Just enjoy yourselves. Miss Martha and I will be back in about ten days or so. Don't fret none if it is a couple of days more. Miss Martha hasn't seen Josephine in sometime. They will have a lot to talk about. And I will have the mill," Porter said, drawing on his pipe. He blew the smoke into the air.

Diana reached for Regina's hand. "I have missed you and Josie so much. I am so glad you could come, but I really hate to see you leave so soon," she said.

Regina smiled. "I know. You have your honeymoon. You just get to know your new husband and be happy. You know where you can find me," Regina said.

Brandon took Diana's hand. "I think we might make a trip to Philadelphia soon, ourselves," he said.

"Oh, Brandon! Could we really? I would love that. Really, I would!" Diana said excitedly.

Brandon nodded. Diana turned to Porter Martin. "Thank you so much, Mr. Martin, for bringing my sister here for my wedding. Thank you so much for everything you have done for me and my family. I don't know what we would have done without you. You have been kinder than anyone could dare to expect," she said. She embraced him.

Porter stood up straight. He smiled down at her and said, "It was a pleasure, Ma'am. You girls are the family I never could have. Losin' Miss Margaret left a big hole in my life. You filled it right well. It is me who needs to be thankin' you all."

Diana stood on her toes and kissed Porter on the cheek.

Martha announced, "How do flapjacks sound this morning?"

Porter smiled. "Flapjacks are my favorite. Sounds mighty fine to me. What do you say, ladies? Let's fill our guts before we head for Philadelphia," Porter said.

They ate their breakfast amongst the gleeful chatter of the four sisters. Porter smiled and said to Brandon. "This brings back memories of when they were all younger. Their Mamma and Little Ruthie were here then. They are missed this morning."

"Oh, no, Mr. Martin," Martha said. "They are here. They will always be here." She smiled.

Porter looked over at her for a moment. He smiled and nodded. "You are right, Miss Martha. I didn't take the time to listen. They are both right here," he said.

The cheerful chatter resumed. Brandon and Porter watched and listened. At times, they broke out into laughter. It was a happy time for the sisters.

After breakfast, the girls all pitched in, cleaning up the kitchen. Even Sofia worked, buzzing around the familiar kitchen. Soon, they were all climbing up into Porter's larger buggy. Brandon drove the buggy while Porter rode his horse alongside of them. Sofia's horse was tied to the back of the buggy. The cheerful chatter continued all the way into town.

When they reached Berlin, they stopped at Martha's dress shop. The girls went inside. Porter and Brandon went to the stables. Stumpy, Marcus, and Parson Gilbert were standing outside watching them as they came into town.

The girls went into the kitchen. Martha began to make tea. Sofia sat down in a chair nearest the window. Diana began to fold her dress from yesterday on the table. It had all been left behind after the ceremony yesterday.

Regina said, "I am having so much fun. I really miss my Maggy, but it was so good to spend the time with you girls."

Diana went to her sister. She put her arms around her and said., "You have no idea how wonderful it was to see you come through that door yesterday morning. I am so glad you came. You tell Josephine we missed her very much."

Martha and Sofia joined her, standing near the stove hugging each other. Tears were in all of their eyes. Then they began to laugh.

Diana said, "I am jealous that you are all going to Philadelphia. Brandon has promised me that we will go. I just wish we could all be together. That is my biggest fear, that we will never all be together again."

Martha hugged her sister. "Remember what we talked about at the breakfast table this morning? Mamma and Ruth Ann would always be there. Remember? We will always be together, Di. As long as we remember, we will be together," she said.

The tears were falling again. They sat down around the little round table, drinking their tea. The conversation went back to their younger years. They spoke about the times they lived in the cabin. The days of hunting and swimming in the shallow stream. The days of milking and bringing the cows in. Soon, it was all gleeful chatter again.

The time seemed to fly by. The noise of the stage arriving interrupted them. They hurriedly cleaned up the kitchen. Martha closed up the shop and they walked to the general store together.

Porter and Brandon helped the driver put the luggage on top of the stage. Zachariah fed and watered the horses. The driver went inside. Grace Hickman fed him. The girls gathered on the porch, saying their good-byes. Before long, it was time for the stage to leave. Sofia and Diana stood watching the stage pull away. Martha and Regina were waving until they were out of sight.

Sofia hugged Diana. "That was so nice of Porter Martin. I hope we get to see Regina again."

Diana smiled. "We will. We will, Sofia. I feel it in my heart," she said with tears in her eyes.

Sofia looked back at the stable. "I really must get back to the house. Jonathan was kind enough to allow me to go to Mr. Martin's this morning. I have things to do," she said. She hugged Diana. "You stop by when you come to town," she said as she turned to walk away.

Diana called after her. "I will, and you remember how to get to Mr. Martin's house. You are always welcome there, Sofia."

Sofia turned and smiled. She nodded her head and waved. Then she continued on her way toward Marcus O'Hara's little house. Soon, she would be living in the house that Porter Martin was building for her and her husband.

Brandon was walking toward Diana. He was smiling. Diana could not help but think how handsome he was. She was happy. He was a wonderful, caring man. He would be a good husband. She thought about her parents. They had a very private relationship. Diana could not remember a time when they embraced, or kissed in front of the girls. She knew the relationship she would share with Brandon would not be that way. She ran to him. She threw her arms around him. "I love you so much!" she said into his neck.

Brandon laughed. He lifted her off her feet. "I love you, too, Mrs. Shively," he said. Then he set her down. He looked down into her eyes. He winked and said, "Let's go home."

Diana nodded. They walked hand in hand to the buggy. They were going back to the house. They would have the farm to themselves until Porter returned. Diana could not stop smiling.

Diana and Brandon spent most of the time inside, even though the days were becoming warmer. Brandon fed the livestock, and Diana cooked their meals. It was a wonderful time in both of their lives. They went hunting one day. They brought home two rabbits and another deer. They took some of the meat to Tilly.

One morning, at the breakfast table, they decided to go for a walk. It was a beautiful day. Porter would be home any day now. He would be working in the sawmill during the daytime. Brandon would be working with him. Diana would not have Brandon all to herself any longer.

They walked hand in hand down the cart trail that led to the log cabin, where Tilly and the children lived. The trees had leaves on them now. Ferns were growing on the forest floor. The smell of spring was everywhere. They crossed the little wooden bridge that Stumpy had built for them. They walked hand in hand talking as they went.

Soon, they rounded the bend and stood at the top of the knob that looked down on the cabin. It looked as though it had been frozen in time. Diana smiled. It hadn't changed, in all this time. Smoke drifted from the chimney. Percy and Gilda were playing on the porch. Brownie and Blackie had been following them. The two dogs ran ahead and jumped onto the children. Diana could hear them giggling and squealing. Tilly and Hoppy came out onto the porch and waved at them. Homer came out of the barn to see what the commotion was. He saw them and ran to meet them.

"Miss Lewis! Miss Lewis!" he called as he approached them.

Diana held out her arms and he ran into them. She laughed. "Good day to you, Homer!" she said. He was nearly nine years old now. He had grown nearly half a foot. His pants were above his ankles. Martha would need to make him some new pants for school. His baby teeth were gone. His new teeth were bigger and slightly bucked. He was growing so fast.

They reached the porch. Diana looked up at Brandon. He was smiling. He lifted Percy. He too, was growing. He was about five now. Diana was amazed. She was so enchanted with her wedding, she had not noticed the change in her students. They were all growing.

"Come in, Miss Lewis, Mr. Shively," Tilly said.

Diana and Brandon went inside. The kitchen had not changed either. The smell of stew cooking in the iron pot filled the cabin. It was spotless. Diana and Brandon sat at the table on the same stools that William had made for his family. Diana folded her hands and placed them on the table in front of her. Brandon reached over, putting his hand over hers.

"Tilly, I am not Miss Lewis anymore. My name is Mrs. Shively now. Do you think you can remember that?" she asked, looking at all of their faces.

They were nodding their heads. "Yes, Miss Lewis. We will remember," Percy said. Diana and Brandon burst into laughter. Brandon rustled Percy's hair.

Homer stepped forward. "We will remember, Mrs. Shively," he said, smiling.

Tilly gave them a cup of cool water. They sipped it. "Thank you, Tilly. This is good water," Brandon said.

Tilly nodded. "I's gets it from the creek out back. It is good water, Misser Shively," Tilly said.

Hoppy stepped forward. Diana noticed that she had a sling hanging from her waist. She wore it exactly like Diana. Diana pointed to it and asked Hoppy, "Do you know how to use that, Hoppy?"

Hoppy put her hand on the sling. She looked at it and then back to Diana. She nodded and said, "Yes, Ma'am, Mrs. Shively. Miss Martha showed me. I bin practicin, and I is gettin pretty good. I kin hit a rabbit on the run wit it."

Tilly said, "We is havin rabbit stew. Hoppy kilt a rabbit yesterdee. She is really good wit the sling."

Diana smiled. "I will have to show you how to use the bow. It will take down bigger game. Perhaps Stumpy will make one for you. He made mine, and it is perfect for someone smaller. It isn't heavy and it fits right over your shoulder. You just climb up a tree and sit real quiet. Then you wait. Sometimes you have to wait for a long time. You will see all sorts of things. Sometime animals can pass by below you and never know you are there," Diana explained.

Hoppy was smiling. "I would like that, Mrs. Shively. I would like that very much!" she said. She stepped closer to Diana. "Kin you help me wit it today?"

Diana smiled. "Not today, Hoppy. Mr. Shively and I are going for a walk. I did not bring my bow. Perhaps after Mr. Martin comes home. Maybe after church one day. We will have to talk to Stumpy about making one for a young lady your size. It will happen, just not today," Diana said.

Hoppy nodded. Homer said, "I wants to learn, too. Kin he make one for me, too?"

Brandon said, "I will ask him to make two of them. I will be going into town tomorrow. I am sure he would be happy to do it." He began to bounce Percy on his knee. Percy giggled. They all laughed.

"Well, Tilly, we are going to continue our walk. Thank you for the refreshments," Brandon said as he stood up, standing Percy on the floor. Diana rose. She smiled at Tilly. They walked outside on the porch.

Brandon took hold of Diana by the waist and lifted her off the porch. The children all giggled. They began to walk toward the creek where the fallen tree would allow them to cross without getting their feet wet. Tilly and the children waved until they were out of sight.

When they came to the cattail pond, Diana's eyes automatically scanned the ground as they passed. "This is where my Mamma was bitten by the moccasin," Diana explained. Brandon held her hand. They made a wide circle around the pond and into the forest beyond.

Diana showed him the peppermint grove. It was just beginning to sprout. They went on until they came to the honey bee tree. Diana told Brandon how she was able to pull the honey out of the tree, only being stung a couple of times. Then they went further into the forest. Diana had not been this far before. There was a clearing ahead. They walked into it. There was tall golden grass that grew waist high on Diana.

They followed the open field in the direction of Berlin. They stayed close to the forest line. Soon, they came to the spot that Diana recognized as being the battleground she stumbled into the day she killed the turkey. She told Brandon about that day as they walked. They continued on until they came out just above Berlin. They stood looking down at the small town. It had grown considerably. There was a covered wagon approaching. It was pulled by two oxen.

"I have never seen anything like those animals before. They are the largest cattle I have ever laid eyes on," Diana said.

"They are called oxen. They are powerful beasts. They are pretty docile. They can pull more than a horse, but they are slow. You won't go anywhere in a hurry with them," Brandon said. "Come on, let's walk down and see who those people are."

They walked down the hill and onto the road that led to town. They watched as the covered wagon pulled up in front of the stables. A man jumped down from the wagon and went around the back. He began helping children out of the wagon. There were five all together. Then he helped a woman, Diana assumed to be his wife, down from the wagon. She was a very pregnant woman, even larger than Concetta, who was due in a couple of months. Diana quickened her step. She was anxious to meet these people.

By the time they reached the stables, the man had disappeared inside. He was talking to Sherman Hickman and Zachariah Dillon. Stumpy was making his way in their direction. Grace was standing on the porch watching them.

Brandon tipped his hat to the lady and went inside. Diana smiled, extended her hand, and said, "Good afternoon. My name is Diana Shively. I am the schoolteacher here in Berlin."

The woman reached out, shaking Diana's hand. "My name is, Madeline. Madeline Hughs. These are my children," she said. She pointed to the children as she introduced them. "This is Winston, Raymond, Shirley, Cecilia, and this here is Franklin," she said, pointing to the baby boy she held in her arms. He appeared to be around a year old.

"Why don't you come rest yourself a while?" Diana said, pointing to the porch on the general store. She led the way, looking back to make sure they all were following.

When they reached the porch, she asked Grace, "Mrs. Hickman, could we have some refreshments for Mrs. Hughs and her children?"

Grace nodded and went inside. "I hope you don't think me too inquisitive Mrs. Hughes, but I was wondering, are you passing through or looking for a place to settle?" Diana asked.

Mrs. Hughes lowered her head. "We were hoping to make it to the mountains before the baby came, but I don't think we will make it. I have been having pains all morning. We were lucky to make it this far," she said.

Diana gasped. "Oh, my goodness! We must get you somewhere to lie down!" she exclaimed.

Madeline waved her hand in the air. "Oh, no! The pains aren't bad enough yet. Trust me, I have been through this enough times to know when it is close to time. I just don't think I could ride any further in that wagon."

Grace re-appeared with a tray. It had a china teapot on it and nine tin cups. Diana looked up at her and frowned. If it had been passengers on the stage, they would have received china cups to drink from. Concetta came out and began to help serving the tea to the little ones.

Upon seeing Concetta in her pregnant state, Madeline Hughes smiled. "When are you due, my dear?" she asked Connie.

"In a couple of months. I am not sure, maybe," Connie stammered. "How about you?"

Madeline smiled. She took a sip of tea and said, "In about a couple of hours, give or take a few."

Connie gasped. Grace stood erect. Their mouths were hanging open. Diana looked at Grace and asked, "Is there somewhere she could rest?"

Madeline interrupted her. "Oh, no, dear! I can have this baby in the wagon. I just don't want it rocking about."

Grace looked down at the children who were gathered around Madeline. She reached out and took the baby from her arms. "I have a room upstairs with two beds in it. I think it would be much more comfortable than that old covered wagon. Much cleaner, too," she said.

Diana took Madeline's hand. "Come along, Mrs. Hughs. I will watch over your children while you rest. You are going to have a baby sometime today," she said with a smile.

They helped Madeline up the steps. She moved effortlessly. "I am not in much pain, really," she said.

"How were your other deliveries?" Grace asked her as she led her to the bed where her son Willie slept in years past.

Madeline sat on the edge of the bed. "They all started out hard and fast. My Shirley came in a matter of an hour or less. The rest were just three hours or so. I've never had a delivery start like this one. But I know the pains have to be much sharper before it is all over. They are just a slight discomfort right now," Madeline said.

Grace frowned. She turned to Concetta. "Connie, I don't think you should see this. It will just scare you. Why don't you go get Sofia and the two of you watch over those children. Mrs. Shively will help me."

Concetta protested. "Mamma, I think I should know what I got comin'. Let me stay."

Grace shook her head. She nodded to the door, giving her daughter a stern look. She said, "You mind me, girl. You get Sofia over here to help with these children. You go right now."

Grace looked over at Diana. She had a worried look on her face. Then she looked back at Madeline and asked, "Have you seen any sign of blood or water breakage?"

Madeline shook her head and said, "I had a spot of blood here and there a couple days ago, but it went away."

Diana was becoming worried. Grace was not herself. She wasn't prying, she was concerned about this woman. Diana had never witnessed a birthing before. She did not know what to expect. Her sisters were all born in the cabin. The older children waited outside. Her father delivered every one of them, except Regina. Agnus delivered Regina by herself. Diana was only two years old and did not remember it.

Concetta gathered the baby boy, Franklin, in her arms and herded the other children back down the stairs. She promised them all some hard candy. They followed without any protesting. Diana and Grace stood next to the bed. Madeline clutched her stomach. She frowned and rubbed at it. "I am getting a sharp cramping feeling right now. No bad pain, though," Madeline said.

Diana looked up at Grace and asked, "Should I get her husband?"

Grace took a deep breath. "We certainly won't be needin' a man pacin' about up here. You should probably tell him she won't be going nowhere. I suppose he has a right to know. Just tell him we got this under control. We will let him know when it is over," Grace said. She put her hands on Madeline's shoulders and lowered her down onto the bed. "You, my dear, are going to lay here until this baby is born. You don't need to be up moving about."

Madeline protested. "I need to walk. That helped with all of my babies. I just walk until it is time."

"All right then, you can walk. But you are staying right here in this room. I will get some water on the stove and some towels. I will be right back," Grace said. She urged Diana toward the steps. They went downstairs.

At the bottom of the stairs, she said to Diana, "You go tell her husband what I said. I don't like the looks of this. Maybe it ain't nothin'. She's had kids before, but I never heard of a delivery like this before. One thing for sure, by tonight we should know."

Grace went toward the kitchen. Diana went outside. Sofia and Concetta were on the porch. Sofia was holding Franklin in her arms. The children were gathered around Concetta. She was passing out hard candy. Diana went toward the stable.

Her eyes had to adjust to the darkness when she entered the stable. She heard the voices and laughter of the men inside. She followed the sounds. Brandon saw her coming. He approached her and said, "Alvin, this is my new wife, Diana. She is the schoolteacher here in Berlin. Diana, this is Alvin Hughes. He and his family are headed for the mountains."

Diana smiled and nodded at Mr. Hughes. "Hello, Mr. Hughes. It is a pleasure to meet you. Grace, I mean, Mrs. Hickman, Mr. Hickman's wife, sent me to tell you, your wife is upstairs. We believe she is in labor," she tried to explain.

Alvin Hughes laughed. "Well, I suppose we could wait a day before heading off again. Lord knows we have done this enough times," he said.

Diana sighed. "Well, I don't know if a day will be enough time," she began.

"Oh, don't worry!" Alvin laughed. "My Madeline pops those young babies out in no time. She walks around holding her belly for a spell and goes off by herself into the wagon for about an hour, and comes out carrying another child. We have done this five times already. She will do just fine," he chuckled.

Diana looked up at Brandon. Then she looked back at Alvin Hughes and said, "Well, I don't know about the last five times, but this one seems to be a little different. I am sure everything will be all right, but Mrs. Hickman seems to feel it may take awhile."

"Well, I hope it don't take too long. I wrote my brother that we would be there before the end of spring. I need to get back on the trail," Alvin said.

Diana tried to hide her dislike for this man. She smiled and turned to Brandon. "I am going to help Mrs. Hickman deliver this baby. Will you be all right on your own for the remainder of the day?" she asked.

Brandon slipped his arm around her waist. He smiled down at Diana and said, "I will be fine. Is there anything I can do to help?"

"Just keep him entertained." She smiled, nodding in the direction of Alvin Hughes.

"I'll walk you back," Brandon said.

They turned and went back out into the sunlight. Diana looked up at Brandon and said, "Brandon, I don't know much about pregnancies, but Grace thinks something is wrong. I don't know what to expect. I don't know how long this will take, but I am worried."

Brandon frowned. He looked in the direction of the general store. He looked back to Diana and said. "Diana, don't worry about me. Just do whatever you have to for that woman. I will help with Alvin and the children in any way I can. We will be fine. You go now." He kissed her on the forehead. She turned and went back to the store.

Diana stepped up onto the porch. She heard a familiar sound coming from beyond the forest line. It was the stage. Porter and Martha would soon be home. Diana felt relieved. Martha would be an enormous help. She waited until the stage pulled to a stop. The door opened and Porter stepped to the ground. He turned and held out his hand. Martha stepped out. She looked up at Diana and shouted. "Diana! Diana! I am so happy to see you. I have so much to tell you." She ran to Diana. Diana threw her arms around her younger sister.

"Martha! I am so glad you are here. I need you. Come inside, I will explain," Diana said. She stopped, turning to see Porter Martin looking at her. He was hunched over, holding onto a cane. Diana smiled and ran to him. She threw her arms around him, kissing his cheek. "Oh, Mr. Martin! I can't tell you how happy I am that you are home. I have missed you so much!" she said.

Porter began to laugh. "I am happy to see you, too," he said. He looked about. "It is always good to be home."

Diana smiled. She took his right hand and squeezed it. "The men are all in the stables. I need to get back inside. We are having a baby today," she said.

"Concetta?" Martha asked.

Diana shook her head. "No. Mrs. Hughes. She came in on that covered wagon just a while ago. Come with me, Martha. We will have a lot of time to talk. She is upstairs, and I need to get back in there," she said, tugging on Martha's hand. She looked back to see Porter Martin making his way to the stable.

Diana continued to pull Martha by the hand, all the way up the stairs to where Madeline Hughes paced around the bedroom.

"Madeline Hughes, this is my sister, Martha Lewis. She has the dress shop across the street. She just returned from Philadelphia, where she was visiting my two sisters," Diana explained.

Madeline smiled. She held her belly with her right hand, and reached her left hand out to Martha. "Hello, Miss Lewis. It is a pleasure to meet your acquaintance; however, I must apologize for my current circumstances," Madeline said.

Martha looked Madeline up and down. She smiled and said, "Please, don't apologize. I am happy to be here. I have never witnessed a baby being born before."

Just then, Grace Hickman entered the room with a pan of steaming water. She had towels draped over her shoulder. "You will not be witnessing the birth of this baby. You will have to wait outside until it is born. There is not enough room for everyone to stand around watching," she dictated.

Martha frowned. Diana assumed Grace was still put off by Martha standing up to her at the church. Martha smiled and said to Madeline. "Well, I will wait outside. It is a pleasure to meet you, Mrs. Hughes. I will see you later."

She turned, leaving the room. Diana could hear her going down the steps. She said softly, "Mrs. Hickman, we may need Martha."

Grace Hickman took a deep breath. She looked over at Diana and said, "We will be fine." She set the pan of water on the dresser and proceeded to fold the towels. Madeline Hughes continued to pace the room.

Diana stood next to the door. She watched Madeline. She looked over at Grace who was also watching Madeline. The room was silent, except for the shuffling of Madeline's bare feet on the wooden floor.

Diana said, "Tell me something about yourself, Mrs. Hughes."

Madeline continued to pace. She rubbed her belly as she went. She smiled and said, "We are from Fredericksburg, Virginia. Alvin was a farmer. My family had a plantation that joined his property. We got married and lived on his farm. His brother was in the war. He went to live in the mountains northeast of here, after the war. Duncan Hughes is his name. He wrote Alvin about the beautiful forests and clear running streams in the area. Alvin began to dream of settling there. He wrote his brother. Duncan wrote back saying he would build a cabin for us and it should be done by the time we get there. We packed up our belongings, and that is where we are headed."

She frowned and Diana suspected that the cramping was getting stronger. She stepped closer to her. Madeline put her hand out and shook her head. "I am fine," she said.

Diana stepped back. "You have a very nice family," she said. She wanted to take Madeline's mind off the pain. Grace looked up at her and nodded.

Madeline smiled and said as she paced. "Thank you, Mrs. Shively. They are all good children. My family was very upset with me for following Alvin. They did not want to let go of their grand children. My father lost most of the slaves after the war. He tried to convince us to stay on and help with the crops. I did not want my children working day in and day out. We felt it was a good move. It looks like it will take longer than we expected to get there, though," she said. She frowned again.

"You had slaves?" Diana asked.

"My parents had many slaves. They have a very large plantation to care for. There is no way they could afford to pay for hired help. Slaves were the best alternative. We furnished them with a place to live. They bred and produced more slaves. They worked all day. Daddy fed them well. When the crops were few, and money was short, Daddy just sold off some of the slaves. That is how it was done," Madeline explained.

Diana became aware that her mouth was hanging open. She looked over at Grace. To her surprise, Grace was covering her mouth with her hands.

Madeline looked up at them and said, "I know it is shocking. You Yankees don't abide by slaves. But that is just the way it was done back home. It don't matter. It is a lifestyle that is gone now. Daddy will do what he can to get by. Without the slaves, there is no crops. Without the crops, there is no food or money. Without money, they can't pay the taxes. I don't know what will happen, but I do not want my children slaving from dusk to dawn on Daddy's plantation. I want them to have a happy life." She bent over and gasped.

Diana rushed to her. Grace, too, was on her feet and hurrying to Madeline's side. They got on each side of her and helped her to the bed.

Madeline laid back and took a deep breath. "Tell me about yourselves," she said.

Grace wiped her forehead with a towel. She smiled down at Madeline and said, "My family settled at Fort Pitt. My father was a military man. There were just four of us. I had a brother who is probably still there. He would no doubt be in the military, too. My Sherman came to the fort with his family when we were young. We have been together since he was in short pants. We moved here right after we was married. There was only one cabin here then. It was old Marcus O'Hara's. He was a trapper. We built the house he lives in, and then we built this place when the stage started passing this way. Marcus moved into our house, and we moved into the store. We tore down the log cabin. Then Zachariah and Stumpy came along. Right about that same time, William Lewis built his cabin about two or three miles out. He was a trapper, too. He went off and got married. He moved his new wife here. That is Miss Diana's family. I mean, Mrs. Shively's family. We had two boys, Willy and Burton. Then we had a daughter, Concetta. My boys went off to fight in the war. Willy was killed, and I reckon Burt was, too, cause I ain't never heard nothin from him, or about him. My daughter, Concetta, met some travelin' actor from England, who was passin' through on the stage. He was a fancy man. A pretty fancy talker, too, for he promised my Connie all sorts of promises, until he had his way with her, and then he just left. We ain't never heard nothin' from him since. Now she is with child. Due in a couple of months."

Madeline nodded her head. "I understand. Poor girl," she said. Grace's face was flaming red. Diana knew it was not easy for her to air out her laundry in front of others. She looked up at Grace and smiled. Grace nodded and continued to wipe Madeline's forehead. Madeline doubled up in pain. She clenched her teeth and gripped Diana's hand. It hurt. Diana frowned and tried not to pull her hand away. "You. What about you? Talk to me, please," Madeline begged Diana.

Diana looked up at Grace. She was nodding. Diana took a deep breath and began. "Well, my Pappa was a trapper, like Mrs. Hickman said. He met my Mamma right after her family came over from England on a boat. Mamma was young, but her parents permitted her to marry Pappa. They moved just a couple of miles outside of town in a log cabin that Pappa had built. Pappa always said he was cursed because he had no sons. He had six daughters. Josephine and Regina live in Philadelphia. Josephine has four children, and Regina has one daughter. She had a complicated pregnancy and can't have any more children. I am the second oldest, with Josephine being the oldest. Then Sofia is married to the preacher. They live with Marcus O'Hara. Porter Martin is almost done with their new house. Marcus is nearly totally blind. My other sister, Martha has a dress shop across the street, like I already told you. My baby sister, Ruth Ann, caught the influenza and died about a year ago. I married a captain in the army and we live with Porter Martin. He has a sawmill out by his house. My husband has been learning the business from Porter and will be taking over when Mr. Martin retires."

"Which will no doubt be soon. Poor man can barely get around anymore," Grace interrupted.

Madeline was doubled over again. She rose up in the bed and groaned. Grace wiped her forehead frantically. She looked over at Diana and shook her head. Madeline had released Diana's hand. Diana reached out and squeezed her arm to comfort her. Madeline fell back onto the pillow. There was a large spot of blood spreading on her skirt. Diana's eyes were wide. She was frightened. Grace was staring at it also. Madeline shrieked out in pain again.

Grace pulled up Madeline's skirt. She looked up at Diana. She had a frightened look on her face as well. Diana asked, "What should I do?"

Grace shook her head again. "I don't rightly know, child," she said. "I don't rightly know."

Diana began again, "Mr. Martin built a beautiful house just over the hill, outside of town. He was originally from Philadelphia. He passed through this way on a stage once, and saw all this timber. He built a house here for Miss Margaret. She was his wife. She was a school…," Diana stopped.

Madeline was screaming now. Diana heard footsteps coming up the wooden steps. It was Sofia. She peered through the door. "Is everything all right in here?" she asked.

Diana looked her way and shook her head. "No," she said.

Grace Hickman interrupted. "Yes, it is fine. This is just a complicated birth, that is all."

"Where is all of that blood coming from?" Sofia asked. She was entering the room.

Grace turned to look at her. "Just go back outside and keep the children calm. You can't help here, and it is crowded enough in this room already. Go on. You can help by calming the children," she said to Sofia.

Diana looked at her sister and nodded her head. Sofia backed out of the room, closing the door behind her. Diana heard her go back down the stairs.

"Who was that?" Madeline asked.

Diana said softly. "That was my sister, Sofia. She is married to the preacher. Remember me telling you about her?"

Madeline nodded. She cried out in pain again. More blood soaked her skirt. Grace began to wipe at the blood. "Something is wrong, isn't it?" Madeline asked through clenched teeth.

Grace sighed. She looked up at Madeline from the bottom of the bed. "Yes, Dear, something is wrong. I am not sure what to do for you. I am not experienced in birthing babies. I do know it is not the usual birth for you, by what you have told me. I don't recall all of this bleeding with my children." She looked up at Diana with a pleading look. She knew she had said too much in all of her nervousness.

Diana rubbed Madeline's arm. "We will do our best for you, Madeline. We will stay right here with you until this child is born. Do you want me to get your husband?" she asked.

"Yes!" Madeline screamed out in pain. "I want Alvin."

Diana rose to her feet and went to the door. Grace called after her, "Send one of the girls after him. I need you here, Diana."

Diana nodded and went down the steps as quickly as she could without falling. When she reached the porch, she found everyone gathered around. She pointed at Alvin and said, "Mr. Hughes, you better come upstairs. Hurry, please!" She looked over at Brandon and shook her head. Then she followed

Mr. Hughes inside. She pointed the way to the room, where the screams were coming from.

When they entered the room, Alvin Hughes cried out. "Oh, my God! Where is all of this blood coming from?"

Diana pushed him toward the bed. She took hold of his hand and led him to the spot she had been sitting in. "Sit here and hold her hand, Mr. Hughes," she said to him.

He sat down. "Madeline, what is happening?" he asked.

Madeline was screaming out in pain again. Grace Hickman said, "I don't know what to do for her. I have never seen a delivery like this before in my life."

Just then, the door burst open. Alda Faulk rushed into the room. "Let me see!" she said. She came close to the bed. She felt Madeline's stomach and then put her hand up inside of her. "The baby is breeched. It is turned the wrong way. It's tryin' to come out feet first and it is ripping her apart inside. We have to turn him," Alda explained.

"I can't do that! I don't know how," Grace said.

Alda nodded. "I've done it before. I just hope it ain't too late," she said in her broken English. She looked over at Alvin. "Do you want to stay or go?" she asked.

Alvin's face was white. "I'm staying. I won't leave her," he said.

Alda reached her right hand up inside of Madeline. She began pressing around her stomach with her left hand. Madeline was screaming. She gripped Alvin's hand. Diana gripped the bottom of the bed. Her knuckles were white. Grace Hickman had turned toward the window. She had tears in her eyes.

Madeline had fainted. She lay limp on the bed. Blood had soaked her skirt and the mattress. Soon, Alda pulled her hand out of Madeline. Blood squirted all over her. There was a cry. It was a boy. Alda handed the baby to Grace. She went to the washbowl and began to wash the blood from him. Alda put her head on Madeline's chest. She stood up. "I am sorry, Mr. Hughes. Your wife is gone," she announced, shaking her head.

"What?" Alvin asked. "What do you mean she is gone? How can she be gone, just like that. The baby is alive, how can she be dead?" He was frantic. He reached over and lifted Madeline's head. He called to her. "Madeline! Madeline, you hear me now! You have a son! You need to take care of him, so you hear me now." He was sobbing. He looked up at Alda. "What am I going to do?" he asked.

Alda shook her head. "That there baby will need to nurse. He will starve if he ain't nursed," she said.

Grace turned, saying to Diana, "You have dairy cows out at the Martin place. You could take him out there," she said, looking from Diana to Alvin.

Alvin stood up. Wiping the tears from his face, he asked, "Would you take care of my baby for me? I can't take him with me. I don't have no way of caring for him."

Diana sighed. "I must speak with my husband and Mr. Martin. I can't make this decision on my own," she said.

Grace turned to her, handing her the baby wrapped in a clean towel. She said, "Well, you better hurry. This boy needs fed pretty soon."

Diana rushed down the steps. She ran to where Porter Martin and Brandon were standing. She saw the startled look on their faces, and realized that she was covered in blood. She said, "Mrs. Hughes did not make it. She had a son. He is fine, but needs milk. Mr. Hughes has asked us to take him home and care for him. I cannot make this decision. It is something we all will have to decide upon."

Brandon nodded and took her hand. They looked over at Porter. He nodded at them. "Of course! We will care for the child," he said.

Diana looked at Brandon. "Of course. We will just start our family a little early, that is all," Brandon said, pulling her to him. Then he said to Porter, "I will hitch up a wagon. We better get home and get some milking done." He went toward the stable.

Martha approached Diana. She said, "I am sorry, Diana. I think I will stay in town at the shop tonight. I brought some things I need to put away. I will ride out tomorrow and tell you about our visit with Josie."

"All right, Martha. I suppose I will be pretty busy tomorrow with the baby and all," Diana said. She turned to go inside when Alvin Hughes came toward them.

"Mr. Martin, I need to bury my wife early tomorrow morning. I was wondering if maybe you could put the children up at your place tonight so they don't have to see it. I would be grateful to you. I know it is a lot to ask, but I am in quite a predicament here," Alvin said.

Porter nodded. He looked over at Diana. "What do you say, Miss Diana? Is there room for them? You will be doing most of the work."

Diana smiled. "Yes. I can keep an eye on them until Mr. Hughes is ready to go," she said.

"Good," Alvin said. "I can't tell you how much this means to me. I will come for them tomorrow after I bury my Madeline."

Brandon arrived with the wagon. He had loaded the supplies that Porter brought with him from Philadelphia. Diana handed him the baby and climbed up beside him on the bench seat. "Change of plans. We will be keeping Mr. Hughes's children until after he buries his wife tomorrow. So they will all be coming home with us tonight," she said. Brandon smiled and handed her the baby. Porter climbed up into the wagon. Alvin helped the children into the back and told them he would come for them in the morning. They waved as Brandon drove the wagon toward the Martin house. Diana looked back to see a blood soaked Alda Faulk enter her house.

When they arrived at the farm, Brandon went to the barn and began milking a cow. He brought the warm milk into the kitchen where Diana was preparing some dinner for all of them. Porter was telling the children stories in the living room. He appeared to be happier than he had been in a long time.

Brandon went back to the barn to unload the wagon. Diana handed Porter the baby while she worked at the stove. He smiled up at her.

The table was full. It reminded Diana of the Sunday dinners. Diana tried to imagine feeding a family this size every day. How did the Hugheses do it? She cleaned up the table while Brandon filled the bathtub. He put the children in the tub, two at a time. They seemed to love it. Then they were led, or carried, upstairs to Diana and Martha's room to be tucked into bed. It was crowded, but no more than what it must have been in that covered wagon. Diana took the baby to bed with her and Brandon. Porter said he would build a cradle for the baby tomorrow.

It seemed Diana had just got to sleep when the baby began to cry. She carried him downstairs to the kitchen. She began to heat up some milk when Brandon joined her. He held the baby until she had filled a bottle that Grace had sent home with her. He began to suck from the bottle making loud sucking noises. Diana looked up at Brandon. He was smiling. "Mr. Hughes forgot to name the little fellow," he said.

"We will get a name from him tomorrow." Diana whispered. Brandon stroked his head until he was fast asleep. They carried him upstairs and put him in the bed between them. Diana fell asleep quickly. It had been quite a day for her.

The next morning, Diana came downstairs to find Brandon and Porter making flapjacks. Porter had all of the children laughing. Brandon was bouncing Franklin on his knee. Diana carried the baby to the copper bathtub. She placed a hide that was near the door inside the tub and laid the baby on it. She went to the stove and began helping with breakfast.

"Are Daddy and Mommy coming here this morning?" Winston asked.

"I think so," Brandon replied.

"How old are you, Winston?" Diana asked as she got plates from the cupboard.

Winston had his fork in his hand. He was obviously very hungry. "I am seven, Mrs. Shively. My brother, Raymond, is six. Shirley is five, and Cecilia is three. Franklin over there is only one," he replied.

"Well, have you ever gone to school, Winston?" Diana asked.

"Yes, Ma'am. Mrs. Green was my teacher. That was before we left Fredericksburg. Raymond and I went," Winston said.

Brandon said. "Mrs. Shively is the school teacher here in Berlin."

"We are going to my Uncle Duncan's. He is building us a house in the mountains. He wrote Daddy a letter telling him all about it," Winston said.

Diana smiled. "You mother told me all about that. It must be pretty exciting for you," she said. She put the flapjacks on the table and their eyes opened wide. Porter led them in a prayer and then they ate. It became rather quiet while they were eating. Every time Diana looked over at Brandon, he was smiling.

After breakfast, Brandon went to do the milking and feed the animals. Winston went with him. Porter took Raymond, Shirley, and Cecilia outside in the morning sunshine, to show them around. Diana fed the baby and played with little Franklin. It was soon time to prepare lunch. Diana thought Alvin Hughes would have been after the children by now. She prepared bacon and eggs for lunch.

"Where's Daddy?" Shirley asked as they ate their lunch.

Porter was holding Franklin on his lap. He looked up and with a smile said, "He will be along soon. Aren't you having a good time?"

"Yeah. This is a nice house. I like it better than that old wagon. I was just wondering where Mommy and Daddy were," Shirley said.

"Well, if he ain't here by the time we get things cleaned up after dinner, I will take a ride to town to see what is keeping him. You can all play out back in the orchard until we get back," Porter said.

That seemed to appease them. They ate and went outside to the orchard. Diana began to clean up the kitchen. The baby slept soundly in the tub, and little Franklin played on the floor between the front room and kitchen. Brandon kissed her and said. "I better go out and keep an eye on them until Porter gets back here with their father. Just you start getting used to a houseful of kids while I'm gone. This is exactly what I meant when I said I wanted a houseful of them."

Diana blushed. She touched his face before he turned to go. He stopped and turned toward her asking, "How about I carry little Franklin outside with me? The sunshine will be good for him, and you will have a few minutes to yourself."

Diana looked over at the baby boy playing on the floor. He was barely able to walk. She smiled and said, "All right, but just for a little while. He is pretty pale skinned. Too much sun would not be good for him."

Brandon scooped him up. He carried him outside to where the children were playing. Diana began washing dishes. She put water on to boil so she could wash diapers.

Brandon carried a fussy Franklin back into the house. He wanted to go back outside. Diana carried him in her arms, walking circles around the kitchen until he fell asleep. She had a stack of hides on the floor in the corner under the window. She laid him there. Soon, she heard Porter Martin returning with the buggy. She ran to the front window and looked down the road for the oxen and wagon. Brandon had told her they were slow. Perhaps it would take them longer. She went to the back window. She saw Porter talking to Brandon. Porter went toward the barn. Brandon was coming to the house. He had a confused look on his face.

"What is it?" Diana asked as he entered the back door.

Brandon removed his hat. He spoke softly so as not to wake the babies. "Porter said Alvin Hughes pulled out early this morning. Sherman said they thought he was coming here. He did not even bury his wife. He just left. Sherman and Stumpy buried Mrs. Hughes this morning." Brandon looked out the window at the children playing in the orchard. "Do you want me to ride out and find him? He would have left a trail with that wagon," he asked.

Diana looked out the window also. Then she looked at the two babies sleeping in the kitchen. She put her arms around Brandon. "How could he leave these adorable children? How could he?" she asked.

Brandon held her at arm's length. He looked into her eyes. He asked, "Diana, they are good kids. He obviously has no way of caring for them alone. Think about it. What would he do with them? We have a decision to make. Do you think we can handle a family this size right off?"

Diana looked up at him. She was speechless. She looked over at the two babies again. "Oh, Brandon! What do we tell them? Of course, they can stay. That is, if it is all right with Mr. Martin. But they will be heartbroken. We need to speak with Mr. Martin before we make a decision." She was pacing the room now. Brandon nodded his head. "He is playing with the children now. I will talk to him when he is alone."

Just then, they heard horses coming. It was Martha and Sofia. They tethered their horses at the front steps and came inside.

"Diana, I just heard Mr. Hughes rode out and left his children. What are you going to do?" Sofia asked.

"Well, we need to speak with Mr. Martin before decisions can be made. This is his home," Diana said.

Brandon said, "He is coming this way now."

Porter entered the back door. He had a smile on his face. "They are some kids, those Hughes kids are." He hung his hat up. He turned to see them all watching him. "What is it?" he asked.

"What do we do with them?" Martha asked.

Porter smiled. He pulled out a chair near where Franklin slept and asked. "Have you forgotten six little girls and their Mamma? When they needed a home, where did they go? Of course, they can stay here. If it is too much work for, Miss Diana, I will pay for someone to help her, just like I did for my Miss Margaret."

Martha said. "I could take one or two of them with me to live at my house in town."

"I will have to ask Jonathan, but I am sure it would be all right if one came to live with us. Perhaps one of the babies," Sofia said.

Porter was shaking his head. "Did I ask you girls to split up? No. They will all stay together. I will pay Tilly to help care for them. They all stay together."

Diana went to Porter Martin and kissed him on the forehead. "You are a wonderful man, Mr. Martin. The good Lord has blessed our family with a neighbor and Christian such as you. Now he has blessed another family with you. Of course, they can stay here. I would be proud to have them," she said.

Brandon smiled. "I wanted a houseful of children, and now I got one," he said. Diana went to him and put her arm around them.

Diana asked her sisters. "Would you two mind staying until after we tell the children? I may have my hands full."

Martha and Sofia agreed to stay. They sat down at the table. Brandon went outside to gather up the children. One by one, they entered the kitchen. They sat around the table.

Winston looked around the table at the faces and asked, "My daddy left us again, didn't he?"

"Again?" Porter asked. "He left you once before?"

"Yes," Winston said. "Once he left us with Mommy, back at the farm. He was going off to war, he said, but he didn't. He came back. He said he thought he wasn't ready to settle down. His daddy, my grandfather, slapped him a couple of times, and he said he wouldn't leave us again. I reckon he took mommy with him this time."

"No. No," Diana said. She went to Winston and put her arms around him. "Your mommy did not leave you, children. She would never leave you. She loved you very much. Your mommy had a very difficult time giving birth to your baby brother. It was more than her little body could take. She passed away," Diana explained with tears in her eyes.

The children looked at each other with confusion on their faces. "Mommy died?" Raymond asked.

"Yes," Diana said.

"Did my baby brother kill her?" Winston asked.

Diana ran her fingers through his unruly hair. "No. She was just too weak. She did not want to die. She did not want your baby brother to die either. If she had been stronger, she would be here with you now. I think the long trip in the wagon was just too much for her," she explained.

Winston and Raymond began to cry. The other children did not understand. They were too young. "What is going to happen to us now?" Winston asked.

"Well, you said you wanted to live in the mountains where there were forests and streams that ran with clear water. We have all of that right here. We would love to have you live with us, that is, if you want to stay," Diana said.

Winston looked around the table. He reached over and took Cecilia's hand. He rose from his seat and went to stand by her side. "If you don't mind, Ma'am. We would work hard to pay for our keep," he said.

Diana smiled at this little boy, who was so much older than his years. She looked up at Brandon and Porter Martin. They were smiling.

Brandon said, "You don't need to worry about paying for your keep. You are part of this family now. We are in this all together, and we will get through it all together."

The baby began to cry. Diana went to the tub and picked him up. She had a bottle all ready for him. When she put it in his mouth, he stopped crying and began to feed. She looked at Brandon. "This little boy has no name. What shall we call him?" she asked.

Brandon went to her. He looked down at the baby in her arms. He stroked his head. "How would you feel about calling him, Robert?" he asked.

Diana looked up at him. She smiled. "Robert," she whispered. She smiled and nodded.

Brandon turned to the children sitting around the table. "What do you say we call your baby brother, Robert?" he asked.

Winston smiled. "Robert is a good name." He looked around at his siblings. They were all nodding. He wiped the tears from his eyes and said, "Robert."

"Now, what do you say we go back outside and make us a couple of swings in that orchard," Porter said. Then he turned to Diana, "After that, I will build a cradle and a crib. It looks like I might want to make a couple more beds, too." He was whistling as he put his hat on his head and held the door for the children. He winked at Brandon and Diana as he turned to follow the children.

"Mr. Martin said once that he wanted children, but Miss Margaret could not have any. It looks like the Lord has blessed him with a houseful," Sofia said.

"Twice," Diana said.

Brandon smiled. "I better go help him. Do you need anything before I go?" he asked.

"We can handle this," Diana said, smiling at him.

Brandon went through the back door. He closed it softly so as not to wake Franklin, who was still sleeping.

"I will make us a cup of tea," Martha said.

The girls sat around the table drinking their tea. Diana held the sleeping Robert in her arms. Martha said, "I have decided to stay in town. It is a beautiful little house that Mr. Martin built for me. I find I like it there very much."

Diana smiled and asked, "Do you like staying in town, or do you like being near Carver Wilks?"

Martha flushed. Sofia looked back and forth between the two of them. "Did I miss something?" she asked.

"Carver Wilks is a very kindhearted gentleman. I enjoy his company very much," Martha said.

"Oh, boy, oh, boy! Is there another wedding coming up?" Sofia asked.

"Shh...," Diana said, nodding toward the stirring Franklin.

"Don't be silly," Martha said. "I don't know him that well. I am just saying I enjoy his company. End of story. I am the last of the Lewis girls. You all have new names now."

"That is true," Diana whispered. "That is sad, too. I guess that was why Pappa always wanted a son. To carry on the family name. It will die with us, girls."

"No, Sir. Pappa said he had a brother somewhere in England. Perhaps he had a son. We don't really know anything about the Lewises actually," Martha said.

Sofia took a sip of her tea. She put her cup down and said, "It rightly don't matter, anyway. There isn't anything we can do about it."

Martha laughed and said, "Of course; Diana here had to go get herself a big family right off. Josephine has four children and she has been married for nearly six years. Di here was married all of two and a half weeks and has six children already. Boy, oh, boy. Build her a schoolhouse, and she will fill it."

They laughed for a while. Robert stirred and continued sleeping. Franklin woke. He crawled toward them. Martha went to him and held his hands so he could walk over to the table. She picked him up. He squealed and squirmed until she put him back down on the floor. He pulled himself up to a chair, and walked about the kitchen holding on to everything within reach.

"He should be walking by the end of the week," Sofia said.

"I think he would have been walking already if they had not been cooped up in that wagon all this time," Diana said.

She handed Robert to Sofia. She picked Franklin up and began to feed him from a bowl of leftovers. He tried to feed himself, so she let him. He made a terrible mess of himself, and her too, but he managed to get most of the food in his mouth.

They laughed as they watched him. The more they laughed, the more he acted up.

"He is a very pleasant baby," Sofia said.

"When are you going to have one of your own?" Martha asked.

"Whenever the good Lord thinks I am ready I guess," Sofia answered.

"Diana will have a houseful if she has children of her own," Martha said.

"I have a houseful now. I am a teacher. I am used to having lots of children around. I am not going to let that stop me," Diana said, laughing.

The three of them laughed. "Leave it to Diana," Martha said.

"They better behave themselves and listen to her, or she will whoop on them," Sofia said.

Again, they laughed. It was time to start preparing the evening meal. Brandon had brought in a pheasant. Diana and Martha began to stuff it with leftover bread and spices. Sofia played with Franklin. Robert was sleeping again. They chatted as they worked.

Sofia left. She had to get home to her husband. Martha stayed to help with dinner and the clean up. It was nearly dark when they all sat down at the table. Porter and Brandon had built a cradle for little Robert. They would work on a crib for Franklin tomorrow. When they all sat down at the table, Diana noticed how lighthearted Porter Martin was. He was happy with a houseful of children. Diana had not seen him like this in a long time. He teased the children and played riddle games with them.

After dinner, Robert and Porter took the children into the front room. Porter would tell them stories, just as he had done for Diana and her sisters, when they moved into the house years ago. Brandon held Franklin on his lap. The others gathered around Porter. He stood in the center of the room telling an animated story that he made up using their names. The children loved it.

After cleaning up the kitchen, Martha announced that she would have to go back to town. It was getting late and very dark. Porter was going to escort her home. Diana began washing the children, preparing them for bed. Brandon kept them occupied until they were all ready to be tucked in. They paraded the children upstairs. Brandon tucked them in. Diana carried Robert to their room and placed him in his new cradle. It still smelled of fresh cut lumber. She smiled. Franklin would have to sleep with them until the crib was finished.

Diana went into the bedroom where the children were all waiting for her to kiss them good night. She bent down kissing each of them.

"Good night," they called as she stood at the door smiling at them.

"Good night," she said. She closed the door. She heard Porter coming in the back door.

Diana followed Brandon down the stairs and into the kitchen. Porter was sitting on the chair next to the back door, removing his boots. He looked up and asked, "Are they all in bed?"

"Yes," Brandon said.

Porter nodded. "I was hopin' to see them before they went to sleep. I suppose it will keep until tomorrow," he said.

The next morning was rather chaotic. It was Sunday. Diana knew that Tilly and her children would be there for dinner after church. She hoped Martha could come help her again. Brandon was going to bring a turkey in from the smoke house. Diana would need all the help she could get.

After breakfast, Porter announced that he would take the wagon to collect Tilly and her children for church. Winston and Raymond wanted to ride along with him. He brought the wagon up to the front porch and the boys climbed up beside him on the front seat. Diana waved at them as they headed toward the shallow stream crossing. She went back inside.

Brandon went to hitch up the larger buggy. Diana changed Robert's diaper. She changed Franklin's diaper, only to change Robert's again. Brandon carried Shirley and Cecilia to the buggy. He came back for Franklin. Diana held Robert in her arms as she sat between the two little girls. Brandon held Franklin on his lap as he drove the team. They were on their way to Berlin.

Once they reached the church, she found the entire town was waiting for them. Stumpy handed the girls to Zachariah and Sherman. He held Franklin while Brandon came down off the wagon. Diana looked around. They were all standing around smiling at them. Grace Hickman approached her.

"Mrs. Shively, I just want to say that it is a noble thing you have done for these children. I admire your grit," Grace said.

Diana smiled. She said, "Thank you, Mrs. Hickman. I appreciate your saying so."

"Well," Grace began. "We are all willing to help in any way we can."

"That is very kind of you," Diana said. She smiled. This was strange coming from Mrs. Hickman. Diana was not sure whether she was genuinely being kind, or setting Diana up for an insult. Diana decided to give her the benefit of the doubt. After all, it was Sunday, and they were at the house of God.

Thelma and Beatrice Faulk had approached Shirley and Cecilia. They were more Winston and Raymond's age, but they were little girls. They were naturally drawn to each other.

Porter was arriving with Tilly and the children. Tilly was smiling. She was dressed in one of the dresses that Martha had made for her. Hoppy and Gilda were wearing new dresses as well. Diana would have to ask Martha to make some new clothes for the Hughes children.

Diana saw Martha walking toward the church. She stopped to talk to Carver Wilks. They talked for a moment and approached the church together. Diana smiled. Martha made eye contact with Diana and smiled back at her. She held her head high.

It was a beautiful morning. Everyone filed into the church. They left the door open. Sofia sat up front next to Concetta. The Faulks sat in the back even though Pastor Gilbert invited them to come forward. Diana thought that it would take time, but eventually, they would become more comfortable with the people in town. Alda had saved Robert's life. It was not her fault that Madeline had died. Madeline would not have survived that birthing regardless.

Martha slid into the pew next to Diana. Diana leaned over and whispered to her, "Martha. Thank you for all of your help yesterday. I don't know what I would have done without you and Sofia's help. Are you coming for dinner today?"

Martha smiled and whispered into Diana's ear. "Not today, Sister. Carver has asked me to go on a picnic with him after church. Will you be able to manage without me?"

Diana felt a lump in her throat. She did not think she would be able to manage without Martha's help. She would have Tilly, but it would be very difficult. She smiled and nodded as she said, "We will be fine. Tilly will be there. We should be fine."

Parson Jonathan Gilbert preached about the love for your fellow man. He welcomed the children into the congregation and announced that their presence was a blessing from the Lord. He urged the entire town to help in the nurturing and caring for the Hughes children. He also praised Alda Faulk for her assistance in the birth of the baby, Robert Hughes. They sang a hymn, followed by a prayer. He went to the back of the church, welcoming each one of the congregation as they exited.

Porter invited the Parson and Sofia to dinner. They accepted. Diana was relieved. She only hoped Sofia wasn't having a dreamy day. She needed her help today.

The ride back to the Martin farm was pleasant. Porter led the procession with the wagon carrying Winston, Raymond, Tilly, and her children. Brandon drove the larger buggy with Diana, the girls, and the two babies. Parson Gilbert and Sofia rode their horses behind.

When they reached the farm, the children went out into the orchard to play. Diana, Tilly, and Sofia began to prepare dinner while the men gathered on the front porch to smoke their pipes.

Porter and Brandon had slid two tables together to extend the length of the one that sat in the center of the kitchen. They also brought in two planks that they rested on chairs to form a bench seat. They all sat down at the table. Parson Gilbert said grace and then they began to pass the food around. Sofia did help with the children. Diana smiled over at her. Sofia smiled back. She was gaining weight. She was nearly as round as she was tall by now. Martha had obviously let the seams out on her dress for Diana could see the stitch marks near the seams. She said nothing. She appreciated Sofia's help.

The day went rather well. The children all played outside until it was time for Porter to take Tilly and her children home. Sofia and Jonathan left early. Tilly helped Diana prepare the children for bed. She promised to come back tomorrow and help Diana. Porter said he would go after her early in the morning. They were going to make it work.

The summer went quickly. Brandon did not have an opportunity to take Diana and her sisters to Philadelphia as he had promised. Diana understood. How would they manage with all of these children? What would they do with them when they got there? She understood why Josephine never made the trip back home now. It would have been exhausting.

School was scheduled to start the Monday following the next church service. Parson Gilbert announced it after his sermon. By this time, Herbert and Alda Faulk were sitting closer to the front of the church. More and more of the citizens of Berlin were going to Alda for their aches and pains. She had become the town's closest thing to a doctor. Her Indian remedies had helped Porter with his gout. Even Grace Hickman had seen her a time or two.

They had a town picnic behind the church this Sunday. The children all played together. Diana, Martha, and Tilly cleaned the schoolhouse to prepare for the next morning. Grace Hickman, Alda Faulk, Concetta, and Sofia watched the children for them. When they had finished, Martha and Carver Wilks went for a walk by themselves. Diana watched them as they went. When they were near the creek, Carver took Martha's hand to help her across. Once they reached the other side, he continued to hold her hand. Diana looked up at Brandon and smiled. He had Franklin resting on his shoulders. Homer was carrying Cecilia piggyback. They went for the buggy. It was time to go home. Porter loaded all of the older children into the back of his wagon. Tilly rode with Diana in the buggy. They had Cecilia, Franklin, and Robert with them. Tilly went to the Martin house to help Diana prepare the children for bed. Then Porter took her and her children home.

The next morning, Porter had left to go after Tilly and the children. Diana dressed for school, while Brandon ate breakfast with the children. When Tilly got there, they were ready to go. Tilly would watch over Shirley, Cecilia, Franklin, and Robert. All of her children would be going to school this year. Porter loaded Diana into the wagon. Hoppy, Gilda, Homer, Winston, Raymond, and Percy sat around her as they went. Porter stopped to pick up Thelma, Beatrice, and Wayne Faulk. This year all of the Faulk children would be in school also.

When they arrived at school, Diana opened the windows. Homer rang the bell, as Porter pulled away with the wagon. Diana began to assign seats according to age groups. In the front row sat Percy, Raymond, and Winston. In the second row sat Homer, Gilda, and Hoppy. Homer frowned. He was the only boy in his row. Diana sat him at the end of the row and told him she was putting him there to watch the door. This appeased him somewhat, but she knew he still would rather sit with the other boys.

She began to go over the alphabet again for the newer students. The older ones were assigned to help the younger ones learn the song. The day went so quickly that she was surprised when Porter came driving the wagon down the hill toward the school.

They piled into the wagon. Porter dropped the Faulk children off. Alda was standing at the door waiting for them. She waved as they pulled away. Diana was anxious to get home. She missed Franklin and little Robert. Porter assured her that Tilly had everything under control.

When they reached the house, Porter helped the children down from the wagon. They were instructed to change out of their school clothes before they went out to play. They would no doubt end up wading in the creek. For some reason, they always came in wet and muddy before dinner. Diana did not mind. She remembered the times they stopped the two-wheeled cart at the crossing so she and her sisters could wade in that creek. It was a good time in their lives. Diana hoped these children would have fond memories such as the ones she had.

Tilly had both babies awake and ready to welcome Diana when she entered the kitchen. She had the stove going with turkey gravy simmering on top. There were biscuits in the oven.

"Oh, Tilly! What would I do without you?" Diana asked as she bent over the gravy, smelling the aroma that filled the kitchen. "You will stay for dinner, won't you?"

"I don't want to be no trouble, Miss Diana. We kin go home an eat," Tilly replied.

Diana shook her head. "Nonsense, Tilly. You did all of this work. There is plenty here to go around. There is no reason why you should go home and cook another meal to feed your family. You will stay and eat with us. I insist. Then you can go home and do whatever you need to do. I appreciate your help so very much. I don't know what I would have done without you," Diana said.

"You is learnin' my kids," Tilly said. "I is glad to help."

"Did you have any trouble, Tilly?" Diana asked.

"No, Ma'am. They is good kids," Tilly replied.

"Good," Diana said. "Are you going to be able to do this everyday? I don't want to take you from your own duties."

"I is fine, Miss. Misser Martin and me have made arrangements. I is to come help everyday, and he will pay me. I kin use the money. I ain't a slave or nothin'. We worked it all out," Tilly said as she played with Franklin.

Diana smiled. She recollected a time when Porter Martin made arrangements with her own mother to come to the house and care for Miss Margaret.

He paid well. Diana turned to Tilly and said, "That Mr. Martin is a very good Christian man, Tilly. If he made arrangements with you, he will stand true to his word. You can bet on it."

"Yes, Ma'am. Tilly knows he is a good man. He is good wit the kids, too," Tilly said.

Diana went to stand in front of Tilly as she sat in a chair at the end of the table. "Tilly, I would like it very much if you and your children would have your evening meals with us. You have been such a blessing to this household. You are like family. You understand what I am trying to say, don't you?" Diana asked.

"Yes, Ma'am," Tilly replied. "The more the merrier. That is what Mr. Martin told me."

"That is right, Tilly. The more the merrier," Diana repeated with a smile.

They gathered around the dinner table that evening with the chatter of the day's events. The children were happy to be in school. The Hughes children went to school in Virginia. They told of a much bigger school with more children their own age. Winston said, "We didn't have no slaves at our school, though. In Virginia, they were not allowed to go to school."

Brandon put his fork down. He smiled and replied. "Winston, Tilly's children are not slaves. There are no more slaves in Virginia either. They were all freed after the war. They are allowed to go to school now, and they should all be doing just that. All of the children sitting around this table are equal. There is not one any better than any of the others. God just made some darker skinned than others. That is all."

Homer smiled at Brandon. Winston looked up at Homer and frowned. "It sure is different here," he said.

Porter reached over and rustled Winston's hair. "It may be different from Virginia, young man. But this is the way it should be everywhere. We are all God's children," he declared.

Homer was still smiling. Tilly smiled, too. Winston went back to eating. It was obvious that he was thinking about what he had just heard.

After dinner, Tilly helped Diana clear the table and wash the dishes. Porter and Brandon had taken the children into the front room for their story time. Diana could hear the laughter of the children coming through the closed door. When they were finished with the dishes, Porter finished his story and loaded Tilly and her children up in the buggy. Diana waved to them as they left.

Brandon stood beside her. He kissed her neck. He would help her wash the children and prepare them for bed. He asked about her day. She talked about it the whole time they were washing the children and putting them into their nightclothes. Porter had returned and Brandon went to the barn to help him unhitch the buggy and bed down the horses.

Soon they were rushing the children up the stairs to bed. Porter held Franklin until he fell asleep. Brandon carried him up the stairs, with Diana following him. She carried Robert in her arms. He, too, was fast asleep. When they reached their bedroom, Brandon held the door for her to enter first. She stepped into the dimly lit room. She placed Robert into his cradle. When she turned, she noticed that Brandon was placing Franklin in a new crib.

Brandon whispered. "Porter finished it today. He wanted to surprise you. We will have the bed to ourselves tonight." He kissed her. She melted into his arms.

Fall turned to winter. Concetta had a baby boy. She named him Burton. Mrs. Hickman doted on the child. She took over as if it were her own child.

Sofia was pregnant. She had gained even more weight. She waddled when she walked. Her face had become round and plump. She was still very pretty, but she did not take good care of herself. Sometimes, she would appear at the general store without even combing her hair. It was obvious that she was even lazier than ever.

Every morning, Porter Martin went to collect Tilly and her children. He was preparing to make a trip to Philadelphia at the end of the week. The stage did not run in the winter months. Porter would be taking a wagon, and traveling alone. Brandon would be picking Tilly and the children up in the mornings until he returned. Porter had instructed Brandon on what he needed him to do at the mill. Stumpy and Carver Wilks would be helping him, unless Carver had work to do at the blacksmith shop.

Martha had been making some coats for all of the children. Porter had promised to return with more fabric for her shop. She had been seeing a lot of Carver Wilks lately. Nearly every Sunday they were at her shop having dinner together, or they would arrive together at Porter Martin's house to have dinner with the family.

It was Friday. They rose to a cloudy, windy morning. Brandon collected Tilly and the children as usual. He had put the runners back on the wagon house, and was taking the children to school. He built a fire and left, promising to return for all of them around two o'clock, as usual. Porter Martin was due to return home today or tomorrow.

Diana had been watching for Mr. Matin's wagon from the window as the students did the arithmetic problems she had written on the blackboard. The younger students were practicing the alphabet on their slate tablets. The wind howled outside. It was snowing so hard Diana could not even see the church, which stood right next to the school. She tried not to show signs of being worried. It was after two. Brandon should have been there by now. She asked Homer to ring the bell. They sat around talking while she watched for the wagon house. Percy declared that he had to go to the outhouse. Diana opened the door and peered outside. The snow was knee deep and rising. She told Percy he would have to use the chamber pot and instructed the children to sit with their backs to him until he had finished. After awhile, she had to put more wood on the stove. Then she declared that they would resume their studies until Mr. Shively arrived to collect them.

After about two hours of going over their daily studies, Diana stopped and they began to sing songs. She knew something was very wrong. She paced nervously, wringing her hands. She could not leave the children. Why hadn't Brandon come for them? She went to the window. The snow was blowing so hard, she still could not see the church. She assumed he was waiting for the snow to let up. The children were becoming concerned. They were whining that they were getting hungry. Diana had nothing for them to eat, only a pot of water on top of the stove and a pouch of loose tea. She decided to make the tea stretch. She took none for herself. This quieted the children for a while.

Diana called Hoppy, Winston, and Homer to her desk. She spoke softly, "The snow is blowing so hard I fear Mr. Shively may not be able to get through until it lets up. I need you to help me occupy the smaller children until it stops. We have plenty of wood for the stove, but we have no food. I do not know how long we are going to be stranded here. Do you think you could help me?" she asked them.

"Yes, Mrs. Shively," Hoppy said.

"We could tell stories like Mr. Martin. He tells the best stories," Winston said.

Diana smiled. "That is a very good idea, Winston. It will keep their minds occupied until Mr. Shively comes," she said.

She sent them back to their seats. Then she tapped on her desk. "Attention, please. That is enough studying for today. Mr. Shively is no doubt delayed due to the heavy snow. I think we will have a story time until he comes. Does anyone have a story they want to share with the class?" she asked.

Homer's hand went up immediately. "Yes, Homer. Would you mind coming up front where we can all see you?" Diana instructed.

Homer approached the front of the room.

"Once when we was in Virginia, our Masser axed my Mamma to cook a chicken for supper. Mamma took me wit her and we was goin to catch us a chicken so she could cut its head off. Well, we chases and chased us some chickens, but we couldn't catch us none." Homer went on with his tale of catching the dinner chicken. The students laughed. Diana's concentration drifted away. She went to the window again. It continued to blow, obscuring her view.

Soon she became aware of the silence. Homer was back in his seat. She went to her desk and said. "That was very good, Homer. Now, does anyone else have a story?"

Thelma Faulk raised her hand. "Yes, Thelma. Come up front, please," Diana said. She stepped back to the window.

Thelma began. "We came here from that way," she said pointing west. "My mother is a full blooded Shawnee Indian. Her grandfather was a chief. Mother says that makes me and Beatrice princesses, and Wayne is a prince. Father married Mother and took her from a reservation. Folks did not like us much I guess because we never had no friends. Anyway, Father decided to move away from there. He said we would be happier in a small town. My mother knows so much about herbs and medicine," Thelma went on.

Diana found herself listening to Thelma's story. She realized the slaves were not the only people who were mistreated. She made a mental note to work on their English. Soon, Thelma finished her story and returned to her seat. "Thank you, Thelma. That was a very interesting story. Who is next?" Diana asked.

Guilda raised her hand. "Yes, Gilda. Come up front, please," Diana said. It was working. The time was passing quickly. Diana lit more candles to put more light into the room. Soon, she heard something outside. It was coming closer. She squinted to see through the blinding snow. It was the wagon house.

The door opened. Snow swirled into the room. Brandon appeared in the doorway. He stomped his feet. He was bundled up with so many clothes it was hard to tell who he was. Diana ran to him. She threw herself into his arms.

"Is everyone all right?" Brandon asked.

"Yes, but I was so worried. Has anyone seen Porter? I hope he is not out in this," Diana said.

Brandon shook his head. "I hope he isn't, either. He is a pretty smart man. I brought some bread and dried turkey for the kids. Tilly sent it. I am going to try to get us all out of here. You feed the kids while I bank the fire and we will be on our way," Brandon said.

Diana took the bread and dried turkey from Brandon. She passed it out to the children. With the help of the older ones, she bundled them up. They stood at the door ready to go. Brandon had pulled the wagon house as close to the door as he could. He carried the children, one by one, to the wagon house. The snow was over his knees by now. There were blankets and hides stacked inside for them to bundle up in. He carried Diana to the wagon last. He climbed up inside after her.

It seemed to be taking twice as much time for them to reach the Faulk house. Thelma, Beatrice, and Wayne stood at the door to the wagon house waiting for Brandon to carry them, one at a time, to their front door. Alda and Herbert waited for them there. They thanked him and waved as he climbed back up into the wagon house.

Diana led the children in songs as they went. It took their minds off of the storm that seemed to be attacking the wagon house. The horses were totally covered with snow. They continued to pull the load in the direction they were instructed. From time to time, they would shake their heads to remove the snow that was building up on them.

"How can you tell where you are going?" Diana whispered to Brandon.

"It isn't easy. The tracks I made coming into town are nearly gone. Hopefully it will let up before we lose them all together," he replied.

Diana could not tell if it was getting dark, or if it was the storm obstructing the sun. Her watch was pinned to her dress. Her coat was buttoned and she was wrapped in so many hides that she could not get to it.

It seemed that it took forever to reach the Martin house. Brandon pulled up at the back door and, once again, he carried them one by one, to the door. Tilly was waiting for them. Brandon pulled the wagon house toward the barn. Diana stood at the window watching for him to return. The snow was letting up, but the wind was still blowing hard.

Soon, she saw the outline of Brandon's body coming through the blowing snow. She ran to the door. He stomped his feet as he entered. Diana pulled a chair over for him to sit down. She pulled at his boots. Tilly wiped up the melting snow that fell off of him. He removed his coat.

"Tilly, could Mr. Shively have a cup of tea?" Diana asked.

"Yes, Ma'am! Already made some for all ya all. Just waitin for ya to get here," Tilly said.

Franklin crawled to them. He pulled himself up until he was standing next to Brandon. He began to bounce and jabber in an unknown language at them. They laughed. Brandon stood up and removed his coat. He walked over to the hooks that lined the wall, hanging his coat on one. He turned to see Franklin walking to him. "He's walking!" Brandon said, surprised.

Tilly smiled. "Little Frank, he bin walkin' all day. Right pleased with his-self, he is."

Brandon reached down, lifting the small boy into the air. "Ba Ba." Franklin laughed.

"I am not sure if he is calling you Pappa, or if he is trying to say your name," Diana said.

Brandon blew onto Franklin's belly, causing the baby to erupt into laughter. They all began to laugh. Only when the baby sleeping in the bathtub began to cry did they turn their attention away. Diana went to Robert, lifting him in her arms. She kissed his forehead. Tilly went to the stove and took his bottle out of a pan of water. She put a drop onto her wrist. It was a test to check the temperature. It was just right. She handed the bottle to Diana, who began to feed him.

Hoppy came into the kitchen through the door that led to the front room. Tilly had sent them all in there so they could play without waking Robert. "Mamma, when are we going to eat?" she asked Tilly.

"Soon child. Soon," Tilly replied.

Diana smiled and nodded her head at Hoppy. She had been listening. The children's English had improved already. They still needed a lot of work, but Diana felt confident that it would happen.

Tilly asked, "Mr. Martin? Is he comin home tonight?"

Diana looked up at Brandon. He said, "Tilly, we don't know. Mr. Martin has not arrived. He may have stayed in Philadelphia to wait out the storm. Until this snow breaks, we will not know." He looked over at Diana. She had a worried look on her face. "Don't worry, Diana. I am sure he is still in Philly. If we have not heard from him in a couple of days, I will ride to Philly to search for him."

He looked out the window. Then he turned to Tilly. "Tilly, the weather is too bad to take you home tonight. Could you, or rather, would you and the children stay here for the night? I doubt there will be any school tomorrow. It will be too risky to take the children back into town with all of this snow," Brandon said.

Tilly looked out the window. She was silent for a moment. Then she turned and nodded her head in the affirmative, without saying a word. She went back to the stove. Diana looked at Brandon and then back to Tilly. "Is there anything wrong, Tilly?" she asked.

"No, Ma'am. We is fine," Tilly said.

"Don't you want to stay here tonight?" Diana asked.

"Yes, Ma'am. We kin stay. I is just worried bout Misser Martin. That is all," Tilly replied.

Diana nodded, "Yes, Tilly. We are worried, too, but unfortunately, there is nothing we can do at the present. We must trust that Mr. Martin had better sense than to try to travel home in this weather. I believe he is still in Philadelphia, like Brandon said," Diana said as she turned to gaze out the window. Then she went on. "What do you say we start getting dinner on the table, and then we will figure out where everyone is going to sleep tonight."

Brandon took little Franklin into the front room. "I think I will check on the children while you two do your magic in the kitchen," he said.

Brandon went through the door that led to the front room. Hoppy followed him, looking back at Tilly and Diana before she closed the door.

Diana began to set the table. There would be a kitchen full of hungry children tonight. Who knew how long they would be stranded here with the storm still blowing outside? The wind blew against the glass windows. Ice was forming on the inside as well as the outside, making it difficult to see through the glass.

After dinner, Hoppy helped Diana and Tilly clean up the kitchen. It was decided that Tilly and her children would sleep in Porter Martin's room for the night. Brandon built a fire in the fireplaces upstairs to warm the rooms.

Tilly washed the younger ones, while Diana carried hides upstairs to place on the floor. It reminded her of the times she slept on hides in the loft with Josephine and Regina. She went downstairs to help Tilly finish with the washing of faces, arms, and legs. Soon, they were all marching up the stairs to bed. Diana could not help but wonder what they were going to do with all of these children tomorrow.

She lay in her bed waiting for Brandon to crawl in next to her. When he did, she turned to him and settled in his arms. He kissed her. Soon, they were making love. They whispered so as not to wake the babies. Afterwards, she lay there staring at the ceiling.

"Don't worry, Diana. Porter is a very smart man. He is held up somewhere safe," Brandon said, kissing her forehead.

Diana kissed his cheek and said. "I know. I guess I am just a natural worrier. What am I going to do with everybody tomorrow?"

Brandon chuckled. "Well, we have plenty of food. I suppose you could just teach school right here in the front room. Why not?" he asked.

Diana looked up at him in the dark night. "Brandon, what a wonderful idea! Why did I not think of that? It will keep us all occupied. They will continue with their studies and stay out of Tilly's hair. And I will have something to think about besides where Mr. Martin is," she said.

He kissed her tenderly. "Now, get some sleep. Tomorrow is going to be a very busy day for all of us," Brandon said.

Breakfast was rather chaotic. Tilly did not seem to be at all rattled by the commotion. She went about preparing breakfast as if it were any other morning. Diana seemed to spend more time retracing her steps. She felt as though she was getting nowhere. Robert was crying. He seemed to want to be held. Hoppy took him, pacing around the kitchen bouncing him in her arms as she went. It did not seem to appease him at all. He wanted Diana. Only when she took him in her arms did he quiet down. Franklin hung onto her skirt. She felt like she was in a bad dream.

Brandon came downstairs. He stood near the door that led to the front room and watched. He smiled. Then he went to Franklin and picked him up. Franklin squealed with delight. Brandon took him and the other children, with the exception of Hoppy into the front room. Diana continued to hold Robert in her arms.

Tilly placed her hands on her hips and said, "Mrs. Shively. You just sit a spell and leave the cookin' to me an Hoppy here. We will do just fine. That baby needs his Mamma."

Diana looked over at Tilly and smiled. "Thank you, Tilly. What would I do without you?" Diana said.

Tilly nodded. She smiled as she said, "You keep sayin' that, Ma'am," she turned her attention back to the stove.

Diana sat down. She looked down at Robert. He was making sucking noises. Hoppy handed Diana the bottle of warm milk. She placed it in Robert's mouth. He closed his eyes and began do drink his breakfast. Diana burped him twice. Finally, he was fast asleep. She placed him in the bathtub. By this time, Tilly and Hoppy had breakfast on the table. Diana went to the front room to announce to Brandon and the eight children that breakfast was ready.

At the table, everyone talked excitedly about having their lessons done at the Martin house. Diana found herself looking out the kitchen window several times. The snow was up over the porch steps. She said a silent prayer for Porter Martin. When her eyes met Brandon's, he winked and smiled. She hoped he was right about Porter being held up somewhere safe and sound.

After breakfast, Brandon took the children into the front room once again. He kept them occupied until Diana and Tilly had the kitchen cleaned up. Hoppy took Franklin so Brandon could go to the barn to feed the animals. Homer and Winston went with him. Diana took the broom and began to sweep the floor. When the two boys returned, she announced it was time to start their studies.

The children sat on the floor around Diana. They did not have their slates or the blackboard. Diana had to be creative. She asked questions and called on those who raised their hands. As she looked down upon their faces, she saw smiles. It made her feel good.

Soon, it was time for lunch. Tilly had baked bread that morning. It was still in the oven. She had about two dozen dough balls that she fried in fat. She passed them around the table for the children. She had a jar of jam made from elderberries. It was a fun time for them all. After dinner, Diana took Shirley, Cecilia, and Franklin up for a nap. Brandon did not come in for lunch. It was normal for Mr. Martin and Brandon to work through lunch at the mill. The sun was shining outside. It was very cold. The ice was still built up on the inside of the windows.

Diana took the older children back into the front room to continue with their studies.

Diana heard the clock chiming. It was two o'clock. She smiled as she excused the class. They all moaned and complained. Diana laughed. This pleased her very much. She placed her hands on her hips and announced. "I just want you all to know how happy I am to see how well you all are doing. You should all be very proud of yourselves, for I am very proud of you."

"Thank you, Mrs. Shively. We like learnin'. I mean, we like learning," Homer said.

Diana smiled and ran her hands over the top of Homer's head. "You are very good students," she said.

They rose from their positions on the floor. They were all talking at once. Diana said, "Shh. The little ones are sleeping. We are not at the schoolhouse. We need to be mindful of the small ones."

They quieted down and went into the kitchen in single file. Tilly was waiting for them. She held Franklin in her arms. When he saw Diana, he held both arms out to her and said, "Mamma."

Diana gasped. She froze in her tracks for only a moment. Then she smiled and went to him. She took him in her arms and held him close. He wrapped his arms around her neck and began to play with her hair. She kissed him on top of the head. He was cutting teeth. He was slobbering and chewing on his fist. Tilly handed Diana a damp cloth. She gave it to Franklin and he began to chew on it. Gilda took him from Diana and began to play with him on the floor.

Diana went to the window and scraped at the ice. The sun was still shining. Her breath fogged up the window. She sighed. "Where are you, Mr. Martin?" she asked under her breath.

As if she read Diana's mind, Tilly went to stand next to her. She placed her hand on Diana's arm. "He be fine, Ma'am," she said, smiling.

Diana went to the pump. She pumped the handle a couple of times until the water began to flow. She placed her hand under the spout and dabbed at her face with the cool water. She smiled at Tilly. She went to the bathtub and peered down at the sleeping Robert. "Franklin called me Mamma," Diana said.

"No one has ever called me Mamma before. It sounded so strange coming from him."

Tilly smiled. "Gilda, Homer, and Percy call me Mamma now. I guess I is their Mamma. At first, it sounded strange, but I reckon all children want a Mammy and Pappy. It just natural," Tilly said.

"Yes, I suppose you are right. I won't stop them from calling me Mamma. However, I would never expect it from them. I know the older ones miss their parents. My heart goes out to them. They are such good children. They have been through so much. I remember losing my parents. It really hurt. I did not lose them both all in a matter of twenty-four hours either. They have a lot of emotion to overcome," Diana said as she continued to look down at the sleeping Robert.

Tilly shook her head and said, "I don't know what that emotion thin is, Ma'am. "

Diana looked up at Tilly. She smiled and said, "Emotions are feelings, Tilly."

Tilly nodded. "Yes, Ma'am," she said.

Shirley was standing in the doorway, rubbing her eyes. Diana went to her. She lifted her up into her arms and kissed her cheek. "Did you have a good nap, Sweetie?" she asked.

Shirley nodded. "May I have a drink, please?" she asked.

Diana smiled at her. "You certainly may, little one." She carried Shirley to the hand pump. She pumped the handle until the water began to flow. She placed the drinking tin under the spout and caught some of the water. She handed the tin to Shirley. She drank the entire cup. She handed the tin back to Diana and said, "I have to pee."

Diana carried her to the corner where a chamber pot sat for the little ones. She supported Shirley as she sat on the pot. When she was done, Diana washed her bottom and replaced her pantaloons. Then she sat Shirley down at the table. Tilly gave her a slice of bread with butter and sugar on it. Shirley began to eat.

Hoppy was changing Franklin's diaper. Tilly had a pot boiling on the stove to wash the diapers. Mr. Martin was going to bring some fabric to make more diapers, from Philadelphia. Diana went to the window and peered out one last time before helping Tilly with dinner.

Cecilia came downstairs from her nap. She, too, wanted a drink. Diana had been trying to potty train her. It was not going very well. Diana changed her diaper and washed her off. She brushed her unruly hair and sat her at the table for her snack. Cecilia was a quiet child. She was content to go off by herself, to play in the corner. She was not at home amongst a houseful of children. She did not talk much either. She looked like her father. Her bones were large. She was short and stout. Her face was round and plump. Her hair was always a tangle of tight, unruly curls. Her eyes were a hazel color, with flecks of brown in them. She was a pretty little girl, but odd compared to the rest of the children. She had not yet warmed up to Diana, or her new surroundings. She ate her snack quietly, then crawled down from her chair, wandering off to play by herself.

Diana busied herself helping Tilly. The day flew by. Diana seemed to be constantly stopping to change a diaper, or help a smaller one on the chamber pot. She stood up, stretching her back. She felt the strain of her activities catching up with her. She sat down at the table and watched Tilly moving about in the Martin kitchen as if it were her own. Diana stood up and went to the stove. "How about a little break for a cup of tea?" she asked Tilly.

Tilly turned to look at Diana. She had a surprised look on her face. "You want Tilly to sit down, Mrs. Shively?" Tilly asked.

Diana nodded. She smiled over at Tilly and replied. "Yes, I do. You have been working non-stop all day. I think it is time for a little cup of tea and a break from all the work. I won't keep you long, Tilly."

Tilly wiped her hands on her apron. "Yes, Ma'am," she said.

Diana made two cups of tea. She set them on the table and nodded for Tilly to sit down. Tilly moved cautiously. "What's wrong ,Tilly?" Diana asked.

Tilly looked up at Diana from her seat and said. "Nobody ever axed me to sit down for a cup of tea afore," Tilly said. She wrapped her hands around the teacup and breathed in the vapor.

Diana smiled at Tilly. "Well, you need a break, Tilly. Remember, you are no longer a slave. Those days are gone forever. In this house, you are as good as anyone else. You are allowed to take a break now and then. It does you good. As a matter of fact, it is required," Diana said, laughing.

Tilly asked, "What is the 'required'?"

Diana took a sip of tea. She put the cup down and explained, "'Required' means it is necessary. It is needed."

Tilly frowned and nodded. She sipped her tea in silence. When her cup was empty, she showed it to Diana. Diana smiled and said, "Okay, Tilly. You may be excused." Tilly smiled and took the cup to the wash pan. She continued her chores as if she had never stopped. Diana smiled. She emptied her cup and took it to the wash pan. She began to wash the dishes that were soaking in the hot water.

Before long, Diana became aware that the sun was going down. She lit the candles in the kitchen. It was time to begin setting the table for supper. Hoppy helped without anyone saying a word to her. Diana smiled at her. Hoppy grinned back at Diana. She was a good worker, just like her mother. Diana wondered what their lives had been like on the plantation in Virginia. She did not mention it. She was determined to make that in the past for them.

Brandon came in, stomping his boots to remove the snow. Hoppy rushed to him. She helped him pull his boots off and wiped up the water from the floor. He kissed the top of her head. She smiled. She liked Brandon. Diana wondered if she had a childish crush on him. Then it occurred to her that there were no other Negroes around this area. What would these children do when they became of courting age? She decided that it was much too soon to fret about such a thing. Like Porter Martin always said, "Things have a way of changin' on you real sudden like." Hoppy was only thirteen. Diana went to the window one last time before sitting down to the table for supper.

After dinner, Brandon took the children into the front room for their story time. Diana and Tilly cleaned up the kitchen. Diana fed little Robert while Tilly bathed Franklin. They carried the babies upstairs to bed. Then they went into the front room to listen to Brandon finish his story to the children. It was bedtime. Tilly rushed her four up the stairs to Porter Martin's room. They closed the door behind them.

Diana and Brandon tucked the Hughes children into their beds. They tip-toed into their own room, closing the door behind them. Diana felt exhausted. She nestled herself close to Brandon. Soon, she was fast asleep. She dreamed.

It was Margaret Martin and Ruth Ann sitting on chairs close to the bed. Diana looked over to find Brandon sleeping soundly beside her, totally un-aware of their presence. They were speaking so softly that Diana had to lean close to hear them.

"Porter is fine, Dear. He is in Quincy. He will be home when it is safe to travel. How could you allow yourself to fret so?" Margaret was saying. "You are doing so well with these children. I am so proud of you. I could not have done it any better myself."

Ruth Ann clapped her hand together. She laughed out loud. "You cer-tainly have a houseful, Diana," she said.

Diana looked over to see if Brandon had heard her. He continued to sleep soundly. She turned back to them. They were gone. She felt sad. Ruth Ann looked just like she did before she became sick. Margaret looked well also. She smiled to herself, feeling comforted to know that they had been watching.

Diana heard footsteps on the wooden floor outside her door. She sat up in her bed. Brandon was gone. The sun was shining through the window. She reached for her watch pin that laid on the stand next to their bed. It was nearly eight-thirty. She jumped up and began to dress. She noticed that Franklin was gone from his crib. Brandon must have taken him downstairs. Robert slept soundly.

After she finished dressing, she scooped Robert into her arms and carried him down the stairs, into the kitchen. Tilly smiled at her as she entered.

"Mornin' Mrs. Shively," she said.

Diana nodded. She smiled at everyone seated around the table, eating their breakfast.

"Good morning, everyone," she said.

"Good morning, Mrs. Shively," the children all replied, just as if they were seated at their desks in the schoolhouse.

"I think we could make it into town this morning if you want to teach school today," Brandon said.

Diana went to the window and peered out. "I think that is a good idea. I am running pretty far behind though," she said.

"I kin do this. You just git ready and I will fix you somethin' to eat on the way," Tilly said. She took Robert from Diana's arms.

Diana looked at the children's faces. They were all washed and dressed for school. She smiled and said, "All right. Just give me a few minutes to wash my face and comb my hair." She turned to go back up the stairs.

She combed her hair and piled it on top of her head. She gazed in the small mirror at her own reflection. Satisfied, she hurried back down the stairs to bundle up for the trip into town. Brandon had the wagon house parked near the back door. The children were filing into it as she opened the door. He carried her to the wagon house. The children all cheered. They were headed for school. It was Thursday. They would get two days in before the weekend. The sun was bright as it reflected off the white snow. Diana kept her eyes averted down to protect them. It made her head pound every time she looked up into the glare. The children sang as they went.

As they approached Berlin, Brandon said over his shoulder. "There is Alda Faulk waving at us. She must have the children ready for school this morning."

Diana tried not to look up. She was getting such a headache.

They picked up the Faulk children and turned toward the schoolhouse. Brandon unlocked the door and lifted the children down from the wagon house. He carried Diana to the door. Inside, Brandon built a fire, while Homer rang the bell and Diana erased the blackboard. Brandon turned, kissing her on the cheek before he left. Again, the children all cheered.

Diana began the day just as if there had been no interruptions. Her head was pounding. She rubbed her temples. She had overslept. She always got a headache when she overslept. That, combined with the bright snow, just made it worse. She allowed Hoppy to take charge of the class. She sat quietly for a while until she felt her stomach turning. She was nauseous. She went to the door, opening it just in time to throw up just beyond the stepping stone. She was aware of Thelma Faulk darting past her. She was running in the snow that was nearly up to her knees. She was headed for her house. Diana could not stop her. She was throwing up again.

When she had finished, she went back inside. Homer handed her a damp cloth. Hoppy was making her a cup of tea. They were all gathered around her, watching her closely. "I am fine now. I just have a headache. Thank you," Diana said to the concerned children.

Soon the door opened and Alda Faulk entered the school with Thelma right behind her. She went to Diana, placing her hand on Diana's forehead. She looked into Diana's eyes. She stood up and smiled. "Dizzy?" she asked.

Diana nodded. "I slept too long. I get like this sometimes. I have never thrown up before though." She dabbed at her face with the cool cloth.

Alda leaned close to Diana's ear. "You are with child, Mrs. Shively." She stood up straight and nodded at the confused looking Diana. She said. "The headache might be the glare from the snow, but the rest is from what I said." She handed Diana a dried root. "Make a tea from this. It will calm your stomach." She patted Diana on the shoulder. "You want me to take the kids home?" she asked.

Diana stared at Mrs. Faulk. She shook her head. "I will be fine," she replied. She could not believe what she just heard. "How do you know?" Diana asked.

"I knows. I have seen this many times. You been feelin' tired? Dizzy sometimes?" Alda asked. Diana nodded. "You missed your monthly visitor?" Alda asked.

Diana wasn't sure what to say. She thought for a moment. Then she nodded. She had been so preoccupied with all that had been happening at the house that she hadn't noticed.

"It is early yet, but I am pretty sure that is what is wrong," Alda said. She turned to go to the door. She smiled as she pulled the door closed behind her.

Diana felt like she was going into shock. How could this be? This is not the right time. She has two babies in diapers now and one that isn't completely potty trained. She has six children already. She did want children of her own, but she wanted to wait awhile. What about the school? What was she going to do?

Hoppy made her another cup of tea from the root that Alda had left. Diana sipped it. Hoppy continued teaching the class for her. Diana had to smile at the young lady as she held herself erect, pretending to be so grown up. The students were very well behaved for Hoppy. Diana was aware of their eyes glancing at her from time to time.

It was lunchtime. Hoppy passed out the snacks that Tilly had packed for all of them. Diana did not try to eat. Her headache was all but gone by now. She was feeling better. After lunch, she took over the class once more. Soon, she heard the wagon house pulling up to the door. Homer rang the bell. Brandon entered to bank the fire. The children all started telling him at once about Diana getting sick and Alda Faulk coming to look at her.

Brandon was concerned. "What is it? Are you all right?" he asked.

"I am fine," Diana began. "She gave me a root to settle my stomach and it helped. I feel fine now," she said.

He loaded the wagon house with the children and carried Diana from the door to the wagon. He continued to frown. He was still worried. He climbed in and drove to the Faulk house to drop off Thelma, Beatrice, and Wayne. Alda met them at the door.

"Is Diana all right?" Brandon asked Alda Faulk.

"She is just fine, Mr. Shively. That root I gave her will calm the morning sickness," Alda said.

"The morning sickness?" Brandon asked.

Alda nodded. She smiled as she closed her door, leaving Brandon standing there, looking bewildered.

As they traveled back toward Porter Martin's house, Brandon said over his shoulder, "I told Tilly I would be taking them all home after dinner tonight. Perhaps she should stay on a couple more days. You might need help with the children," he said.

Diana was still in shock. She could not believe this was really happening to her right now. She looked up at Brandon and said, "Let's wait until after supper, and see how I feel then."

"How are you feeling now?" he asked, still concerned.

Diana smiled. "I feel fine right now," she said. "I really don't think it is anything to worry about."

"You just let me be the judge of that," Brandon said. He winked at Homer who was nodding his head.

"Mrs. Shively was pretty sick this morning," Homer said in perfect English.

Diana smiled at him. "Your English is improving, Homer. I am very proud of you," she said, patting his hand.

"Yes, Ma'am," Homer said.

Brandon pulled the wagon house up to the back door. One by one, the children jumped down and went inside. They all began telling Tilly about Diana's being sick at school.

Tilly was waiting for her when she entered the house. Brandon had gone to put the team away. Tilly rushed the children into the front room. She closed the door and turned to Diana, who was removing her coat.

"You has the mornin sickness?" Tilly asked.

Diana looked up at her in surprise. "How did you know?" Diana asked.

"Tilly has seen it afore. I seed you was actin' odd like yesterday, when you wanted me to sit wit ya for a cup of tea. I thought that was what it was. I didn't say nothin', though, cause it ain't none of Tilly's business," Tilly said.

Diana went to the table and sat down. "What am I going to do with all of these children?" she asked.

Tilly sat down beside her. "You will do just fine. Tilly will always be here for ya to help. I will be here everyday. That is, unless you don't want me here," she said.

Diana reached over, taking Tilly's hand. "Oh, Tilly! I have told you before, I don't know what I would do without you. You are a blessing to this household. We are all grateful that you and your children are here. You are like family. Of course, I want you here. We all want you here. I couldn't do it without you," she said, smiling at Tilly.

Tilly nodded. "I is happy to hear that, Miss. Tilly is happy to be here. You has made me feel like family." She stood up and went to the stove to stir the pot of stew that was bubbling in a large pot. The smell filled the room. Diana felt her stomach turning. She moaned. Tilly replaced the lid on the pot and went to Diana. "You just go up and lay yourself down for a spell. I got everythin' under control here. I kin do this with my eyes closed. Misser Shively will be in soon. He don't need to be seein' you like this. Do he know yet?" Tilly asked.

Diana shook her head and said. "Not exactly. Well, not for sure, anyway. Alda Faulk kind of hinted to it. I don't know what he knows, to be honest with you."

"You go on up. Ifin he aks about ya, I will tell him you is tired and I sent you up for a nap," Tilly said.

Diana stood up and turned for the door that led to the hall and stairs. She said over her shoulder as she went. "Thank you so much, Tilly."

She climbed the stairs slowly. She heard the back door. Brandon was back from the barn. She had just lain down on the bed when she heard his footsteps on the stairs. He tiptoed into the bedroom. He sat on the bed next to her. She opened her eyes, smiling at him.

"Diana. I am worried about you," Brandon said.

Diana reached up, stroking his cheek. "I am fine Brandon," she said.

Brandon kissed her on the forehead. "I know you have been worried about Porter. But I don't want you worrying yourself sick over it," he said.

Diana smiled and said. "Porter is fine, Brandon. He is waiting the storm out in Quincy."

Brandon sat up straight and frowned down at her. "How do you know that?" he asked.

Diana said, "Miss Margaret and Ruth Ann told me last night. They came to me in a dream. They knew I was worried. They wanted to put my mind to rest."

Brandon smiled. "Well, they could have let me in on the little secret," he said.

"They didn't want to wake you." Diana laughed.

"How are you feeling now?" Brandon asked.

"I am feeling better. I am just so very tired. My stomach does not like the smell of food. They call it morning sickness," Diana explained. She smiled up at him.

Brandon frowned. "Is that what I think it is?" he asked.

Diana asked, "What do you think it is?"

"Are we having a baby of our own?" Brandon asked her.

Diana smiled. "I think perhaps we are. How do you feel about that?"

Brandon took a deep breath. He held it until he was about to burst. He let it out quickly and smiled. "I'm the luckiest man alive!" he said, smiling from ear to ear.

Diana asked. "It doesn't bother you that we already have a houseful of children? Are you sure you are ready to start a family of our own?"

Brandon placed his hands on her shoulders. "What do you mean, of our own?" he asked. "Those children downstairs are ours. We have already decided that. We knew we both wanted more children someday. Well, someday just snuck up on us, that's all."

Diana took a deep breath. "You are right."

"Now, you just rest awhile. I am going out to the barn. I haven't done the milking yet. I am taking Winston and Raymond with me to the barn. Homer has been such a help in the mill, but it is time Winston and Raymond learn the ropes, too. Porter will be happy to see them out there when he gets back from Quincy," Brandon said with a wink.

Brandon closed the door behind him. Diana closed her eyes and listened as his footsteps descended the stairs. She dozed off. She woke with a startle. It was quiet. She turned to face the window. It was still daylight. She picked up her watch pin, to see what the time was. She had only dozed for twenty minutes. She felt better. She sat up and rubbed her eyes. She went to the window. She could see the smoke puff clouds rising in small grey clouds from the mill. She heard the constant chugging and puffing noises that were so familiar to her. She went downstairs.

The children were playing in the front room. They smiled at her as she entered.

"Please, go on with your game. I am going to help in the kitchen. I believe I saw beef stew on the stove. Is everybody hungry?" she asked.

"We are very hungry, Mrs. Shively," Percy said.

"Good. I think you are going home tonight after dinner, Percy. Do you miss home?" she asked.

"No, Ma'am. I likes it fine right here in Misser Martin's house," Percy said.

Diana laughed. "I understand exactly how you feel," she said.

Diana went through the door, into the kitchen. Tilly, Hoppy, and Gilda were preparing dinner. Gilda rushed to Diana.

"You just sit down, Mrs. Shively. We are almost finished. I just have to set the table. May I make you a cup of tea?" Gilda asked.

Diana shook her head. "No, thank you, Gilda. I will wait until dinner. Is there anything I can do to help?" she asked.

Hoppy turned toward her and replied. "No, Ma'am. You just rest. Tomorrow is Friday. We have one last day of school this week. Then you can rest up."

Diana smiled. Tilly nodded in agreement. "Hoppy kin help ya wit the learnin' the kids tomorrow ifin ya need her," Tilly said.

Diana said. "Thank you, Hoppy. You did very well today. I may need your help from time to time. You study real hard and maybe someday you will be a teacher yourself."

Tilly looked from Hoppy to Diana. "Miss Shively, I don't think we is allowed to do that. We ain't supposed to be goin to school nohow. How kin Hoppy be a teacher? We don't want no trouble wit the law."

Diana smiled as she said, "The law says you are free. You are allowed to learn to read and write. Why would it stop you from teaching others? You are not breaking any laws, Tilly. Some day, Hoppy is going to marry and have children of her own. She will want her children and your grand-children to be educated."

Tilly nodded. "Yes, Ma'am," Tilly said. She turned her attention back to the stove. Diana wondered if she understood what being free really meant. Tilly had been born into slavery. It was all she knew.

Just then, the door opened and Raymond came in. He removed his coat and boots. Gilda began to clean up the melting snow.

"Pull my boots off," he demanded. Gilda knelt down before him.

Diana rose and went over to them. "Gilda, you can help your Mamma and Hoppy. I will do this," she said. Gilda turned to go back to the stove. Raymond stared up at Diana from his chair.

Diana smiled as she knelt down to remove his boots. "I didn't mean you, Ma'am," Raymond said.

"Why not? Why is Gilda any different than I?" Diana asked.

Raymond began. "Because she is"

"She is what, Raymond? She is not a slave. Do you understand what the war was all about? All Negroes are free now. There are no more slaves. Remember our conversation on this matter? Tilly and her children have all of the same rights as the rest of us. They are equal. Do you know what equal means?" Diana asked.

Just then the door opened and Winston, Homer, and finally, Brandon entered from outside. Raymond looked up at them. He returned his gaze to Diana. "Yes, Ma'am. It means exactly the same," he said.

"That is right. No one person is any better than any other in this house," Diana explained.

Brandon frowned. He had a confused look on his face. Diana smiled at him. She rose and proceeded to help him remove his coat. He kissed her cheek. "How are you feeling?" he asked.

"Much better, thank you," Diana replied. She hung Brandon's coat on the wooden peg near the door. Raymond got up from the chair so Brandon could sit down to remove his boots. Homer and Winston removed their boots. Gilda was back with the cloth to wipe up the melting snow. Just then, the door to the front room opened. Franklin could be heard crying. Percy was carrying him. At the sight of Brandon, Franklin began to squirm. Percy put him down. He walked to Brandon. He was cooing and smiling. Brandon picked him up and hugged him. Diana smiled. Brandon was going to make a wonderful father. Suddenly, she realized he already was a wonderful father. She sighed. It was going to be all right. Somehow, she knew they would get through this just fine indeed.

Dinner was a cheerful time, with everyone around the table. Diana listened to the chatter with a smile. She looked up from time to time to catch Brandon watching her. She smiled at him. He returned the smile.

After dinner, Brandon took the children into the front room for a story. The girls cleaned up the kitchen. Tilly helped Diana bath the babies and dress them for bed. Finally, it was time for Brandon to take Tilly and the children home. He kissed Diana. "I will be right back. I will stay until I get the fireplace going, and once I am sure they are settled in, I will be right back," he said.

"Just be careful and return safe and sound," Diana said. She watched from the window as the wagon house pulled around to the trail that led across the stream, and on toward the log cabin. She picked Franklin up. He was chewing on the cloth. She kissed him as she began to pace the floor singing softly. Soon, he fell asleep. She carried him up the stairs to his crib. She checked on Robert, who was sleeping in his cradle, before closing the door to go back downstairs.

She heard the sounds of a team and wagon approaching. "Brandon?" she whispered. She hurried down the stairs, trying to be as quiet as she could. He could not be returning so soon. Something must be wrong. She caught a glimpse of the wagon approaching the stables. It was dark by now. If he still had Tilly and the children, he would have stopped at the back door first. Why was he back so soon? She could not leave the house. She could not leave the children unattended. She stood frozen at the window, watching for him. It seemed to take forever before a shadow appeared, making its way toward the back door. Through the darkness, it moved in a familiar gait to the back porch. It was Porter Martin. Diana rushed to open the door. He stomped his feet before entering.

Diana threw her arms around his neck. "Mr. Martin! We have been waiting for you!" she cried.

Porter pulled his coat off. Diana hung it on a peg. He sat down in the chair. She began to pull his boots off. "Where is everybody?" he asked.

"Brandon just took Tilly and her children home. Winston rode along with him. The babies are in bed, sleeping, and Raymond, Shirley, and Celia are getting ready for bed. They should be in the front room," Diana replied.

"Did the storm give you any trouble?" Porter asked.

Diana was wiping up the melting snow. "Some, but we got through it. We had school here in the front room yesterday, but today it was just another day. Were you held up in Quincy?" Diana asked.

Porter looked up at her from the chair. "How did you know that?" he asked.

Diana laughed. "I know this sounds strange, but Miss Margaret and Ruth Ann came to me in a dream. They knew I was worried. They told me you were safe, and that you were hold up in Quincy until the storm passed," she said.

Porter rubbed his balding head. "That is a might queer. Miss Margaret and Ruthie came to me as I was napping. They told me to stay over in Quincy until the storm had passed. They told me that Brandon had everything under control here," he said, watching Diana.

"They have been watching over us, haven't they?" Diana asked.

"Yes, Ma'am, I believe they are, indeed. I suppose it is like you girls have always been sayin'. They are always with us. They never really left," Porter said.

The door to the front room opened. Raymond, Shirley, and Cecilia ran to Porter.

"Shh." Diana said as she pointed up, indicating that the babies were sleeping over head.

Porter hugged them. Cecilia stood back watching. Diana went to her holding out her arms. Cecilia went to her. Diana lifted her into her arms. They stood watching as Porter fussed over Shirley and Raymond. He went to the kitchen table. Diana sat Cecilia down on the table near Porter and the children. She began to prepare a cup of hot tea for Porter. "Have you eaten?" she asked.

"Naw. I was anxious to get home. I didn't stop for nothin'," Porter said.

Diana began to reheat the stew. She heard the wagon house approaching. "Brandon and Winston are back," she replied. Raymond went to the window. He sat on the chair watching.

Porter sipped his tea. He tugged on Cecilia's hair. She whined. Porter put her down onto the floor. She went to Raymond. He lifted her up onto his lap. "Here they come," Raymond said.

The door opened. Winston was the first to enter. "We saw your wagon in the stable," he said as he began to remove his boots.

Brandon closed the door behind him. "Everything all right?" he asked Porter as he tugged on his coat.

"Yep. Everything is fine. I was in Quincy at the Anderson place. I just waited until I figured it was safe to travel," Porter said.

Brandon looked over at Diana. She was smiling. He raised his eyebrows and smiled. He went to the table and sat down across from Porter. Diana sat a bowl of stew in front of Porter, and handed him a spoon.

"Thank you, Miss Diana. How did you make out with the children while I was gone?" he asked.

"We managed just fine. Tilly and her children stayed a couple of nights. We had quite a houseful, but it wasn't any trouble. The storm kept us home yesterday, but we did our studies right in the front room. Tilly was a wonderful help. They slept in your room for the two nights they were here. She washed the bedclothes today while we were in school. She has just been wonderful. I really don't know what I would have done without her," Diana said.

"Mrs. Shively was sick at school today," Raymond said.

Porter looked up at Diana. "Sick?" he asked.

"It was nothing. I am fine now. Brandon can explain later," she said, flushing.

Porter looked from Diana to Brandon. He smiled. Diana poured him another cup of tea. "I think it is time for you children to go to bed. Tomorrow is the last school day this week. You can stay up late tomorrow night," Diana said.

The children kissed the three adults before going upstairs to bed. Cecilia whined and fussed all the way up the stairs. Diana followed to tuck them in. Brandon and Porter had things to talk about. She kissed the children's foreheads as she pulled the covers up over them. Cecilia continued to whine. Finally, Diana lifted Cecilia in her arms and carried her to her room. Cecilia sucked her thumb. She put her small hand on Diana's face. Finally, she fell asleep. Diana lifted her, carrying her back to her own bed. She tiptoed back into the hall, closing the door behind her. She dressed for bed. She would leave Porter and Brandon talk for as long as they wanted. She needed her sleep. She had to take good care of herself. She was going to have a baby. She was anxious to write to Josephine and Regina.

It was Friday. The children sat in their designated seats inside the schoolhouse. Diana had a fire blazing in the stove. It was quiet. They were practicing their writing skills. Diana took advantage of the time, writing letters to her sisters in Philadelphia. It saddened her that she was not going to be able to make the trip to see them when the weather broke. Brandon had promised, but she could not hold him to his promise now. Everything had changed. She looked up at the faces intent on their studies. They were all good children. They had come a long way. She was proud of every one of them, especially Hoppy, Gilda, Homer, and Percy. They had been so intent on learning. They have progressed further than any of the others. Diana shuddered to think of what their lives must have been like before.

It was lunchtime. The children had all brought their own lunches today. None of Tilly's children knew exactly when they were born or how old they were. Diana guessed at their ages and gave them each a birth date. Today was Percy's seventh birthday. She had brought a small cake and a jug of fresh milk. After lunch, they were going to have a party. The children were excited.

They were enjoying their meal when the door burst opened and Sofia entered. At first, Diana did not recognize her. She was bundled up in so many clothes. As she removed her scarf, her brunette hair raised straight in the air from the static electricity. The children laughed. She looked about at their laughing faces. Diana pointed to her hair. Sofia laughed and smoothed her hair with her wrapped hands. The laughter died down and she approached Diana, still smiling.

"Did you come to celebrate Percy's birthday with us?" Diana asked.

Sofia looked back at Percy and smiled. "Of course," she lied.

Diana motioned for her to sit down on one of the benches. She sat down beside her. "Percy is seven years old today. After they eat their lunch, we are having cake and milk to celebrate," Diana explained.

Sofia looked at Percy once more and smiled as she said, "How wonderful! Happy birthday, Percy."

Percy smiled back at her. "Thank you, Mrs. Gilbert," he said politely.

Diana smiled in approval at him. She turned to her sister and whispered. "What brings you here?"

Sofia lowered her voice. "I have news. I am pregnant. I am having a baby, Di. I am so excited, I could just burst. But I am also very frightened. I will never forget Madeline Hughes and how she suffered. I can't stop thinking about it." Sofia smiled at the children as she spoke.

Diana took her sister's hand. "Congratulations! Try not to allow yourself to dwell on what could happen. Be happy, and accept the news with the thought of all the successful births. Just look around this room. Madeline had five healthy deliveries before Robert was born. I like to think that the odds are five to one in favor of a normal birth. I too, have news. I am also pregnant," she whispered to Sofia.

Sofia gasped. She put her hand over her mouth. Her eyes stared at Diana in disbelief. "My goodness! What a surprise! When did you find out?" Sofia asked.

Diana smiled. She whispered. "Just yesterday. I am guessing it will be due sometime around Thanksgiving. When do you expect to deliver?" Diana asked.

Sofia lowered her head and whispered. "Around July, maybe a little sooner. I am not really sure. Alda Faulk said I was about four months along, but she is not certain. Oh, Diana! This is the best news ever. I was so frightened, but I think I will be all right, just knowing we will be going through it together." Then as an afterthought, she looked up at Diana and asked, "Oh, my! I just thought of something. What on earth are you going to do with all of those babies in diapers at the same time?"

Diana smiled. "Well, we are trying to potty train Cecilia. She isn't co-operating at this point, but hopefully, she will before the baby comes. If we are successful, we will still have three babies in diapers at the same time. We have three now," she said.

"But there won't even be a year between little Robert and the new baby. That is going to be really hard. How are you going to manage?" Sofia asked.

"I have a secret weapon. It is called Tilly. As long as I have Tilly, I will be fine. If anything were to happen to her, I don't know what I would do. I would lose my mind, for sure," Diana said.

Sofia shook her head and replied. "I am surprised that you haven't already. You are a very special person, Di."

Diana patted Sofia's hand. She looked about the room. The children had finished their lunches. They were sitting patiently, waiting for Diana to serve the birthday cake and milk. She rose from the bench and went to her desk. "It is time for our birthday cake. Shall we all sing "Happy Birthday" to Percy?" she asked. She began to sing. The children joined in, as did Sofia. Diana cut the cake. Sofia passed the slices around the room on bits of cloth that Diana had sewed to make napkins. They each had their own tin cups. Sofia poured the milk. Each of the students took a turn, standing, to say something special about Percy. He smiled as they each said something nice about him.

Sofia left. Diana asked her to wait until Brandon arrived with the wagon house to take her home. She did not want to wait. The sun was shining and it was warming up outside. She wrapped herself up and left after hugging Diana. Diana watched her as she waded through the snow, back toward the house that Porter Martin had built for her and Jonathan. Sofia was nearly two hundred pounds by now. Diana remembered how beautiful her sister used to be. Now, her face was full and round. Her hair was hardly ever brushed or pulled up on top of her head. It hung in disarray.

Diana turned back to her class. "Who knows what holiday is coming up soon?" she asked.

Homer, Hoppy, and Raymond raised their hands. Diana pointed to Homer. Raymond's face went white. Diana knew he had not accepted the fact that he had to live amongst Negroes.

"Easter, Mrs. Shively," Homer said.

"And what is Easter?" she asked. Again, Homer, Hoppy, and Raymond raised their hands.

"Raymond?" she asked.

"It is the day we celebrate Jesus' death on the cross," Raymond said.

"What does his death signify?" she asked. No hands went up. "Does anyone know why Jesus died on the cross?"

Winston raised his hand. Diana nodded at him. "Because he was a Christian? They crucified Christians," Winston said.

Diana nodded. "Yes, they did. But he died for something far more meaningful than because he was a Christian. For homework this weekend, I want you all to do some research into the reason Jesus was put to death on the cross. We will have a discussion on the matter when we come back to school Monday," Diana said. She heard the wagon house pull up out front. Brandon entered through the door. The students cheered as he entered. He waved at them.

"Is she teaching you anything today?" he asked the class as he went to bank the fire.

The students all began to chatter at once. Diana raised her hand into the air, and they all quieted down. "You may erase your slates and begin to dress to leave. Homer, you may ring the bell," she announced. She glanced over at Raymond, who had bowed his head. He had a displeased look on his face. This worried Diana.

Soon, they were on the familiar road to Porter Martin's house. The sun was brightly reflecting off the snow. Diana had a headache from the glare. She rubbed her temples. Brandon glanced back at her from time to time with a worried look on his face. Diana smiled back and shook her head, indicating that all was well. He was not so convinced. He had been doting upon her ever since she announced that she was pregnant.

Once they reached the Martin house, she sighed. She was tired today. She knew that Tilly would have things under control at the house. Diana had a craving for cherry pie. Just the thought of it made her mouth water. There would be no cherry pie until summer. Cherries were not to be had this time of the year. Diana knew of no cherry trees nearby either. She smiled up at Brandon as he lifted her from the wagon house to the back porch. He drove off to put the team away. He would go directly to the sawmill. Winston, Raymond, and Homer would join him after they changed out of their school clothes.

Inside, Tilly had everything under control, just as she always did. "How do you do it?" Diana asked as she removed her hat and coat.

"I is used to it. The plantation was bigger n Misser Martin's house. The family was bigger, too. Masser Harmon had somethin like twelve kids. They was a handful. There was four of us that cared for em. Annie and me looked after the littlest ones," Tilly said as she wiped up the melting snow from around the pile of shoes near the back door.

Diana shook her head. She touched Tilly on the top of the head ever so lightly. Tilly looked up at her from her kneeled position. "Do ya feel better today?" she asked Diana.

"Yes, I do. Thank you for asking," Diana said. She looked around the room. Franklin was jabbering in his unknown language as he followed Gilda and Shirley about the room. Gilda bent down and lifted him in her arms. The girls took him through the door that led into the front room.

Tilly called to Hoppy as she went through the door after them, "Hoppy, child, put a log on the fire in there."

"Yes, Mamma!" Hoppy called back to Tilly. The door closed and Tilly and Diana were alone in the kitchen. Diana went to the copper tub and peered down at Robert. He was awake. He was sucking on his fist.

"I just changed him. His milk is warming on the stove. You want me to feed him, or do you want to do it?" Tilly asked Diana.

"I will do it, Tilly," Diana replied as she lifted Robert in her arms. "I missed you today," she said to Robert. Tilly handed her a bottle of warm milk. Robert's little mouth opened like a baby bird until he was sucking on the bottle. His little eyes rolled back in his head as he closed them. Soon, he would fall asleep. Diana smiled down at him.

Tilly sat a cup of tea on the table for her. Diana felt better today. She smiled at Tilly. "Thank you, Tilly," she said.

"You is quite welcome, Miss Shively," Tilly said. She turned, going back to the stove.

Diana burped Robert twice. She laid him back in the copper tub. She looked up just in time to see Porter Martin come into the kitchen from the stairs.

"Good afternoon, Ma'am," he said.

Diana smiled. "Good afternoon, Mr. Martin. I thought you were at the mill. Are you feeling all right today?" Diana asked.

Porter smiled. He nodded his head and replied. "I am fine. I am headed that way right now. I just want to say hello to the younguns before I go back outside." He went through the door that led to the front room. Soon, he reappeared. He put his coat and hat on, turned to Tilly and Diana, and said, "Ladies, I will see you later." Then he went out the back door.

Dinner was somewhat quieter this evening. It appeared as though they had all adjusted to the new life at the Martin house. The children behaved well. They were polite. They all cleaned their plates. Franklin was content to sit on Brandon's lap and eat from Brandon's plate.

After dinner, Winston brought Blacky and Brownie into the house. They took the dogs into the front room with them for story time. Diana was about to object when Porter told him it was all right. The dogs were getting old and did not jump around as much. Still they had an unpleasant odor to them from being outside all day.

When the kitchen was cleaned up, Porter loaded Tilly and her children into the wagon house. Winston rode along to keep him company. Blacky and Brownie also rode along. It was time to begin washing the children for bed. Brandon was a big help. He played games with them so they did not fuss so much at getting their ears washed. Cecilia was the only one who cried. She ended up with soap in her eyes. Diana tried to cuddle with her to comfort her. Cecilia would have none of it. She wanted down. She went off by herself and cried until finally she lay sleeping on the floor. Brandon lifted her in his arms. He carried her up the stairs to bed.

Upon descending the stairs, he joined Diana in the kitchen. "How do you feel? Are you tired?" Brandon asked.

Diana smiled. "Some. I feel all right though. Just tired," she said.

Brandon began to rub her shoulders. He towered over her as she sat at the table. She allowed her head to drop forward as he massaged her neck. She closed her eyes and smiled.

"Sofia stopped by the schoolhouse today. She is pregnant," Diana said.

"Did you tell her you were pregnant, too?" Brandon asked.

Diana nodded. She rolled her head around. "She was surprised. She is worried about what happened to Madeline Hughes," Diana said.

Brandon sat down next to Diana. He reached out to take her hand. "So am I," he said.

Diana smiled, saying, "I try not to think about it." She could hear the wagon house returning. "Porter is back," she concluded.

Brandon went to the window. He wiped at the steamed glass. He walked back to the table where Diana sat. "Perhaps you should go on upstairs. I will see to it that Winston gets to bed all right. You need all the rest you can get," Brandon said.

"Thank you. I think I might do just that," Diana said. She rose and went to Brandon. He kissed her tenderly. She turned to go upstairs. Brandon watched her as she went. Diana heard the back door open. Winston and Porter were back.

The next morning was cloudy. Diana went to the window and peered out. She saw puffs of smoke coming from the mill. She had overslept. She dressed and made the bed. She peered into the crib. It was vacant. The cradle was empty as well. She stepped out into the hall.

The children's room was empty. The covers were thrown all about the beds. Diana went into the room and began to make the beds. She stopped. "What am I doing?" she asked herself. She went out into the hall and down the steps.

She found them all gathered around the table in the kitchen. Brandon sat at the table holding Robert in his arms. He was feeding him his morning bottle. Franklin was standing next to Brandon, bouncing up and down. He wanted Brandon to pick him up. Diana went to Brandon and took Robert in her arms.

"How did you sleep?" Brandon asked her.

Diana smiled. "I slept really well, thank you for asking. I did not hear Robert at all last night," she said.

Brandon lifted Franklin high over his head. "He slept all night," he said.

Diana looked over at him and smiled. "I hope that becomes a habit," she said.

Brandon nodded. He began to tickle Franklin. "Do you want me to go collect Tilly this morning?" he asked.

Diana looked about the kitchen. She smiled. "I think I would like to handle it myself. If I have any trouble, I will come for you," she said.

"Well, you certainly won't be able to leave the kids alone. I will check in on you every couple of hours. How does that sound?" Brandon asked.

Diana nodded as she replied. "Sounds good. Thank you." She kissed Brandon's cheek. Shirley began to laugh. Diana smiled at her. "You finish your breakfast young lady," she said, smiling at the little girl. "Then I will show you how to make your beds."

Brandon placed the whining Franklin on the floor and began to bundle himself to go outside. Diana went to the stove. She prepared a bowl of oats for herself and poured herself a cup of coffee. She had to eat. It was very important that she kept herself in good health. Madeline was probably malnourished from traveling. Being jostled in that wagon probably did not help her any either. Diana was determined to have a healthy pregnancy and delivery. She sat at the table eating her breakfast.

Winston and Raymond were out at the mill with Porter and Brandon. Shirley and Cecilia were playing with Franklin. Robert had fallen back to sleep. Diana continued to hold him while she ate her breakfast. When she was finished, she put Robert in the bathtub. She began to clear the table and wash the dishes. She would have to go upstairs and make the beds soon. She decided to put the children down for a nap and make the beds when they got up. It seemed that the time flew by, when Brandon stuck his head in the back door. "How is it going?" he asked.

Diana smiled. "We are all just fine. Thanks," she replied.

He closed the door and went back to the mill. Diana went to the stove. They were having bacon and eggs for lunch. She was slicing the bacon when she heard a noise at the back door. *Brandon must have forgotten something*, she thought to herself. She went to the door.

It was Tilly and the children. "Tilly. How did you get here?" she asked.

Tilly began to remove all of her fur wraps. She was wet. It had begun to rain. "Tilly walked. Mr. Martin did not come for us so we walked," Tilly said. "Homer went to the mill to help Mr. Martin and Mr. Shively."

Diana helped her with her wraps. She said, "You did not have to come today, Tilly. You should have at least one day a week for yourself. I can manage."

Tilly shook her head and said, "Tilly told you I will always be here for ya, Miss. Tilly would never let you do all this by yourself."

Diana remained silent. She was managing fine, but she was grateful that Tilly was here. She would have to make a larger meal for lunch. The men would not come in for lunch, but they would send the boys in to eat.

Tilly went right to the stove. She began to poke at the fire that burnt inside the stove. She added a piece of split slab wood that was piled next to the stove on the floor. Percy was carrying the laughing Franklin around the kitchen.

Diana put her finger to her lips, indicating that they needed to be quiet. Robert was still sleeping. Percy carried Franklin into the front room. Hoppy took Cecilia in her arms and followed. She closed the door behind her.

The day went by very quickly. Diana was glad that Tilly had come to the house. The children all took a nap, except for Hoppy and Percy. They remained in the front room.

The evening supper was just like a normal day. Porter took Tilly and the children home after everything was cleaned up. Again, Winston rode along with Blacky and Brownie.

The days passed and so did winter. Easter Sunday arrived. Martha and Carver Wilks were getting married after the Sunday services. Martha had made her dress. It was beautiful, even more so than Diana's. Martha was becoming one of the best seamstresses Diana had ever seen or read about. She made all of their clothes. They all sat in Church that Sunday morning, dressed as well, if not better, that any high society family in the large cities, like Philadelphia. Diana felt proud of all of them.

Porter gave Martha away. Carver was taking Martha to Philadelphia to see Josephine and Regina before they went on to Boston for a honeymoon. Diana held Martha tight before they left. Martha whispered just before she climbed up into the wagon. "Keep an eye on Sofia. I can't let her dresses out anymore. If she gets bigger, she will bust. Don't tell her, but I have two new dresses in the shop for her. That fabric only comes so wide." They giggled. Then Martha and Carver climbed up into Porter Martin's finest carriage and drove off. Diana watched them leave. Brandon came to stand at her side.

Porter loaded Tilly and all of the children into the wagon. Brandon drove the buggy with Diana and Robert. They were headed back to the Martin house for their usual Sunday dinner. Diana wished that Regina and Carver had waited another day to leave. She enjoyed the celebrations at the Martin house.

After dinner, Brandon asked Diana to take a walk with him. The children all begged to go along, but he told them he wanted to talk with Diana privately. Tilly and Porter agreed to watch over them until Diana and Brandon returned.

It was a beautiful day. The daffodils were in full bloom. The smell of spring filled the air. It was a bit muddy in places. Brandon lifted or carried Diana through the mud to drier ground. They held hands and talked.

Brandon stopped and turned to Diana. He put his hands on her shoulders and said, "Diana, Porter has been teaching me everything about the mill and the entire business. I really like working with the smell of fresh cut lumber. He has made out his will, and, well, he has left everything to us. He told me he has willed the mill in Philadelphia to James and Josephine. He is tired and wants to retire."

Diana pulled herself close to Brandon. She held on tight. She said, "Oh, Brandon, Mr. Martin is like a father to me. I can't bear to think about such things. I don't know that I ever will," she fought back the urge to cry.

Brandon kissed the top of her head. "I know. But you need to hear this. Also, there is one more thing. I promised you I would take you to Philadelphia to see your sisters. Of course, a lot has happened since I made that promise, but Porter and Tilly are willing to watch the children so we could go. The weather is much better now, and I thought perhaps we should go before the baby comes," Brandon said.

Diana held her breath. "I don't know, Brandon. Madeline was jostled in that wagon so much. I am not sure it is safe to go," she said.

Brandon nodded. "If you don't want to go, I understand. We may never get another chance. Porter spoke with Alda Faulk about Madeline. She said it would have happened regardless. It wasn't the jostling, it was just that Robert wasn't turned the right way to be born. If Alda had been there earlier, she could have turned Robert before he tore Madeline up so bad inside. I am not trying to convince you to go, I just want to help. I guess I just want to make you happy," he said.

Diana took his hand. They walked awhile in silence. Then, Diana stopped. "Let me think about it, Brandon. What would I do about school?" she asked.

"We could go as soon as school is out for the summer. I do think if we are going, we should do it before Porter decides to retire completely. He can run the mill while I am gone. Stumpy will help him. Tilly seems to be able to manage well enough while you are gone all day at school. And Hoppy is big enough to help out at the house," Brandon said.

Diana nodded. "All right. I really want to see my sisters. Maybe by then Martha will be back and she can go along. I don't know if the buggy is big enough to take Sofia," she giggled.

Brandon laughed out loud. "I am not saying anything. Lord knows, Jonathan Gilbert has his hands full. Literally," Brandon said.

They both laughed. They were headed back to the house. Diana saw the children playing in the orchard from a distance. They were waving at them. Diana waved back. "They are such good children. We have truly been blessed," she said as they neared the house.

The rest of the spring went rather quickly. Diana could not help but think that their lives were flying by. It seemed when she was a young girl, the days passed slowly. Even though she was busier then, it seemed that the older she got, the faster time passed.

School was out for the summer. Franklin was talking some, Cecilia was potty trained, and little Robert was sitting up on his own. Today was the day Brandon was to take Diana to Philadelphia. They had loaded up the big carriage. Martha was riding along. Sofia decided it wasn't a good idea for her to go. She was due to deliver in a month or so. Brandon drove the carriage into Berlin. Martha and Carver were waiting for them outside of Martha's dress shop. Carver kissed his wife goodbye. He loaded her bag into the carriage. He stood waving until they were out of sight.

The weather was beautiful. It was a dry sunny day. Perfect for traveling. The team of horses moved slowly and effortlessly along the rutted trail. It was the same route the stage traveled when Diana made the trip with her mother and Porter Martin. She closed her eyes. She could almost hear Porter Martin snoring as he slept in the stage. Martha had brought some embroidery with her. She worked continuously as the carriage rocked from side to side. Once, she even pricked her finger with the needle. Diana was content to take in the scenery. It was a beautiful day. She caught Brandon looking back at her occasionally. She smiled to reassure him that she was fine.

They stopped at Quincy. Mr. Anderson was no longer there, as he had eaten the poison mushrooms his wife fed the confederate soldiers and died, years ago. His son was nearly a grown man now. He watered the horses and gave them some grain. Mrs. Anderson invited them inside for a slice of sugar bread and a cup of tea. Diana would know her anywhere. She had aged considerably, but her red face and wide hips were the same. She was no doubt a very handsome woman when she was young.

They were back in the carriage and headed for Harrisburg. Martha dozed off. Diana watched Brandon from behind. His shoulders were wide and square. His dark hair curled under his hat. He was a very handsome man. Her heart fluttered as she watched him. She wondered what he had been like as a boy. Would she have a son? If she did, she hoped he would be just like his father. Tall, muscular, and very handsome. Diana's thoughts went to Robert. He was very much like Brandon, except, he was not as tall. He was more on the lean side. His features were pretty much the same. She had not thought of Robert in a long time. She felt guilty thinking of him now. She tried to think of something else.

The carriage swayed as they moved across the dirt road that led to Harrisburg. Diana looked about as they went. Nothing looked at all familiar. It had been a long time since she made this journey. Martha was humming as she worked on her needlepoint again.

They were passing a farm on the right. Martha put her needlepoint down. Two young boys ran to the road, running alongside of the carriage. "Where you headed, Mister?" they called out to Brandon.

"Philadelphia, son!" Brandon exclaimed.

They waved as the carriage pulled away. Diana and Martha turned and waved until they went around a bend in the road and the boys could no longer be seen. Martha put her needlepoint into her bag. She folded her hands in her lap and smiled. "Those same boys greeted Carver and me when we passed this way on our honeymoon," she said, smiling.

Diana looked up at the sky. It was the brightest blue with large puffs of white clouds hovering high. "Was it this pretty that day?" she asked.

"No. It was cloudy. It did not rain, but it looked threatening nearly the whole way," Martha said.

Brandon began to whistle. He looked back over his shoulder at the two women now and then. Diana felt her face flush. He would smile then turn his head back towards the dirt road. They were coming to a clearing. There were four Negroes walking alongside the road. Two women and two children. They were dirty and barefooted. They nodded their heads as the carriage approached them. Brandon pulled to a halt beside them. "Whoa. Whoa, now. Would you ladies be needing a ride somewhere?" He asked them.

Their eyes opened wide. They looked at each other in surprise. "We are going to Philadelphia. If you need a lift, we would be happy to oblige," he said.

"We is going a far piece down this here road, that's all" the oldest woman said.

"Well, climb on in the carriage. We would be happy to take as far as we can," Brandon said.

The four of them climbed into the carriage. Diana and Martha sat close, making room for the four of them. Brandon urged the team onward. The four riders sat huddled close to one another. They were all sitting on the same side of the carriage even though there was room for one of them next to Diana. They watched Diana and Martha closely.

"My name is Diana Shively. This is my sister, Martha Wilks. That gentleman," Diana said, pointing to Brandon, "is Mr. Brandon Shilely, my husband."

The oldest of the riders nodded her head. She remained silent. They just continued to watch Diana and Martha.

"What is your name?" Martha asked.

The oldest woman spoke. "My name is Rita," she said. Then it was quiet once again.

"And you, what is your name?" Martha asked the youngest. He was a little boy, about four or five.

"He don't say nothin'. He cain't. Never has said a word to nobody," Rita said. Then after a pause, she went on, "His name is Gordy. He cain't talk."

"Well, Rita, do the rest of them speak. What are their names?" Martha asked. Diana continued to smile at them.

Rita pointed to the other adult woman, "This here is Delila. She kin talk just fine. And this little un here, her name is Nesta. She kin talk, too. She is just shy around strange folks," Rita said.

"Well, now that we know your names and you know ours, we are not strangers any longer," Martha said laughing. She placed the tip of her index finger on Gordy's nose. He smiled wide at her.

"We are going to Philadelphia to visit with our sisters. We live in Berlin, which is quite a ways from here. Where are you going?" Diana asked.

"We is just goin'. We don't know where. We is lookin for some kind of work. We ain't ate in some time now, and we is gettin mighty hungry. But we ain't stole nothin'. No, Ma'am. We might be hungry, but we is honest people. We is just lookin for honest work," Rita said.

Brandon looked back at them from over his shoulder. Diana reached into her bag. She unfolded the paper-wrapped sugar bread that Mrs. Anderson had given them for the road. She began to break it off into four pieces for the four strangers. She looked up at Brandon, who was still looking back at them.

"Perhaps, they should come with us. Maybe we can find something for them in Philadelphia," he said to Diana.

"Of course," Diana replied.

Rita began to shake her head. "No, Ma'am. Don't want no trouble. Folks has told us to stay out of the big cities. They says folks don't like our kind in big cities. We is supposed to just keep to this here road," she said.

"Well, Rita," Diana began. "This road will lead you directly to the big city. It will lead you to Harrisburg, which is a big city. It isn't all that far either," she said.

Rita looked over at Delila. Her eyes were opened wide. "What is we gonna do, Delila?" she asked her friend.

Delila shook her head. "I don't rightly know, Rita. They didn't say what to do if we came to a town. Just go around it I reckon," Delila replied.

"No need to do that, Delila. We will stop in Harrisburg and get you all something to eat. Then you can travel with us on to Philadelphia. We have family there who might know someone who has work for you. You will be safe with us," Diana said.

Martha agreed. "Yes, Delila. You can't just walk around every town you come to. If there is any work to be had, it will be in a town. Trust us. We will look after you."

The Negro women sat quietly as the wagon continued to sway down the dirt road. Soon, the rocking had put Gordy to sleep. "Why don't you put him over here next to me?" Diana asked. "It will make more room over there."

Rita lifted Gordy to the other side of the carriage, next to Diana. Martha began to hum once more. Delila smiled at her. Nesta began to clap her hands softly. Martha began to sing out loud. She clapped her hands along with Nesta.

Brandon called back to them. "Harrisburg is just ahead." Fear came upon the faces of the two women sitting across from Diana.

Diana reached out and patted Rita on the hand. "It will be all right, Rita. We will look after you."

Brandon drove the team through the dusty streets to the livery stable. He pulled the team to a halt. Brandon jumped down from the carriage and helped Martha and Diana down. Rita and Delila were reluctant to exit the carriage. The stable hand approached them.

"Good afternoon. My name is Frank. You look a little familiar to me. Have we met before?" he asked.

"Yes, Sir," Brandon replied. "My name is Brandon Shively. I have passed this way many times with Porter Martin from Berlin to Philadelphia."

Frank said, "Awe, yes! Porter Martin. I know him well. He stops here pretty regular. Ain't never brung no Negra's with him before, though. These here your Negra's traveling with you?" he asked.

Brandon looked at the women and then back to Frank. "No. They don't belong to anybody. We are just helping them out. Do you know of anywhere that might need someone? Someone to work for them, that is," Brandon asked.

"Naw. Not off hand. Let me think on it a spell," Frank said.

"Well, Frank, we will be at the Café over yonder. If you think of anything, we would be obliged," Brandon said.

"You can't take them into the Café," Frank said. "They won't let you. They won't serve them or you, either, for that matter, if they are with you."

Brandon stopped. He turned around and looked at Frank. "Slavery was abolished, Frank. You are a Northerner. You should know that. I fought in that war. I lost a brother in that war. We paid a mighty high price so people like these women right here could be free. Why would they not be served food in a Northern state, for crying out loud?" Brandon asked, agitated.

"Now, don't get huffy with me, Mr. Shively. I lost a son in that war, too. I agree with what you are saying. I'm just stating a fact. You can go on in the Café and they can stay here with me. If you want to bring them something to eat, they can eat it in the stable over here where nobody will bother them. I'll look after them myself," Frank explained.

Brandon looked at the women standing before him. He looked at Diana with a question in his eyes. Diana nodded at him. "All right, but you keep an eye on them. Anybody messes with them, I want you to come get me," Brandon said to Frank. He turned to Rita and said, "Rita, we are going to the Café over there. You wait inside the stable with Frank here. I will bring some food out for all of you. Do you understand?"

Rita nodded. "Like I said before, we don't want no trouble. We is honest folk. We just want to work somewheres so we kin eat. That's all," Rita said.

Brandon patted her on the back. He took Diana by the arm and they, along with Martha, went in the direction of the Café.

Inside, they found a table near the window that looked back toward the stables. The same oriental woman who served them when Diana made the trip with Porter and her mother years ago approached the table. They ordered a bowl of soup for themselves and asked for four more bowls in something that could be taken to the stables for their friends. The woman looked them over closely. They were very well dressed, thanks to Martha. They had an important look to them, so she agreed. She insisted that the bowls and spoons be returned, and that the ladies would remain in the Café until they were returned. Brandon laughed, but agreed. He carried the soup to the stable on a tray. Gordy was awake. When they saw the soup and a slice of bread for each of them, their eyes opened wide. Brandon watched as they gobbled up the food. He carried the tray back to the Café. Then he joined Diana and Martha in their meal.

Once they had finished eating, they returned to the stable to find the four Negroes still where Brandon had left them. They were huddled in a corner. The sun would be going down in a couple of hours. Brandon was anxious to arrive in Philadelphia before dark. The carriage was ready to go with a pair of fresh horses. They climbed aboard. It took some coaxing to get Rita and the others to get back into the carriage, but at last, they agreed. They were once again on the road.

It was nearly dark when they pulled to a halt in front of Josephine and James' house. There were candles burning in the window. Josephine hurried outside when she heard them approach. She had been expecting them. Behind her stood three of her children. James stood in the doorway. Diana waved from the carriage.

"Come on down, children, and greet your Aunt Diana and Aunt Martha," Josephine called back to them as she hurried toward the carriage.

James moved them aside and took the reins of the team, holding them. Brandon jumped down. He helped the ladies out of the carriage. Rita and the rest sat fast to their seats, not sure what to do. In all of the excitement, they were nearly forgotten. Diana turned to Brandon and said, "What should we do with them?" she whispered.

Josephine asked, "Who are they?"

Diana smiled and said, "We came upon them walking along the road. They have nowhere to go. They are looking for work. They were tired and hungry. Do you know of anyone that may need help?"

Josephine thought for a moment. "Not right now. I can't think of a soul. Let me think on it for a while. They can sleep in the barn loft for tonight. Tomorrow, we may be able to come up with something more suitable. Right now, I am just so happy that you are here. I can't think of anything else," she said, bubbling with joy.

Brandon and James took the team to the stables. Rita, Delila, Nesta, and Gordy remained glued to the carriage. The women went inside with all three of Josephine's children behind them.

"Isn't someone missing?" Martha asked.

Josephine smiled and said, "Pauline is asleep. She was fussy so I put her down early. We are trying to potty train her. It isn't working out very well."

Diana laughed. "I know how that is. We just got Cecilia potty trained. I was so worried that we would have three in diapers all at the same time. She fought it, but finally she gave in. Thank the good Lord above for that."

Josephine put her arm around Diana. She smiled and said. "The good Lord smiled down on those children the day they came to Berlin. Lord knows where they would be now, or what would have become of them if it were not for you and Brandon. I heard from Porter Martin how their father just up and left in the night, without even a goodbye."

Martha spoke up. "There were a couple of families who were willing to take them. Even Sofia, if you can believe that. But Porter Martin would not hear of it. He would not allow them to be separated. He is a good Christian man."

"That he is," Josephine said. "Let me make you a cup of tea. I have been baking all day. I really expected you to arrive tomorrow."

Diana hung her coat over the chair in the kitchen. "We made really good time." She looked at Josephine's children gathered around the fireplace. Again, it reminded her of the days in the cabin when someone would come calling. She and her sisters did the same thing. "Who have we here?" she asked.

Josephine placed her hand upon the heads of her children as she said, "This is Will. He is five now. This is James Porter, four years old, Agnus Diana, who is three, and Pauline is sleeping upstairs."

Diana nodded at the children. "You have all grown so much since last I saw you."

Martha laughed and said, "They have grown since I saw them last, and that wasn't even a full month ago."

Just then, the door opened and Brandon and James entered the kitchen. James was carrying an arm full of split wood. He placed it near the fireplace. He lifted Agnus into his arms and sat down at the table. Brandon sat next to Diana. The other two children moved closer to the table, gathering near their father.

Josephine poured tea for them all. She unwrapped a small bundle of cheesecloth that contained cookies. She broke the cookies into pieces and gave each of the children one. They remained quiet.

"They are very well behaved," Brandon said.

"They better be. I have been coaching them for the last four days or more," James said laughing. Then he continued. "I'll bet it gets pretty festive at your table. Porter told me that Tilly and her children are there nearly every day. That makes about fourteen of you at the table in the evenings."

"Well, not quite. Little Robert isn't big enough to sit at the table yet. And I must say, those children are all very well behaved. They listen well. We really don't have much trouble with any of them. Winston and Raymond have been helping at the mill. Shirley is only five. The rest are pretty much babies," Brandon exclaimed.

"I see," James said. He turned to Martha. "Well, Martha, when are you and Carver going to start giving us some more nieces and nephews?" he asked.

Martha flushed. "Oh, James, please. We have only been married a few weeks. When the Lord thinks we are ready, I reckon," she laughed.

Josephine sat down beside Martha. She took her hand. "Don't let James embarrass you, Dear. He is such a tease. He thinks everybody should have a big family," she smiled at her sister.

"Well," Diana laughed, "maybe not as big as ours. Or at least, not as quickly," she said.

Everyone laughed. They were enjoying their evening. Then James asked, "What are we going to do with that group in the stables? We can't leave them out there. We have to find somewhere for them to go."

Brandon asked, "Do you know of anyone who needs some hired help? They said they were willing to work. I imagine they have been wandering about for a long time. They are all pretty malnourished."

"Yeah, they need a bath and some clean clothes, too," James said. "If we clean them up some, we may be able to find work for them somewhere. But looking like they do right now, I don't think anyone would hire them," he replied.

"What about at the Main Street Restaurant?" Josephine asked her husband. "There is a sign in the window, "COOK WANTED.""

"That would be great," Diana said.

"Yeah, but they still have to be cleaned up, and where are they going to stay?" James asked.

"We can clean them up tomorrow. I will give them a couple of my old dresses. As for a place to stay, I haven't a clue as to what to do with them. We do not have the room here, and they can't stay in the barn this winter," Josephine said.

"If Porter were here, he would just build them a house," Martha said, laughing.

The room grew quiet. Then, James spoke up. "You are right, Martha. That is exactly what Uncle Porter would do. We have the lumber at the mill. We have the hands to do it. We could build them a house. There is a community of Negroes just outside of town. We could build them a house out there amongst their own people."

Diana looked around the table. "Why do they all live outside of town? They are free people. They are equal in the eyes of the Lord, aren't they?" She asked.

James pursed his lips together. He shook his head as he said, "This is not Berlin, Diana. Folks here think they are free from slavery and mistreatment, but not equal to white folks. At least they don't treat them as equal."

Diana gasped. "What? Why did all of those boys die in that war? What were they fighting for?"

Josephine covered Diana's hand with her own. "Di. I understand how you feel. We all feel the same way. But we can't change the way everybody else feels. The colored folks have their own community, just outside of town, with their own school and everything. They come into town to work and do their shopping, but they keep pretty much to themselves out there. To be honest with you, I think they want it that way. Some of them have strong ties to their past. They have their own religion, even," she explained.

It grew quiet again. Then, James said, "They can stay in the barn for awhile. I will try to find a place for them in the company of their own kind. I think they will be happier there. Then I will get some men together from our church and we will build them a small place out there."

"Thank you, James. That is kind of you," Brandon said.

"Well," Josephine said, "let's turn in for the night. I will show you to your rooms. Don't worry about the china, I will wash it in the morning. Come along, children." She stood and waited by the kitchen door while the children filed past her toward the stairs. Diana, Brandon, and Martha followed behind. James began to bank the fire.

"I'll be along," he said.

Josephine had put all of her children into one bedroom. She had four bedrooms, one being for Porter Martin when he stayed with them. It was the house Porter had built for himself and his beloved Margaret. They had hoped for a large family. He had a barn and the mill, which James and Thomas had been running for him. When Margaret had her accident, and there were no longer any hopes for children, they did not need such a big house. That was when Porter had decided to build another house, much smaller than this one. He moved her to Berlin and built another mill to expand his business. Porter had become a very rich man, but childless.

Now, Porter found himself with a very large family. None of the children was his own, but no one would ever know it. He was happy, except he missed his one true love, Miss Margaret. All of this was passing through Diana's mind as she slept next to her beloved Brandon in Porter Martin's large brick house on a side street in Philadelphia. Just before sleep overtook her, she counted herself very blessed. Porter was a man she admired very much. She was living his dream. She smiled to herself before she dozed off.

The next morning was somewhat chaotic. When Diana and Brandon went downstairs, the kitchen was already full. Martha was helping Josephine prepare breakfast. All four of Josephine's children were seated around the table. It had been extended to make room for the guests. James sat at the head of the table next to the fireplace. Brandon was seated at the other end. Martha and Diana sat on one side with William sitting next to his father. Josephine sat across from Martha with Little Jimmy on one side of her and Agnus on the other. Little Pauline sat in her high chair. She was crying because the food was not coming fast enough.

"Good morning, Aunt Diana," William said. He was almost six years old by now. Diana could remember the last time she saw him. Josephine was pregnant with Little Agnus. Will was about three years old then.

"Good morning, Will. Did you sleep well?" she asked him.

"Oh, yes, Ma'am," he replied. He was so polite. Diana made a mental note to work on the manners of her children when she got home.

Martha pulled out a chair and sat down. Josephine finished pouring the coffee and she too sat down. They bowed their heads. James said grace. "Amen," they all said afterwards. Pauline cried through the whole thing. Josephine handed her a slice of toasted bread with jam on it. She began to eat. Once her mouth was full, she quieted down. She was happy now.

Diana smiled. Josephine winked at her. "She likes to eat, this one does," she said.

"She takes after Sofia," Martha said, laughing.

They all laughed. "I hope she isn't as dreamy as Sofia," Josephine said.

Martha went on, "Josie, you should see Sofia. She is due in a couple of weeks, but she looked like she was pregnant before she even got pregnant. She is so fat I can't let her dresses out anymore. Her house is a mess. One Sunday she came to church without even combing her hair. It was matted in the back and all disarrayed." Martha sighed. "I apologize. I know it is poor manners to talk about her behind her back in such a vulgar manner, but it is the truth."

Diana nodded. "Unfortunately, it is the truth, Josie. If Mamma could see her now, she would whoop on her something terrible," she replied.

Josephine just shook her head. "I am so sorry to hear that. I think deep down, I always suspected that would happen. Mamma said she was dreamy, but I always suspected she was just plain lazy. I declare, I do not know where she got that from," Josephine said.

"Poor Jonathan Gilbert. I don't think he expected her to turn out the way she did," Diana said. "He seems like a very tolerable man."

"He must be. From what you have told me, I reckon he is a very tolerable man. What is he going to do when the baby comes? I hear that Concetta Hickman gave birth to a baby. Porter doesn't normally gossip, but he did tell us an actor came through on the stage and took advantage of her innocent nature. Porter told us that the actor has never been seen or heard of since. He says that Grace and Sherman are raising the child because poor Concetta has nowhere else to go. That must have been something to see. I mean, Grace Hickman's face, that is. She has always been so high and mighty. She always talked down to us when we took milk into town. How humiliating it must have been for her." Josephine talked as she kept spooning food into Pauline's constant opening mouth.

"Oh, excuse me," she said, finally. "I did not mean to go on so. I am sure you men folk do not appreciate listening to our chatter. I will save my dull conversation for when we women are alone," Josephine said, flushing.

Brandon laughed. "It is all right, Josephine. I can't say that any of it has gone unnoticed by myself and other men around Berlin. I think even old Sherman himself has spoken about his wife's high and mighty attitude toward others around Berlin. For some reason, she always speaks highly of Porter, though," he said.

Diana laughed. "Because Porter Martin has money. More money than her," she said. She took a drink of her coffee.

"Uncle Porter does not act high and mighty, though. He doesn't even pay no mind to financial matters. He does his job and expects to be paid for it. If someone less fortunate than himself needs help, he is happy to oblige," James said as he scraped his plate. "That was a mighty fine breakfast you girls gave us this morning."

"Mighty fine, indeed," Brandon said. He scooted his chair back and crossed his legs. He held his full coffee cup in his right hand. Diana thought he looked so grand. She was so proud of him.

After the men drank their coffee, they went out to the mill. James sent Rita and the others in for breakfast. They came to the back door. Josephine invited them inside and asked them to sit at the table. She and Martha began to prepare another breakfast for them. Diana cleared the table of the dirty dishes and set clean ones out for the four guests, who watched with their mouths hanging open.

"Nobody ever served us afore," Rita said.

Rita, Delila, Nesta, and Gordy ate everything Josephine and Martha put on the table. When they had finished, Delila insisted on cleaning up the mess. Josephine showed the two women where everything went. Josephine led

Martha and Diana upstairs. "Help me find some clean clothes for them. Then we will have them bath and change. Perhaps if they look more presentable, we will be able to find work for them."

Josephine went through an old trunk that sat in the corner of her bedroom. It was full of children's clothes. She didn't have anything for Nesta because she was older than any of Josie's children. She found some old clothes for Gordy and the two women. Martha took an old dress of Josephine and said she would cut it down for Nesta. They busied themselves preparing and planning. After a couple of hours, Josephine straightened up and said, "I don't hear the children. I better go check." She turned and quickly ran from the room. Diana noticed the panic in Josephine's eyes. She ran after her.

They descended the stairs quickly. They ran right into Delila, who was waxing the stair railings. "Where are the children?" Josephine asked, holding her hand at her throat.

Delila pointed toward the parlor. "Nesta is wit em in there," she said.

Josephine hurried past her. "Dey is all right!" Delila called after her. She looked up at Diana who was still standing on the stairs, "Nesta is real good wit younguns."

Diana touched Delila on the shoulder. "I am sure she is. Mrs. Harris just wants to check on them. What are you doing, Delila?" Diana asked.

Delila smiled. "I is cleanin' house. Rita is doin' the kitchen and I is doin' the hall. We is grateful to you all for lookin' out for us. We just want to pay you back some. We is honest folks. We don't expect notin' for notin'," Delila said.

Diana looked up just in time to see Josephine coming back toward her. She was smiling. "They are all fine. They are playing in the front room. What is going on here?" Josephine asked, looking at Delila who had resumed waxing the spiral posts that supported the railing.

Diana spoke, "Rita and Delila are repaying you for breakfast."

"An for lettin' us sleep in the barn," Delila said, smiling up at Josephine.

Josephine looked up at Diana. She smiled. Diana said, "That is really nice of them, Josie. Don't you think?"

Josephine looked back at Delila and then toward the kitchen door. "Indeed, it is. It is going to be hard to let them go after we find work for them."

Delila looked up at Josephine. "Oh, Miss. We is willin to work for our keep. We will do anythin' you need done. Maybe you will let us just stay in the barn. We like it there mighty fine."

"Well, I don't know, Delila. I have to talk to my husband about that. But I don't think the loft in the barn would be warm enough in the winter. You really should have a place of your own. Wouldn't you rather have your own house?" Josephine asked.

Delila nodded and said, "Yes, Ma'am. That would be nice, but it ain't necessary. We ain't never had a place of our own, so we ain't missin' nothin'. We is happy here."

Josephine looked up at Diana. Diana shrugged her shoulders and smiled. "What have you gotten me into?" Josephine asked.

They went back up the stairs. They found Martha sewing an old dress of Josephine's. It was one that she had cut down for Nesta. They began to explain to Martha all that had transpired downstairs.

"Well, maybe you could work something out with them. We would be lost without Tilly and her children. Look how well they are caring for your children. My guess is that if it were not for Nesta watching over your children, you would not have the time to spend up here with us. Am I right?" Martha asked without looking up from her sewing.

Josephine looked over at Diana. "Yes. That is true. But I could not allow them to work for us without paying them. Just room and board would not be enough. People here would talk. It is just not done," she said.

Diana slipped her arm around Josephine. "You will figure something out. James is building them a house, right? It could be payment for the house. I don't know. You don't have to let them stay if you would rather not. It is your decision to make, not ours," Diana said. She picked up a needle and began to thread it.

"It sure is nice to have a few minutes to myself. I can't tell you how long it has been. I need to talk to James about it," Josephine declared as she too, picked up a needle and began sewing. "One thing is certain. We need to get these clothes ready. They need to bath and change into clean clothes."

The three sisters worked diligently on the sewing. It was about an hour later when they held up the finished product. They smiled, satisfied with their work.

"Come on. Let's get them some hot water to bathe," Josephine said.

"I would really like to visit with Regina today," Diana said as the hurried down the stairs.

"We will take a walk over there," Martha said as they reached the bottom of the stairs.

Rita had been dusting the baseboards. "If you need to go somewhere, Miss, we kin watch the younguns for ya," she said.

Josephine looked up at Diana who was still on the stairs. "Well, perhaps we could all go together after they clean up. It would be so nice to go with you," she said.

"Of course. We can wait another hour, I suppose," Diana replied.

The three sisters instructed Rita, Delila, Nesta, and Gordy on how and where to bathe. They handed them each clean clothes. Then they retired to the front room to look over the children. They sat sipping a cup of tea while William and James played on the floor, pushing their homemade toys about. Martha held Agnus on her lap, while Josephine held Pauline.

"How do you feel?" Josephine asked Diana.

Diana smiled and replied. "I feel fine now. At first, I had the morning sickness. It was awful. But it has passed."

"You have hardly gained a pound. You would never know you were due in about four more months," Josephine said.

"You should see Sofia," Martha said, laughing as she bounced Agnus Diana upon her knee. "She looks like she is going to burst. But then she was looking like that before she became pregnant."

They chuckled. Diana said, "That isn't fair. She is very frightened. She is afraid because of what happened to Madeline Hughes. I haven't forgotten that day, either. I was in the room with her when it happened. It was just awful."

Josephine said, "Porter told us about that. It really was awful. I think it would frighten me also. She isn't having any problems is she? Sofia? I mean, there are no signs of any problems are there?"

"No. She is fine, I guess. But Madeline showed no signs of problems either until right at the end," Diana explained. "She said her pains had been coming all day. Normally they just started kind of quick like. She said she just walked around in circles until she felt the baby coming. I don't know that I would call that trouble. Little Robert did not turn like he was supposed to. He was coming feet first and he tore her up too bad on the inside. Alda Faulk said if she had been there sooner, she could have turned him around and Madeline would have lived. All I know is I want Alda Faulk there at the first sign of pain."

"How is Regina's little girl, Margaret Agnus?" Martha asked. "She was sickly when Carver and I were here last."

Josephine nodded. "She is always coming down with something. I think she is over that. I don't see much of her. Regina stops by now and then, but she is mostly busy doing something at the printing shop, or with Delbert's mother. She isn't well. Since her husband died and she had a stroke, she's taken to her bed. James said she always was frail," Josephine said.

"I swear. I never thought Regina would last here. I thought for sure Delbert would send her packing. She hasn't calmed down any, either. She still talks all of the time," Martha said.

Josephine laughed and said, "You should see them together. They are perfect for each other. Delbert hardly ever says a word. If you ask him anything, he just says, Yes, Ma'am or no, Ma'am. Then Regina jumps right in there and answers the question for him. She finishes any sentence he may find the nerve to start. He just sits there with his hands folded in his lap while she goes on and on."

Diana laughed at the thought. "Remember all of those times when you wanted to just smack her in the mouth at the general store? Old Grace Hickman knew, too. She knew that Regina would tell everything she knew. You couldn't shut her up. You had to cover her mouth with your hand," Diana said, laughing.

"Just listen to us gossiping about our sisters. Aren't we wicked?" Josephine said, laughing.

"I guess we are," Diana replied. "I apologize. That is very rude of me to talk about them when they are not here to defend themselves."

Josephine waved her hand in the air. She laughed and said, "Don't worry, Diana. I enjoyed it so much. No one ever comes to visit with me. I am so busy with the children I don't have any social life. I don't have one friend here in Philadelphia. Porter and the letters he brings to me from you girls are the only source of news I have. You can talk about anything or anyone you want. I won't repeat a word of it, I swear."

Soon, there was a slight tap at the door. It was Rita. "Come in, Rita," Josephine said.

Rita stepped into the room. Josephine nodded and said, "How nice you look, Rita."

Rita pulled her skirt up slightly and dipped in an attempt to curtsy. Diana thought that perhaps she had seen some southern lady curtsy at some point in time. Rita turned around, saying, "The dress is mighty fine, Miss. I ain't never wore anythin' as fine as this here dress. I be thankin' you for lettin' me wear it, Ma'am."

"The dress is yours to keep, Rita," Josephine said.

Rita placed her hand over her mouth. She whispered. "Why, thank you kindly, Ma'am."

"How are the others coming along?" Josephine asked.

"They is dressed. They is wonderin' what you want us to do? Kin we fix you all anythin'?" Rita asked.

Josephine stood up. She passed Pauline over to Diana. "No. I would like to go calling with my sisters. We have another sister who lives down town. It would be very kind of you to watch after my children so I could go," Josephine said.

"Yes, Ma'am. We kin do that for ya. We would be obliged to look after the younguns. We will be right here when you get back. You just take your time and have a nice visit with that sister of yourun. You tell Rita what you want for your evening meal, and I will git it started for ya. I is real good in the kitchen, Ma'am!" Rita exclaimed.

Josephine smiled. She looked back at Martha and Diana. "I have some salt pork in the cellar. I will show you where it is." She turned to her sisters. "I will be right back." Then she led Rita out of the room.

Nesta and Gordy came into the front room. Nesta took Pauline from Diana. "Mamma says you is goin' out. We is to look after these here younguns," she proclaimed.

"Thank you very much, Nesta," Diana said. She winked at Gordy. "Thank you, Gordy."

Just then, Josephine returned. She smiled. "All right then. Nesta, you take Pauline into the kitchen so she doesn't see me leave. Then we can go," Josephine said.

"Yes, Ma'am," Nesta said. She lifted Pauline higher on her hip. She took Agnus by the hand, and Gordy took James and William's hands. They went into the kitchen, with Will looking over his shoulder at his mother.

"It is all right, William. I am not going far, and I will not be long. I am just going to visit your Aunt Regina with my sisters," Josephine explained to her oldest son. He waved at her. Josephine blew him a kiss. She turned to her sisters. "Let's go before I change my mind," she laughed.

They walked slowly down the streets of stone. Diana recalled the red brick houses that lined the streets, with their grand lawns. Plants sat in large pots on the porches. It was a beautiful day.

Now and then, a carriage would pass them. The passengers always called out a greeting. "It is such a friendly place for being as big a city as it is," Diana commented.

Josephine nodded. "It is here, but once you get into the city itself, it isn't as friendly. Actually, I must warn you not to venture there alone. I don't believe I would venture into the main part of the city without a man to accompany me. It is pretty rough there. Daytime isn't nearly as bad as night time, though," she explained.

Martha asked, "But doesn't Regina live right over the print shop? Isn't that in the city?"

Josephine nodded again. She replied, "Yes, it is, but not on the main street. We will walk to the back entrance. Regina and Delbert's apartment is upstairs over the shop. They have a stairway that goes up the back of the shop. It isn't near the saloons or gambling casinos, either. That is where it gets dangerous."

They continued to stroll along the cobblestone sidewalks. The tall brick houses were becoming smaller. More and more wooden buildings lined the streets. There were less and less glamour on the lawns. Picket fences separated the yards from the street. Soon, the noise of the city could be heard in the distance. Josephine pointed to the left. "We must go this way," she said.

The cobblestone sidewalks disappeared all together. It was just dusty, dirty, streets. Soon, they came to a wooden sidewalk that went behind several buildings. Stairs went up the second floor of most of them. After they came to the fourth building, Josephine began to ascend the stairs, with Martha and Diana following her up. She knocked on the door at the top.

The door opened just a crack. Diana could see the familiar hazel eye peering through at them. Then the door swung open all the way, "Martha, Diana!" Regina cried out.

She began hugging them. She was saying something, but Diana did not hear a word of it. She was looking down at little Margaret Agnus. She was five years old now. She was beautiful. Her hair was light, not quite blonde, but much lighter than Regina's. She had blue eyes, a perfect oval shaped face, with just a few freckles on her nose. She was the image of Sofia when she was young. Diana smiled at her. She stepped behind her mother and peeked out from behind her skirt.

"I am so thrilled to see you! Please, come in! And Josie? How did you manage to get away from that family of yours? What a wonderful surprise. You know I never really expected you to make it, what with all of those children you have to care for now. May I make you a cup of tea? What a wonderful surprise. Wait until you see Delbert. He has lost all of his hair on top. He is a little sensitive about it, but I think it makes him look more distinguished. Oh, where are my manners, please come sit down. You must tell me all about your trip!" Regina said, barely breathing between sentences.

Diana burst into laughter. "Regina, calm down. It is so good to see you. Yes, we would like a cup of tea, thank you very much. Let me help you make it," she said, still laughing.

Josephine and Martha were also laughing. "I swear, Regina. You would think you never get to talk to anyone the way you go on," Josephine said.

Regina went to the cupboard. She pulled down a tin containing loose tea. She put the kettle on the stove and turned it on. Diana was going from cupboard to cupboard, until she found the cups and saucers. Martha took the spoons from Regina's hands and began to place them on the table. Josephine was playing with Margaret.

"When did you come in?" Regina asked.

Martha answered. "We got in last night just after dark."

"Did you have good weather? Did anyone else come with you?" Regina asked.

Diana replied. "The weather was very pleasant. It was sunshine nearly the entire way. It was beautiful. Brandon came with us. He brought us. He is working at the mill with James and Thomas this morning. We picked up four riders. They are back at Josephine's."

"Four riders? Oh, Diana! Did you or Brandon know these people? Who are they?" Regina asked.

"They were just two Negro women and two of their children. They were looking for work. Do you know of anyone who needs two hardworking Negro women?" Martha asked.

Regina stood perfectly still while she thought a moment. Then she raised her eyebrows and replied, "Well, Delbert mentioned that he could use someone to stay with his mother full time. Since her stroke, she has been confined to a wheelchair, just like Miss Margaret was. Only she doesn't move her left arm at all. She doesn't speak very well, either. But I don't know about two children. He would never allow children running amuck in the house."

"Well, perhaps he could hire Delila. The children belong to Rita. That would help some," Martha said.

Regina started up again. "I will mention it to him. I will have to come visit with you tomorrow. How long are you staying? I could get away tomorrow for sure. They are staying at the house, you say? Are they watching out for your children, Josie? You trust them that much, do you? They must be honest for you to trust your children in their care, because I don't recall you ever doing that before. What are they like? How old are they? I don't think Delbert wants some young, inexperienced woman looking out for his mother. No one too old, either. She can be a handful when it comes to lifting her. They have to be clean, too. We have to think of what the neighbors are going to say.

Being Negroes isn't a problem. Lots of folks here abouts has Negroes working for them. They work real cheap. Some work real hard, too."

Josephine interrupted. "They are clean, hardworking women, Regina. I would not leave my children with just anyone. You know that. As far as cheap goes, that is something you will have to work out with them. I know they have just taken over the chores and caring for my children as if they have been doing it for years. I think they would be a good choice for Delbert's mother. But then, that is for Delbert to decide."

Regina picked up where she had left off. "Well, as I said before, some are really hardworkers. They seem to have a desire to please. The rich folks in this town prefer to hire white housekeepers, but they usually have a few darkies work for them, too. White housekeepers are hard to come by these days. They charge more, too. It seems the Negroes are content to get whatever they can. They work just as hard, but accept less. They just want to eat and care for their families."

Diana sipped her tea. "This is very good tea, Regina," she said.

"Thank you," Regina said. "I will talk to Delbert about hiring one of the women to stay with his mother. I can't think of anyone who needs someone with two children, though. So how are those children of yours Diana? You never did tell me how you managed to get away from them. And how is Porter Martin?"

Diana began to laugh. She looked over at Josephine, who was trying not to laugh as well. "Well, they are all fine. Cecilia is finally potty trained. Franklin is walking and Robert is sitting up by himself, although he isn't very steady yet. Tilly and Hoppy are looking out for them. Porter is fine. He is retiring soon. He has taught Brandon the business. He seems to be content with just playing with the children all day," Diana said.

"Oh, yes, Tilly. What would you ever do without her? She has been a blessing hasn't she? You really got lucky the day she came into your life, didn't you, Di? Porter has told me that he is happy with you and your family staying at the house. He said he would not want you to be anywhere else. Although I thought for a while there that you bit off more than you could chew when you took in all of those children. Hughes? Is that their names? Are you going to adopt them?" Regina babbled on and on.

Diana found herself rudely interrupting her sister. "Yes, their names were Hughes. As far as adoption goes, Brandon and I have not discussed it. It is something to think about. They are all very well behaved children, and I can't say that they are any trouble at all."

"What about you, Martha? How do you like married life? Carver seemed like a very nice man. I got to meet him before he moved to Berlin, you know. He had a blacksmith shop right down the street. It was a small one, but he did very well for himself. I think he would still be there if it weren't for Lester Fullton. He opened a big smithy right up the street from where Carver's shop was. Porter talked him into moving to Berlin. I don't think it took much talking, though. Then he met you and the rest is history," Regina said.

When she stopped talking, everyone looked at one another. They weren't sure what had happened. Regina had been talking nearly non-stop since they arrived. Diana reached down and lifted Margaret up onto her lap.

"She will be ready for school in another year or two," Diana said, looking at the beautiful little girl she held on her lap. Margaret smiled up at her.

"Yes, I suppose she will. How are you feeling? I understand you are due in about four more months," Regina asked.

"Yes, that is right. I feel pretty good actually," Diana said, running her fingers through Margaret's curly hair.

"What about Sofia? When I came home last time, I couldn't help but notice how big she was. I thought she was pregnant then. But of course, she wasn't. She should be due soon. Is she still heavy?" Regina asked.

Martha laughed. "I can't let her dresses out any more. She is huge. It isn't all baby either. I think it is mostly laziness. We were just talking about the morning she went to church without combing her hair. Mamma and Daddy would whoop on her if they were alive to see how she has turned out," Martha said.

"I suppose you were right all along, Di. You tried to tell Mamma that Sofia was just lazy. Mamma kept saying she was dreamy, but you knew all the long. I feel sorry for that preacher husband of hers. Perhaps motherhood will change her. I hope so, anyway," Regina said, sipping her tea.

She stood up and went to lift Margaret out of Diana's arms. "I am sorry, Di, but it is time for Maggy to take her nap. If I wait, she will fall asleep too early and then we will be up all night. Kiss your aunties, Dear. You will see them again tomorrow," Regina said.

They each kissed Maggy and Regina disappeared into another room with the child. Soon, she re-appeared to sit at the table with them again.

"Are you teaching school next year, Di? With a new baby and all, how are you going to manage? Perhaps someone could fill in for you. You could hang a notice up in the shop asking for help. Sometimes people do that when they are looking for help. That reminds me; we should go down and look at the wall. Perhaps there is a help wanted for that Negro woman who has two children. We will have to stop down there before you leave. Now, again, what are you going to do when the baby comes? Are you still going to teach?" Regina began to go on and on, again.

"I think I can manage. Porter has built a cradle for Robert. He will be too big for it soon. I will take it to the schoolhouse. Hoppy has been most helpful with filling in for me when I need to step out for a while. I think I can handle it. If not, there is always Tilly. She is my God-given angel. I don't know what I would do without her," Diana responded.

Regina turned to Martha. "What about you, Martha? How is the seamstress business coming along? Do you know how many times I am stopped on the street and asked who my seamstress is? Everyone comments on how well I am dressed. You really should consider moving here. You could make a fortune," she said.

"No, thank you. Big city life is not for me. Just living in Berlin gives me enough work to keep me busy and cash in my pocket. At times, I find even it's too busy, and I long for the cabin back home. I know that sounds silly, but I never really liked a lot of activity around me. I could never do what Diana is doing," Martha said. Then, as an afterthought, she said, "Although I admire what she is doing very much. I just know I could not do it."

"I wonder if Sofia is up to parenthood," Regina said. She went on, "I think she may come around after awhile. She never was any good on the farm. She couldn't or wouldn't do much of anything. You never saw her jump in and try anything. She always hung back and watched everybody else do it. It was kind of like, if she didn't learn how to do anything, no one expected her to. Did anyone else ever notice that? I often wondered why Mamma put up with it. Even on the day when Mamma got bitten, Mamma knew Sofia was in the wrong. She knew Diana was the stronger of the two, so she sided with Sofia. Then it turned out badly for Mamma. Sofia felt guilty about that, too. She tried hard after that to make it up to Di, but it didn't last long. The old lazy Sofia came back."

Diana put her hand on Regina's arm. She said, "Regina, please. That day is very difficult for me. I feel so terribly guilty myself. If I hadn't fought with Sofia, Mamma would not have been out there. And if I had just seen the second bite under her arm, I might have gotten most of the poison out and she may have lived. I don't think we should be gossiping about Sofia in this manner. I just don't feel comfortable with it. Especially about that day. I think of it enough without reliving it again."

Regina looked at Diana for a moment. It was the first time today they heard nothing coming out of her mouth. After a few sips from her teacup, she changed the subject. "Delbert's mother isn't well at all. Did I tell you that? She can't speak. Least wise in a manner that is understandable. She mumbles and drools. Her left side is completely paralyzed. Delbert goes over there each afternoon after he closes the print shop. He sits with her for a while. I try to make it over every day, but with Maggy and all, I just think it isn't the healthiest environment for Maggy. Delbert has hired a woman to sit with Mother Gordon. She is very expensive. I will definitely mention your Negro woman to him. Perhaps I will have an answer for you by tomorrow. Speaking of tomorrow, what are you all doing for dinner? I would love to have you all over, but there isn't enough room here for all of us. I was thinking maybe we could go to his mother's house and I could prepare something for all of us there. What do you think?"

Josephine spoke before Regina could take a breath and start up again. "I was going to invite you over to our place for dinner. I thought it would be nice to have the whole family there. I have the room. We have plenty of room and now we have plenty of help."

Regina perked up. "Help. What help?" she asked.

"Well, the two ladies and their children are staying in the barn for now. That is until we find them more suitable housing. They are watching the children for me right now. They are wonderful in the kitchen. They can help. Maybe if Delbert sees how good they are he will be more inclined to hire one of them to take care of his mother," Josephine explained.

"Why, of course. What was I thinking? We would love to come for dinner. Just give me a time," Regina said.

"Regina," Martha began, "Don't you want to discuss it with Delbert first? Perhaps he has other plans."

Regina laughed. "Oh, no! Delbert will not have other plans. We will be there. Just give us a time. Whatever I say is all right with Delbert. He is very considerate to my wishes. He never says anything."

Diana and Josephine's eyes met. They both smiled and lowered their heads. Martha must have read their minds for she, too, was smiling. She folded her hands in her lap and sat in an upright position. The stiffness in her spine indicated she was about to burst into laughter.

Regina went on. "Isn't it a glorious day? I was going to take Maggy for a walk after her nap. She needs to get more fresh air. She has been sickly ever since she was born. Would you girls like to join me in a walk later? We have a beautiful park here. I would love to show it to you. I don't have many friends, but there are a couple of ladies that I meet daily in the park. I would love to show you off to them. They will just die when they see those dresses you are wearing."

Diana spoke up. "I am sorry. I don't think we have time for a walk in the park."

Josephine agreed. "That is right, Regina. We really should be getting back. I think that Pauline has figured out that I have left by now. She will be crying and throwing a tantrum. I really need to get back. As a matter of fact, I am ready whenever you girls are."

Diana stood up. Martha carried the teacups to the wash station. "Thank you for the tea, Regina," Martha said, hugging Regina.

Diana hugged her, too. "It was so good to see you again, Regina. I am so looking forward to tomorrow night."

Josephine hugged Regina also. "Dinner will be around six-thirty. Is that a suitable time for you?"

Regina nodded. "Yes, it is. We will be there," she said as they walked to the door. Josephine opened the door and stepped outside onto the landing. "Should I bring anything? I can bake tomorrow and bring it with me."

Josephine shook her head. "No, no. That is not necessary. We have plenty. Just come and relax." She started down the steps. Diana and Martha followed her lead.

Regina was still talking as they were leaving. "I am so sorry you could not go for that walk with me. I will have to tell the girls at the park all about you. I am sure they will not believe me when I tell them about your sewing abilities, Martha. Although, they do ask about my dresses often enough."

Soon, she was out of hearing distance. They turned to wave at her. She was still on the landing. "I wonder if she is still talking?" Martha asked. They laughed.

When they returned back at Josephine's house, they found that the children were all taking a nap. Even Gordy, who was sleeping on the floor in the kitchen.

"How was yourn visit wit you sister?" Rita asked.

"It was very nice, Rita. Thank you for watching over the children so I could have an afternoon with my sisters," Josephine said.

"It were not nothin'. They was no trouble. That little one cried some, but she cried herself to sleep, n the others went up for their nap wit out even bein told twice," Rita said.

"What is that smell? It smells heavenly," Martha asked.

"That be yous salt pork, Ma'am," Delila said from the stove.

"It's making my mouth water," Martha said.

"We may have a job for the two of you. Maybe just one of you. I am not sure. My sister said her husband needs someone to stay with his mother full time. She is not well and cannot do for herself. They are coming to dinner tomorrow and perhaps we will know more by then," Josephine said.

"That be fine, Ma'am," Rita said.

Diana asked. "Rita, are those your children or Delila's?"

Rita smiled. "They is mine. I had more. Lots more, but they all got sold off afore we was freed. I don't know where they is. Just Nesta an Gordy is all I have now," she said.

The room grew quiet. "How awful! I don't know what I would do if someone took my children away from me. Oh, Rita. I am so very sorry that happened to you," Josephine said, choking up.

"Do you have any idea who bought them or where they may be?" Diana asked.

"No, Ma'am. Masser jus took em on a wagon. I didn't even git to go wit em or says goodbye. We was not allowed," Rita explained.

"How terrible!" Martha said, wiping at her eye.

"It is what it is, Miss. That's how it was on the plantation. Now we is free. Masser says we has to go. We don't know notin'. Just start to walkin' up that long road," Rita said.

"Mmm, hmm," Delila said from the stove.

"Do you know the name of the plantation where you lived and worked, Rita? Maybe they kept records," Josephine said.

"What is records, Ma'am?" Rita asked.

Josephine answered. "Written reports of where the slaves were taken. Who bought them and where they lived. Things like that may help us to find your children."

Rita shook her head. "No, Ma'am. Don't know notin' bout records. Don't know no names of plantations, neither. Just know Masser and Missus. Never called em notin' else," she said.

Josephine sat down on a chair. "I am so very sorry. If I just had something to go by. Maybe James would have some idea as to what to do. I just want to help in some way."

Rita smiled. "It is all right, Ma'am. Don't need to be worryin' bout it. I gots Nesta and Gordy. They needs me, and I is here. Bein free, they cain't be sold. We kin stay together."

"Yes, you can, Rita," Diana said. "Nobody can separate you anymore."

Martha rubbed her forehead. "I think I need to lie down. The bright sun gave me such a headache. Now, this, on top of it, is just too much. It is very upsetting. Do you mind if I lie down for awhile, Josie?"

"No, not at all. I understand. This is indeed most upsetting. You go on up. I'll check in on you in an hour or so," Josephine said.

Diana and Josephine watched Martha leave the kitchen. They sat across from one another at the table. Delila had poured them another cup of tea. Josephine sipped at hers. Diana stared into the cup. "Rita," she began, "Do you recall anyone being called by a name from, perhaps, a visitor, or someone else who lived on your plantation?" She asked.

Rita thought for a moment. "Misser Boggs comes to the house once a week. He aks for Misser Higgins or Missus Higgins. I reckon that be Masser's name. Never thought of it afore."

Diana looked up at Josephine. "So. All we have to do is look for a plantation that belongs to a Higgins. We should be writing this down. Who was Mister Boggs, Rita?" Diana asked.

"Misser Boggs? He lived somewheres else. I ain't sure who he is. He just comes to see Masser every week. It be fo business," Rita said.

"Monkey business it was," Delila chimed in. "He used to mess around wit some of the slaves in the fields. Masser looked the other way, too."

Josephine gasped. "What? Mr. Higgins permitted such a thing?" she asked, looking over at Diana.

Delila turned from the stove to face them. "Yes, Ma'am. Missus used to fuss about it. Masser said it was good for business."

"Whatever did he mean by that?" Diana asked.

"Some of us was for workin, some of us was for breedin. Masser said sellin' his slaves brought as much as the tobacco crop," Rita said.

"You said some of us. Rita, is that why you had so many children? Did your Mr. Higgins breed you?" Josephine asked in shock.

"Yes, Ma'am. Sometimes when Missus went to visit her sister, Masser breed me hisself," Rita said.

"Oh, good Lord!" Josephine said, covering her eyes with her hands. "I am so glad Martha went upstairs. This is just awful. I had no idea."

Diana wiped the tears from her eyes. "I think we need to talk to James and Brandon about this. I don't think I have the strength to take on such an ordeal on our own," she said.

Josephine nodded in agreement. "Yes, I think you are right. But first, I need to know something. Rita, do you want us to find your children? Do you want to be reunited with your children who were sold off into slavery?" Josephine asked.

Rita wiped her hands on her apron. She looked over at Delila. She turned back to Josephine and smiled. "No, Ma'am. I don't reckon I do. They is off somewhere's I don't know. I think it be best left alone," Rita said.

"Rita," Diana began, "If you want us to, we can do this. It may take awhile, but we can do it. But only if you want us to do it."

"Naw. Rita don't need no more children to look after. What is I gonna do wit more kids? I cain't do for the ones I got. Poor Gordy will likely need me all his life. It is best left the way it is," Rita replied.

"What about you, Delila? Do you have any children out there somewhere?" Diana asked.

Delila had her back to them. She shook her head, and without turning around, she replied. "I ain't never had no babies, Ma'am. Missus watched me real close. I ain't never been wit no man."

Diana sighed. She looked over at Josephine and whispered. "Thank the Lord for that."

Josephine nodded. She rose from her chair and walked to the window. "I suppose we have led a pretty sheltered life, Di. I had no idea that went on in the world. Just imagine what is out there that we don't know about. I suppose it is a blessing, because now I will never forget this sick feeling in my midsection that will eat at me for a very long time," she said. Tears streamed down her cheeks.

Diana was so choked up she could not speak. She just covered her face and sobbed.

Rita went to stand behind Josephine. She touched her shoulder lightly and said, "Ma'am, I didn't mean to make you cry. I ain't cryin. My younguns will do fine. Just Gordy is all I is worried bout right now."

Josephine wiped her eyes. She turned to Rita and smiled. "Gordy will be fine, Rita. So will you. I personally will see to it," she said. She looked over at Diana. "I can't send them away. I will have to talk to James, but I just can't send them away. We have an attic. They could stay up there," she said with a sigh.

Diana smiled and nodded. She could not find her voice. Her thoughts went to Tilly. She was like a sister to Diana. What hardships had she seen? Whose child was Hoppy? Did she even want to know? She swallowed hard. Today started out to be such a perfect day. Now all she wanted was for it to end.

A noise at the kitchen door got all of their attention. It was Will and Gordy. They stood at the door looking about the room. Josephine rushed to Will and hugged him close to her. Tears streamed down her face. The boy looked over her shoulder at his Aunt Diana. He was confused.

"Mamma, why are you crying?" he asked.

Josephine smiled and looked at him as she said, "Because I am so happy to have such a fine young man as yourself for my son. Mamma loves you so much," she said. The boy smiled back at her. He still looked confused. He wasn't sure if he believed her. Diana smiled and cleared her throat. She opened her arms to Gordy. He ran to her. She lifted him up onto her lap.

Gordy looked over at his mother, who was still working at the stove with Delila. He watched her as she moved about. He was such a well-behaved child. Diana wondered if he heard any noise at all or if it was total silence. She whispered his name. He did not respond. She said his name louder. Nothing. He began to play with a string hanging from his pants.

"Is there a library here in Philadelphia?" Diana asked.

Josephine sat down across from her. She lifted Will onto her lap. "Yes. It is right down the street from Regina's house. On the same side of the street. Why?" Josephine asked.

"I would like to do some research on deafness. There has to be a way to communicate with Gordy. I am sure this has been researched somewhere. I would like to go to the library. Do you mind if I go out for awhile?" Diana asked.

Josephine reached over and took Diana's hand. "You can't go alone. It isn't safe. I will go with you. Do you mind watching the children again for me, Rita?" she asked, turning to Rita.

"I watch em for ya," Rita said with a nod.

"I will have Thomas hitch up the buggy and take us in," Josephine said. She went to the door. Will ran after her. She smiled down at him and said, "Come along, Will. You can walk out to the mill with me. But you can't go into town with me. You stay and play with Gordy." They went through the kitchen door. Diana heard the outside door close behind them.

Diana sat at the table holding Gordy. He smiled up at her. She smiled back at him. "You said he was born deaf?" she asked.

"Yes, Ma'am. He never did act like he heard anythin around him. Missus said he was stone deaf," Rita said.

"I would like to take him to a doctor or some kind of specialist. I am going to the library to do some research on the subject. A library is a place that has books on everything. I might find one on deafness and read up on the subject. I want to help him," Diana said.

"Ma'am, I mean no dis-respect to ya. I just think Gordy is blessed wit not hearin' the evil in the world," Rita said, smiling at Diana. She ran her fingers through Gordy's hair. He looked up at her and put his arms up for her to take him in her arms. She shook her head and he lowered his arms, going back to playing with string on his pants. Diana could not help but feel that she would never turn away from one of her children. She smiled at Rita. Rita turned back to the stove.

Diana kissed the top of Gordy's head and put him on the floor. She heard Josephine coming back. She straightened her skirt and patted at her hair. Josephine came through the kitchen door carrying Diana's cape and hat. She handed it to Diana. "Thomas will collect us out front, straight away. He has to run into town anyway, so the buggy was already hitched up. I caught him just in time," she said, smiling at William. "You stay here, Will. We will be back soon."

Diana turned to Rita. "I am just researching it, Rita. I would never do anything with Gordy that you don't approve of. I will let you know what I learn. I will be a couple of hours." She turned and followed Josephine out the door.

The buggy ride was pleasant. It was still a beautiful day. The sky was bright with large white clouds clustered about in groups. The sun shone down on them as if to bless them. Diana said to Josephine, "Rita thinks Gordy is blessed with his deafness."

Josephine nodded. "I can understand that. Just imagine the hardship she has known. My heart breaks at the thought of what they have endured." She swallowed hard. She fought back the tears. "I am going to talk to James tonight when we are alone. I cannot send them away. If Delila wants to work for Delbert or his mother, that is fine, but those children," she broke off, gulping back the tears.

They rode the rest of the way in silence. Thomas pulled the buggy to a halt in front of a large two-story brick building. The stone steps went up to an overhang with large white pillars. "How grand," Diana said.

"I will be right here when you come out, Miss Josephine," Thomas said.

"Thank you, Thomas. We may be some time. If you want to come back later, that will be fine," Josephine said to him. She turned and followed Diana up the steps, into the building.

Inside, they found a desk with an older woman sitting behind it. Diana announced herself and told the woman what she was looking for. The older woman directed her to go up the steps to the second floor. She said she would find it in isle F on the right side. Diana was impressed that she knew exactly where the books were. This building was filled with books everywhere. To memorize them all would be nearly impossible. She made her way up the steps. Josephine followed.

"Have you ever seen so many books in your life?" Josephine asked.

Diana shook her head. They reached the top of the stairs. Each isle was marked with a letter from the alphabet. They found isle F. Diana went to the right and ran her fingers along the book titles. She found four books on hearing and deafness. She handed two to Josephine, taking two for herself. She pointed at a table with three chairs along the far wall. They went to it and sat down.

Diana leafed through the books. Josephine did the same. "I found something," Josephine said. She passed the book to Diana. Diana read out loud. "A form of communication called sign language. Each letter of the alphabet has a sign used to spell words. A series of hand signs indicate whole words." She smiled at Josephine. She leafed through the book some more. "Here is a chart." She turned the book so Josephine could see it. Josephine moved her chair closer.

"Oh, I wish I had thought of some writing paper and a pen," Diana said.

"We will just have to take the book with us," Josephine said.

They put the other books back where they found them. They carried the book down to the desk.

"Do you have a library card?" the older woman asked.

Josephine shook her head. "You will have to fill out an application." She handed Josephine a form. She filled out the paper, asking for her name and address. The woman looked it over. "Oh, you are Mrs. Harris. Your husband has the sawmill. I suppose it would be all right for you to take the book with you today. I know where to find you," she said, smiling.

"Thank you," Josephine said. They went outside. Thomas was not back yet. They had found what they needed much quicker than they had expected. They sat down on a bench and began to look through the book. Time passed quickly.

Diana was looking down at the pages when she became aware of a pair of shoes right in front of her. They were a man's shoes. It was Thomas. "Ma'am, I did not mean to frighten you," he said.

"Oh, Thomas. You did not frighten us. We were just distracted," Josephine said.

"Whenever you are ready, Ma'am. I really do need to get back to the mill," Thomas said.

"We are ready, Thomas," Josephine said. They went down the steps to the buggy. Thomas followed behind them. He held their hands as they climbed into the buggy. He, too, climbed into the driver's seat and clicked his tongue. The horse jumped and began to pull the buggy back in the direction of home.

Thomas pulled the buggy to a halt at the front door. He helped the ladies down from the buggy and drove off toward the mill. Diana and Josephine climbed the steps to the front door. The door burst open. William and Little James were waiting for them. Gordy was standing behind them.

"Were you good boys for Miss Rita and Delila?" Josephine asked them.

"Oh, yes, Mother. We listened to everything and did as we were asked. Mostly, we just played out back. Nesta watched over us," Little James said.

"Good, boys. You make your Mamma proud," Josephine said, smiling down at her sons. "Where is Aggie and Pauline?"

"They are having a tea party in the front room with Nesta. We are not allowed to join them. It is just for girls. We don't mind, though. We would rather be here with you," William replied.

Diana laughed. She rustled Williams hair as she passed him. He held the door for them. "What a little gentleman you are, Will," Diana said.

"Thank you, Aunt Diana," William said.

Inside, Josephine took their capes. She hung them on pegs near the front door. They removed their bonnets and hung them up as well. Gordy went to the kitchen door and stood watching them. Josephine bent down and smiled at him. She made the sign for hello that she saw illustrated in the book they brought home. She said as she signed. "Hello." Gordy smiled. She stood up and turned to Diana. "This is going to be a challenge."

Diana laughed. "What makes you think that?' she asked jokingly.

They went through the kitchen door. Both ladies were bustling about. "We almost have dinner ready, Ma'am," Delila said.

"No hurry, girls. The men haven't came in from the mill yet. Will it simmer awhile?" Josephine asked.

"Yes, Ma'am. It will simmer. The longer, the better," Delila said.

Martha came through the kitchen door. "Why did you let me sleep so long? I will not sleep a wink tonight," she said.

"I am sorry, Martha. Di and I went to the library to research deafness. We did not realize how long we were gone," Josephine said.

"Did you find anything?" Martha asked as she sat down at the table.

"Oh, yes, we did. We found a wonderful book on sign language. If we can find a way to teach it to him, we will be able to communicate with him," Josephine answered.

Delila turned from the wash station and asked. "What is dis communicate?"

Diana sat down beside Martha. "Communicate is how we talk to each other. This book shows sign language. It is a way of moving your hands and fingers to spell out words or say words. If we all learn it, and if we can teach it to Gordy, we can talk to him and he can talk to us in return," she explained.

Rita lifted Gordy into her arms. "We cain't read. How is we gonna git it?" she asked.

Diana responded. "Josephine will teach you. She will read the book and teach you how to do it. Everyone in the house will have to learn how to use sign language. It might be fun."

Rita looked at Gordy. He knew they were talking about him. His eyes went from one to another in the room. He smiled finally, satisfied that he had not done anything wrong. He wiggled until Rita put him down.

Josephine touched Diana's hand. "It probably wouldn't hurt to teach them to read while I was at it. What do you think? You are the teacher in the family," she asked.

"I think it is a wonderful idea, Josie. Who said there could only be one teacher in the family?" Diana replied.

Martha stood up and stretched. "Did someone say there was a tea party going on? I haven't been to a tea party in a very long time. I think I will just drop in on the girls." She winked at William and went through the kitchen door that led to the front room.

Josephine looked up at Rita. "My sister, her husband, and daughter are coming for dinner tomorrow night. Would you mind helping us with your wonderful cooking skills, Rita?" she asked.

Rita smiled widely. "Yes, Ma'am. I is happy to help. Rita likes it here real good. You treat us nice. We like it here mighty fine. We don't mind cookin' at all. We likes to cook," she said proudly.

"Good," Josephine said, smiling at the two Negro ladies. "Because I like having you here very much." She looked over at Diana and said, "Di, would you mind coming up to the attic with me for a minute?"

"Of course," Diana said. They went through the kitchen door that led to the front hall. They climbed the stairs. The upstairs hall was lined with closed doors on both sides. In the center, on the right side, were three doors close together. The center door was a closed in stairway that led to the third floor. It was dusty and narrow. They climbed the stairs to the top.

The attic was a maze of boxes and old furniture shoved close to the slanting ceiling, which was the roof of the house. There was one small window on each end of the large open room. It was drafty and very hot. The smell of stale dust filled the air.

"What do you think? A little insulating and a good scrubbing," Josephine said, looking at Diana.

"It is perfect, but don't you think you should talk to James first?" Diana asked.

"Of course, I will talk to James first. I would never do it without his permission. I am not Regina, and he is not Delbert. But I am sure he will go along with it. Especially when he comes in tonight and smells what those girls have done with our salt pork. I am a good cook, Di, but I can't cook like that," Josephine said, smiling.

"I know what you mean. My mouth has been watering ever since I stuck my head in the door," Diana replied. "Do you want me to help you clean up here?" she asked Josephine.

"Oh, no. I just wanted your opinion. I wouldn't touch a thing until I have James's permission," Josephine said.

"Well, I'll say this: once you get settled into a routine with them here, you won't be able to imagine how you lived without them. I don't know how I survived without Tilly. I miss my children, Josie. I am having a really good time. I am glad I came, I really am. It is good to see you and your family again. I have missed you all so very much, but I miss my children, too. I am ready to go home. Do you understand?" Diana asked.

Josephine hugged her sister. "I understand perfectly. You don't have to explain." She began to descend the stairs. Diana followed her. Josephine closed the door behind her. They walked down the hall to the stairs that led to the first floor. The men would be coming in soon for dinner.

Dinner was a buzz of excitement. It appeared as though the smell of dinner inspired James, Brandon, and Thomas. They were in such a lighthearted mood. Diana was right about the effect Rita and Delila's cooking skills would have upon them. They all ate until they could hold no more. Josephine had instructed Rita and Delila to dish a plate out for themselves. Rita objected that it was not proper, but in the end, she conceded. They ate at a small table in the corner.

When dinner was completed, Rita and Delila insisted that they be left alone in the kitchen to clean up. The ladies joined the men in the front room while they smoked their pipes. The children played around them. Josephine brought Nesta and Gordy into the front room with them. Soon, Delila came, carrying a tray of tea, into the room. James retrieved a bottle of brandy from the mantle, offering it as an additive for their evening tea. Brandon, Thomas, and Martha accepted the offer.

"I will need it to help me sleep tonight, after that nap," Martha said.

The conversation went to the dinner and the four Negroes. "What should we do with them?" James asked.

Josephine cleared her throat. "Regina said that perhaps Delbert could use one of them to look after his mother full time. She would have to live at the Gordon house. She said she would let us know tomorrow night when they come for dinner," Josephine said. She glanced over at Diana. Martha kept her head bowed, staring into her teacup.

"What about the children?" James asked.

"They belong to Rita. That is a sad story. I will tell you about it later when we are alone," Josephine said. "I do not want to discuss it in front of the children."

Brandon said, "I can just imagine. You can't imagine what I saw and heard during my internship in the military. Those poor people suffered dearly at the hands of their masters. At least some of them did. Some were treated well, but I found that to be only a handful."

"I suppose I did not miss much by staying here in Philly," James said.

"You did the right thing, James," Brandon began. "Besides, you were needed here at the mill. You did more for the cause by keeping the mill active. We needed you right where you were."

Thomas was nodding. He remained silent. Diana looked around the room. This was not an easy conversation for any of them.

Josephine glanced over at Diana. She cleared her throat and said. "I went to visit with Regina today with Martha and Diana. It was the first time I have been out of the house, without the children, in I don't know how long."

James looked over at her. "You left the children with Rita and Delila? I am surprised that you felt that comfortable with them."

Josephine blushed. "James, they are wonderful. They would never harm our children. They are amazing. I trust them completely," she said in her own defense.

James watched Josephine for a moment. "Well, I suppose you have spent more time with them than I have. You also have that woman's intuition thing going for you. Don't get upset, Josie. I know you would not leave the children with just anybody. You are a very good mother. If you feel they are trustworthy, then who am I to challenge your opinion?" he replied.

Josephine squirmed in her seat momentarily. James noticed her uneasiness. "What is it, Josie?" he asked.

Josephine was still blushing. "It's just that they have no place to go, James. They are both wonderful cooks. They are clean and they are wonderful with the children. I was just thinking that perhaps they could stay here," she said softly.

James raised his eyebrows. He asked, "Here? In the barn? It is unbearably hot in the summer and freezing in the winter. I don't think that is such a good idea, Josie."

Josephine squirmed again in her chair. "You are right, James. I was thinking about possibly putting them up in the attic. Perhaps we should discuss this at another time." She lowered her head to watch her shoes.

The room grew quiet. James coughed and said, "The attic wouldn't be so bad. Are you asking me if they can stay here full time? I am not so sure we could afford two women. One, possibly, but not two."

"I was thinking about Rita and the children. They have nowhere to go. Delila can find work somewhere else. It would be nearly impossible to find work for a woman with two children. Unless, you have an idea," Josephine said softly.

James flushed. "Perhaps we should discuss this when we are alone. We have guests to entertain. Let's change the subject for now."

The woman sat quietly. Even the children had begun to speak softly. They seemed to sense that something important was being discussed amongst the adults. Thomas went to the mantel and poured more brandy into his cup. Just then, the door that led to the kitchen opened, and Delila entered the room to take the tray and cups back to the kitchen to be washed.

James smiled. "That beats all. It appears as though those two ladies in the kitchen have just ascended from heaven. I see what you mean, Josie. Perhaps, I owe you an apology. We will discuss this later tonight."

The conversation then changed to the mill and the railroad. The ladies gathered the children and went into the kitchen to wash them off before bed. Rita was lighting the candles in the kitchen. Delila had found the fuel for the lanterns and was filling them. No one seemed to want to talk much. Finally, Martha excused herself and went up to bed.

Diana smiled. She leaned close to Josephine and whispered, "I think James will concede to allowing Rita and the children to stay." She nodded and continued to smile. Josephine smiled too. She remained silent.

They placed the candles in the window. Josephine went to the cellar door. "What should we have for dinner tomorrow night?" She asked herself out loud. Diana stood at the door as Josephine went down the stairs carrying a candle. Soon, she came back up the stairs. "I have a nice ham down there. It looks cured enough. It is the only thing I have big enough for all of us. What do you think?" she asked Diana.

Diana smiled as she replied. "I think a ham will do nicely. Do we need to go to the market? I would like to help in any way I can."

Josephine shook her head as she said, "I have plenty of potatoes and we have canned goods down there in the cellar. I think it will do nicely. I will leave the selection of vegetables up to our two miracle cooks," she laughed.

Rita and Delila were washing their faces and arms at the washing station. They appeared not to have heard the conversation, although Diana knew they certainly had.

Josephine called out to them. "Rita, Delila. I have a ham in the cellar. There are potatoes and cold packed vegetables down there as well. I am going to allow you ladies to decide the menu. Do you have a problem with that?"

They turned to look at the sisters. They shook their heads. Then they looked at one another. Josephine laughed. She took Diana by the hand and led her through the kitchen door. "Come now, Di. Let us go up to bed and allow those men to carry on in the front room. I am tired," she said.

Diana followed Josephine up the stairs. When they reached to top of the stairs, Josephine asked, "Would you come into my room and read from the Bible with me?"

Diana smiled. "Of course," she replied.

In Josephine's room, they sat on the bed. Josephine read from the Bible just like her mother had done when they were young and lived at home. Diana's thoughts went back to the cabin. She could see them all gathered near the fireplace. Her father sitting on his three-legged stool, smoking his stone pipe. She could almost smell the fresh tobacco. She closed her eyes. She could hear Josephine's voice, but the words were lost to Diana's memories. Their faces were all clear as if they were real. She had a smile on her lips.

Finally, it was Josephine touching her on the arm that brought her back. "I read to my children nearly every night. Tonight was the exception," Josephine said.

"Oh, Josie! I am so sorry. I did not mean to keep you from them," Diana said.

Josephine laughed. "It is all right, Diana. They miss a night every now and then. Tomorrow night, we will read to them together. You were remembering the nights around the fireplace at the cabin, weren't you?" she asked.

Diana nodded her head. "Yes, I was. It was all so real," she replied.

Josephine put the Bible on the nightstand. "Sometimes, they come to me. I mean, not really. I suppose it is just the memory of them, but at times they seem to know when I am at my lowest, and they are there," she said.

Diana gasped. She put her hand on Josephine's and asked. "You, too? I haven't said a word to anyone except Brandon and Porter Martin. Mamma and Ruthie has come to me before. It was just like you said. When something is troubling me. Porter Martin said they have come to him also. They really are watching over us, Josie. It is so enlightening to know that they come to you as well. They haven't left us at after all."

Josephine smiled. "Mostly when I am sleeping. That is when they come. They give me advice, or say something when I am troubled, to put my mind at ease. Like you said, Di. They have never left us," she said. "It is getting late. We best get to bed. The men are likely to talk all night, but we need our rest for the children. Would you like me to pray with you?"

Diana wiped a tear from her cheek. She nodded. "Yes, please," she said.

They knelt near the bed. They prayed together. Then Diana kissed her sister on the cheek and left the room to go to bed. She undressed and pulled the nightgown over her head. She had just crawled under the covers when Brandon entered the room. He kissed her lightly on the forehead. Soon, he was snoring. Diana smiled and rolled over onto her side. She put her arm over Brandon's chest. It wasn't long until she, too, was sleeping soundly.

The next morning, Diana woke early. Brandon was still sleeping soundly. She dressed and tiptoed out of the room. She descended the stairs as quietly as she could. She could hear the laughter coming from the kitchen. She went through the door to find Josephine, James, and the four children gathered around the table. The table was spread with an abundance of sausage, eggs, biscuits, and fresh buttermilk. The aroma of coffee filled the air. Delila was at the stove working on a fresh pan of scrambled eggs, while Rita was buttering the tops of a tray of biscuits.

"What a wonderful vision first thing in the morning," Diana said.

James stood up. He pulled a chair out for her; he waited for her to be seated before he sat back down at the table. "Good morning, Diana," he said. He looked over at his children.

"Good morning, Aunt Diana!" they all chimed together.

Diana smiled. She nodded at them and said, "Good morning to all of you as well."

"Your sister and I were just telling Rita that we feel she and the children should move into the attic. We have decided that they can stay here. Delila is welcome to stay, too. How could we pass up such an opportunity as this?" he said, spreading his hands over the center of the table.

"I know what you mean," Diana replied. "As I told Josephine yesterday, soon you will not know how you did it without them. I know I would be lost without Tilly."

"Tilly?" Rita asked. "Tilly and Annie are wit you?"

Diana looked up at Rita. "You knew Tilly?"

"Yes, Ma'am," Rita said. Delila came to stand at her side.

"Tilly an Annie were on the plantation wit us. Annie had some younguns. Tilly just had Hoppy. Annie was one of them breeders the Masser had," Delila said.

Diana covered her mouth. "Annie died. She left her children with Tilly. They live in our cabin in Berlin. Tilly is one of my dearest friends," Diana responded.

"Annie died? She was my sisser," Delila said.

"What a small world!" James said.

"She is my sisser an you is Miss Josephine's sisser. I be derned," Delila said.

"Well, you may rest assured that your sister's children are in good hands, and they are loved very much," Diana said to Delila.

Delila nodded. "Mm hm. I is."

Josephine placed her hand over Delila's. "I will introduce you to Mr. Porter Martin the next time he comes to Philadelphia. He is looking out for Tilly and the children. He is a good man." She smiled as she spoke.

"Yes, Mm," Delila said.

"You may also be pleased to know that Hoppy, Gilda, Homer, and Percy are all students in my school. They have learned to read and write. They are doing quite well," Diana added.

Delila covered her mouth with her hand. She looked over at Rita. "They is readin and writin? That is ginst the law," she said.

"No, no. Not anymore. You are free now, remember?" Josephine said. "You are allowed to attend school. As a matter of fact, I recommend it for Nesta. Hopefully, we will have Gordy communicating soon, and he will learn to read and write as well."

Delia shook her head. "Lordie, Lordie. I declare. Readin n writin. My, my," she said, amazed.

Diana laughed. "Your whole world changed with the war. You are bound to no man. You never will be again. Things are not all worked out yet, but it will get there. Someday, you will find Negroes owning their own businesses and farms. They will be teachers and lawyers. It will come slowly, but it will come," she said.

"My. My. Cain't hardly think of it right now. Just thinkin' bout schoolin' is mo then I kin magine. I is proud of Annie's chillren. I know she be proud, too," Delila said.

"Mm hm," Rita added.

Delila turned her attention back to the stove. Rita put the biscuits in a bowl. Just then, Brandon entered the kitchen. He sat down next to Diana. "What is going on in here? It smells devine," he said.

"Oh, Brandon!" Diana began, "Delila was Annie's sister. They were on the plantation together. She is Gilda, Homer, and Percy's, aunt."

"How did they get separated?" Brandon asked.

Delila looked over her shoulder. "Tilly n Annie left way afore wes did. Wes was in da house wit the Missus. She kept us til she couldn't no mor," she responded.

"They's no food fo us all to eat. Missus had ta let us go," Rita said. She piled scrambled eggs onto Brandon's plate.

"Thank you, Rita," he said.

"You is very welcome, Misser Shively, Sir," Rita said.

Diana began to repeat the previous conversation to Brandon. He listened as he ate his breakfast. After he had finished, he drank his coffee. Soon, he was ready to go to the mill with James. Thomas was already out there. He was an early riser.

"Today, we are going to the attic and make a place for you to sleep," Josephine said. "The barn is no proper place for you. James said it was all right," Josephine said.

They were just finishing their coffee when Martha entered the kitchen. "I am sorry I slept so late. I fell right to sleep, thanks to the brandy, but I did not sleep long. I tossed and turned all night. Now, I am ready to sleep. I suppose I will sleep good tonight. What are we doing today?" she asked.

"We are clearing the attic to make room for our friends," Josephine said with a smile.

"They are staying? Oh, good! I knew James would not turn them away. Especially after that dinner last night," Martha said with a smile.

"There is more," Diana began. "Delila was Annie's sister, Martha. She is Gilda, Homer, and Percy's aunt. Can you believe that?"

"What? Sisters you say?" Martha looked around the room at the faces staring back at her.

"Yes, it is true," Diana said.

"What a coincidence that we should happen upon them in our travels. I wonder if the good Lord above had a hand in it," Martha said as she took a drink of her buttermilk.

"No doubt he did," Josephine responded.

"Wait until we tell Porter Martin. He is going to be amazed," Martha said.

Rita served Martha with breakfast. They all chatted until everyone had finished. Rita and Delila had begun cleaning up after them. Josephine shooed the children into the front room. The sun was shining brightly outside. "As soon as the grass is dry, you may go out to play in the backyard. We will be in the attic if you need us," Josephine explained to the children.

The three sisters made their way to the third floor. Diana carried a broom, Martha a bucket of water, and Josephine carried a rag mop with a handful of rags. They laughed and teased each other until finally they had the attic cleaned. The smell of dust still lingered in the air. Both windows were opened to air out the room. The furniture and items that were not being used were stacked into one corner. They stood in the room surveying their deed.

"It looks pretty good to me," Martha said.

"It looks good to me, too. All that is missing are some beds," Diana said.

"I am afraid they will have to sleep on the floor until we come up with something better. I don't think they will mind, though, considering where they have been sleeping lately. After it is aired out a day or two, it won't smell of dust. It has to smell better than the barn," Josephine said.

They went back down the stairs. The sound of laughter came through the opened windows. Josephine went to peer out at the playing children in the backyard. There were two swings that James had fashioned hanging from a large maple tree in the backyard. She smiled as she watched them playing.

Delila had poured them each a cup of tea. They sat at the table drinking their tea, and taking a break. Josephine went to the cellar and returned with Rita following her. The preparation of the evening meal was about to commence.

"Let's take a walk around the yard. These ladies don't need our help. We are no doubt in their way anyhow," Josephine said.

They went out the back door. The children ran to them. Josephine pulled the book she had gotten from the library out of her pocket. She looked through it. She made a gesture with her hands. "Hello," she said out loud. "Now, you all try it."

The children watched her again. They made the gesture back and repeated after her. "Hello."

Josephine took Gordy's hands. She gestured again. He smiled and copied her movements. "Hello," she said. She said it again, very slowly and distinctly. "Hello." She made the gesture as she spoke. Gordy smiled. He made an attempt to form the sign with his hands. Josephine said it again, while gesturing. Gordy gestured with a smile. Everyone cheered. Gordy looked around at them. He was pleased with himself. He gestured again. They cheered him on.

"This isn't going to be as hard as I thought. Thank the Lord above he can hear," Josephine said. She looked up several more gestures in the book. She made the signs and repeated the words over and over as she did. All of the children responded to the lessons. Even Diana and Martha joined in. The time went by quickly.

"It is time to go wash up for dinner. Your Aunt Regina and Uncle Delbert will be arriving soon with your cousin, Margaret Agnus. Perhaps you can teach her what you have learned today," Josephine said to the children.

"Gordy smiled and signed, 'Thank you.'"

Josephine smiled. She was quite proud of herself. Diana was proud of her as well. She had always admired and looked up to her older sister. She had come to miss her very much. She knew she would continue to miss her once she returned home. However, she was still anxious to get back to her home and her family. Her heart ached to hold little Robert in her arms again. She smiled as they shooed the children into the back door.

The men had returned from the mill early. They were washed and dressed for the expected guests. "It isn't often we receive company. I am not sure how the children will behave with all of the excitement," James said as they went into the front room to await the arrival of Regina and Delbert.

It wasn't long before they heard the carriage pull up out front. The doors were open to allow a breeze to flow through the house. The screen doors kept the flying insects outside. Diana thought of asking Brandon to put screens on their doors when they returned home.

Regina entered first. Delbert followed, carrying Margaret in his arms. "What a wonderful aroma you have coming from your kitchen. We could smell it even before we pulled up to a stop out front," Regina said. Before Josephine could respond, Regina went on. "I suppose those two women you were telling me about are the ones responsible for the aroma. It smells absolutely divine, Josie. I did have that talk with Delbert about employing one of them to take care of his mother. He will want to meet her, of course, but he was favorable to the idea. As I said before, white help is so very expensive these days, and you did vouch for these women." She turned to Delbert, "Oh, Delbert, do put Margaret down. She wants to play with the children." She turned back to

Josephine and said, "She seldom gets out to play with other children. I try to take her to the park every day, but we don't always make it. This is such a treat for her. She hasn't seen your children in months and months. Thank you for inviting us."

Before she could suck in enough air to get started again, James spoke up. "Please, come in and sit awhile, Delbert. Would you like a smoke?" he asked.

Regina turned to face James. "Oh, Delbert doesn't smoke, James. He has never acquired the taste for tobacco. Although he did try it once. He just never liked it much. It is a good thing I suppose. It smells up the house so," she said.

Josephine spoke up. "I always enjoyed the smell of Pappa's pipe. I find myself missing it sometimes," she said, smiling as she glanced over at Diana.

Diana smiled. She nodded her head, but said nothing. Regina took advantage of the pause. She said, "I remember the smell of Pappa's pipe as well. It didn't seem to bother me much at the time, but I find now that I have grown, my tastes have changed. However, please don't allow me to stop you gentlemen from smoking. I know how you enjoy it, and I don't really mind all that much. These warmer days, the windows are open anyway."

James pulled out a chair for Regina. When she had seated herself, he motioned for Delbert to sit as well. Regina ran her hands over the blond pelt that hung over the back of the rocking chair she was seated in. "Is this the mountain lion fur that James gave you back on the farm, Josie?" she asked.

Josephine nodded her head. She had no time to answer, for Regina had already began talking again. "I remember that day well. I thought Pappa was going to kill you. I think we were all frightened. No one had ever stood up to Pappa like that before. I suppose you did the right thing. You got your way anyhow. You were braver than I would have been, I can tell you that. Look at you now. I suppose Mamma and Pappa would be pleased with the way it turned out. Yes, I am sure of it."

The door to the kitchen swung opened. Rita stepped into the room wiping her hands on her apron. "Excuse me, Ma'am. We has supper ready," she said.

"Oh, good!" Regina said. "I don't know how much longer I could tolerate that mouth-watering aroma. I can hardly wait to try it!" She stood up, along with everyone else in the room.

"Thank you, Rita," Josephine said. She turned to Diana and said, "I will get the children; you get everyone seated in the kitchen and we will be right with you."

Diana nodded. Martha was standing at the kitchen door. James opened the door and one by one, they filed into the kitchen. Diana felt herself smiling, for Regina began talking again and continued until they were all standing around the table. Josephine came through the door carrying Pauline in one arm, and Margaret in the other.

"Oh, Delbert. Do take Maggy. I am so sorry, Josie. Was she any problem?" Regina asked.

"Not at...," Josephine began.

Regina interrupted. "Here now, Maggy. You go to Daddy. Are you hungry? Aunt Josephine has a very nice meal prepared for us. You be a good girl now," she said pushing a stray strand of hair from little Margaret's face. Delbert took her in his arms. He held her on his lap as they sat at the table.

Finally, Regina fell into silence as James said a prayer. Then the food began to be passed around the table. They ate in silence for only a brief moment when Regina began talking once more. "This is heavenly, Josie. Isn't it heavenly, Delbert? I think your mother would like a meal like this, don't you think? Which one of these ladies would you recommend to take care of Mother Gordon, Josie?"

Josephine put her fork down. She swallowed the food in her mouth and smiled as she responded. "Delila. Rita has two children. Delila has no children. You would want her to move in with Mrs. Gordon, wouldn't you?" Immediately, she regretted asking the question. Regina jumped at the chance to respond.

"Of course! Mother Gordon needs full time care. I hope this Delila is clean. I can tell that she is a good cook, but she really must be clean. That is one thing we really must insist upon. Mother can't speak for herself, of course, but Delbert, nor I, either, will tolerate an unclean person living in the house." Regina took a moment to take a bite of food. Diana spoke before Regina could start again.

"Delila and Rita both are very clean. They keep a clean house as well. Perhaps you are not aware of it, but Delila was Annie's sister. Remember the woman who was traveling with Tilly, who died. She was the mother of Gilda, Homer, and Percy. Isn't it a small world we live in?" Diana said.

"How can that be?" Delbert asked. Everyone stopped eating and stared at the man. No one spoke. They were surprised to hear him speak.

Diana smiled. She looked over at Brandon and then Josephine. She turned back to Delbert and replied. "They all came from the same plantation. They left at different times. The sad part of it is when I told Delila that Annie had died, she seemed sad for only a moment. It was as though they were not permitted to show emotions. I can hardly bear to think of what their lives must have been like."

Regina started once more. "I have heard awful stories. It must have been simply awful indeed. But now that all of that is over, I am sure they will all be fine."

Brandon cleared his throat and said, "I am not so sure. It will take some time to sort all of this mess out. They have been brought here from who knows where. They were treated like animals, sold and resold over and over again. They don't know where their families are. Most of them have nowhere to go. It is a mess. I fear it will take some time to straighten it all out. They may be free, but they are still bound by their lack of education and misfortune." He lowered his head and began eating again.

"Well, Brandon, what is to be done with them? Surely, we can't employ all of them. And heaven knows we can't house them all. We would all be belly up broke, ourselves, in no time. It isn't our problem. We freed them at great cost to many. We can't be expected to do any more," Regina said.

Delbert reached over and squeezed her hand. Again, he spoke. "Gina, Honey, perhaps we should just change the subject. I will come for Delila tomorrow morning. For now, we should talk about something else."

Regina stared at her husband for a moment. She swallowed hard. "Well! I see. I suppose the politics of it all are way over my head." She took a bite, and fell silent.

"I am sorry," Delbert said. "This meal is very good, Josephine. I would like to take this moment to thank you for inviting us."

Josephine nodded. James spoke up. "It is good, indeed. We are blessed that you could make it tonight. Our guests will be leaving tomorrow morning, and this house is really going to be quiet."

Josephine looked over at Diana. Martha snickered. She lowered her head. "Quiet indeed," she said with a chuckle.

Regina looked from sister to sister. She did not get the joke at all. They all finished their meal. The conversation went to Porter Martin and the two sawmills. Then the men excused themselves. They went onto the front porch to smoke their pipes. The women went to the back porch to watch the children play in the backyard.

Josephine spoke while watching the children playing a game of Red Rover. "Di, Martha, I am going to miss you both so very much. I promise to write every month to keep you up on things. Please promise you will do the same."

Diana took Josephine's hand. "I promise, Josie. It is much easier now that the stage delivers the mail to the railroad. The train is always on time and much faster, too. If, for some reason, the stage doesn't come, Porter Martin just takes the mail to the train station. He is always traveling somewhere to get something anyway. Lord knows, I don't know what we would do without him," Diana said.

Martha spoke up, "I will be back every couple of months too, Josie. I will make some dresses for you and the girls. I will be making some school clothes for your children, too. They will all be in school this fall, except for Pauline. What are you going to do with yourself?"

Josephine shook her head as she replied. "I honestly do not know." She never took her eyes from the playing children.

Regina spoke up, "Well, I don't know what I'll do when Maggy starts school. She pretty much occupies my entire day, everyday. I do enjoy our time at the park, though. I will certainly miss that. Of course, I have another two years before I need to worry about that. You will make her school dresses also, won't you Martha? Of course, you will. How silly of me to even ask. I know the ladies in town will be just green with envy. You should see the looks on their faces when we dress up for the park. They look us up and down. Some even approach us, asking who our dressmaker is. I just smile politely and say we have our own personal dressmaker and tailor. You can just see the green coming over them. It is difficult not to smile at times."

Martha interrupted. "I am really going to miss you, Regina. Do you remember all those times we sang songs while we rode that two-wheeled cart to and fro from Berlin? I think of it so often. There was one song you sang more than others. I can't remember the words, though. I have tried and tried, but it fails me," Martha said, smiling over at Josephine.

Josephine frowned and shook her head at Martha, who sat with her hands folded in her lap and a smile planted on her face.

"Oh, I remember it very well," Regina said. She took a deep breath and began to sing. "Do, Lord, oh, do, Lord, oh ,do remember me."

Her voice cracked and squealed. Diana grit her teeth as Regina continued. Even the children stopped playing, staring at the women as Regina continued. "Do, Lord, oh, do, Lord, oh, do remember me."

Josephine reached over, and taking Regina's hand, she said, "Oh, yes, we remember now. Thank you, Regina, for that. Now tell me, will Delila be living with Mrs. Gordon, or will she be reporting there on a daily basis?"

Regina took a breath and replied. "Oh, Josie, she will be living at the house. She will have a room right next to Mother Gordon's. If you think she is to be trusted, that is. We are taking her on your word that she is trustworthy. She certainly seems capable enough. That meal was wonderful. Delbert certainly seemed pleased. I am anxious to get her started, to be quite frank. Mother Gordon's current housekeeper reports every morning, leaving her alone at nights. As I said before, she is very expensive. She will be excused from her duties first thing in the morning. I don't think it will hurt her feelings any, to be quite honest with you. She is a pleasant enough woman, but she gets huffy if she is asked to do anything around the house. She is constantly reminding us that she is paid to watch over Mother Gordon, not be her housekeeper. Delila is perfect for what we need."

Martha was smiling again. She watched her shoes while smiling. Diana reached over and pinched her arm. "Ouch!" Martha squealed as she rubbed her arm.

Regina leaned forward to look over at them. "What are you two doing over there?" she asked.

Diana smiled as she replied. "I didn't do anything. I think something must have bitten Martha on the arm. Perhaps we should move around a little bit." She stood up. "I am going to play a game of Red Rover with the children. Anyone wants to join me?" she called out as she jumped from the porch. She ran toward the children.

"I'll play," Josephine called out as she ran toward them. Martha rose and nodded her head at Regina. She jumped from the porch and ran toward the rest of them.

"I suppose I am playing, too. I don't want to be the only bystander, by no means. It has been quite some time since I have played a child's game. I am accustomed to sitting on a park bench and watching Maggy play with the other children. I certainly hope I can run with this dress on," Regina said.

"Oh, hush up and play!" Martha called to her. "The exercise will do us all good."

They played and laughed like children. Diana felt as if the clock had been turned back. She pictured them all as they had been when they were young. She could see her mother sitting on the porch watching them play. Her father sat on the porch steps, smoking his stone pipe. She could not stop smiling.

Soon, Delbert was standing on the porch watching them. "Regina, what on earth are you doing?" he called out.

Regina laughed. "I'm playing Red Rover, Delbert. Have you never played in the yard before? You really should try it sometime. It feels good. Come play with us!" she called back.

"No, thank you. Have you not noticed the sunset? It is time for little Margaret to get ready for bed. I am sorry to spoil your fun, but we really must be going," Delbert called.

Regina was out of breath. "All right," she said. She bent over, placing her hands on her knees. She was trying to catch her breath. They all gathered at the back porch. Regina hugged her sisters. Diana lifted Margaret into her arms and held her tight.

"Good bye, Margaret. Your Aunt Diana will miss you very much," Diana said.

Martha hugged the child as well. "I will be back soon, Maggy," Martha said.

They went back through the house to the front door. James had gone for their buggy. He had it waiting for them. They hugged each other one more time before Delbert lifted Regina and Margaret up into the buggy. Soon, they were waving as they made their way down the cobblestone street toward home.

Martha turned toward the others standing on the porch. "Lord Almighty! That Regina can talk. Poor Delbert hardly said a word all night," she laughed.

"Neither did anyone else," Josephine added. They all laughed. Diana and Martha helped Josephine wash the children for bed. They all went upstairs. They gathered in their beds, while the women sat on the bedside, listening to Josephine read from the Bible. Soon, the children were sleeping. They tiptoed from the room and said their good nights. They were tired as well.

The next morning was a blur to Diana. Delbert arrived to collect Delila, just as he had promised. They said their good-byes to her before they sat down to breakfast. The time went by so quickly that Diana, Martha, and Brandon were in their buggy and traveling down the cobblestone street before she knew it. She sighed. "I will miss them," she said to Martha. "I envy your coming back to see them soon, but I miss my children so much, I can't wait to get home."

"I understand," Martha said. They rode in silence for a while.

Diana was just about to doze off when Martha spoke. Diana jumped at the sound of Martha's voice. "I can't, for the life of me, figure out where Regina came from. It appears as though she had been dropped off onto our doorstep when she was a baby. No one in our family talked that much. Mamma was so quiet, and Pappa spoke mostly with his eyes. One glance from Pappa and you knew if he was pleased or displeased. Regina just goes on and on as if she can't stop," Martha said laughing.

"Well, no one in our family was ever lazy, either, yet look at Sofia," Diana replied. She turned her head to look at the city growing further and further behind them. "I wonder how she is doing. I hope she hasn't had her baby yet. I want to be there for her. I know she is frightened," Diana said.

They traveled through the winding road until they reached Harrisburg. Brandon took the horses to the stable for a cooling down and to be fed. He met them in the little café where the oriental woman waited on them. They each had a bowl of soup and some sugary rolls. They drank hot tea from very small cups. Then they were on the road again.

The afternoon sun beat down on them. Diana and Martha both fanned themselves with decorated fans that Porter Martin had bought for them years ago. Diana thought of Porter as they rocked back and forth in the buggy. She missed him as well. It was late afternoon when they reached the inn in Quincy. Mrs. Anderson made them a cup of tea. She brought out a bowl of cool water and a cloth for each of them to wash the dust off themselves, and cool down. They took their sugar bread with them, as they wanted to get home before dark. Once again, they were on the road. The trip from Quincy to Berlin was the shortest stretch of road, but the roughest. They rocked to and fro as the buggy bounced across the rutted terrain. The sun was low in the sky when they pulled up at the general store in Berlin. Diana was anxious to see her children.

Brandon helped Martha down from the buggy. Carver was making his way down the street towards them. Concetta had appeared on the porch of the general store, carrying her sleeping baby. Diana spoke softly as not to wake the child, "How is Sofia doing, Connie?"

Concetta nodded her head. She whispered. "She is fine."

Diana smiled. "You tell her I will see her sometime tomorrow. I want to get home to my family," she whispered back. Brandon climbed up into the buggy. They were headed for Porter Martin's house. It would be dark soon. They would be home just in time for supper.

Brandon stopped at the back door. He helped Diana down from the wagon. Porter came out onto the back porch. "Well, will ya look at what the cat dragged in," Porter said, laughing. Soon, the children were all standing around him, still chewing on their supper.

Diana rushed to them. She received hugs from each of them. They were all talking at once. "Were you good for Mr. Martin and Tilly?" she asked. "Yes, Ma'am, we were very good!" they replied.

Diana noticed red welts on Percy's arms and legs. "What happened to you?" she asked him.

"Nothing, Mrs. Shively. I am fine," Percy said. His voice cracked as though he was about to cry. He swallowed hard and lowered his gaze.

"We had a kind of incident, I suppose you would call it," Porter Martin said. "I took care of it, I hope. I will tell ya about it later."

Diana looked from Porter to Percy and back to Porter again. "I am going to help that boy unhitch the buggy. I don't want his dinner to get cold," Porter said, going down the porch steps and across the backyard toward the stables.

Diana hugged the children again. "Let us all go see Miss Tilly. I have news from Philadelphia that she will be pleased to hear," she said, smiling. She noticed that Raymond's face was flushed. "Are you all right, Raymond?" she asked, placing her hand on his forehead.

"Yes, Ma'am, I am fine," he answered. He followed her into the kitchen. Tilly was standing just inside the door. She had a big smile on her face. Diana threw her arms around her, hugging her. "Oh, Tilly! I am so very happy to see you. I missed you and the children so much," Diana said, holding Tilly in her arms.

Tilly smiled. "Yes, Miss Diana. I was missin' you, too. I took care of thins fo ya. I did my best to make sure the younuns was cared fo real good," Tilly said, still smiling.

"I knew you would, Tilly. I never doubted it for a minute. I don't know what I would do without you," Diana said, holding Tilly at arm's length.

Tilly laughed. "Ya keep tellin me that, Miss. Ya keep tellin me that," she said.

Diana hugged her again. "I love you like a sister, Tilly," she said over Tilly's shoulder.

Tilly pulled back. "Me? Yo's sister? Why, Miss Diana, I's ain't got the words," Tilly said. Her eyes were tearing up. Diana hugged her once more, then released her hold on her.

"How did the children behave?" Diana asked Tilly.

"They was fine, Ma'am. Little Robert is awake. He is in the tub over there," Tilly said nodding toward the tub. Diana rushed to him. She lifted the baby boy into her arms. He had food all over his face. He had been feeding himself. Diana laughed. She kissed his face and went to the pump. She pumped the handle, putting her hand under the spout to catch a handful of cold water. She wiped it across Robert's face. He shook his head, trying to avoid the water.

Diana laughed at him. The children had gathered around, watching. They were laughing as well. Hoppy was holding Franklin on her hip. He squirmed until she put him down. He hurried toward Diana with his arms in the air.

"Here, Hoppy. You take Robert for a moment," Diana said. Hoppy took the baby from her arms. Diana reached down and lifted Franklin into her arms. He was drooling. She wiped at his chin. He held his mouth open for a kiss. Diana kissed him and hugged him. Just then, the door opened and Porter and Brandon entered the kitchen. Upon seeing Brandon, Franklin began to wiggle and bounce in Diana's arms. He held his arms out to Brandon. "Da. Da Da!" he called out to Brandon. Brandon went to Diana, taking Franklin in his arms.

Diana took Robert from Hoppy. "Oh, Tilly! Supper smells very good. We are very hungry," Diana said.

"I will set two more places at the table," Hoppy said. She went to the cupboard and began lifting dishes down, carrying them to the table. Tilly got the silver from the drawer. Soon, everyone was seated at the table. The children each told Diana and Brandon how much they were missed. They conveyed all the events of the past four days.

Shirly said, "Yes, and Mr. Martin had to talk to Raymond. He was the only one who was bad."

Porter shook his head at the little girl, and she went silent. Raymond was staring at his plate. He had not touched his food. His face was red. Finally, he got up and ran from the room.

Diana looked over at Porter Martin. She noticed that Tilly kept her eyes averted on her plate as she ate. "What happened?" Diana asked.

"I think we should discuss it after dinner," Porter said. They all grew quiet and went back to eating their meals. After dinner, the children were sent into the front room for story time while Diana and Tilly cleaned up.

"I forgot my news," Diana said to Tilly. Tilly looked up at her from washing the dishes. Diana was drying them, placing them on the table. "We picked up two women and two children on our way to Philadelphia. They were looking for work. We took them to Josephine and James's house. Their names were Rita, Delila, and the children were Nesta and Gordy," Diana smiled as she watched Tilly's expression.

Tilly's mouth fell open. "Delila and Rita ya says?"

Diana nodded. "They were from the same plantation you and Annie came from, weren't they?" she asked.

Tilly nodded. "Yes, Ma'am, they wus. They worked in the big house. They wus the Missus favorites. Delila was Annie's," Tilly fell silent. She stared down into the dishpan.

"Delila was Annie's sister. Nesta and Gordy are her niece and nephew," Diana finished the sentence for Tilly.

Tilly nodded. "Yes, Ma'am." She continued to was the dishes. After a moment, she continued. "Me n Annie hepped in da kitchen sometimes, but Delila and Rita stayed in the big house. They wus special to Missus." She stopped washing the dishes, looking up at Diana. She swallowed hard and asked, "Is ya takin Annie's chilren ta Philly?"

Diana turned to face Tilly. "Oh, no, Tilly. I would never take those children from you. Delila cannot take care of them anyway. She is living with my sister Regina's mother-in-law. She is going to take care of her, living with her. She will not have time or the means to care for three children. Gilda, Homer, and Percy are staying right here with you in Berlin. Rita and her children are staying with my other sister, Josephine. She is going to be her housekeeper. I thought you would like to know that they were safe and cared for," Diana said, watching Tilly.

Tilly nodded again. She smiled at Diana. "Dat's good t know, Miss. Thank ya fo tellin Tilly. I's preciate it. I's wus wonderin bout what happened ta da others what worked on the plantation. I is lucky ta found a good home wit ya all," Tilly said.

Diana hugged Tilly. "Now you can put your mind to rest on the matter. Everything is going to be fine. Are you and the children staying the night with us Tilly?" Diana asked.

Tilly shook her head. "I thinks we best be goin to ours own house tonight, Miss," Tilly replied.

"I understand," Diana said. "It has been awhile since you slept in your own bed and cooked in your own kitchen."

"Yes, Ma'am," Tilly said. She went back to washing the dishes.

After the supper dishes were cleaned up, Porter went to the stables to get the buggy. He was going to take Tilly and the children home. Diana and Brandon washed the children in the kitchen. When they had finished, they took them upstairs to bed. Raymond lay in his bed with his face to the wall. They decided not to disturb him. Diana kissed his cheek softly. He did not stir. They heard Porter on the back porch as they had finished tucking the children in for the night. They quietly made their way downstairs to meet Porter in the kitchen.

Diana poured Porter Martin some brandy. Brandon pulled a chair out for her, waiting for her to be seated before he sat down next to her. He held an empty cup in his hands. The jug of homemade brandy sat in the center of the table.

"How was your trip?" Porter asked them.

"It was fine. We did not have any trouble at all. The weather was pleasant for traveling. I was worried on the trip to Philly. It looked pretty cloudy at one point, but it was very nice," Brandon said.

Diana squirmed in her seat. "Tell him about Rita and Delila, Brandon," she said excitedly.

Brandon smiled. He poured himself some brandy and said. "Oh, yes. We picked up two Negro women and two children just outside of Harrisburg. They had been slaves on the same plantation that Tilly and the children came from. We came to find out that one woman, Delila was her name, was actually the sister of Annie. She was the woman who was traveling with Tilly. Gilda, Homer, and Percy's mother. She is their aunt. Well, Delila is now employed by Delbert Gordon. She is looking after his mother. The other woman, Rita was her name, is staying at Josephine and James's house. She is going to help Josephine out. They made a place in the attic for her and the two children." Brandon took a drink from the cup. He held the brandy in his mouth a second before swallowing it.

"What a small world," Porter said.

"Oh, Mr. Martin, that is just the beginning. The little boy, Gordy they call him, cannot speak. Josie and I went to the library and we found a book on sign language. Josie is going to teach it to everyone in the house so they can communicate with the boy. He looks to be about four years of age, but he is already catching on. We are very grateful that he can hear. If he were deaf, it would be so much harder." Diana paused. She folded her hands in front of her on the table. Then she said, "Josephine is going to teach them all. William and Little James will be going to school this fall, but Nesta would be so far behind that Josie felt she could teach her at home. So now, we have two teachers in the family."

Porter smiled. He said, "Margaret would be so proud of you girls. I hope she can see you from where she is." He poured more brandy into his cup.

"She can, Mr. Martin. She can. I just know it. I feel her with me at times when I am teaching the children. I know she is there," Diana said, smiling over at Porter Martin. "Now what on earth happened to little Percy? He looked like he was whipped or something."

Porter set his cup down on the table. He looked over at Diana. "He was," he said.

"What! Someone whipped Percy?" Diana shrieked.

Porter nodded. "Yes. It was Raymond. They were all playin' in the orchard. I was just makin my way to the stables when I heard Percy screamin'. I ran to find Raymond whippin' the daylights outta him with a leather belt. He kicked him a couple of times, too. Homer got there before I did, but the poor lad was frozen in his tracks. I think he was afraid to interfere."

Brandon spoke up. "I imagine he has seen a good whipping before. Who knows what their lives were like on that plantation in Virginia? I cannot tell you some of the horror stories I have heard. Not in front of Diana, anyway."

Porter nodded. "I've heard a few myself. Anyhow, I had a talk with Raymond. He did not take it well. Prejudice has been instilled in that lad long ago. He ain't likely to get over it over night. This might take awhile. The other children don't seem to have a problem gettin' along. That Raymond has a big chip on his shoulders. He's been a poutin' 'bout the whole thing ever since it happened," Porter said.

Diana looked over at Brandon. "How do we handle this?" she asked him.

"We will have a talk with him tomorrow. Maybe by example. I really don't know, but we cannot tolerate such behavior," Brandon said.

"I agree. Lord Almighty. Poor little Percy," Diana said.

"Well," Porter said standing up. "I'm sure you two are tired after that trip. I am goin up to my room. You get some rest. I told Tilly I would be by to collect her in the mornin'. Good night, you two," he said.

Diana rose from her chair. She went to Porter and gave him a kiss on the cheek. Then she hugged him. He hugged her back, laughing. "It is good to have you back, Miss Diana. We all missed you," he said before going towards the stairs.

Brandon took her hand and pulled her onto his lap. He kissed her tenderly. He placed his hand on her stomach, which was only slightly protruded. "How are we doing after that trip?" he asked her.

Diana smiled at her husband. "We are feeling very well, thank you for asking." She kissed him again. "I am very tired though," she whispered.

Brandon smiled. "Oh, I see. Okay, let's get you up to bed. Tomorrow is another day," he said.

Diana smiled. "Well, I am not all that tired," she said, smiling up at him. He towered over her. "I love you so much, Brandon," she added.

Brandon hugged her. Then he lifted her into his arms. He carried her to the stairs. "Please, Brandon. Please let me walk upstairs on my own. I am so afraid you will drop me," she giggled.

"Drop you? I couldn't. You're still as light as a feather." Brandon laughed as he continued to carry her up the steps. When they reached the top, he put her down. They tiptoed into their room. They undressed hurriedly. Soon, they were lying on the bed in each other's arms, making love. It felt good to be home. Afterwards, Diana lay with Brandon's arm under her neck. She could hear his steady breathing. He was asleep. Sleep did not come to her so easily. What were they going to do about Raymond? It would have to be dealt with, but with love. Raymond seemed to have a problem with Tilly's children right from the beginning. Tears filled her eyes.

It was almost morning when sleep finally came to her. She had slept in. When she finally made her way down the stairs, Tilly was in the kitchen cleaning up. The children were all outside playing. Winston, Raymond, and Homer had gone to the mill to help Porter Martin and Brandon. Little Franklin hurried to her. "Mamma, Mamma, uppie!" he said, holding his hands up to her.

Diana laughed. She lifted Franklin. Little Robert began to cry. He, too, was holding his hands up to her from where he was sitting on the floor. He had begun to crawl everywhere now. Hoppy hurried to him. She lifted him up to rest on her left hip. He was chewing on a wet cloth. He was cutting teeth.

Diana kissed Little Franklin on the forehead. "Aren't you a big boy, Frank? I missed you so much. You are talking so much better now. I am so proud of you." She kissed him again. Then she put him back down. She went to Hoppy, taking Robert from her. "And you, Little Man. You are cutting teeth, aren't you?" she rubbed noses with the baby.

"Mamma. Mamma, uppie," Little Franklin said as he pulled on her skirt. Hoppy lifted him into her arms.

"Should I take him outside to play?" she asked.

"That would be very nice of you, Hoppy. I'll have a bite to eat, and then I will be out myself. Do you mind terribly?" Diana asked.

"No, Ma'am! I like to play with him. He is funny. He makes me laugh. We will be out by the swing," Hoppy said. She carried Franklin on her hip as she went out the back door.

Tilly set a cup of coffee on the table for Diana. "Breakfast will be ready fo ya, Miss Diana. I almost done," Tilly said.

Diana smiled up at her. "Don't hurry none, Tilly. I am feeling very tired this morning. I am not at all hungry anyway, but I know I should eat," Diana said as she sat down at the table. She sat Little Robert on the table, playing with him until Tilly brought her a plate of eggs and toast. She handed Robert over to Tilly.

Diana ate slowly. Her head pounded as she remembered what Porter Martin had told her the night before. She watched Tilly as she moved about the kitchen. How did she feel about what Raymond had done? She hadn't said anything. Was such treatment tolerated, even now? Diana closed her eyes and tried to block it out. She could not.

"Tilly, Mr. Martin told me what Raymond did to Percy. I am so sorry. I am also very ashamed. I want you to know that such treatment will not be excusable in this house. Brandon and I are going to have a talk with Raymond, and it will never happen again. Do you understand what I am saying?" Diana asked.

Tilly had her back to Diana. She said. "Mm hm. Tilly knows. It weren't nothin. Percy is fine, Miss Diana. He is all healed dis mornin'. I put salve on his welts last night fo bed. He is all better now," Tilly said.

"No, Tilly," Diana said. She held her fork in the air. "It is not fine now. It is bad enough to harbor prejudice feelings, but to take out acts of violence on another human being, no matter what color they are, is not permissible. There will be none of that here. We will not allow it," Diana took a bite of her egg.

"Mm hm," Tilly replied. She did not turn around.

Brandon appeared at the back door with Raymond behind him. "Tilly, would you mind stepping outside with the children for a moment. Diana and I would like a private moment with Raymond. I will come for you when we are finished," he asked.

"Mm Hm," Tilly replied. She took her apron off and draped it over a chair. She went out the back door. Brandon waited until she was off the porch and out of hearing distance. He pointed to a chair, signaling Raymond to sit down.

Raymond plopped down in the chair. He hung his head. He was obviously, still, very upset. Brandon pulled out a chair next to him, opposite Diana.

"Raymond," Brandon began. "Do you know why we are having this little talk?"

Raymond remained silent. He nodded his head, but did not look up. Brandon went on. "Porter told us about the incident that happened in the stable yesterday. Why did you whip Percy?" he asked the lad.

Raymond shrugged his shoulders, remaining silent. Brandon looked over at Diana. She was watching Raymond for some sign of remorse. There was none. Brandon turned his attention back to the boy. "I believe I have made it quite clear that we are all equal in this house and we are all to be treated as equals. We do not whip on any of you children when you misbehave, and we will not tolerate you whipping on one another. Is that clear?" Brandon asked.

Raymond gritted his teeth. "They are just niggers," he said softly through clenched teeth.

"No, Raymond. They are human beings just as you and I are. We are all the same. Percy may have darker skin than some of us, but if you were to see inside, under that skin, you would not be able to tell us apart," Brandon said.

Raymond looked up at Brandon. His cheeks turned red. He squinted his eyes and said, "My Pa would not want me living with no niggers. He would never stand for us eating at the same table. They belong in the stable. They should be doing the work, and we should be watching over them, lest something comes up stole." He was breathing hard as he spoke.

Brandon reached over to touch Raymond's arm. Raymond pulled it back and put his hands in his lap under the table. Brandon glanced over at Diana and then back at Raymond. "I am sorry you feel that way, Raymond." Brandon spoke softly. "In this house, things are different. You are no longer living in the south. There are no longer any slaves. They have been freed by the war. Many men died so that they could be free. My brother was one of those men. Things are going to change all over the country because of that war. Negroes will work right alongside of white folks. They will own their own farms and plantations. White folks may even end up working for them. You might as well accept that," Brandon said.

"Well, I ain't acceptin' nothin'!" Raymond said. He stood up and shouted. "I hate it here! I hate school, I hate working in the mill, and I hate livin' with niggers! I am not your son. I am Raymond Hughes, son of Alvin Hughes. I want to find my father. I don't want to live here!" he shouted.

Diana had enough. "Raymond! That will be enough. Sit down right this minute!" she said.

"You ain't my mother! You might have the others fooled, but not me. You ain't nothin' to me. I hate you! I hate all of you!" he shouted. He ran for the back door and slammed it shut behind him.

Diana was white and trembling. Brandon went to her. He held her tight as she began to sob. "There now," he said, trying to sooth her. "He just needs to cool down. It will be all right. He knows he was wrong. He is just too proud to admit it. It will all be forgotten in a day or two." Brandon spoke softly. Diana cried for a few moments. Finally, she wiped her eyes.

"I know you are right. I just have never had any child speak to me that way before. Except, of course, Sofia. Then I whooped her a good one. I can't do that to a seven-year-old. Not one I love as my own," Diana said. She wiped her eyes again and blew her nose into her handkerchief. "I am fine now. I suppose if we just pretend it never happened, he will get over it quicker. We really need to talk to Percy and Homer about what happened."

Brandon nodded. "Would you like for me to talk to them?" he asked. Diana nodded her head. She went to Robert, lifting him up into her arms. Brandon went to her, kissing her cheek. He turned at the door before exiting, "I will have a talk with them later. I need to get back to the mill. Stumpy is helping Sherman carry some items into the store and Marcus is the only one out there with Porter right now. Will you be all right?" he asked.

"I'm fine now. Please, ask Tilly to come back in, on your way to the mill," Diana said.

Brandon went out the door, closing it softly behind him. Diana went to the window. She watched him approach Tilly, then head for the mill. Tilly was making her way towards the back porch. Diana scanned the area for Raymond. She did not see him. She imagined him off somewhere by himself sulking over his outburst. She smiled at Tilly as she entered the back door.

Diana went back to the table. She sat down to finish her breakfast. It was cold now, but the coffee was still warm. Tilly hummed as she began to clear the dishes from the table to wash them. Robert was chewing on a piece of Diana's toast. She smiled down at him. "What are we doing today?" she asked Tilly.

Tilly turned to face her. "I was thinkin' on pickin' some blackberries when I was done here, Miss Diana," Tilly said with a smile.

"Wonderful! Then we can make some jam later. I will run into town and get some sugar. Do we need anything else?" Diana asked.

Tilly smiled. "Ifin ya git some flour, we might have a pie or two after supper tonight," she said. She turned her attention back to washing the dishes.

"I can do that. I will have Homer hitch up the carriage. I will take Robert with me. Maybe even Hoppy and little Franklin. Do you mind?" Diana asked.

"No, Ma'am. Just send Hoppy out ta hep me onest ya git back. She knows where ta go," Tilly said.

"Okay. I will get ready to go now," Diana said. She went to the back door. When she stepped out onto the porch, the morning sun shined into her eyes. She placed her hand over her eyes to shade them as she called out for Hoppy. "Hoppy, would you run up to the mill and ask Homer to bring the carriage down? We are going into Berlin for some supplies."

"Yes, Ma'am!" Hoppy called back. She put Franklin down near the porch steps. She ran in the direction of the mill.

Diana stepped off the porch. She placed Robert down next to Franklin. They began playing together. Soon, Hoppy was back. Diana asked, "Would you keep an eye on them while I get ready? I will be right back."

"Yes, Ma'am," Hoppy replied. She knelt down next to Robert. "We are going into town," she said to the little boys.

Diana went back inside. She went upstairs to her room. She fussed with her hair and placed a bonnet on her head. She would not need a shawl, for it was already nearly eighty degrees outside. She heard the carriage pulling up to the back porch as she was coming down the stairs. She hurried to the back door. "Hoppy, would you like to come along to help with the babies?" she called out.

Hoppy smiled. She nodded as she ran, carrying Franklin on her hip towards the buggy.

Diana stepped back inside the kitchen. She carried Robert in her arms. Tilly began to put a dry diaper on him. Diana placed a bonnet on his head, and out the back door they went. She stood on the porch watching the remaining children. They had all stopped playing and gathered by the carriage. There was only Gilda, Percy, Shirley, and Cecilia left. "Would you all like to ride into town?" she asked them. They all began to shout out in excitement that they wanted to go. "Well, get up in the carriage," she said laughing. "Homer, would you mind driving us all into town?" she called out over the children's voices.

"Yes, Ma'am!" Homer replied with a smile on his face. "I would be happy to. Mr. Martin has been letting me drive the wagon when he takes us home in the evenings."

Diana nodded. They bumped and swayed as the buggy full of children bounced along the rutted trail that led to Berlin. Diana began to sing. "I got a home in glory land that outshines the sun." The children joined in. "Do Lord, oh, do, Lord, oh, do remember me." Diana smiled as they went, remembering a time when her sister Regina squeaked out the verses long ago on this same trail, and recently at Josephine's, she gave them an encore performance.

Soon they were pulling up at the general store. They all piled out of the carriage. "You children wait out here. I will get something special for you from inside," she instructed them. She stepped up onto the porch of the general store. Marcus O'Hara was helping Sherman Hickman carry a large crate to the back of the store. They both looked up at Diana as she entered. "Good morning, Miss Diana, Ma'am," Sherman called to her. "Good morning, Ma'am." Marcus echoed.

"Good morning, gentlemen," Diana said with a smile.

"Grace! Grace, you have a customer!" Sherman called out looking toward the curtained doorway that led to their private quarters.

Grace appeared through the curtain carrying her grandson in her arms. He, too, was teething and chewing on a damp cloth. "Good morning," Grace said with a smile.

Diana could not help but notice that Grace seemed to be back to her old self. She held her head erect, and her nose in the air. "What can I do for you?" Grace asked looking down her nose at Diana.

"I would like a penny's worth of hard candy and a jar of cold lemonade for the children outside," Diana said politely. She walked around the store looking over the new items that rested on the shelves. "Also a sack of flour and a sack of sugar. I think I may need some more cloth for diapers. And, oh, yes, give me a few buttons from that jar on the shelf, please," Diana said, looking around.

Grace went back to the curtain. She called out, "Connie, come get Burt. I have a customer!" She looked back at Diana with a smile.

"Have you seen Sofia this morning?" Diana asked.

"No. Alda Faulk was in earlier. She was on her way over there. She has been checking in on Sofia every morning this past three or four days. Apparently, Sofia has taken to her bed. I am surprised you didn't know that, you bein' her sister n all," Grace said, grinning at Diana.

"I just arrived later yesterday. I was anxious to see my children. I didn't want to interrupt their dinner, so I went straight home," Diana explained. Why she felt she needed to explain herself she did not know. She made a mental note not to let Grace Hickman talk down to her.

"Well, I see you brought nearly the whole brood with you this morning," Grace said with a frown. "Even that Negro bunch."

Diana did not respond to the remark. She continued to inspect the goods on the shelves.

Grace placed the candy on the counter. She poured a quart mason jar full of lemonade. "I suppose you will be needin' something for them to drink from," she said, looking over her glasses at Diana.

"Oh, yes, please. That is, if you do not mind," Diana answered.

"I suppose it wouldn't hurt much. Of course, it is a lot of extra work, washin', all of those tin cups," Grace said.

"Oh, Mrs. Hickman. Of course. Just give me three tin cups, and we will wash them at the pump when we have finished with them. Thank you very much," Diana said, smiling at Grace.

Diana went to the doorway and called out, "Gilda, Percy, would you please help me carry this to the buggy?"

"Yes, Ma'am!" They called back. They ran into the general store. Diana smiled back at Grace Hickman as she said, "They are so well behaved. And such a big help, too." Grace frowned at her as she watched them all from over her glasses.

They carried the purchased goods outside to where the children were waiting. Hoppy was practicing with her sling. She was hitting the fence posts with her stones every time. She was quite good with the sling. Diana reached down at her waist for her own sling. It was not there. When had she stopped wearing it? She could not remember. It had been so long since she had used it.

"Do you mind if I try?" she asked Hoppy. Hoppy held her sling out to Diana. She gave her a handful of rounded stones. Diana placed the stone in the leather pocket and began to swing it. She flicked her wrist and let it fly. She missed. She stood there staring at the post. She could not believe it. She tried again. Another miss. She handed the sling back to Hoppy. "I suppose I need to practice. Let that be a lesson to you, Dear. Keep up with your skills. You never know when you will need it," she smiled at Hoppy. They passed the drinks around. The babies were not allowed to have the hard candy, but they did not miss it. They were playing in the shade of an old oak tree that stood next to the store. It shaded a large watering trough. There was also a well there. "Keep the little ones away from the well," Diana instructed.

When they had finished, they washed their cups just as Diana said they would, and returned them to Grace Hickman. Then they rode over to Sofia and Jonathan Gilbert's house, which stood next to Zachariah's little two-room house.

Diana knocked on the door. Alda Faulk opened the door. "Good morning, Mrs. Shively. I see ya got back from yo trip okay. It is good to see ya," she said as she stepped aside to allow Diana to enter.

"How is Sofia doing?" Diana asked.

Alda pointed toward the bedroom. "Come n see fo yourself. She has taken ta bed as her feet are swelled mighty big. I told her she needs ta keep em up," Alda said.

Diana entered the bedroom. Sofia was propped up on the pillow. "Diana! Oh, I am so glad you came to see me. I was wondering and wondering how the trip went. You really must tell me all about it!" Sofia said excitedly.

Sofia looked like she was about to burst. Her face glowed a bright red that seemed to travel on down her neck to her bosom. She was even heavier than she was the last time Diana had seen her. Her feet and legs were swollen so much that she wore no stockings or shoes. Even her toes were fat. Diana hoped the shock did not show on her face. She smiled at Sofia and asked, "How are you feeling, Sofie?"

"I feel like I am about to burst. I have no pains or anything, but I can't hardly get around at all. If this baby doesn't come soon, I may become permanently attached to this here bed," she joked. Diana was not laughing.

"Is this normal?" she asked Alda.

Alda shrugged as she replied. "I have heard of it, but ain't never seen it myself. I don't rightly know what to expect when her time comes. We's just takin' it a day at a time and hopin' it comes soon. The baby is moving about just as it should be, so I reckon it's okay."

Diana looked back at Sofia. She was struggling to raise herself up higher on her pillow. "Tell me, Diana, tell me about Josie and Regina. How was your trip?"

Alda pulled a chair over for Diana. She backed towards the door. "I will be back in a little while to check on ya, Miss Sofia. Good ta see ya, Mrs. Shively," she said before turning to exit the room.

Diana sat down. She told Sofia all about the trip to and from Josephine's. She told her about Delila and Rita. She told her about Regina's constant talking. They laughed. Then Sofia told Diana how Jonathan had been working on a cradle for the baby. Porter Martin had stopped a couple of times while they were gone to check on her. He gave Jonathan a few suggestions on the cradle. He said he would show Jonathan how to build a crib for when the baby was older.

"That Porter Martin. What would we ever have done without him?" Diana asked.

Sofia took a drink from a cup that sat next to her bed. "Think on it, Di. Where would we be today if Porter Martin had not come to this area to settle? He is like our guardian angel. That is how I think of him," Sofia said, smiling.

Diana thought for a moment. "You know, Sofia, I have never thought of it that way before, but you are right. That is exactly what he is. Our own personal guardian angel," Diana smiled back at her sister. "So, you don't think that baby is coming today?" she asked.

Sofia shook her head. "I don't think so, but Alda said when it is ready there won't be any stopping it."

Diana patted Sofia's hand. "I have the children all outside. I need to get them back home. If you have any signs of labor starting, you send someone for me right away. I want to be here when that little niece or nephew comes into this world," Diana said.

Sofia nodded again. "You bet I will send someone for you. You may even hear me a yelling from Porter Martin's house. I got to tell you Di, I am not looking forward to the pain that goes with having this baby. I am truly frightened near to death," she said with a serious look on her face.

"Just thank the Lord for Alda Faulk. I have confidence in her. She will take good care of you. I really have to get going, Sofie. I love you," Diana said as she bent down kissing her sister on the forehead. "I'll be here as soon as I can." She winked at Sofia as she exited the room. She let herself out the front door to where the children were all waiting for her. "Come along, Homer, let us get back to the house. Your mamma is picking blackberries, and she will be waiting on Hoppy to help her." They climbed up into the carriage. Once again, they were traveling the rutted trail to Porter Martin's house. They could see the puffs of smoke from the sawmill, off in the distance. Diana smiled. It was good to be home.

Homer stopped the carriage at the back porch. Once everyone was unloaded, he drove the team on toward the stable. He would unhitch the team, turn them loose in to pasture, and then go to the mill to help. Diana watched his back as he drove on in the direction of the stable. He was growing into quite a man. She was proud of him. She tried not to think of the things he had seen in his eleven years. She climbed the steps of the porch. Hoppy followed carrying Franklin.

Once inside, Diana removed her bonnet and the bonnet she had placed on Little Robert. He had fallen asleep on the ride back. She laid him in the copper tub. She took Franklin from Hoppy. "You best help your mamma with the blackberries, Hoppy. She will be expecting you," she said. Hoppy turned to go outside. Franklin whined, wanting to go outside again. Diana carried him out onto the porch.

Shirley and Cecelia took his hands, walking him toward the swings. Diana sat down on the steps. She could see Percy walking in the direction of the mill. Gilda was swinging on the closest swing that hung in an old sugar maple tree. Diana looked for some sign of Raymond. When she did not see him, she assumed he was at the mill also.

She watched the children playing. Little Franklin was walking very well now. As a matter of fact, he was running after Gilda as they played around the swings. Diana could not stop smiling as she watched the girls playing with the little boy. She was proud of her family. She imagined her own mother watching her six girls playing in the yard of the log cabin with the sod roof.

She could smell the honeysuckle vines that grew up the porch post. She could see the cows grazing on the knob above the barnyard. She could hear the laughter. She placed her hand on her small stomach. She was hoping for a boy. The boy her father had always wanted.

Diana went inside. She tiptoed past the copper tub and up the stairs. In her room, she found her sling lying on the dresser. Four small round stones lay scattered around it. Diana clutched them in her hand. She put the stones in her pocket. She went back downstairs and outside as quietly as she could. She went to a spot near where the children were playing. She began to practice hitting a small apple tree. Shirley retrieved the stones. After about a half hour or so, she began to hit the tree a couple of times. It was coming back. Slowly, but surely. She continued until she heard the sound of Robert crying from inside the house. She gathered her stones, placing them in her pocket. She hung her sling on her waist, just as she had worn it for years. Then she went inside to Robert.

Diana had changed Robert's diaper and washed him down with a cool damp cloth. She made him a sugar bread, placing him back in the copper tub while she prepared sugar bread and peppermint tea for the other children. They were all sitting on the back porch when Tilly and Hoppy appeared, carrying three baskets of black berries.

Hoppy took the babies outside to play. Tilly and Diana began to wash the berries. Tilly was rolling out piecrusts while Diana began to stem and clean the berries. She placed them in a large pot and added sugar. Once Tilly had two pies in the oven, the two of them began preparing jam. Tilly hummed as she worked. Diana smiled. Tilly appeared happy. Diana knew it had not always been this way for Tilly. Diana had always tried to suppress the thoughts of Tilly's past. It made her happy to be in a position to make life better for Tilly.

The pies were done. Tilly placed them in the window to cool. She placed a cloth over them to keep the flies off of them. By the time the jam was finished and the kitchen was cleaned up, it was time to start supper. Diana went to the smoke house and returned with a pheasant. Tilly got the potatoes from the root cellar, which was a hole dug deep in a dirt bank near the side of the house. Several wooden barrels were buried there to hold potatoes, apples, onions, and other perishables.

The kitchen was very hot by this time. Diana and Tilly carried the table outside. They set it up in the backyard. The children grew excited. It was going to be a family picnic in the backyard. There were more flies in the kitchen than there was outside by this time. Gilda had a fly swatter. She was dancing around the kitchen as she swatted the flies. She giggled and sang as she worked feverishly to rid the house of the pests. Shirley had joined her. They sounded like they were having a good time.

The men arrived from the mill. Stumpy was with them. They gathered around the table. There was a vacant chair where Raymond usually sat. "Have you seen him?" Diana asked Brandon.

"Not all day. I thought he was sulking upstairs," Brandon replied.

"I'll go see if he is in his room," Winston said. He ran inside the house.

Soon, he reappeared shaking his head. "He ain't in there. I mean, he is not in there," he said as his face turned red.

Diana smiled at him. "Thank you, Winston." She looked over at Brandon. "Where could he be?" she asked.

Porter said, "If he can smell this food, he'll be along. If he ain't here by the time we finish our meal, I will go lookin' for him."

Porter led them in a prayer. The conversation went to the events of the day. Diana tried not to let the other children see her concern. When they had finished, Porter announced he was going off to look for Raymond. Stumpy agreed to accompany him. Brandon and Homer carried the table and chairs back into the house. Then, they too, went off to look for Raymond.

Tilly, Hoppy, and Diana cleaned up the dishes. Everything was done and put away when Brandon and Homer arrived back at the house.

"No sign of him anywhere," Brandon said. "Maybe Porter and Stumpy had better luck. I think I will take Tilly and the children home."

He went to the stable. Homer ran after him. Franklin cried when Brandon left. Hoppy carried him around the kitchen, trying to find something to take his mind off of being left behind.

Diana paced the floor. She tried to think of where Raymond might have gone. He said he wanted to be with his father. Surely, he would not be able to find Alvin Hughes? He was only seven years old. He would never survive in the wild all alone. Diana dabbed at the tears welling up in the corner of her eyes. She continued to pace.

Brandon pulled up to the back porch. Tilly and her children climbed up into the wagon. Winston rode along. Brandon let him drive the wagon. Diana could see the disappointment in Homer's face. She winked at him as she waved good-bye. He smiled, waving back.

Diana was alone with her children. She washed Shirley, placing a clean nightshirt over her head. Shirley played with Franklin while she washed Cecilia. Then she began washing the babies. They were going up the steps when they heard Brandon and Winston pulling the wagon around the house to the stable.

Diana read the Bible to the children. Cecilia went to sleep first. Then Franklin. Finally, she kissed Shirley goodnight and exited the room. She passed Winston on the stairs as he was on his way to bed.

"No sign of Ray, Mom," Winston said.

Diana smiled. He had called her Mom. She kissed his forehead. "We will find him, Winston. Good night, Son. I love you," she said to the nine-year-old who stood before her looking like a young man.

Winston went on up to the bedroom he shared with the other children. Diana continued on down the steps. She found Brandon in the kitchen. He looked up as she entered. He was pouring a cup of cold water from the pump. "Don't worry, Dear. Porter will find him. If he doesn't, I will look again to-morrow," Brandon said.

"Oh, Brandon, do you suppose he went looking for his father? He may have left early this morning right after our talk. That gives him the whole day's head start. We may never find him," Diana said, wringing her hands.

"How could he find his father?" Brandon began. "All we know is his uncle lives somewhere in the hills near Pittsburgh. I could go to the fort there and ask if anyone knows of him, but I doubt that Ray would know to do that. I don't recall them mentioning that they had ever been there before. That boy wouldn't even know which direction to head into. He's probably just lost somewhere in the wilderness. We will find him. He gets a good dose of the cold and hungries, he'll change his attitude," Brandon said, taking a drink of the cold water.

They heard Porter on the porch. He entered the back door taking his hat off his balding head. He looked up at Diana. He shook his head as he said, "No sign of him."

Diana sobbed into her apron. Brandon went to comfort her. He held her in his arms. "Di, he isn't a stupid boy. He will be fine. Just be grateful it isn't the dead of winter. Tomorrow, at first light, I will go look for him. I won't come back without him," he said into her hair.

Diana nodded, but continued to sob. "I am going up to bed," she said. She turned and went up the stairs.

In her room, she read from the Bible for a while. She could not stop crying. The windows were open, and she kept going to look out, hoping to see Raymond standing in the backyard, or off near the stables or mill. Finally, she fell to her knees next to the bed, praying. Then she crawled into bed. The air was still hot. She could hear the peep frogs singing her to sleep. To her surprise, she fell asleep quickly.

The next morning found Diana up early. She had breakfast on the table when the children began to filter down into the kitchen. Brandon was up before Porter, which was unusual. He ate his breakfast and drank his coffee. Diana had packed him a saddlebag full of food. "When you find him, he will be hungry," she said. She kissed Brandon before he left. She stood on the porch until he had ridden out of sight.

She had just returned to the kitchen when Porter arrived downstairs. She explained where Brandon had gone. Porter said, "After breakfast, I will ride into Berlin. Maybe I can rustle up a few men to help search for him. We have a better chance of finding him if we spread out the search. No tellin' which direction the boy went."

Diana hugged Porter. "Thank you, Mr. Martin," she said. Porter patted her on the arm, then he turned his attention to his cup of coffee.

Diana packed a saddlebag full of food for Porter, too. Winston begged to go along. "You need to stay behind and protect the women, lad," Porter told him.

Winston thought on it a moment, and then smiled. After Porter had left, he asked Diana. "May I hitch up the wagon and go after Tilly and the children?"

Diana thought on it awhile. She smiled as she stroked his hair. "I would feel more comfortable if you stayed here with me and the little ones," she said.

She could see the disappointment in his eyes. He nodded. "You're a good lad, Winston. I am so proud of the young man you have become. You are growing so fast. You're going to be a man before we know it." She rustled his hair again. "What do you say we give you a haircut this morning?"

Winston nodded. Diana carried a chair out onto the back porch. Winston sat perfectly still while she clipped away at the large curls forming around his ears. She had just finished when she saw Tilly and the children walking through the orchard toward them. They waved as they came closer.

"Tilly," Diana began as they approached the porch. "You needn't have walked all that way in this heat. We could manage one day without you," she smiled.

Tilly shook her head. "This is where Tilly belongs. I tol you I's would always be heres fo ya. I keeps my word. I ain't got notin' to do at home least ways. Hoppy heps me git everythin done. She's a good girl," Tilly said.

Diana smiled. "Yes, she is a good girl. You have taught her well," Diana said. She had finished with Winston's haircut. He stood up dusting the hair from about his shoulders. He had been sweating and the hair had stuck to his neck and face. "You best go wash off and change your shirt, Winston," Diana said. "If you don't, you will itch all day."

"Yes, Mamma," he said. He disappeared into the house.

Diana smiled. She was getting used to the children calling her Mamma. Her thoughts went to Raymond. It must have shown on her face, for Tilly said, "They will find the boy, Miss Diana. They will find him."

Diana nodded. "I hope so, Tilly," she said. Tilly took the broom and began to sweep the loose hair off the porch. Diana sat down on the chair Winston had occupied only moments ago. She watched the children playing. They laughed as they chased one another around the backyard. Diana remembered playing with Josephine's children in Philadelphia. She missed her sisters, but was so glad to be back home. She became aware of Tilly standing at the bottom of the steps in the sun.

"Oh, Tilly. Do come up out of the sun. I have some sassafras tea made. Would you like some after that long walk in the heat?" Diana asked.

"Yes, Ma'am," Tilly replied. "That would be mighty kind of you."

Diana stood up. She laughed as she replied, "Now, Tilly, you do not have to wait until I offer it to you. You and the children are welcomed to anything we have here. I told you once before, you are family."

Tilly smiled widely. She stepped toward the back door. She held it open as Winston passed out onto the porch, all cleaned up. "I's git it Miss Diana. You rest awhile," Tilly said before she went into the kitchen. She returned with a tray full of tin cups, about half full of tea. She passed the drinks around to the children. Hoppy helped little Robert drink his tea. Diana smiled down at them. Franklin was climbing the porch steps to get to Diana. She met him half way. He rested his head upon her shoulder as she sat back down on the chair. She fanned herself as she sat holding him. Soon, he was breathing steady. He was asleep. She carried him inside, placing him on a pile of hides that was stacked near the window in the kitchen. She closed the shutter to block the sun from shining in on him as he slept. She went back outside.

Diana and Tilly spent another hour or more watching the children. Soon, Tilly went inside to prepare a light lunch for the children. Diana took some needlework with her when she went back outside. It was too hot to sit indoors today. Soon, Franklin was standing at her side. He was cranky from his nap. Hoppy rushed up onto the porch, taking him in her arms. Diana smiled. She was so grown up for a young girl about to turn fifteen. She was near marrying age.

The afternoon passed slowly. The children continued to play near the orchard. At least it was shaded there. Diana gave the older ones permission to go to the creek that passed in front of the house. Now and then she could hear them laughing. She remembered the days when she, herself, splashed in that creek with her sisters. They were on their way back from Berlin. She stepped off the porch. "Who wants to go wading in the creek with me?" she asked. Gilda was the first to respond. "Me, me!" waving her hand in the air as if they were in the classroom.

Diana handed Franklin to Tilly. "Come on, Tilly! Let's go cool off with the children." Tilly had a shocked look on her face. Diana laughed. "Come on, Tilly. It is hot. The water will feel really good. Just tuck your skirt in like this. You hold Franklin, and I will hold Robert. A little play time will do us all good," Diana laughed. She watched Tilly as she folded the hem of her skirt in at the waist. They hurried around front to where the older children were playing.

Winston, Homer, and Percy were splashing one another. They stopped and watched as the rest of them approached. "We've come to play in the water, too!" Hoppy shouted at them as the women and smaller children approached. Soon, they were all laughing and playing together. Tilly smiled widely. She was enjoying herself.

They caught a few crayfish and placed them in a wooden bucket. They would boil them for dinner. Diana could not remember the last time she had eaten crayfish soup. It was something they usually had when nothing else could be found, for her father never really liked it much. Again, her thoughts went to the days when she and her sisters would catch the crayfish in this very stream on the way back from taking the milk to Berlin. She could remember watching Porter Martin's house as it was being built. She remembered James meeting them as they passed by this way. She smiled to herself as she remembered her sister, Josephine, blushing at the sight of him.

Soon, the sun was in the western sky. It was time to begin preparing supper. They carried the bucket of crayfish to the back porch. Tilly pumped a bucket of clean water from the hand pump in the front yard. She dumped some salt into the water. Hoppy fished the crayfish from the wooden bucket and placed them in the salt water. Tilly poured the water into a pan on the stove. She started a second pan with potatoes and onions in it. The vapor rose high above the stove, making it even hotter in the kitchen. Once the salt water was boiling and the crayfish floated to the top, Tilly scooped them up, placing them in with the potatoes and onions. The salt water was discarded. Diana and Tilly carried the table outside into the backyard. The children carried the chairs. It was too hot to eat inside today.

They ate in the shade of the sugar maple tree. Diana wondered where the men were. Porter Martin and Stumpy had gone in one direction, while Brandon went in another. Porter had taken the dogs with him. Hopefully, they were not too old to track Raymond's scent. Brandon had gone in the direction of Pittsburgh. He would not return for several more days, unless he happened to find Raymond. Diana said a silent prayer as she sat under the sugar maple tree. Dark clouds were forming overhead. A bolt of lightning flashed across the sky.

"We best be g'tting' inside, Miss Diana," Tilly said, jolting Diana from her daydream.

"Yes. That would be a good idea," Diana responded. "Winston, Homer, you boys help with this table and chairs. Hoppy, you help your Mamma and I clear the dishes. We are about to get wet."

They worked frantically to get everything inside before the rain started. They had just brought the last of the chairs inside when the rain started. They were all gathered in the kitchen when a knock came at the front door. Diana went to the door, followed by all of the children, hovering behind her to see who it was. It was Concetta Hickman.

"Diana, Alda Faulk sent me to fetch ya. It is Sofia. She has started into labor," Concetta said. She was soaked to the skin. Her horse was tied to the hitching post just off the porch.

"I'll be right there," Diana said. She turned to Homer. "Homer, you get me a horse. No need for a saddle, just a bridle. I will make better time on horseback. The rest of you stay with Tilly. I will be back when I can. We are having a baby!" she said, smiling at them.

Diana grabbed her bonnet. She placed it on her head and tied it securely. "You may wait here if you like until the rain stops, Connie," she said.

Concetta shook her head. "Not on your life. Sofia is my best friend. I may not be of much help to her, but I will be there for her," she said.

Diana went back into the kitchen. She informed Tilly of the latest events and assured her she would be home as soon as she could. She told Tilly they could sleep at the Martin house tonight. Then she saw Homer approaching with one of Porter's fastest horses. Diana ran to meet him in the rain. She climbed the fence railing and swung her leg over the bare back of the horse. She dug her heels into its side and galloped toward Berlin. Concetta Hickman was close behind.

She reached Sofia and Jonathan's house, soaked to the skin. Concetta took the reins of her horse. She raced inside without even knocking. She found Jonathan sitting at the kitchen table with Zachariah Dillon sitting across from him. Jonathan stood up. "Diana!" he said. He pointed toward the bedroom just as Sofia let out a scream. Diana went to the door.

She opened it softly. She took a deep breath before stepping inside. Sofia was propped up on three feather down pillows. Her hands were wrapped around two rawhide straps that were tied to the head of the bed. She gripped them tightly. Her legs were spread wide with Alda Faulk on her knees between them. Grace Hickman was dabbing Sofia's forehead with a cold wet cloth. Martha stood just inside the door. She was pale and wide-eyed. Diana squeezed her hand. Sofia opened her eyes to see Diana standing at the foot of the bed. "Di ann aaaa!" she called out as another pain took hold of her. Diana could see the mounded stomach moving with the pain. She went to her sister's side. Grace handed her the cloth and stepped back out of the way. Diana looked down at Alda Faulk.

"She is doin just fine, Mrs. Shively. Everythin is as it should be," Alda said.

The pain had passed. Sofia was panting as she said, "I was so worried that you would not make it in time. I didn't want to have this baby without you." Another pain took hold of her and she screamed again. Then she began to sob.

"You stop that cryin!" Grace Hickman said. "You take it like a woman. There is nothin' for you to be cryin' about."

Alda looked up from over Sofia's spread legs. "Let her cry. I found that cryin' heps with the pain sometimes. You cry if ya want to Miss Sofia," Alda said.

Grace huffed as she went to the door. She stood next to Martha, watching from afar. Her feelings had been hurt. Diana could not think about that right now. She felt sick at her stomach, watching Sofia in such pain. She felt helpless. She reached up to where Sofia gripped the leather strap. She covered Sofia's hand with her own. Another scream.

"It's a comin'!" Alda shouted. "Give me a real hard push now."

Sofia took about four more quick breaths, and pushed hard. "Ahhhh!" she yelled out as she grunted with the pain that gripped her body.

"Again!" Alda called from the bottom of the bed.

Grace stepped closer. "I can see its head," she announced. "It is coming, Sofia," Martha began to pace, wringing her hands.

Diana leaned close to Sofia's ear. "Come on, Sofia. You can do this. It is almost over," she whispered to her younger sister.

Sofia panted a few times. "Ahhhh!" she yelled as she pushed again.

"Here it comes!" Grace called out in her excitement.

The thunder boomed outside. The lightning flashed a bright light into the room. A baby's cry filled the air. "It's a girl!" Alda called out. She laid the wet baby girl on Sofia's stomach. She cut the cord and tied it close to the baby girl's belly. Sofia was crying and laughing at the same time. Martha let out a sob, covering her mouth with both hands. Diana wiped the tears from her eyes, as she watched. Alda handed the baby to Sofia. Grace took a blanket and covered them both. Sofia was sobbing hard.

Grace stepped out of the room. Moments later, Jonathan was standing in the door. Alda took Diana's hand and led her out of the room so Sofia and Jonathan could be alone. Martha followed them into the kitchen.

Grace Hickman and Concetta stood near the door. It stood open to let some fresh air pass through the humid house. Grace had her arm around her daughter. Alda went to the washbasin and began to wash her bloody hands. Diana sat down next to Zachariah. "It's a baby girl," she whispered to the blind man. He smiled, nodding his head.

Jonathan appeared in the door to the bedroom. "She wants to see her sisters," he announced. He turned to disappear back in the bedroom. Diana and Martha went through the door and stood at the foot of the bed.

"Come look at her. She is perfect in every way," Sofia said, motioning for Diana and Martha to approach them.

Diana went to the bedside. Martha hung back. Diana smiled down at the nursing baby. "What are you going to name her, Sofie?" she asked.

Sofia looked over at Jonathan and then back at Diana. She smiled. She looked down at her daughter as she said, "Rose Marie Gilbert."

"That is a beautiful name, Sofie," Martha said as she stepped closer, taking hold of the baby's hand.

"It fits her perfectly. She is like a perfect, beautiful, little rose. I like that name very much," Diana said. A tear formed in the corner of her eye.

"Would you like to hold her?" Sofia asked.

"Oh, my. Shouldn't Jonathan hold her first?" Diana asked, wiping her eyes.

"I can hold her anytime," Jonathan said. "You hold her first."

He took the baby from Sofia and held her out to Diana from across the bed. Diana took the sleeping baby in her arms. She kissed her on the forehead. Her damp hair clung to her head. It appeared to be light, like Sofia's. Diana wondered if she had blue eyes like her mother. She was going to be quite beautiful, just as Sofia had always been.

Alda Faulk appeared in the door with a basin of warm water. "We need to wash her up before we put her down to sleep. She's gonna cry some, but that is normal. When I git her cleaned up, I will help Miss Sofia git cleaned up as well," she said, placing the basin on the dresser.

"May I wash her?" Diana asked.

Alda looked over at Sofia. Sofia nodded. "Course ya kin," Alda said. "I kin get started on cleanin up Miss Sofia and this bed."

"Well, you won't be needing me any longer," Jonathan said. He bent down to kiss Sofia. "You did really well, Sofia," he said. Then he left the room.

Diana held little Rose Marie in her arms. Martha stood by, watching closely. The color was coming back to her cheeks. She wiped her with a warm damp cloth. The baby shivered. She squirmed with every wipe. Diana laughed. "She is a feisty one, Sofia. Just like her mamma," Diana said. Diana laid her on the bottom of the bed, rolling her over to wash her from behind. The baby squirmed, thrashing her arms and drawing up her legs. She let out a loud cry. Diana worked quickly so she could wrap little Rose in a blanket. As soon as she had the baby wrapped tight and held her close, she quit crying. She handed her to Martha. Tears were streaming down Martha's cheeks. She sniffled, smiling down at her little niece. "Rose Marie Gilbert," she whispered, "so nice to meet you. I am your Aunt Martha," she said softly.

Martha held the baby out to Diana. Diana took her, holding her close to her bosom. She thought of her own baby. What will it be? A boy or girl? She had been feeling her baby moving about more and more lately. It wasn't due to be born for another five months. Diana had barely began to show. She kissed little Rose again. "I can't stop kissing her, Sofia. I love her so much," Diana said. A tear was forming in her eye.

Alda helped Sofia into a chair so she could strip the bed of its sheets. Diana carried the baby to Sofia. As soon as Sofia took little Rose into her arms, the baby seemed to know that she was with her mother. Sofia began to nurse Little Rose once again. Diana turned to help Alda with the bed.

"The storm's passed. It is still rainin' mighty hard, though," Alda said as she shook a clean sheet over the bed, allowing it to fall across the top. Diana began to tuck her side under the mattress, while Alda did the same on the other side. Soon, the bed was made. Diana held the baby, while Alda helped Sofia back into bed. "She will sleep now," Alda said as she went toward the door. Diana followed her, watching Sofia with her baby from over her shoulder.

In the kitchen, Diana went to the open door. Rain was blowing in on the porch. Grace and Concetta were cleaning up the pans that were used to boil water.

When they had finished, they turned to Jonathan. "If you don't need us any longer, we have a baby waiting at home who needs us. Sherman will be pacing the floor with Burt. We really should be getting back," Grace said.

Jonathan stood up. "Thank you so much for coming. I don't know what I would have done without you ladies. All of you," he said, turning to look back at Alda, Martha, and Diana.

"I wouldn't have missed it for the world. Sofia is my best friend," Concetta said.

"Come along now, Connie. We must make a run for it before another storm comes through," Grace said. She nodded at Diana and Martha before they disappeared into the rainy night. Diana could hear their footsteps splashing through the muddy streets as they ran toward the general store.

Diana stepped into the open doorway. It was very dark outside. "I really need to get back home. Tilly is waiting with the children," she said.

Jonathan went to stand behind her. "It looks like it is an all nighter. You can't be thinking on riding your horse back to the house. You are still wet from the ride in. You may need to just wait it out. You can stay the night if you need to. You can sleep with Sofia. I can sleep out here. I don't think Tilly would mind staying the night. It is raining too hard for her to go home anyway," he said.

Just then, Carver appeared in the darkness as he made his way through the pouring rain to Jonathan and Sofia's house. He hurried up the steps. "I passed Grace and Concetta. They said we have a girl," he said, smiling.

"Yes, you are an uncle. Again," Diana said, laughing.

"Is Martha ready to go home? I have her supper warming on the stove," Carver said.

Diana raised her eyebrows. She turned to her sister. "What a lucky woman you are, Martha. Your knight in shining armor has come for you. He has a hot meal awaiting in your castle," she teased.

Martha smiled. She hugged Jonathan, then Diana before she stepped out onto the porch. She waved before splashing off into the darkness. Diana watched until they, too, were out of site.

Diana continued to watch out into the darkness as she said, "I wish I had asked Winston or Homer to come for me. I didn't think in my rush to get here. We have the wagon house. Mr. Martin put the wheels on it for the summer. He uses it to transport Tilly and the children on days like this. He takes the wheels off in the winter and uses it as a sled. I wish I had thought of it before I left. I was in such a hurry to get here. Oh, well, it is done now. I will either have to stay or make a run for it in the rain."

Jonathan shook his head. "You Lewis girls have a mind of your own. You are welcome to stay if you want. If you want to stay, I will take your horse to the stable for you. He has been standing out there in that storm all this time. That isn't good for him," Jonathan said.

"Oh, my. I didn't even think about the horse. That is one of Mr. Martin's best, too. I better just go home. He will need a good rub down and some dry hay.

She turned to face Jonathan. "I think I will make a run for it. The lightning has stopped...."

Before she could finish, she heard the sound of a wagon approaching the front porch. "Whoa!" A voice called out. Diana and Jonathan stepped back out onto the porch.

It was Winston driving the wagon house. "Mamma! I came to give you a ride home. Has Aunt Sofia had her baby yet?" he called out from the narrow window that was cut in the front of the wagon house. Diana began to laugh. Jonathan laughed, too.

Diana went to the edge of the porch. "Yes, she has! A little girl. Rose Marie Gilbert. Your new little cousin. Would you like to see her?" she called back to Winston.

"Yes, Ma'am!" he said. Soon, the doors on the back of the wagon house opened, and Winston jumped down. He ran through the rain to meet them on the porch.

Diana turned to Jonathan. "Do you mind, Jonathan?" she asked.

Jonathan shook his head. "Don't mind at all. Come on in," he motioned with his hand as he stepped inside. Diana followed, with Winston behind her. Jonathan put his finger to his lips as he glanced back at the boy. They tiptoed inside the bedroom. Diana went to the bed and pulled the covers that wrapped Rose back so Winston could see her face. Winston bent down close. A smile came upon his face. He kissed his fingers and then placed them on Rose's forehead. They went quietly back into the kitchen. Jonathan closed the bedroom door behind them.

"She is beautiful, Pastor Gilbert," Winston said.

"Uncle Jonathan to you, son. I am only Pastor Gilbert on Sunday mornings," Jonathan said. He placed his arm around Winston's shoulder. Winston smiled.

Winston looked over at Diana and said, "I will hitch the horse to the back of the wagon house. Whenever you are ready, Mamma."

Diana hugged her son. "I am ready, son," she said. She hugged Jonathan. "I will try to get back tomorrow if this rain lets up. When Sofia wakes, tell her I said she did a good job, and I love her very much." She turned to leave. She waited on the porch until Winston had hitched the saddle horse to the back of the wagon house. He opened the door and climbed up inside, holding the door open for her. She made a run for the opened door. She climbed up inside, waving to Jonathan before closing the door. Winston crawled to the front of the wagon. He took the reins in hand and began to drive the wagon house back toward Porter Martin's house. Diana smiled as she thought back on the night. Sofia had been so worried about the pain. It was horrendous, but once Rose was born, Sofia seemed to have forgotten all about the pain. Diana began to hum to herself. She was happy. Winston began to hum along. Soon, the two of them were singing as they rode home. Diana said a silent prayer that Brandon, Raymond, and Porter would be there when she got home.

Winston dropped her off at the back porch. "I am going to rub down the horses and feed them before I come in, so I may be awhile," he told her.

"Just be careful. Don't dally any longer than you have to," Diana called as she ran up the porch steps. The wagon house moved off toward the stables. The saddle horse trotted behind. Diana went inside to find Tilly sitting in the kitchen.

Tilly hurried to Diana with a blanket. She draped it around Diana's shoulders. She had poured a cup of sassafras tea when she heard the wagon house outside. "You is soaked to da bone, child. Ya need to git outta dem wet clothes," Tilly said.

"I will. Oh, Tilly. Sofia had a beautiful little baby girl, Rose Marie. She looks just like Sofia," Diana said, smiling.

"Mm hm," Tilly said. "She is smaller, though."

Diana burst into laughter. "Yes, she is a whole lot smaller. Poor Sofia. She has gained so much weight. I hope she loses some now that Rose has been born." Diana laughed again. "Jonathan will have to put heavy duty springs on their buggy if she doesn't." They both laughed.

Diana drank the tea. It was so humid in the house. The windows were steamed up. The rain continued to pound against the outside of the house. "I hope Brandon is dry. I hope they are all dry. I am so worried, Tilly. It has been nearly three days. I don't know how long I can wait. Brandon said he would not come home without Raymond. Now I am wishing he had not said that," Diana said, sipping her tea.

Tilly sat down across from Diana. "You is like a mother hen. You is not happy least all your chicks are close ta ya," she said, reaching for Diana's hand.

Diana smiled at her. "I suppose you are right. Did the children give you any trouble?" she asked.

Tilly smiled. "Now ya know better n dat, Miss Diana. They is good kids. They listen good, too. They is all sleepin away in deir beds. They is never trouble ta Tilly. I loves em like my own," Tilly said, still smiling.

Diana finished her tea. Tilly stood up. She had two pots of boiling water on the stove. "I gots water fer ya to bath. It will warm ya up," Tilly explained.

Winston came through the back door. He removed his wet clothes. Diana went to him. She hugged him and kissed the top of his head. "Thank you so much, Winston. You go on up to bed now. Tomorrow is another day," Diana said.

Winston nodded. He went toward the stairs. He said over his shoulder, "Hopefully, it is a drier day."

"Mm hm," Tilly said as she poured the hot water into the copper tub. Diana undressed. Tilly pumped a bucket of cold water. She added some to the tub. She continued to test the temperature of the water as she added more cold water. Diana climbed into the tub. She rested her head against the back of the tub, slipping down as deep into the water as she could. Sweat beads formed upon her forehead. The humidity, along with the hot bath water, was making her sweat. She slipped her head under the water. Tilly began to rub a bar of lye soap over her head, working it into a lather. Diana closed her eyes. Even though it was hot, it was soothing. She slipped under the water again, thrashing her head from side to side to rinse her hair. She soaked a little longer. She felt like she could go to sleep. Her body aches were slowly fading away. She found she was very tired. She stood up. Tilly handed her a dry cloth. Diana dried off.

Diana stepped from the tub and wrapped herself in the towel. Tilly had brought her a clean nightdress from upstairs. Diana pulled it over her head. She wrapped her wet hair in the towel and sat down on a chair. She looked up at Tilly. "Tilly, you should try taking a warm bath before bed. It feels wonderful," she said.

Tilly looked up at Diana. "Go on, take your clothes off and get in. I will get you a dry towel. It feels wonderful," Diana said.

Tilly smiled widely. "I ain't never had me a tub bath afore," Tilly said.

"Well, that will never do," Diana began. She stood up. "You get undressed and step into that tub. I will go upstairs to get you a clean night gown and a dry towel."

Tilly was still smiling. She hesitated only a moment. Then she began to unbutton her dress. Diana went upstairs. She got a clean nightgown from her drawer. She grabbed a clean towel and softly made her way back down the stairs. She found Tilly in the tub. Her head was resting on the back splash just as she had seen Diana do only moments before. She slid under the water. When she came back up, Diana worked her head into a lather with the bar of soap. She worked on scrubbing Tilly's many braids. Tilly slipped back under the water. Diana stood holding the towel as Tilly stepped out of the tub. She wrapped herself in the towel.

Tilly looked up at Diana. "You was right. I feels real good. I feels clean all over."

Tilly and Diana emptied the tub. Tilly wiped it out, and dragged it back to its spot near the fireplace. They went to bed. Diana was so tired. She fell asleep quickly.

The next morning was Saturday. Diana and Tilly both were late rising from their beds. The children were in the kitchen, wrestling and playing around the back door. It was still raining, although it was not anywhere near the downpour they had the night before. Diana sighed. She thought about the men out searching for Raymond in this weather. Her heart sank.

Hoppy had a pot of coffee brewing. She had made biscuits and was in the process of frying scrambled eggs when Tilly and Diana entered the kitchen. She smiled up at them as they entered the room. The children all quieted down. They each hurried to Diana and Tilly, giving each a morning hug. Diana kissed Winston on the forehead. "Thank you, again, Winston for rescuing me last night in that storm," she said.

Winston blushed. "I asked Tilly if it would be all right. She said it was a good idea. Actually, it was Homer who thought of it. He wanted to come with me, but Tilly said she needed a man to look after them while I was gone," Winston said, smiling.

"That was a good idea, Homer. Thank you. You boys are quite grown up for your ages. I am very proud of all of you. What good children you all are," Diana said.

Just then, Hoppy began to spoon the scrambled eggs onto the plates. The children all sat down around the table. The back door was opened to allow some fresh air into the room. There was a chair laying on its side across the doorway to keep Franklin and Robert from going out the opened door. They had all just began to eat when Brownie came jumping over the chair. He jumped up on Percy, licking his face. Blackie came in right behind him. He was limping slightly. The children shrieked as the wet, smelly dogs darted from child to child.

Diana stood up. "Mr. Martin is back!" she said excitedly. She ran to the door, peering out toward the stables. She watched for the familiar posture to appear through the light rain. "Tilly, get some dry towels. Hoppy, start another batch of eggs on the stove. And would someone please put those smelly dogs outside? Give them something to eat out on the porch!" she called over her shoulder.

Then she saw him. He was trying to rush through the rain. Age had slowed him down considerably. He appeared soaked through. Diana could hear Tilly rushing down the stairs. She came up behind Diana, carrying dry towels just as Porter Martin came up the steps, and onto the back porch.

He removed his hat, exposing his balding head. He shook his head as he said, "No sign of him, Miss Diana. I am so sorry. We searched high and low, but we came home empty handed," he said, standing before Diana.

She sighed. She hugged the wet Porter Martin, who stood before her looking like a defeated man. "I know you did your best, Mr. Martin. I know you did. Come in and get dried off. We have some hot food and coffee for you. You go upstairs and get some dried clothes on first. We can't have you getting sick," she instructed.

Porter nodded his head. He started for the stairs, then stopped. He turned and asked, "Has Brandon returned yet?"

Diana swallowed hard. She shook her head. She could not bring herself to say the words. Porter shook his head as he ascended the stairs, slowly, with the look of defeat. Diana swallowed hard, again. She did not want him to see her tears. Tilly stood by her side. She placed her arm around Diana's shoulders. No words of comfort came, because she, too, was near tears.

Diana sat quietly at the table, waiting for Porter to come back down. She bounced a teething Robert on her knee. Franklin stood next to her, playing with his baby brother. He was chewing on a piece of toasted bread with jam on it. Diana had to laugh at the sight of him. He had jam all over his face and even in his hair. He smiled up at her showing a mouth full of teeth. Diana went to the pump. She wet a cloth; she was wiping Franklin's face when Porter Martin appeared into the kitchen.

Hoppy poured him a cup of coffee. Tilly placed a plate of scrambled eggs before him. He sat down at the table. He held the coffee under his nose. "You have no idea how good this smells," he said. He took a drink. He did not speak again until he was scrapping his plate clean with his fork.

"That was mighty good, ladies. We didn't eat last evening. We just headed home. Poor old Stumpy's caught a cold out there sleepin on the ground. He'll need a couple of days to get over it. We camped out every night. Couldn't find anywhere else to sleep. That boy just up an disappeared. Ran into some folks passin' through by wagon. They was headed to some place in West Virginia. Said they had folks there. I reckon Raymond went the other direction. I sure hope Brandon has better luck than we did," Porter explained. Hoppy poured him another cup of coffee.

"Well," Diana said softly. "I'm glad you're back, Mr. Martin. I've been so worried about you. I know you did your best. I am sure it is like you said; Raymond just went the other direction. Perhaps Brandon will find him. I just want things to go back to the way they were. I want you all home where you belong," her voice was cracking.

"Mr. Martin," Hoppy began, "We have a new baby. Miss Sofia. She had a baby girl last night. We are hoping the rain will stop so we can all go to town later. Miss Diana says she is beautiful," she said, smiling, as she looked from Porter Martin to Diana.

"A baby girl ya say?" Porter asked, with a smile.

"Yes!" Diana replied. "A baby girl! You should see her, Mr. Martin. She is the very image of Sofia. She is fair complected, with light hair. I didn't see her eyes, for she didn't open them. I'll bet they are blue just like Sofie's. She is the sweetest little darling. They named her Rose Marie. You must rest up for a while, then go see her for yourself. Sofia would love to see you," Diana concluded.

Porter smiled. He nodded his head, as he said, "I will do just that. If you ladies and gentlemen don't mind, I think I will go upstairs and rest a spell." He stood up, stretching his back.

"That is a good idea. You rest as long as you like," Diana said.

"Mm hm. Rest will do ya good," Tilly added.

Porter went up the stairs. Again, he walked about half bent over. Diana watched him as he went up the stairs. "Thank you, Lord, for bringing Mr. Martin home safely," she whispered.

It rained until early afternoon. Diana took the large carriage into town. They all went to see the new baby. Tilly had baked an apple pie for Sofia and Jonathan. They stayed only a while until Porter Martin rode up on the very horse that Diana had rode into town on the night before, in the storm. After visiting with Sofia, they went to visit with Martha.

Martha measured each of them for some new clothes. She would be making school clothes for the children who would be starting school in the fall. This year Cecilia, Franklin, and Robert would be the only children left at home. Martha was going to be very busy. She had also promised Josephine and Regina to make new clothes for them and their children as well. Rita, Delila, Nesta, and Gordy would all be needing clothes also. Before leaving for home, Hoppy had promised to come by every day. Martha was going to teach her to sew. She would help Martha in the dress shop. Martha promised to pay Hoppy for every garment she finished. Hoppy was very happy. She promised Diana that she would not allow the dressmaking to interfere with her schooling.

They rode back to Porter Martin's house. It was time to begin supper. Porter was off to see how Stumpy was doing. Tomorrow, he had planned on firing up the engine that powered the sawmill. He would need a few helping hands. Winston and Homer both volunteered. Porter said he needed another hand, and would have to check with Marcus and Sherman. He would be home in time for supper.

The dark clouds disappeared, leaving the sun to shine. A light vapor seemed to rise from the wet grass due to the heat of the day. The mud flew up at them as the wagon wheels turned, leaving ruts in the muddy trail. Soon, they were back home. Diana's heart sank when she realized that Brandon was still not home.

Supper that night was a blur to Diana. She was aware of the children and Porter Martin teasing one another. Her mind was not on the goings on around her. Now and then, a laugh would jar her out of her mental distraction. Even Tilly seemed to be having a good time. Supper dishes were washed and put away. Porter and Winston drove Tilly and her children home. Diana went through the motions of washing the faces, arms, legs, and feet of each child. She dressed them for bed. Porter and Winston returned. Winston prepared for bed. Diana read the Bible to them and tucked them in. She said her good nights to each of them, as well as Porter Martin. It was her plan to go to sleep as quickly as possible. Time passed faster while she slept. She was anxious for Brandon and Raymond to return home. Tonight, sleep did not come as easily. Diana cried until early in the morning. Finally, sleep fell upon her, only for the sounds of the birds outside her window to wake her early. She dressed. It was Sunday morning. They would all be going to church this morning.

Diana prepared pancakes for Porter Martin. It was her way of saying she was very glad to have him home again. She dressed herself and then the children. Porter had taken the wagon to collect Tilly and her children. He would pick her up on the way back through. Winston and Franklin rode along with Porter Martin. Diana only had Shirley, Cecilia, and little Robert to care for. She moved quickly.

Porter pulled up at the front door. Diana and the children climbed up into the wagon. The mud had dried some, and the ride into town was not as messy as it was coming home the day before. The sun was shining again. It was going to be a hot one.

Sofia was not in church this morning. Jonathan made the announcement that they had a new addition to his family, as if the whole town did not already know it. Diana tried hard to concentrate on the Sunday sermon. It was the birth of Joseph to Abraham and Sarah. Diana's mind wondered. She found herself watching out the window. Where was Brandon? How much longer would he be gone? Would he come home with Raymond? She tried not to be angry with Raymond for turning her world upside down. She knew she would welcome him home with open arms, but for now, she was very angry with him. Not only for what he had done, but for taking Brandon away from her. It had been five days. Five long days. The longest they had been apart was five days. That was a trip Brandon had made with Porter Martin to Philadelphia.

"Amen," she heard everyone saying. She had not realized they were saying the concluding prayer. She hoped God would not punish her for missing the prayer. She bowed her head, saying a silent prayer to God, asking for his forgiveness, and asking him to bring Brandon home to her soon.

She stood up, following the rest of the congregation to the door, where Jonathan stood. He took her hand. He kissed it and said, "Tell Brandon we missed him this morning."

Diana nodded. She could not bring herself to speak. She went to the wagon, where the rest of them were already piling in. Porter Martin took her hand, helping her up into the wagon. Suddenly, she was aware of Porter

Martin's house looming into view. She did not remember the trip home. She would have to snap herself out of this. She noticed Tilly watching her. Tilly smiled at her. Diana smiled back.

The Sunday dinner was celebrated outdoors, under the shade of the large maple tree. Diana smiled when spoken to. She could not bring herself to concentrate. Little Robert had pulled himself up by her skirt. He was crying. She stared down at him, totally unaware of what was happening. Tilly hurried to him, scooping him up into her arms. She comforted him until he was sleeping over her shoulder. Tilly carried the sleeping child inside. When she emerged from the house once again, she said to Diana, "Miss Diana, Ma'am. I thinks maybe you should go upstairs and lay yo self down fo a spell. Yo is lookin peekid."

Diana looked up at her. She nodded as she stood up. Without saying anything, she made her way slowly towards the back porch. She went up the stairs to her bedroom. It was very hot up there. She stretched out across the bed. She burst into tears. She could not hold them back any longer. Where was Brandon? What if he did not come back, like his brother Robert? She cried for the longest time, then she fell asleep. She did not sleep long. It was too hot up there. She sat on the side of the bed. She smoothed the wrinkles from her dress as she stood up.

Diana went back down the stairs. She peered in on the sleeping Robert. She pumped a handful of water from the hand pump, splashing it on her face and neck. She did not bother to wipe it dry. The cool water felt good. She went out onto the back porch.

Porter sat in a chair under the shade of the maple tree. He held a laughing Franklin on his lap. Tilly and Hoppy had the dinner table completely cleared off. They were playing some game with small stones. Shirley sat on Tilly's lap, watching. Winston, Homer, and Percy were playing a game of keep away with a leather ball in the orchard. Cecilia was playing with the dogs under the table. They all stopped, watching Diana as she walked down the porch steps and toward the shade tree. She felt her face flush as she approached them.

"How are ya feelin'?" Tilly asked.

"Much better. Thank you. I don't know what came over me. I was suddenly so very tired. I did not sleep long, but I feel so much better now," Diana said with a smile.

"Well, yo is with chile," Tilly said with a nod. She went back to her game with Hoppy.

Diana sat down in a chair next to Porter Martin. "It's a hot one today," Porter said.

"Yes," Diana agreed. "I hope it is cooler wherever Brandon is." She folded her hands in her lap. "How much longer do you think he will be, Mr. Martin?" she asked, staring at her hands.

Porter reached over, patting her hands. "I suppose he will be along soon. That is if he's found the boy. Ifin he didn't, a day or two, longer. Give him another week. Ya want me to go lookin' for him?" Porter asked.

Diana looked over at him. Tears were swelling up in her eyes. She shook her head and said, "No, Mr. Martin. Then I would be worried about both of you again. You are home, I am glad of that. I only have Brandon to worry about now. Just don't you go anywhere until he comes back. I couldn't bear it right now, thinking that I may have lost both of you."

Porter smiled, and said. "Miss Diana. You have not lost anyone. Don't you be frettin' bout such things. Brandon is a smart man. He knows that area. He was there during the war. I am confident that he will return. With the lad in tow. You just stop dwellin' on such nonsense."

Diana swallowed hard. She nodded her head. "You are right, Mr. Martin. It's only been five days. I have been unfair to Brandon. Five days is hardly enough time to get to the fort in Pittsburgh and ask around, let alone find Raymond and be back home. I am sorry. I will try to be more patient," she said, smiling over at Porter Martin.

"When does school start up again?" Porter asked, changing the subject.

Diana looked over at the boys playing in the orchard, as she replied. "In about three more weeks."

Porter shook his head. "My, my. Time sure has a way of flyin' by," he said.

Diana laughed. "I suppose it does. Unless, of course, you are waiting for someone to come home."

Porter smiled. He began to bounce his knee again. Franklin burst out into laughter. He giggled and said. "Pappap. Bounce more."

Porter laughed and bounced the child again. He blew onto Franlkin's belly, which caused the boy to squeal with excitement. Diana found herself laughing.

Franklin placed his head on Porter's chin. Still laughing, he said, "Mamma, bounce Frank." He leaned toward her with outstretched arms. Diana took him in her arms. She began to bounce the laughing boy on her lap. They were laughing when Hoppy jumped up.

"Little Robert is crying, Mamma. I will get him." She ran towards the back porch. Diana lifted Franklin in the air. "Your brother, Robert, is awake. Hoppy went to get him. Now, you have someone to play with." She blew onto his belly. Again, he burst into laughter.

"Robert!" Franklin said with a laugh.

Hoppy emerged from the house carrying a sweating Robert in her arms. She laid him on a blanket to change his diaper. Then Diana put Franklin down. He ran to his little brother. Robert crawled to meet him. They were playing and talking in baby talk that Diana could not understand.

Porter rose from his chair. He reclined onto the blanket that was spread under the tree. Before long, he was asleep. Diana went to the table. Tilly and Hoppy began to explain the game they were playing with the stones. They invited Diana to play with them. "It will hep ya git yo mind offa ya's troubles," Tilly said.

Diana nodded. "Okay, I'll play."

The rest of the day was enjoyable. Later in the afternoon, Martha and Carver rode out to visit with them. They ate again, outdoors under the maple tree. Before Carver left for home, he helped Porter to carry the table back inside. Porter then hitched up the wagon to take Tilly and the children home.

It was such a hot afternoon they all decided to ride along. Porter drove the wagon through the orchard and under the shade of the trees as he went to the log cabin with the sod roof. Diana had not been here in awhile. The place looked different to her now. The barn was all but caving in. There was no grass in the front yard, only mud and dirt. The weeds behind the house loomed up high. Only around the three graves, under the big tree, was neatly cared for. This was no longer Diana's home. It was Tilly's now.

They dropped Tilly and the children off. Porter drove the wagon back to his house. He pulled up to a stop near the stream that ran in front of his house. "Anyone want to cool their feet off?" He called back to them from his seat on the wagon.

They all jumped off the wagon. They removed their shoes, rolled up their pants, tucked in their skirts, and waded into the water. Porter held onto Franklin. Diana dangled Robert in the water. The water was high from the rain. It was muddy, but cold. They played for a while, then climbed back up into the wagon. Porter dropped them off at the back porch. It was getting dark.

The children fussed about getting washed for bed. They reasoned they had just been in the stream. Diana would not listen to their excuses. She washed the faces, necks, ears, arms, legs, and feet of the smaller ones. Winston and Shirley washed themselves. Porter went upstairs with them. He lay across one bed, while Diana lay across another. She read from the Bible. Then Porter went to the door, holding it for Diana.

"When is Pappa coming home, Mamma?" Shirley asked.

Before she could reply, Cecilia asked. "Yes, Mamma. We miss Pappa. Is he bringin' Ray home with him?"

Diana looked over at Porter. She smiled back at the children. "Pappa is out there searching for Raymond. As soon as he finds him, he will bring him home. It shouldn't be much longer," Diana said.

"Is Raymond going to get a whoopin'?" Shirley asked.

"Shirley! Pappa never whooped any of us," Winston said.

Diana smiled and said, "Winston is right. Your Pappa, nor I, have ever whooped any of you, children. You know when you've done something wrong. There is no need for whooping in this house. Now, you children get to sleep. Tomorrow is another day."

She pulled the door shut. Porter waited for her to descend the stairs first. Once they were in the kitchen, he poured himself a tin cup of brandy. He held the jug up to Diana. She smiled. "I don't normally drink the stuff, but tonight I believe I will have just a sip to help me sleep," she said, reaching for a tin cup of her own. They sat at the table discussing the day. Then Diana went up to bed. To her surprise, the brandy did help her to sleep. She dreamed.

It was winter. She was chasing the cows down the knob toward the barn. Her father was standing in the corral, motioning for her to come. She ran for she felt an urgency in him. As she approached him, his features began to change. It was Robert, Brandon's brother. He was smiling. "Hurry, Diana!" he called. Diana ran as fast as she could. The cows seem to scatter in all directions.

"What is it, Robert? Where is Brandon?" she asked as she drew near to Robert.

Robert smiled down at her. "You are the strongest woman I have ever met, Diana. You just need to be strong a little longer. Brandon will be here soon," he said as he turned to go into the barn.

"Has he found Raymond, Robert?" she called to him.

He did not answer. He went into the barn. Diana hurried inside to find him. "Did he find Raymond?" she asked again. He was gone. Diana looked around. The barn was falling down. She hurried outside, just in time to see the roof fall. "Robert!" she called out. "Robert, where are you?"

Diana found herself sitting up in bed. She was soaked with sweat. She hung her feet over the side of the bed. She remembered the dream. Was Robert trying to reassure her in the same manner that Miss Margaret and Ruth Ann had done in the past? She went to the washbowl. She was wiping her face when a knock came at her door.

"Mamma? Mamma, are you all right?" Winston asked.

"Yes, Winston. I am fine. I had a bad dream," she said as she opened the door. Winston entered the room.

"I heard you calling out to little Robert," Winston said as he went to the crib near the wall. The baby boy lay sleeping through the whole thing.

"Yes, well, it was just a dream," Diana said. He kissed Winston on top of the head. She turned him around, leading him to the door. "I am very sorry I woke you. I am fine, and little Robert is fine. You go back to bed now, and thank you for checking up on me," she said. She hugged the lad and closed the door behind him. She checked on Robert one more time before going back to bed. Sleep came quickly. The morning found her sleeping in again.

Porter Martin was at the stove. He had a mess on the table. The children were seated around, laughing and teasing him as he attempted to cook their breakfast. Diana stood in the doorway watching for only a moment.

"What is all this?" she asked with a smile.

Porter turned to look at her. He grinned. "Thank goodness you are here! Pancakes I can handle, but all of these eggs, and browning toast, and making coffee and cocoa!" He said waving a large wooden spoon in the air. "I don't know how you ladies do it. Everything is getting ready at the same time." He turned back to the stove. He lifted a piece of burnt toast in the air for Diana to see.

Diana went to the stove. "I have this, Mr. Martin. You pour yourself a cup of coffee and sit down. I will have breakfast on the table in no time," she winked at Shirley who was watching very closely. "I'll make more toast," she said as she worked.

Before long, Diana had the table spread with breakfast. The children were quiet while they ate. Robert sat on Diana's lap and ate from her plate. She hardly ate much these days anyway. Little Franklin had his own chair that Porter and Stumpy had made for him from a picture they saw in an advertisement at the general store.

After breakfast was finished, Porter said to Winston. "Come on, boy. I'll help you hitch up the wagon and you can go collect Miss Tilly and her children, while I get the engine fired up at the mill."

Winston smiled. He was given a task that had, up until now, been for the adults. Diana thought of protesting. He was only nine years old. But one look at his beaming face told her to hold her tongue. She sipped at her coffee. Porter rose from the table. He stretched his back and walked toward the back door. Winston hurried to follow. Diana watched them as they disappeared off the back porch. Just then, Robert tipped her coffee cup over. Hot coffee ran across the table and dripped down onto her skirt and leg. It was hot, but not enough to seriously burn her. Luckily for Robert, she was able to move him out of harm's way. She placed him on the floor. She went to the pump and pumped the handle until the cold water was flowing into the trough. She cleaned up the dripping coffee and began to wipe away at her skirt. She would have to wait until Tilly arrived before she left the children alone to change her skirt.

Diana began to clear the table. Franklin squirmed and fussed until she put him down onto the floor. Cecilia took his hand, leading him onto the porch. There they played with the dogs until Winston began to drive the wagon through the orchard toward Tilly's house. The dogs ran from the porch to follow the wagon. Diana stood on the porch watching until the wagon was out of sight.

Tilly arrived, taking control of the household. Diana took a buggy, going into Berlin to see Sofia and the baby. Hoppy rode along so she could help Martha with some sewing. She had a taste of what it felt like to have her own money in her pocket, and she liked the freedom it gave her.

The day went by slowly, until once again Diana was washing faces, arms, legs, and feet for bed. She just went through the motions. Brandon was forever on her mind.

Another morning found Diana sleeping in again. She sat on the side of the bed, staring at the floor. She felt exhausted. She did not remember dreaming or waking in the night, yet she was not getting the restful sleep she longed for. She rose slowly, going through the motions of dressing and brushing her hair. She slowly made her way down the stairs.

This morning, she found Tilly in the kitchen already. "Mornin, Miss," Tilly said with a smile. She sat a cup of coffee before Diana.

"Thank you so much, Tilly," Diana said as she sat down at the table. "You are here early this morning."

Tilly smiled. "Mm hm. That Winston, he likes to come fo us. He's comin earlier and earlier," she said, winking at Diana.

Diana looked up at her as she said, "He likes driving the wagon by himself. It makes him feel so grown up. I will have a talk with him."

Tilly was shaking her head as she said, "No, Ma'am. We is ready anyhows. It ain't no bother. We just eat our breakfast here with you all, that's all. That's okay, ain't it?"

Diana smiled as she sipped her coffee. She put the cup down and said, "Of course, it is all right. We love having you here. I told you, you are all like part of the family."

Tilly smiled. "Yes, Ma'am. Like a sisser," she said.

Tilly sat a bowl of cracked wheat before Diana. Diana took a deep breath before taking a bite. She was not hungry. She was only eating so she could keep her strength up. She ate half of the wheat, then pushed the bowl away. "I am sorry, Tilly. I cannot eat any more. I have no appetite this morning."

Tilly passed the bowl over to Cecilia. She began to eat the remaining wheat. Diana smiled. Tilly refilled Diana's coffee cup. "Why don't yo take yo's coffee out on the porch an rest a spell. The mornin' air will do ya good. Lift ya up some," Tilly said.

Diana smiled. "I think I will. I think I will have my coffee on the front porch. I just need some time to myself, to clear my head, so to speak," Diana said as she went toward the front door.

"I will have Hoppy keep the yunguns out back," Tilly called to her.

Diana sat in a rocking chair on the front porch. She could see the bend in the road that led to Berlin. Butterflies floated about the climbing roses that grew over the fence near the porch. She looked out at the crossing in the stream. She remembered Porter stopping the wagon there for them all to cool off before going in for the night. She closed her eyes. She could hear her sisters laughing as they splashed in the stream on the way back from a milk run to Berlin. Josephine was there. She was as Diana remembered her, before she left for Philadelphia. Regina was there. Diana laughed as she remembered Regina's squeaky voice as she sang. Diana heard the dogs barking. She looked up. She shaded her eyes from the sun with her hand. Someone was coming around the bend on horseback. She watched as they trotted closer to the house.

Diana stood up. She walked to the steps, watching as the figure approached. It was a man with broad shoulders and a straight back. She was aware of the children coming out onto the porch and standing behind her. She knew that silhouette all too well. It was Brandon. She ran to meet him.

Brandon dismounted, running to meet Diana. They fell onto the ground in each other's arms, laughing as the children piled on top of them. Diana began to cry. Brandon helped her to her feet. "Are you all right?" he asked, placing his hand on her stomach.

"I am fine now," Diana said. "Oh, Brandon, I was so worried."

"Did you find Raymond?" Gilda asked.

Brandon shook his head as he said, "No, I could not find him. I went all the way to the fort in Pittsburgh and beyond. I swung around in both directions on my way home. I couldn't find him," Brandon said.

"Let's not worry about that now. You children run inside and tell Tilly to prepare Mr. Shively something hot to eat," Diana said. She turned to face Brandon again. She smiled and said. "You must be starved nearly to death."

Brandon smiled. The children ran toward the house. Brandon tied the horse to the hitching post near the front porch. "That wasn't true, Diana. What I said about not finding Raymond. That was just for the children's sake," Brandon said, holding Diana by the arm.

Diana put her hand over her mouth. She looked up into Brandon's eyes, as she asked, "He's not...," she could not finish.

"No," Brandon said. "I found him. He made his way to the fort. Lieutenant McGillis knew where his uncle's cabin was. He sent some soldiers to take the boy out there. I rode out to the cabin and Raymond was there with his father and uncle. He didn't want to come back with me. I had to leave him behind, Di. I had no rights over his father. I told his father what happened. It didn't seem to have any effect on the man whatsoever. I told him his children were being cared for and was loved as though they were our own. He said we could keep them because he had no way of caring for them. He asked me not to mention him to them. I think that is the best thing for them, anyway. It would only hurt them to know they were not wanted by their father. So, on the way home, I decided it was best just to tell them I did not find Raymond."

Tears were streaming down Diana's face. "He can't be happier there. How could he? How could his father just leave his children like that?" she whispered.

"He clearly wasn't happy that Raymond had found his way there. He was using the boy more like his own personal slave than a beloved son," Brandon said, shaking his head.

Tilly interrupted them by appearing on the porch with Cecilia and Franklin behind her. "Pappa!" Franklin cried as he hurried to the edge of the porch. He lunged into the air. Brandon caught him, laughing.

"Hey there, my little man. Look how big you've gotten while I was gone," Brandon said, hugging Franklin.

Tilly laughed. "Yo has some cracked wheat n coffee waitin whenever ya is ready."

Brandon darted up the steps. He put Franklin down and lifted Tilly off her feet. He spun her around. "Tilly. Oh, Tilly, I missed you so much!" he said.

Tilly laughed. "Yo jus missed Tilly's cookin'. That's all," she said when he set her down.

They were all laughing. Brandon lifted Franklin again. He put his arm around Diana's waist and they went inside. Brandon ate his breakfast. He talked about the fort and how he saw more settlers building houses as he traveled to and from the fort in Pittsburgh. When he finished his breakfast, he went back out the front door. He took his horse, leading it to the stables. He was going on to the mill. Diana stood on the back porch watching him as he went. She felt the fluttering in her stomach. She covered herself with her hands. "Yes, baby. Pappa is home," She said softly.

Diana suddenly had a burst of energy. She began to help Tilly. They decided to bake a couple of apple pies for supper. Gilda and Shirley went to the orchard to find some apples. Hoppy was in town. She would be surprised to find Brandon there when she came home in the late afternoon. Cecilia and Franklin went outside to play on the swings. Robert was content to crawl around on the kitchen floor. The boys were all at the mill helping Porter Martin and Stumpy. Life was suddenly the way Diana remembered it. She was happy. She tried not to think about Raymond. Maybe it was for the best. She decided to leave it in the hands of the Lord, for there was nothing she could do about it anyway.

With Brandon home, things fell back into the normal routine. The next three weeks went by quickly. Winston drove Diana, Hoppy, and Gilda into Berlin to the schoolhouse. They worked all day scrubbing and preparing it for classes the next Monday. At the end of the day, they rode back to Porter Martin's house. Diana could smell the fall. Rotting apples, and dried leaves were the smells that filled the air. The leaves were just beginning to turn. Soon, they would be falling and the snow would cover the ground. And her baby would come. Diana patted her stomach as the wagon swayed to and from along the rutted dirt road to Porter Martin's house. The smoke from the mill rose in little puffy clouds. Diana smiled. She would be back to teaching in just two more days.

All three of Alda and Herbert Faulk's children would be there this year. All four of Tilly's children would be there. Then, there would be three of her own there. Only Franklin and Robert would be left at home with Tilly now. They were all growing so quickly. Soon, there would be another baby in the house.

Margaret Martin would be so proud of her. Her own mother would be smiling down on her with her household full of children. Diana could not stop smiling as the wagon rocked on over the hill. They went around the bend in the road. Porter Martin's house came into view.

Diana began to sing. "Do Lord, Oh, do, Lord, Oh, do remember me." Soon, all of them were singing. Just as it had been years ago, when she was a young girl. So very long ago.